THE ORENDA

Joseph Boyden

ONEWORLD

A Oneworld Book

This paperback edition published in Great Britain and Australia by
Oneworld Publications, 2014
First published in Great Britain and Australia
by Oneworld Publications, 2013

ISBN 978-1-78074-440-7
ISBN 978-1-78074-436-0 (eBook)

Printed and bound by CPI Group (UK) Ltd, Croydon, CR0 4YY

Oneworld Publications
10 Bloomsbury Street
London WC1B 3SR
England

AMANDA
Gnaajiwi nwiidgemaagan

BLANCHE
Gnaajiwi nmama

ONE

We had magic before the crows came. Before the rise of the great villages they so roughly carved on the shores of our inland sea and named with words plucked from our tongues—Chicago, Toronto, Milwaukee, Ottawa—we had our own great villages on these same shores. And we understood our magic. We understood what the orenda implied.

But who is at fault when that recedes? It's tempting to place blame, though loss should never be weighed in this manner. Who, then, to blame for what we now witness, our children cutting their bodies to pieces or strangling themselves in the dark recesses of their homes or gulping your stinking drink until their bodies fail? But we get ahead of ourselves. This, on the surface, is the story of our past.

Once those crows flew over the great water from their old world to perch tired and frightened in the branches of ours, they saw that we had the orenda. We believed. Oh, did we believe. This is why the crows, at first, thought of us as little more than animals. We lived in a physical world that frightened them and hunted beasts they'd only had nightmares of, and we consumed the mystery that the crows were bred to fear. We breathed what they feared. But they watched intently, as crows are prone to do.

And when they cawed that our magic was unclean, we laughed, took a little offence, even killed a few of them and pulled their feathers for our hair. We lived on. But that word, unclean, that word, somehow, like an illness, like its own magic, it began to grow. Very few of us saw that coming. So maybe this is the story of those few.

HUNTED

I awake. A few minutes, maybe, of troubled sleep. My teeth chatter so violently I can taste I've bitten my swollen tongue. Spitting red into the snow, I try to rise but my body's seized. The oldest Huron, their leader, who kept us walking all night around the big lake rather than across it because of some ridiculous dream, stands above me with a thorn club. The weight these men give their dreams will be the end of them.

Although I still know little of their language, I understand the words he whispers and force myself to roll over when the club swings toward me. The thorns bite into my back and the bile of curses that pour from my mouth make the Hurons convulse with laughter. I am sorry, Lord, to use Your name in vain.

They'd all be screaming with glee, pointing and holding their bellies, if we weren't being hunted. With a low sun rising and the air so cold, noise travels. They are clearly fed up with the young Iroquois girl who never stopped whimpering the entire night. Her face is swollen and, when I see her lying in the snow, I fear they killed her while I slept.

Not long ago, just before first light, we'd all paused to rest, the leader and his handful of hunters stopping as if they'd planned this in advance, the pack of them collapsing against one another for the heat. They whispered among themselves, and a couple glanced over at me. Although I couldn't decipher their rushed speech, I sensed they talked of leaving me here, probably with the girl, who at that moment sat with her back to a birch, staring as if in a dream. Or maybe they talked of killing us. We had slowed them down all night, and despite trying to walk quietly I'd stumbled in the dark through the thick brush and tripped over fallen trees buried in the snow. At one point I removed my snowshoes because they were so clumsy, but then sank up to my hips in the next steps, and one of the hunters had to pull me out, biting me hard on the face once he'd accomplished the deed.

Now the snow covering the lake glows the colour of a robin's egg as sunlight tries to break through cloud. If I live through this day I will always remember to pay attention to the tickle of dryness at the back of my throat at this moment, the feeling of a bad headache coming. I've just begun to walk to the girl to offer her comfort, if she's still alive, when a dog's howl breaks the silence, its excitement in picking up our scent making me want to throw up. Other dogs answer it. I forget how my toes have begun to blacken, that I've lost so much weight I can barely support my gaunt frame, that my chest has filled with a sickness that's turned my skin yellow.

I know dogs, though. As in my old world, they are one of the few things in this new one that bring me comfort. And this pack's still a long way away, their voices travelling easy in the frozen air. When I bend to help the girl up, I see the others have already disappeared into the shadows of trees and thick brush.

My terror of being left behind for those chasing me, who will make sure my death is slow and painful, is so powerful that I now weigh taking my own life. I know exactly what I must do. Asking Your divine mercy for this, I will strip naked and walk out onto the lake. I calculate how long all this will take. It's my second winter in the new world, after all, and my first one I witnessed the brutality of death by freezing. The first ten minutes, as the pack races closer and closer, will certainly be the most excruciating. My skin will at first feel as if it's on fire, like I'm being boiled in a pot. Only one thing is more painful than these early minutes of freezing, and it's the thawing out, every tendril of the body screaming for the agony to stop. But I won't have to worry about that. I will lie on the frozen lake and allow the boiling cold to consume me. After that handful of minutes the violent shaking won't even be noticed, but the sharp stabs of pain in the forehead will come, and they will travel deeper until it feels my brain is being prodded with fish spines. And when the dogs are within a few minutes of reaching me, I will suddenly begin to feel a warmth creeping. My body will continue its hard seizures, but my toes and fingers and testicles will stop burning. I will begin to feel a sense of, if not comfort, then relief, and my breathing will be very difficult and this will cause panic but that will slowly harden to resolve. And when the dogs are on the lake and racing toward me, jaws foaming and teeth bared, I will know that even this won't hurt anymore, my eyes frozen shut as I slip into a sleep that no one can awaken from. As the dogs circle me I will try to smile at them, baring my own teeth, too, and when they begin to eat me I won't feel myself being consumed but will, like You, Christ, give my body so that others might live.

This thought of giving, I now see, lifts me just enough to pick up the girl and begin walking away from the lake's edge. After all, if she's alive, won't her people—my pursuers—consider sparing me? I will keep her alive, not only because this is what You demand but also to save myself. The thought of betraying Your wishes feels more an intellectual quandary than what I imagine should physically cause my heart to ache, but I'll worry about that later. For now I follow the others' footsteps as best I can, my thick black robe catching on the branches and nettles, the bush so thick I wonder how it is that the men I follow, and those who follow me, are not part animal, contain some black magic that gives them abilities beyond what is natural.

You seem very far away here in this cold hell, and the Superior's attempts to prepare me before I left France, before my journey to this new world, seem ridiculous in their naïveté. You will face great danger. You will most certainly face death. You will question Jesus' mercy, even His existence. This is Lucifer whispering in your ear. Lucifer's fires are ice. There is no warming your body and your soul by them. But Superior doesn't have any idea what true cold is, I realize, as I allow myself and the girl to be swallowed by the darkness of trees that the bitter sun fails to penetrate.

A MAN SHOULD FEEL HAPPY

I stop to look up because the sun breaks, puffs of my breath shimmering in the first light. It's you who shimmers, my love, in this first morning light. The sun will illuminate all of it. I know this most of all. The sun will show the Haudenosaunee who chase us exactly where to go, how many of us there are, what condition we're in, and especially that we drag a crow with us. The sun today is not a friend. If we all die today, it will be because of it. And the sun won't give true heat for three more moons, so it's useless. The Crow who tries to follow is worse than useless. And the girl. Taking her was a bad idea. I knew this yesterday like I know it now. I'm older, my love, but still haven't learned to listen to what my chest tells me.

I ask Fox to set a sinew snare where the path narrows, just high enough to strangle the first of their dogs, now howling across the lake and not so far away. With any luck, the others will be hungry enough to stop and tear apart their friend, for surely they've not been eating much this last while. I dreamed all of this and spoke of it as the sky began to darken last evening. I know, my love, that yesterday you watched from somewhere above when my group stumbled across the smaller party of our enemy, both pursuing the same deer. Luck and the bit of tobacco I'd offered to Aataentsic the Sky Woman the night before allowed me to find our enemy's tracks first, and we followed nimble and fast. By the drag of the Haudenosaunee's snowshoes I knew they were close to starving. And by the lack of dog prints I knew what their last meal had been.

I tied the Crow to a tree and then attacked the hunting party when we found them in a gully. It was almost too easy. We shot arrows through two and the other two could barely put up a fight. They didn't even seem to care when Fox clubbed down one of the women, who at least bit him hard through his hide. I myself walked up to the biggest man, already singing his death song, and swung my thorn club into his temple, angry he wasn't willing to fight for his woman. I will not forget having to stand on his head to wrench my weapon free. Yes, I'm older, but still strong. The only one as tall as me is that Crow who I can now hear stumbling through the snow and whining, trying to catch up. He's big, thick through the chest and clearly strong, but is he not the most awkward man I've ever met? He is a holy one, though. I've watched him pray to his sky people for long stretches at a time, thumbing wooden and white metal beads that I think I want to possess once I understand their power.

I took no pleasure yesterday in killing the last two women. They were already so wounded we knew they wouldn't survive the trip home. Even though I asked Fox to do it, my asking is the same as if I myself had done it. Fox cut their throats with his knife so that they'd die quickly, ignoring the taunts of Sturgeon and Hawk and Deer to make it slow. When the three called Fox a woman for making the first leave so fast, he positioned the second woman, who was quite pretty, so the blood from her throat sprayed their faces. That shut them up, and despite feeling badly for these dead, I laughed. For all I knew, it was this group who was responsible for the slow and awful deaths of you, my wife, and you, my two daughters. There's been no peace since. I no longer care for peace.

As we gathered the few Haudenosaunee possessions worth taking, I caught the sound of a sniffle behind me in a clump of cedar. I didn't turn immediately, for I was too tired to have to chase what was clearly a child through the forest. Fox looked at me and then walked away and around behind the cedar, circling it in a wide arc and cutting off the child's escape. He emerged with the girl in his arms, her body as straight and stiff as if she were frozen solid. She stared ahead with eyes that didn't seem to see but maybe saw everything. Was it this that stopped me from killing her, allowing Fox to suggest that I take her and make her my own child? Despite the pock scars from an old sickness, she's beautiful, and will only become more so in the next few years.

We shouldn't have followed our own tracks back out. This certainty of direction gives away too much to an enemy who's quick to learn. By late last night, a much bigger group of Haudenosaunee had found the killing grounds and were following us. It's not that I could hear or see them. The cold air took on another quality, though, and the hair at the back of my neck had begun to stick out, something tickling me like blackflies buzzing my ears, waking me from an afternoon slumber. That's when I hurried my pace last night and my hunters knew then, too, what we all now faced.

Despite her slowing us down all night and as her people pursue us this morning, I still don't regret taking her. She contains something powerful. This has become more and more clear in the last while. I'm willing to take this great risk because of the promise of what's inside her. And if the Crow is able to not only keep up with my hunters but also keep the girl alive, he will have proved to me that both of them have something worth studying.

Now that the Crow appears through the trees, the girl in his large arms, I decide to push forward. It's a good plan. If the Haudenosaunee catch up, they'll find the Crow first, and when they see their child in his arms they'll celebrate her survival with a feast that ends in the consumption of the Crow. Yes, they'll immediately send a much smaller party to pursue the rest of us, but these odds are better than what we now stare at. I point out the snare to the Crow as he stumbles up, breathing heavily.

When he sits in the snow, the young girl stiff again with her eyes staring straight ahead, my men and I stand. The Crow's confused expression fast turns to anger, and I like this sign very much. He has energy left and maybe he will make it through today after all. My four hunters and I walk to where I see a sharp drop to a creek below. Crouching and leaning back, I slide down the hill on the heels of my snowshoes, and feel like I'm flying as I pick up speed to where the creek will offer us a much faster route. I feel happy. A man should feel happy on the day that will be his last.

DREAMS

I dreamed all of this. I told my father but he was too tired, too hungry, I think, to listen. I told my mother as well, but she, too, was tired and hungry. I see the arrow that strikes my father's neck before it even flies. I see the blood on the snow, steaming for just a bit before freezing into something that looks like a soup he fed me when the shaking sickness came. Before my mother bites the small man who is like a lynx or maybe a fox and he smashes her head and she falls to the ground and shakes like she dances in the snow, I have already dreamed her being held roughly by them and finding my eyes as I hide in the cedar. She tells me with her eyes that she's going to do something important, and when she does I am to run as fast as I can and not stop until I find my father's brothers and their children who aren't far from here. I will run faster than I ever have and I won't stop until I find my father's brothers or I am dead. Her eyes flash to me that if these ones here catch me I will wish I had died already. And then she bites the man like she's a crazed wolf and he screams out and begins smashing her in the head with his club and she flops in the snow like a pike pulled from a hole in the ice or maybe a rabbit that has been clubbed and shakes toward her death, feet thumping the ground. It's a good thing my father lies dead on the ground near her with an arrow through his neck or he would not stop until all of them are dead. But he is dead and my mother shakes toward him and my oldest brother, who is blind and deaf and cannot see or hear our parents dying, leaves the world with them when the big older man clubs him in the head. My whole family shakes on the ground today before leaving me and this is something I've already dreamed, the shaking of my family in the snow, feet and arms thumping, then vibrating, then humming before eventually going still.

I will not shake into my death, I tell myself in my dream, and again when I'm swallowed up in the arms of the fox man, who sneaked up behind me quick as a lynx, so I go stiff and wait for him to smash me on the head. Instead, he carries me to the big man who struck down my brother, and as I pass the others who are dead, my father, my mother, his two young hunters and their wives who squirted blood onto the men laughing at them, I keep my eyes forward and try not to see any of it, pretend I am my brother who cannot see, who I've mimicked since I can remember, that look of seeing nothing and seeing everything. But I do see. I see that my father lies in the snow, a ring of blood circling his head like a bright ring around the moon in autumn, and his arms stretch out from him as if he's pointing with one to where the sun rises and with the other to where the sun sets, and I see one foot crossed over the other as if he can finally relax now that he has slipped through to the other side. I remain stiff, though, believe that if my body stays still and hard as I can make it that these men will lose interest and they'll think I've turned to wood or ice and they'll leave me in the snow because my weight is not worth carrying, especially when my father's brothers and their sons and their dogs find out what's happened. These men who have killed my family, these men who I've dreamed of, they better start running now, for my father's brothers and their sons who will pursue them soon will never stop chasing until they're done with it. And so I'll stay heavy and stiff and let my feet and arms and head catch on the branches as these men try to carry me away. If I stay frozen they'll eventually be forced to drop me.

This morning my plan has worked and I watch my family's killers leave me soon after my father's brother's strongest dog sings out that he can smell me. But the other prisoner bends down to me, and he smells so bad that I want to throw up, his breath stinking like rotted meat. The wolf's hair on his face and his clothes the colour of charcoal scratch me and there's no way I can stay stiff and dead anymore and just when I open my mouth to scream, when I begin to swing at his face and claw at his eyes and bite like I watched my mother bite, I see my father, grown tiny and sparkling, hanging on a leather cord from this thing's neck.

It's my father, lying in the snow with a circle around his head and his arms stretched out and his feet relaxed, one crossed over the other. As the hairy man bends over me, I watch my tiny father arc toward me, his face catching the first morning light and his body meets my lips and it feels warm and I see now that he's still alive because he's warm and I try to kiss him as he swings away and the stinky man picks me up and I hear my father's brother's dog in the distance sing out once more.

PROTECTION

I know that the one called Bird and his warriors can't be far ahead. I wish to God they'd wait. The dogs mustn't be far behind either, having gone quiet now that they're closer to me, their prey. The stiff girl in my arms is brutally awkward to carry, and as I follow the Hurons' snowshoe trail to a steep embankment, I pause to calculate the best way down. So steep, this drop, that I wonder if Bird hasn't tried to trick his pursuers and taken another route. I look around for other tracks. Nothing. Christ, please help me. The dogs will come soon, they will howl out my presence, and with that noise will come the men who pursue, with their flashing teeth, their red and black and yellow painted faces and hatchets and flint knives to cut off the tips of my fingers in preparation for the true torture. I know all about these ones I've never met. They love to caress their enemies with red coals and razor flint so slowly that days pass before Jesus comes to take the victim.

The small of my back spasms as I stand looking out at the frozen stream beneath me. I consider dropping the rigid girl and letting her tumble down to the bottom, and am sick to realize I might consider this because if she makes it then I, too, will survive it unscathed.

And then I see the tracks below, Bird's snowshoe tracks, small as pigeon claws, etched along the distant bank and disappearing into thick brush. I lift my charge higher in my arms and step forward to test the footing, feeling steadier now with a faint glow of salvation.

The toe of my snowshoe catches a bit of branch or rock, something below the white, and I tumble fast, over and over, down the hill, my ribs and left arm hitting rocks at the bottom in the frozen creek bed.

I stand and feel the shock of snow down my back. The girl is clearly no catatonic. Quick as a hare, she scrambles to her feet and begins scratching her way up the embankment, its incline steep enough that when she makes it no farther than her own length, she slips back down again. It would almost be comical if not for the glare she shoots back at me, her eyes alight like some animal's. These ones can behave so inhumanly. Despite our dear Pope's teachings that possession of a soul raises all of us to men, I have seen with my own eyes what they'll do to an enemy. Forgive me, Lord, but I fear that they are animals in savagely human form.

I sit in the snow of the creek and fit the snowshoes back on my feet, tying the hide cords as best as I remember the Hurons showing me. I stand up and think to say something in parting to the desperate girl still struggling desperately to climb away, but then think better of it. She won't understand my French, and my head is far too panicked to attempt the Huron tongue, which Bird claims she understands. I will leave this girl to her people, to my pursuers, and surely this will quell their appetites.

But no more than ten paces along the creek and I realize that to leave without her leaves me without protection. My legs ache so badly and my breath already comes in such short spurts that I know today might be the beginning of my last. The ones behind me are too strong. I turn back and shuffle through the snow to the girl who still frantically tries to climb up and toward her people. She looks at me as my arms reach out, and as I tense for her to claw at my eyes, she instead goes stiff as if dead and drops to the snow with a thump. I would laugh if I had the energy. I bend over and pick her up, struggling now with her scant weight, then turn and drag my heavy and awkward snowshoes along the trail left by Bird.

LIKE PRAYERS

By mid-afternoon my warriors and I begin to lag. We've had nothing warm in our bellies for two days, and the idea of even a small bowl of ottet makes me groan for it. The wind from the east has picked up and the freeze in the air relents some. I see the low clouds on that horizon. Snow considers coming, and I know that snow is what will save my life today. If it comes hard enough it will cover first my tracks and then my direction, and finally it will offer me its safety of cover to slip into the protected lands of our home village, a place the pursuers will not dare enter. I whisper to the Sky People for their help.

My reflecting on possibilities causes my pace to slow and I watch Fox slip by to take the lead, looking at me as he does and spitting his mock disgust on the snow, which makes me smile. Fox is a good man. A very good man. He is a great war-bearer. He is a great friend. Smaller than the others, he's always had to prove himself. This he's done well. There's no better war-bearer in all the Wendat nation, and if he is to be captured today, the Haudenosaunee will rejoice as loud as they ever have, and they will pay close attention to Fox, torturing him with a love saved only for the truly special ones. They'll keep him alive for days because they know he has the strength, and he will die a particularly brutal death. As will I. I push these thoughts away and focus on one step after the other, following the trail Fox has cut into a stand of birch as the first snow, like prayers, tickles my face.

SPARKLING FATHER

My chance to get back to my father's brothers is gone now. The snow falls so thick it will cover our tracks fast. I stare up and it makes me blink my eyes. The shining thing that my father has become rides on the chest of the hairy man, tied to a cord around his neck. My father remains outstretched, and I picture his real body in the snow, his arms to east and west, his legs relaxed. The shining being he has become is nearly naked, I now see, and in this way he tells me what I must do. I wasn't strong enough to climb that hill, so now I decide I will go to the place where my mother and father have gone. The hairy one who carries me doesn't notice when I pull my mittens off with my teeth and spit them into the snow. He just keeps breathing heavily and whispering to himself, sometimes choking on his spit and crying. I don't understand this creature. Despite how large he is and the obvious strength of his body, he acts as if he's in the skin of a child younger than me. When he should be focusing his stride, he whines to himself instead. He'll never make it in this world. Yet he somehow manages to follow those who killed my family. It's just dumb luck, I can hear my father say, that this one walks the route he's supposed to.

My hands are numb enough now that I can't feel my fingers as I try to remove my rabbit and deer robe. At first I do this slowly so the hairy one won't notice, but he doesn't see much as he stumbles and whines and struggles through the heavy snowfall. His black beard is covered in white and I can imagine him as an old man, but he won't live long enough for his hair to turn white. I try harder now to pull my robe over my head and only when my elbow digs hard into his gut does he stop and lower to his knees and drop me. His eyes stare down into my own, searching for something as his breath rasps into the air in white puffs. I sit up. He wants to ask what I am doing, I know. Instead, I pull off my robe and then my rabbit leggings. He stares strangely at me as I remove the last of my fur. I lie back shivering into the snow, and I stretch my arms out, one to the east, the other to the west. I place one foot over the other and try to relax into death. I stare up at the hairy man, for surely he will understand, stand up and walk away. I smile at him, my teeth chattering beyond my control, and it's only then that his hands reach down and take mine with something like anger.

He tries to put my leggings back on and reaches for my robe, and when I struggle against him, he raises his arm high and slaps me hard across the mouth. I freeze now, for real, unable to move. The only thing I can feel is the warmth of blood on my chin. I can't move as he pulls the robe over my head and picks me up. I've never been struck before. My hands are numb and I try to tuck them into my sleeves. I look up at him for just a second, and his eyes are focused like I've not seen them before, slitted against the falling snow as he pushes along a stretch of birch that tells me a big lake must be nearby. We're entering their country. I know now I will die soon and only wish it was how I had decided.

I want my mother to hold me. I want my father to rub my nose with his. I want my brother to carry me across the creek so my feet don't get wet. I want my father's brothers to kill all these men who have killed my family. I want my father's brothers to make these men feel the same pain I do. I want my father's brothers to take days to do it.

There is nothing now but hard snowfall and then the smell of distant fires. My end must be coming quicker, and I reach up to this man's chest and struggle with my frozen hands to take my sparkling father into them, his body so small and perfect, and I think I can feel his heat leak into me like a burn that doesn't hurt. I clutch my tiny father harder and his warmth begins to crawl up my arms and into my body until I feel like I'm lying under a summer sun. My teeth still chatter and my body keeps shaking, but I'm warm. I look up at the man and he looks down at me and sees that I hold my father in my hands. The stinking man stops walking. I'm scared he will yank my father away but instead a white flash of teeth blossoms in the black hair on his face and he whispers something to me that I don't understand, caressing my forehead with his long thumb. We stare at each other, not afraid anymore.

Our stare is broken only when I feel others around us. I can smell their anger before I see them. A gang of Wendat emerges from the birch, as silent as the trees themselves. Their hair rises up from the centres of their heads proudly, and all of them carry weapons. They've been waiting for us. I know this for their faces are painted in strips the colour of charcoal and squash blossom. The hairy one continues to stare down at me, whispering to me and running his thumb over my forehead every few seconds, his voice droning in a tongue that sounds like a fast spring creek. He has no idea that these others have surrounded us until one Wendat rips me from his embrace and another behind raises a club to strike him down.

WHEN THE BEAR HAS HER YOUNG

My welcome home is at first muted by what I've brought back with me. The winter's been quiet here, with little drama, I'm told, and my neighbours seem as content as I remember them being this late in it. Normally, food supplies are running low and the promise of spring is distant. But the autumn harvest was a good one for all of us this last year, and the Anishnaabe came down from the north in strong numbers, their hunters loaded with deer meat and pelts to trade for Wendat corn, their medicine people building shaking tents in the birch forests outside my village in order to communicate with their families back in the north.

I'm a respected man in this community, but I know that my decision to take a war party out when the boredom of winter set in was frowned upon during the moon when the bear has her young. Relations with the Haudenosaunee have always stunk like sick bowels, though for the last while, raids between us haven't been an issue. Why stir up a sleeping bear in the months when we all should be fasting and dreaming and gathering strength? I'll tell you why, my love. For you. To avenge you. It really is as simple as that. When the pain of you not being beside me in bed at night is too strong, I can do nothing but walk and walk until I find them and kill a few. A hundred will die for each member of my family taken by them. Three hundred will die before I even consider resting.

My heart's darkest in the long winter months. In that moon when the cold settles so deeply into the poplars that it causes them to moan their pain out loud, my own pain at the loss of you, beautiful wife, and of you, beautiful children, makes my legs ache so badly that nothing stops it except a long walk to their country.

I don't like to brag, but these vengeance walks have become the stuff of legend among the young men of the village, who wish one day to warm their hands in the split chests of our enemies, and I'm never short of those who wish to test their mettle on that path. I'm old enough now that I know if Fox were ever to refuse this walk with me, I'd probably quit doing it too. But, like me, he still remains thirsty for adventure and for bounty. And certainly two captives are a decent haul.

At first I'm forced to keep the Crow guarded at all times, not allowing him to wander freely but instead making the curious of the village come to see him. And there are many. They bring little gifts to leave by my fire, woven baskets, ochre for face paint, strips of leather soft from chewing, even smoked fish. All of this I share with the other members of the longhouse, for they, too, have much to put up with; day and night the longhouse is lively with those who sit cross-legged and watch the Crow try to speak with them in their own language, something that never ceases to bring amazement and laughter. He speaks as if his mouth is full of birchbark, and his vocabulary is less than a child's, but I only need remind the ones who laugh the loudest to try and speak even a few words of the Crow's tongue to see how gifted this one truly is.

Few pay attention to the girl, who seems to blend into the walls and smoke of our house. I see that she's sad for her family and misses them very much. When she is ready, I'll apologize to her for what I did to her blood, and then explain that her life can be full and happy and content now that she is my daughter. I will throw her a great welcoming feast and invite all the important people of the village and will exhaust my riches in doing so, for riches can always be replaced. And in this ceremony the girl will become my new daughter, and my heart will heal just a little bit from the loss of my own.

But for now she remains curled up in her sleeping robe, a special one I had sewn for her from many beaver pelts. She spends her days wrapped in it, listening to the Crow caw out his words. She won't eat. She barely drinks water. I'll have to intervene if this behaviour continues.

Since your departure, dear one, our longhouse now contains eight fires, eight families, mostly nephews and nieces and their little ones who constantly run around playing, chasing one another and the dogs that wander in. Fox and his wife and four children keep their fire beside mine since your death, closest to the door, a good place for a man like Fox, a natural protector. Now that all of you are gone, I like nothing more than to return home from a long journey with my friend and watch him become like a child again, wrestling and chasing his children, telling them stories of his adventures that are carefully stripped of the violence he has perpetrated and witnessed. A child's life is too short for such lessons just yet. My life at home is good, despite no longer having you here, and I'm like a grandfather to dozens, a grandfather who will teach them the laws of the humans and the laws of the forest.

———

THIS MORNING, I wake up early to wind whistling along the longhouse. I look beside me and am relieved to see that the girl finally visits the place of dreams. Sitting up, I climb from my perch where the warmth accumulates. Peering into the dark corner where the Crow sleeps, I can hear the rhythmic draw of his breath. This, too, is a good sign. We've been back home for five days now, and this is the first that I've seen either of them sleep. These two are strange beings indeed, but something in my chest tells me that they both will prove worthwhile. At least this is what I hope. A niggling doubt has been worming into my ears the last days, and maybe this is what causes me to wake so early. Am I holding on to these two for the wrong reason, for only the pleasure of ownership?

I stoke the fire with more wood and lift my robe to my shoulders. You would understand, dear one, what I need right now. After all, we made the promise to each other that if one were to die too young, the other, after appropriate mourning, should feel free to take care of physical needs. It's time to pay Gosling a visit.

No light yet, and the snow blows sideways, building high against the west side of the longhouses, helping to insulate them from the lake's wind. This is the time when our people go to the dream world most deeply, and normally I'd be there too. But I awoke to Gosling's image in my head, and I knew she beckoned me. She lives alone near the southern palisades, and no one dares build a home near her. She is the only one in a community of thousands to live alone.

She's not born of our people but is an Anishnaabe, a Nipissing from the north. She arrived one winter with a group of their traders on a day not long after you were killed. These ones were very slow and careful with the building of their shake tents and had something stronger in their magic than I'd ever seen before. They knew of the last year's troubles with the Haudenosaunee, and of my pain, and some of them invited me to their shake tent and told me they'd spoken to you, that you and the girls had moved safely to the spirit world. They knew details of our enemy's raids on our hunting camps that late autumn that they had no way of knowing. They talked of how you were killed last, after the girls had been killed in front of you while I battled for my life a hundred steps away. They told me this not to brag but to allow me to understand you were now safe. With no reason to offer such kindness, they still did. The Anishnaabe medicine people told me that one day they'd take many of us in after we were dispersed like cornhusks in the wind.

After their holy people left with the gift of all the corn they could carry, we began to notice that one had stayed behind. This woman, Gosling, had for days managed to walk by the sentries as if invisible, was seen entering and leaving different longhouses before disappearing again. Each home that she visited contained a person close to death. Within a week, each of them sat up and took food again by the fire.

She continued these visits through the winter, living alone outside our palisades in a bark wigwam, and each time she was spotted in the community, something else seemed to bless us. We became used to her presence over the cycle of moons that followed. The harvest that year was bountiful, not one warrior perished to the Haudenosaunee or in fast waters on the long summer trek to trade with the Iron People so far away by the great rapids. We Wendat gathered and agreed to build her a true home in the hope that she'd stay with us and continue to bless us.

When I slip in, she's sitting by her fire, facing me with a coy smile on her face. She allows the beaver robe around her shoulders to fall down, and in the firelight her naked body appears to me that of a young woman, her breasts plump and high, the nipples hardened, and in turn I harden at this sight. It's been too long since our last visit. I allow my own robe to fall to the floor and then walk to her, kneeling for her embrace. I've often wondered if I am the only one allowed such pleasure with her, or simply one of many. In a village where nothing goes unnoticed, no one's ever mentioned, even in jest, my visits to Gosling. And I've never heard of another bragging of exploits with her.

After, she lies on her back with her eyes closed and a half smile on her face as I tell her of my most recent adventures, tracing the outlines of the tattoos on her arms. My favourite is the carefully depicted owl that perches with large eyes, peering from the crook of her arm.

"The Crow you've brought home with you like some pet is the talk of the community," Gosling says. "Be careful, though. Crows are very difficult to tame."

I frown at this. I have no desire, I want to say, to own this Crow.

"They are tricksters," Gosling continues. "They love to steal. You won't even know what you're missing until it's too late."

"He's got something to him," I say. Something I might be able to use.

"It's the girl I worry about most," Gosling says after a time.

"What do you mean?" I ask this too quickly, suddenly fearing that Gosling senses some illness in the girl that I can't see yet.

"She comes from rare blood. Her people miss her. They want her back. They'll go great distances to get her back."

I'm about to answer defensively, but pause.

"You should give her back before you allow her to become your daughter."

"I'd rather give the Crow back," I finally say.

"No. We need to keep the Crow, unfortunately," Gosling says. "Keeping him here is good for relations with the foreign ones. He will draw their traders to us rather than to others." She laughs. "The more crows you allow, the stronger your ties with them will become."

On my back now, I know she stares at me after saying this, daring me to follow the path of her reasoning. She's left the obvious unspoken. It's what the crows bring with them that our people haven't yet seen that Gosling is asking me to consider.

I'd rather not think of this now and slip to my stomach, lifting myself above her as she arches to me and takes me inside.

CHASTISEMENT

They are beautiful people. I cannot ignore this fact. I write all of this down in the bound book I've carried tucked in my robe, one of the very few comforts I possess. To bring Jesus into the lives of these people is one mission. To report my findings back to my Superior in Kebec, who will in turn send it to his back home in France, is the other. Ultimately, I write of my journeys and my struggles and my suffering to glorify You. I will die here for You if this is what is requested of me.

These sauvages, they are shameless in their lack of modesty. When the fire burns hot, the children run naked around the longhouse and the women strip down to their waist. The men often walk around in simple breechclouts, and a number of times I've witnessed couples I am quite sure aren't married embracing and then slipping away. The light of the fires, the thick smoke, the primal grunts of passion, the laughing children, the chatter of this language that I struggle so hard to master, I think I might very well be in one of Dante's rings.

I record in my journal that each longhouse is the length and width of a small ship, and families related through the women reside within. As far as I can tell, eight or ten families, each with its own fire, fill these residences with the noises of humanity. I've estimated anywhere from forty to sixty souls in each longhouse, and I believe there to be at least fifty longhouses in this community. What's more, I've been told that this village is just one of many in what I've termed Huronia, this land they call Wendake. While it's possible to walk the length of Huronia in just a few days, I've learned that five separate and yet unified nations populate this fertile country, each with its own name. The people I reside with call themselves the Bear, and the other nations are named Rock and Cord and Swamp and Deer. Their sworn enemies, the Iroquois, also consist of five nations, but it seems that the Huron refer to them collectively as Haudenosaunee in their language.

The Huron are, as Champlain so duly noted a number of years ago, the key traders in a very large geography, controlling their business with the keen eye of a banker. They dominate the trade of tribes as disparate as the Montagnais to the north and the Neutral to the south. Their main currency is the vast quantity of corn that they grow each summer. I'm fascinated to watch how their different systems work as time allows, but from what I can see, they trade their produce with the Algonquin and the Nipissing for those hunting people's furs, mainly beaver, which the Huron then paddle all the way to New France in the summer, where they trade those furs for staples such as iron axes and copper kettles and all form of glass beads, which to the Huron are as valuable as gold. They in turn bring back these treasures from New France and again trade them with their neighbours to the north and south. Yes, they are indeed the lynchpin to the economy of this new world.

Now that it's winter, each family sleeps up off the ground on raised platforms, mother on one end, father on the other, children squeezed in between. They are smart enough to peel the bark from the wood they burn but it's still sometimes so smoky that my eyes are often irritated. These longhouses are truly a wonder, like giant beehives woven together with saplings and covered in sheets of bark. Up in the rafters hang corn and beans and squash and tobacco and dried fish and all manner of food that I've never seen before. The Huron winters are clearly the time of relaxation and enjoyment. All day long the mothers play with their children, and the dozen or so dogs that wander through the longhouse are treated as members of the family as well, eating from their hosts' kettles and sleeping in their beds, and all this madness of life surrounds me while the men stand in groups, taking turns visiting one another's longhouses to talk and laugh and smoke pipes of tobacco.

The men are tall, some nearly my size. I've always towered over my companions in France. Wasn't it the dear Bishop who nicknamed me the Brittany Giant? But these ones have a musculature that's impressive, taut stomachs and strong arms, their brown, hairless skin in the winter firelight like oil paintings that have come alive. Some have their women pluck and shave the hair from both sides of their heads with sharpened and intricately decorated clamshells, leaving a thick brush of it running down the centre that they grease until it stands on end. An ancient sailor on the miserable voyage over from the old world to this new one regaled all of us with his experiences in this land, going so far as to claim he was the one to first name these people Huron, wild boars, for how he thought the men's hair bristles like a pig's. Other warriors grow their hair long and shave off only one side of it, which leaves them looking frightening and half-mad. On the warpath, Bird and his soldiers paint their faces in red and yellow and black ochre. I am sure this was meant to stir the same fear in their enemies that it did in me.

The women are as striking as the men with their long shining black hair, their white smiles flashing against brown skin. They go to great lengths to decorate themselves, sometimes spending hours chattering as they braid feathers and tiny painted clay beads into one another's hair. Some of them have even tattooed their bodies with the images of animals, and these women seem held in high regard. Many of them love to flirt with me, regardless of their age. They smile coyly, and the younger ones think nothing of touching my hand or my arm, as if to prove to themselves that I'm indeed real. Word has gotten out that my vows prevent me from being with women, but obviously their simplicity prevents them from understanding the complexity of Catholicism. As I preached the other day, after much confusion in our mutual understanding, a man dared to ask me if I preferred boys, causing all the others to laugh hysterically. This childlike comprehension of the world will be both my greatest test and a wonderful tool. I'll treat them as I once treated young children back in France when I was given the rather odious mission of teaching them the catechism.

These first ten days, I feel like a prisoner in this glowing longhouse filled with smoke. Bird is clearly an important man in this community. I've watched people bring him gifts and come to visit now that he's back. And I understand the crowds come as much to see me as they do Bird. I take this opportunity to try to bring a little of God's light into this dark corner of the world. For months last year back in Kebec, I worked on learning the Huron language, a converted sauvage with the Christian name of Luke teaching me its guttural intricacies.

He explained that I had to begin to grasp the natural world around me if I were ever to conquer the language. The Huron, Luke said, don't live above the natural world but as a part of it. The key to their language was to make the connection between man and nature. I scoffed at this. A language doesn't exist that can't be learned by rote. And You, Lord, have given us the natural world for our use and our governance. Man was not meant to grovel in the dirt with animals but to rise above them. I make note in my relations to be sent back in due course to you, my dear Superior, that this is a lesson paramount for the conversion of the sauvages. I had long ago proved myself masterful with languages. Thanks be to God, I've been given the gift of Latin and Greek, a little English, some Dutch. In fact, dear Superior, did you not choose me for this mission to New France because of my ability to learn new tongues?

Just one more reflection for now, something I find both fascinating and appalling. In matters of the spirit, these sauvages believe that we all have within us a life force that is similar, if you will, to our own Catholic belief in the soul. They call this life force the orenda. That is the fascinating part. What appals me is that these poor misguided beings believe not just humans have an orenda but also animals, trees, bodies of water, even rocks strewn on the ground. In fact, every last thing in their world contains its own spirit. When I pushed Bird about this, he explained it to me in a rather odd way. He told me of a recent hunting trip in which he pursued a deer for a long time. Eventually he caught up to and killed it. "My orenda overpowered its orenda," he said. "The deer's orenda allowed me to take it." He then looked at me as if his words might explain with final clarity this strange belief of theirs. I have to admit, dear Superior, that I'm still left confused.

———

TODAY, A DOZEN of them sit on the ground in front of me, staring and whispering amongst themselves, watching my every move and studying me with such intensity that I begin to sweat. Those closest to me hold their noses or fan their faces as if I'm the one who reeks, despite their overpowering smells of smoke and hide and what I can only describe as lustful intention. A couple of young women sitting at my feet try to peer up my cassock and then laugh as they mimic me blessing myself. An old man near the wall sits with a rigid back and his arms crossed, his thin lips scowling.

Like a child struggling for words, I slowly begin with the holy lamb. But there is no such thing as a lamb in the world of these people, and so Jesus becomes a fawn, a fawn whose blood is spilled so that we might live eternally. One heckler, an old woman, says loudly that the thought of fawn's blood makes her hungry in this winter when fresh meat is scarce, and why do I torture her so? The others laugh at this. I've learned quickly that they laugh often, even at the most inappropriate times.

"If you take the fawn that is Jesus into your life," I say slowly and then stop, straining for the words. "Your hunger. Gone."

They scoff at this. "Not go hungry ever again?" one young man asks. "Does this mean we are dead?" Again there is more laughter and more discussion in their tongue, all of it too quick for me to understand.

When the crowd breaks down like this, usually after only a few minutes of my speaking, I know I've lost them. And that's when I take my chalice and white cloth from my bag, and I use a bit of their sagamité, the horrid corn mush they call ottet that's the staple of their diet in the winter and on travels. With this mush that I've flattened and dried and rounded into a small Host, I perform the most sacred of sacraments, lifting the chalice of melted snow water to Heaven so that it might become Your blood, raising the corn wafer to the sky so it transforms into Your flesh. This always silences them. They watch every little move with the eyes of hawks, all humour gone from their faces. Apparently, they're more susceptible to my actions than to my words. I've made careful note of this, and wait patiently for the day when one of them will dare ask that he or she might also take a sip from the chalice, a nibble from my outstretched hand.

And yet there's one who watches everything, who misses nothing, who doesn't rudely interrupt when I preach. The young Iroquois girl hides beneath her sleeping robe, the girl I carried in my arms through that nightmarish day. In all the time we've been here, I can't remember seeing her move from her perch above me in the bed beside Bird's. I desperately hope that no ill intention exists in Bird's loins. I find it very strange indeed that he's the only one in the longhouse without a wife or family. Has the sauvage taken this girl to be a child bride? I will keep a close eye on this.

———

EARLY THIS MORNING I wake up in the dark, the wind blowing hard and Bird stoking the fire before sneaking out of the longhouse. Sleep beckons me back to its warmth and comfort, and it's exactly this I know I must fight. I deserve neither of these as long as those around me remain heathen. Forcing myself up from my blanket, I kneel on the hard ground in the corner away from the fire in just my nightshirt, shivering through my morning prayers and contemplation. The girl troubles me. She troubles me deeply. The image of her stripping naked in the snow and offering herself to me is burned into my memory no matter how hard I try to erase it. It was her smile as she lay exposed there, asking me something I couldn't comprehend. And then the wickedness of what she wished me to do dawned on me and forced my hand harshly across her mouth. I've already made careful note of this in my relations to dear Superior, which I can only hope will eventually reach him. The one conclusion I can draw from the depravity and brutality I've witnessed so far is that these beings, while certainly human, exist on a plane far lower than even Europe's lowest caste.

I must remember, though, that all of us are God's creatures. It is my mission to begin to help these poor souls rise up. The only way that their eternal souls might be saved is to accept Jesus, and to do this they must accept the Eucharist.

As if Christ Himself speaks directly to me on this frigid morning deep in this troubled land, I can see a vision materialize through the fog of my breath. The girl will become my first convert. I know this as surely as anything I've ever known. I remember her hand clutching my crucifix as we walked the last miles and were accosted by the Huron sentries. The poor thing is in desperate need of redemption. Her tempting me is evidence. And I have been brought here to offer it to her.

When I am finished my morning vespers, I don my heavy black robe, noting that it's saturated with my scent, the heavy stink of hard labour, the sour odour of sheer fear, and suddenly I feel self-conscious. I push this worry away. I must rise above the physical stains of humanity. My mission is more than the mundane facts of everyday life. I am more than that.

The sounds of sleep still echo through the longhouse as I climb the ladder to the young girl's bed. It strikes me I don't even know her name. No need. Soon enough, I will give her a Christian one. This will be a first for this territory, and word of it will travel far.

The girl lies on her back, tucked into a plush beaver robe. Her mouth is slightly open and I can't help but smile to notice a thin string of spit runs from the side of it. She appears deep in sleep, and for this I'm thankful. She's been through so much. We all have. Though Bird tied me to a tree out of sight of her family's massacre, the sounds of struggle and screaming and slaughter still haunt me. The girl has gone mute for good reason. At her age she saw what no one should ever have to witness. The brutality these people are so willing to show their enemies astounds me.

I stare at the girl for a long time in the dim light, trying to understand her. I suddenly realize that I am trying to see her humanity. She's not very beautiful, at least in comparison to the other children around her. She'd be better looking if not for the scars of some childhood disease that ravaged her face. Epidemics have begun to sweep through these people the last few years. I can only take this as a sign from God, a divine message. Any fool can see that when great change comes, the weak and the wicked will suffer. But the converted will live on.

I bless myself and whisper prayers of devotion and of gratitude and of guidance. I pray most fervently for the salvation of the soul of the young one sleeping in front of me. When I'm done, I raise the silver crucifix, a gift from my dear mother before departing on this voyage, and kiss it, then decide to lower it to the girl's lips. After all, she's already shown such fascination with the cross.

As Jesus touches her mouth, I'm shocked to see her eyes dart open. She raises her arms and pushes against my chest. Only now do I realize how closely I'm hovering over her. Her fists are a flurry of punches against me, and as I lean away, the crucifix in hand, she begins screaming. Panicked, I clap my hand over her mouth before she wakes the others. They'll see me up here with her and will not understand. I plead with her in whispers to be quiet but her eyes only widen more. When she bites my hand, the pain shoots up my arm and I pull it away. The girl's screams pierce my ears, ringing through the longhouse, and just under them I can hear the sounds of people awakening abruptly all around me, of men scuffling for their weapons. A rush of cold air sweeps up to send chills down my back and I hear feet scrambling up the ladder, then feel a hand grab my cassock and yank.

Now I'm falling, and I close my eyes and grit my teeth just as my shoulder slams into the unforgiving earth with the crack of what must be a bone breaking, the dull throb followed immediately by a sharp pain that sucks the breath from me. Bird stands above, his face contorted in anger, a knife in his hand. He raises it as he straddles my chest. I can see that he'll do it, and my first reaction is regret that I've come all this way only to fail in converting a single sauvage. I close my eyes and whisper to Jesus for another chance, wait for the burn of the knife across my throat.

But it doesn't come. Instead, I hear a strange voice, young but gravelly, speaking calmly, rationally, in Huron. It's not quite human in tone, more like a small animal that's learned to speak like a two-legged being. I pick up certain words. Spirit. Father. Illness. I slowly open my eyes. Bird stares at me, and, over his shoulder, up in the rafters on her sleeping perch, the girl peers down, talking to the back of Bird's head, her thin face hovering above us in the early light that comes in from the smoke holes of the longhouse. Her face shimmers in the glow of morning and fire smoke so that I can't help but think of her as a spirit, a ghost who's appeared to intervene. Bird stands up, with one foot on either side of me. He says nothing, but his look tells me as surely as if he were screaming it. Never touch this girl again. He turns then and strides out. I look around and see the other families have risen from their beds and stand in a ring at a distance, staring. I look up to glimpse the strange sight of the girl once more, but already she's disappeared.

———

FOR THREE DAYS, no one visits or speaks to me. I assume this is Bird's punishment. And so, unsure if I'm even allowed to leave the long-house, I sit in a corner that offers some privacy and spend long hours in prayer and reflection. At least I attempt to, but a growing sense of isolation, of what by the second day I realize is malaise, sets in. Like snow built up on a roof too long, I fear I creak with too much weight. I fear I will collapse. My shoulder was dislocated in the fall, and the right arm hangs limply, now longer than the left. The pain is breathtaking. If only I had another Jesuit here to re-set it. If only I had another Brother here to speak with, another priest with whom I might seek confession and absolution. I try to sleep but it's fitful, shot through with a deep-seated fear that I've gone so far into this bizarre and brutal land that even God has lost contact with me.

What of the others? I set out from New France with the plan of reaching Huronia late last summer. I was promised that a group of Jesuits who were due to arrive soon from Normandy would follow if the season still permitted.

In the best of conditions the trip from Kebec to Huronia is a three-week-long act of brutality, back-breaking work of paddling and portaging great distances, which means lifting everything from the canoes and making multiple trips, sometimes of miles, through bogs or up steep embankments, half the weight of a man strapped to your back. Living daily with swarms of insects that sting and itch and bite, hoping for the short respite of rain and, when it comes, shivering in the downpours, then wishing for some sun again, despite this meaning the return of the insects. Starving even as the sauvages seem to grow stronger from the scarcity of food, waking before dawn each morning and bending their backs against the currents in their flimsy, wobbly craft until dark, smoking their wretched tobacco in place of meals. They grew more muscular as I began to wither.

But the worst aspect of my journey was certainly the Iroquois, enemies of us French. To get to Huronia, one must pass through their country. Yes, being hunched from dawn to dusk on scabbed and bloody knees, the painful monotony of paddling into wind and rain, never resting or stopping to eat until light faded, this was simply crushing. The abject fear, though, that I tried to constantly quell was of being surprised by an Iroquois raiding party. I did all that I knew to do. I tried to place myself in Your hands. And I am so sorry that, for a time, I failed.

I'd left New France last year with a small party of Algonquin who promised Champlain himself that they would deliver me safely to the Hurons. I forgive them now, as I write this to dear Superior in my book. After all, I admit I'm a weak paddler and despite my size, couldn't carry nearly as much as them. I remember them grumbling and complaining amongst themselves for the ten days. One heathen even began to loudly suggest I was a demon in human form. But it's when we came across a barely cold Iroquois campfire that the Algonquin made their decision. That afternoon, after they inspected the camp, silent and cautious as wolves, and just as I was relieving myself behind a clump of willow, they climbed into their canoes. They'd deposited my black cloth bag containing my chalice and diary and few personal possessions on the shore, along with a small sack of food. I emerged from the bush and watched as they paddled away at speed.

The more I shouted for them to come back, the faster they worked to get away. I quit only when it dawned on me they wouldn't return and that my shouts might very well alert the Iroquois, who couldn't be far away, to my presence.

The terror consumed me those first hours as I huddled behind that same clump of willow, peering out at the lake in hopes the Algonquin might return for me, pleading to You, Lord, that this not be the way I was to perish. Might not dying alone, slowly starving and going mad, lost in the tangle of forest as the mosquitoes ate me alive, be even worse than to die the death of a martyr at the vicious hands of the Iroquois? This morning, as I sit ignored in the corner of the longhouse, I truly come to understand that my life, and my death, are preordained, and I come to the understanding that fretting over all of this will not aid my mission but cripple it.

This third morning of chastisement, I kneel on the hard ground shivering, and I finally feel the fear that's consumed me release and begin to lift from my back, a fear that's burdened me since I first set foot in this foreign and desperate place. With my left hand, I force my right arm up the wall until it's above my head, my shoulder braying its anguish. I whisper now to You as I throw my weight hard into the wall. I feel the ball popping into its joint again as I collapse. I fall to the floor and bite my hand to stop a scream from escaping and awaking the house.

I will die. We'll all die. How many times have I narrowly escaped it in the past few months? The last few days? My death most probably will happen here in this foreign world, away from my family, at the hands of these people. So be it, Lord. So be it.

THE WESTERN DOOR

I am the western door of my people. My mother's and my father's brothers will not forget about me. They will rescue me. I don't know how to mourn my parents properly. I miss my mother's kisses, her whispering my name so close in my ear that it tickles. I miss my father kneeling down and rubbing his nose against mine. When I'm sad and scared like this, I remember what he told me to speak out loud. I am Snow Falls. I am the western door of the five nations of my people. I am a Seneca, an Onondawaga of the Haudenosaunee.

Near the end of my grandfather's long sickness, he told my father and his brothers that he'd die in seven days, and so they showed him the fine leggings and robe and moccasins he'd wear at his burial, and on the sixth day he asked my father to paint his face the colour of blood because his closest friend had been to the afterworld and saw that this is how the people looked, and on the seventh day, just as he said, he slipped into that world. There was a great rain of sadness. The women in my family wailed all night and for ten days after. My father and his brothers didn't cry but made very sad faces. They painted my grandfather more, and then curled him up like a baby in his mother's stomach, and then they wrapped him snug, tight in his robe, and laid him back on his sleeping mat. I watched all of this. I watched my father cover him with bark. My father and his brothers, they stood guard over his body all through the snowmelt. And all this allowed everyone to say goodbye properly. But how do I say goodbye to my family? I didn't know they'd be taken away so suddenly. So quick. Despite the dreams, I didn't know it was the morning when I awoke on the trail that today would be the last day of my family's life. The sun shone bright on the snow, and braver winter birds came close in the hope I'd offer them a tiny scrap of deer fat. It's only now I realize they came to forewarn us of what soon approached. But we paid no mind, for we didn't expect to find our enemy in our winter place, so far away from his own home. But he came. And he took. And now he wants to become my father. But what he doesn't yet know is that I have special gifts, and it won't be long before I'm ready to show them.

I've stayed up on my perch, hoping the people in this longhouse will forget about me, forget that I exist. Those first few days when I arrived, I planned to try and escape, but the one named Bird watches me too closely, even though it appears he doesn't. Now I know I can't escape, and a death song begins to form in my head and I try to find the song by humming just under my breath, but it won't come to me. I want to be with my parents and my brother. I don't want to be here surrounded by those who slaughtered them. I am trying, now, to learn how to die.

The deepest night is when I sneak out of my warm robe to go outside and relieve myself, only having to do this every other night since I barely drink any water or eat any ottet. Despite how quiet I am, I know Bird awakes and listens for me to return. He can read my thoughts. He knew about my wanting to slip away. He knows about my wanting to die. He's a smart hunter. He watches everything. But I watch, too.

Early, early, before the light today, he awoke. I didn't hear him right away but felt the cold on my face when the door to the longhouse opened, and when I searched for his form in the dark I saw it wasn't there. I considered running away into the storm blowing outside but soon slipped back into bad dreams, flashes of things that scare me. Wolves. Being alone and lost in the forest. The spirit that lives under the water. And then I awoke to cold on my lips and the smell of sickness in my throat. I opened my eyes to see the bearded man hovering over me like a great charcoal bird, his eyes burning and wet, his whispers spitting onto my face. He held my father against my mouth, against my lips, as if to take the breath from me. My father didn't want to do this to me. I know it. And so I began to scream, to struggle to get the Crow away from me, biting his hand hard until he let go, and when I screamed again it's as if he flew backward, my father flying away with him, too. He just sprang backward like he wasn't human at all, disappearing to the ground below.

I crawled from my robe and peered down to see Bird crouched over the Crow. I could tell by the tension in his body that Bird was preparing to kill him. And despite not wanting to, I opened my mouth, and in a voice I hadn't used in many days, I spoke aloud, my throat strained from the lack of water and the lack of talk.

I told Bird that my name is Snow Falls and that this Crow had stolen the spirit of my father, that he kept him imprisoned in the glowing being around his neck, that if Bird killed the Crow now, my father would be his prisoner forever and I could never become Bird's child. I don't know where the words came from, but they came, and I watched the killing tension ease in Bird's shoulders. I told him, finally, what I've been dreaming, what only right then I could put words to. An illness was slipping into this village, into this very longhouse, and even if he killed the Crow now, it was too late to stop. It had arrived. Killing him would only make things worse. The words, they poured out of me and were beyond my control. To kill this one would simply make those who sent him angry and eager to punish the Wendat. It was better to allow this one to live and to study him, to try and understand him in order to prepare for what was coming. Bird, he listened. Slowly, he stood up, and his stare, as pointed as an arrowhead, warned the Crow never to touch me again.

I went back into my robe after that, my face warm, my stomach warm, my back feeling like it had the heat of the sun on it. For the first time since my family's murder, I felt heat, as if a coal that I'd thought had gone cold in the pit of my belly had been fanned and come to life. I wanted to close my eyes and feel this warmth in my sleep, but I couldn't.

I am alive now with the understanding of something important. I have power over this one called Bird. I have power over the Crow. The coal in my belly begins to burn the edges of my deep sadness. This coal licks my pain with fire so that I can feel my pain becoming sharp as the lip of a clamshell. I can feel it turning into something else. Something coloured like blood and charcoal, and these colours ease my pain just a little. I can sense my hurt becoming something else, and in the warmth of my robe I can see what it is. The coal ignited in me creates a weapon, one that I will use against my enemies when the time is right.

———

A WIND THAT isn't very cold blows in from the west. It takes the storm away with it and brings a sun so bright it calls me outside. I don't ask Bird's permission. I just rise from my sleeping mat, slow because my body hasn't moved in so long. My body doesn't want to listen to me as I try to get down the ladder and my legs feel as if they're frozen but eventually I'm on the ground again. Children playing in the longhouse stop and stare. I rise up on my toes and stretch, making a sound that begins in my belly and escapes like a loud hiss. The children's eyes go wide. They go wider when I crouch by the fire and rub soot on my face until it's dark as night. I stand and glare at them until, one by one, they turn away in fear. A couple of old women who watch over the children study me as they sew, glancing up every few seconds to see what I'll do next. I find my outside clothing stiffened and hanging, ready. Bird is off somewhere this morning, and I'm sure word will travel to him fast.

The possibility of spring is in the snow. I walk through it as it softens in the sun, the bright line of it outlining the paths of the village, and it scares me how big this place is. It's bigger than my own by far. Many, many longhouses with the smoke of the fires of all the families reaching into the air. How will my father's brothers defeat all of these people? Although not too many are outside yet, I can tell that as many as a great flock of finches live here.

My darkened face must stand out because people stop and look as I walk by. I growl deep in my throat when a young man laughs. He'd be good-looking if he wasn't so stupid. I move around the village for a long while, circling its outside twice before exploring the pathways inside. The palisades are three rows deep and tall and thick and the tips are sharply pointed. The longhouses are built well, are built much like our own. A few bored lookouts stare at me as I walk by them. I can feel their eyes on my back. I must learn the place of my enemy.

When I begin to tire, I sense someone following me. I had no real plan in all of this but to get outside and look around, then imagined I'd walk until I fell to the ground with exhaustion. I'm weak from so little food, but I want my enemies to think I'm even weaker than I am. I want them to pity me. I want them to worry for me.

I know who it is that follows. Word has reached him. He'll certainly worry for my head, and this is what I want. I'll keep him wondering about me until I've figured out how I'll return to my people and he's so confused by me that he'll be happy I'm gone. He makes no secret of walking behind me. He hums a song that sounds like spring, and I like it despite wanting to hate it. I walk faster, but he keeps pace. After a while, I begin to feel as though he's leading me, not me him. I don't like this man. I don't want to admit it, but he has powers too.

I turn down a smaller path that by the sun's place I think will take me back to his longhouse, and I consider slowing so that he'll catch up and walk with me. Kneeling in a snowbank, I begin to draw circles and wait for his shadow to stretch across me, blocking out the glare of sun on snow. As I turn my eyes to him, all I can see is a black outline. It isn't his. Bird is tall and this one who follows is small, her form as thin as a snake's. My head tells me to stand, and I do, but when it tells me to run, my legs go weak, weaker than when I climbed down the ladder from my bed this morning. As if commanded, I sit on my haunches, my hands folded on my knees, though my eyes remain on the thin woman who has been following, my eyes adjusting so I can make out the strands of her messy hair, the cheekbones that look sharp enough to cut me, the bare hands with long fingers. She stares at me, and this stare holds me down. My legs begin to shake, my knees knocking against each other. She raises her hand and my legs go still.

"You aren't afraid?" she asks. "Cold?" She doesn't wait for my response. "My name is Gosling. I could ask if you wanted to be here but I already know you don't."

I look up at her, the sunspots dancing, her face becoming focused. I think it's beautiful, but her words, her voice, make my legs start shaking again. She raises her hand once more. They stop.

"You will cause your new father much pain," she says. "I can see this, too." She smiles.

"He's not my father," I tell her. The idea that he is makes me sad and confused.

Although her mouth stays the same, I see her own confusion in her eyes. "I didn't ask you to speak, Snow Falls," she says.

I want to tell her that she isn't my mother, either. And how does she know my name? I try to find it in me to open my mouth and say this but it's as if it's been sewn shut with deer sinew.

"You're a strong girl, but not that strong," she says. "If you would like me to prove this to you, I will."

I suddenly feel as if my head's been shoved under water. I stare up at her, struggling with her, and I'm gasping for breath. The confusion in her eyes is now gone. She looks at me blankly, watching me drown. My mouth moves like a pike's that's been tossed onto shore. I feel my eyes bulge.

She blinks, and a rush of air fills my lungs so fast that I begin coughing and gasping.

"I'm not cruel," she says. "But I won't allow you to think that your strength can defeat mine." She sits beside me. I want to run screaming but I'm paralyzed.

She cups snow and pats it. "Spring will come earlier than last year. If you concentrate you can feel it in this." She nods at her hands. "The last night's snowfall was like our bodies when they reach that time. It's breaking down. It's dying." She keeps patting the snow as she speaks, one palm cupping the other. "Your brother," she says. "The special one." Her hands stop moving and she cradles the packed snow now. I look, and my brother's face stares back at me, as if carved by the most talented artist. His mouth slopes down at the edges, and his eyes, a little sunken, just as in real life, stare at me, unseeing.

The woman talks again. "If your brother hadn't been killed by Bird, if you'd all made it home this winter, he would have drowned two summers from now on a trading mission with your dead father."

She covers my brother's face and begins patting the snow again. When she opens her hands once more, my mother's face, her small nose, even the laugh lines at the edge of her eyes, astonishes me. "Your mother still had twelve or thirteen more winters but then would have been taken away by the coughing sickness."

She pats the snow again and there is my father, smiling at me as he always had when I climbed into my parents' sleeping robe and tugged his hair to wake him. "This is the most difficult loss of all," Gosling says. "Your father, had he not been killed, would have lived to be a very old man. He would have seen you marry, would have seen you give birth to many grandchildren, would have seen your hair begin to turn grey." I can feel her looking at me, but my eyes remain on my father's face in her hands. "And what's most difficult to realize," she says, "is that had he lived past this winter, he was to become the one strong enough to prevent the slaughter that now approaches."

Before I can protest, she covers my father's face with her hand. I want to ask her to tell me more but my mouth remains sewn shut. She pats her hands quickly, showing me glimpses in the packed snow of my cousins who were killed with my parents, explaining their other deaths, too, some by warfare, some by disease, one by old age. "The time's finally arrived," she says. "It's the most brutal that we'll ever witness. Your father's death has sealed that."

We sit in the snow, both of us quiet now, and watch as the day unfolds. Chickadees land close to us and blink, opening their beaks as if to say something important before flying away. The sun crawls across the sky almost fast enough that I can see its slow march. And yet for hours we sit there silently, the woman studying me without having to look at me. I don't feel cold or cramped or damp from the snow.

When she finally stands up, the sun is already weakening, and her shadow looks long. I stand too, and it's only now that I feel the winter has seeped into my bones and made me heavy with it.

"Don't worry," she says. "Spring is close." She turns to me. "You can speak now."

"Make my family alive again," I blurt, and my voice sounds old and scratchy.

She gives me that blank look once more, and I become frightened she'll take my breath away again, or worse. "I can't do that. That isn't my world." She smiles, but it isn't warm. I don't know if she can smile that way. "I've heard word that the Crow openly tells people that he can, though. He says to anyone who'll listen that the man he most admires came back from his murder three days later. I'll have to go and listen to him speak."

My ears perk at that. I, too, will have to start listening to the Crow and his sad attempts with Wendat words.

"Go back to your father now," she says. "He'll be worried for your safety."

"He isn't ..." But then I stop, fearful of her reaction.

She stares at me, and her lips curl a little at the edges. "You think I mean Bird." She looks away. "I'm not referring to him," she says. I want her to look back at me but she won't. Then she says, "I'm talking about the Crow."

———

AND SO AN IDEA begins forming in my head as winter thaws, dripping into spring. I take long walks every day, sneaking out by squeezing through a break I found in the palisades, and I know this makes Bird mad. He tells me I'm not to do this anymore. It's dangerous beyond the village, he says. Out there is a place the humans don't control. I tell him I'll wander where I please, and if he doesn't like it, he'll be forced to tie me up, for that's the only way he'll keep me in his stinking home.

The village lies on a river that, if you walk it for not very long at all, takes you to a great lake that looks so big it must be impossible to cross. I walk out onto the ice, listening as it moans, speaking, I guess, to the season about to come. I go as far as I can before my feet refuse to take me out any farther, and I gaze down at the black river of water that snakes through the lake where the stronger current must be. It grows wider each day, lapping at the ice that sometimes cracks so loud it makes me jump. I speak to the water, asking if it wants me to come into it. My father told me never to do this when I was a child because the spirit that lives in the water will hear me and want to meet me, and if that happens, well, it would be the end of me. But I do it anyway, in part because if I'm to leave this world for another, I can't imagine it being worse. Maybe I'll find my family. Maybe I'll find the place where the path turned in the wrong direction.

On my walks, this idea continues to form, and I find something like peace away from my enemy's home. I will make him hurt for hurting me so badly. Today, instead of following the river to the lake, I cut into the forest where the women collect wood. I want to memorize all the details of this land so that when the time is right and my people swoop in, they'll know it, too.

Just ahead of me, I see bloody snow where something was killed. As I get close, tufts of fur blow when the wind picks up. A large deer, it must have been, by the mess that's left behind, fur and so much blood that of course I think of your deaths. I search out the area with my eyes, trying to imagine what happened so recently. Last night, maybe? A pack of wolves must have followed a deer this big for a long time, bothering it, nipping at the tendons in its legs when they got close enough, biting at its belly, keeping a wary eye for the quick flick of hooves that can break ribs or crack skulls. The wolves would take turns pursuing, a couple driving the deer at a fast pace, the others hanging back and holding on to their energy. My father was careful in teaching me all of this.

You told me, Father, that wolves will pursue for days, will wage a war that's slow and patient, that wolves are so frightening not because of their fangs and claws but because of their intelligence, because of their hunger. I see this now, right here. I see the moment in the snow when the deer finally has nothing left, and the wolves join together as a pack, hungry and smart. I see the deer knowing that its fate has arrived and yet it prepares itself to fight as hard as it can for the slim chance its gut is telling it wrong, for the simple fact this is what it's meant to do, this fighting to live. The deer's tongue sticks out from its mouth it's so tired, and in this clearing in the half moon of last night, the wolves slip around the animal, weaving like shadows, growling directions to each other, the lead wolf holding back, allowing the younger ones to keep the deer's attention. And then the time presents itself. The lead wolf, having slowly, slowly crept close as the others snap and growl, the deer pawing snow and pinned between them and the cedar too thick to pass through, then lunges low and hard and from the side when the deer turns its head away, and the lead wolf latches onto the deer's thigh as hard as he can, feeling his teeth penetrate the coarse fur of the winter coat. He holds on to the thick strap of skin and muscle he's taken into his mouth and the others know as sure as they know anything that he has the deer as it tries to bolt away through the pack, screaming out in fear as the others descend and begin biting, too, their teeth as sharp and pointed as flint knives, the deer being dragged to the ground now, trying to kick itself back up but exposing its belly in the process and the strongest of the pack, so hungry, so desperate to feed, snap hard at the soft flesh, ripping skin and tasting the blood that drives them to snap and rip more.

This animal's death wasn't a pleasant one. But I begin to understand it probably never is. How can it be? But it has to happen, doesn't it? Can you hear me, Father? Do you believe what the woman named

Gosling said? That your dying will cause so many more deaths? It's not fair. This world isn't fair.

The wolves eat, and when they're so stuffed they can barely move, they drag what's left of the carcass away from this place that smells of humans and fire, leaving only the fur. If it were up to them they wouldn't have eaten here at all, but they're happy to be given the gift of more days of life. Wolves can't live on berries and twigs, after all, and their viciousness is what allows them to keep going, and will allow those who will one day follow to do the same. I bend to pick up a tuft of the deer's fur and lift it to my nose, and it's then I see that had this deer not died last night it would have before spring, in just as panicked and horrible a way, by breaking through the ice as it crossed a lake, kicking and struggling for a long time to get out, its eyes wide with terror until the exhaustion consumed it and it allowed itself to slip under, its last snort bubbling the water, its last breath drawing the cold water into its lungs. No, it's not that life isn't fair.

I lift the fur and let the wind take it away. I realize something important. Something you want me to see. It's a big decision, isn't it? I can hear your voice asking it, Father. Do I grow up to become a deer? Or do I grow up to become a wolf?

———

THIS MORNING WHEN Bird awoke early again, sneaking from the long-house to do what he does so early like this every few days, I crawled out from underneath my beaver robe and into his, taking in his scent. I had to piss, and so I climbed back out, crouched over his thick fur blanket, and released a long stream.

I lie awake now, waiting for him to return and discover what I've done. I consider how he'll choose to punish me. He'll probably not say anything at all until the longhouse gathers for our meal, and then he will announce this insult to everyone.

I wait and wait but he doesn't return. It must be noon when my legs begin to bounce with boredom, so I crawl down from my sleeping place and see that no one's inside. That's strange. I can't remember a time when there weren't at least a few people in the longhouse, tending to the fires or preparing meals or talking and laughing. I can tell that outside the sun is bright by the way it pierces the shadows in what are usually the dark corners of this place.

Pulling my coat over my head, I walk out and am amazed to find the ground brown and muddy all around me, as if winter's disappeared overnight. Is it possible I slept for days? Weeks? I'm suddenly confused and feel the fear come padding back around me on its large paws. No one's outside, either. It's as if I'm the only one left in the world. I walk through the deserted village, little mounds of snow in the shadows of longhouses the only evidence of winter.

When panic is about to consume me, I look up and see smoke coiling from the longhouses into the blue sky. People must be around, then, must be close. It's too warm for my coat, so I take it off and walk to the gap at the palisades. When I squeeze through, I finally hear the noise of humans, people speaking and walking and digging through soil with their tools. All across the fields that stretch out over the rolling hills, the people of the village stand or walk on the black earth, the ground muddy and rich, heavy with the smell of spring, of past crops, of worms and seeds and the sweat of those who've worked it. For a long time I watch all the people who live here, thousands of them. Most don't do much, just hold their faces to the sun or to one another, enjoying this first day of true spring. The air's filled with their happiness, their relief that they've made it through another winter and the good spring is upon them. Not wanting to, I lift my face to the sun as well and let its warmth fill me, the smell of loam so strong in my nose that I crouch down, lift handfuls of it to my face and breathe in deeply. My people are a farming people, just like these Wendat. We are a part of this earth. We speak similar tongues and grow the same food and hunt the same game. Yet we're enemies, bent on destroying one another. I don't understand it. But then I think of you lying dead, my family, the snow soaked with your blood, the same snow melting with your blood into the black earth at this very moment, and the anger rises in my throat and I do understand. Standing, I turn and throw the handfuls of mud at the palisades, watch as it speckles across a few of the sharp poles. I turn my back on these people. I will not let them change me. I won't let him become my father. The sun on my scalp is warm like blood trickling down onto my neck, making me shiver in the bright light.

———

AGAIN I AWOKE EARLY this morning. Yesterday, that first day of the new season, feels like a long time ago. When everyone had returned from the fields for their evening meal, I sat among them and waited for Bird to announce what I'd done to his sleeping robe. I waited for the reactions, the staring adults, the children laughing at me and pointing. But Bird never uttered anything, even though I knew he'd discovered what I'd done when he went up to his sleeping place earlier to retrieve his pipe and came down wiping his damp hands on his legs.

I waited until the meal was finished and the Crow stood and began to speak in his child words about his god being the one who brought the sun to the people today, most of the longhouse ignoring him, standing and going off to their night games and stories, the few who remained laughing at the idea of a maggot-pale god bringing sunshine to the Wendat world. Bird stood with the rest and left the longhouse without so much as looking at me. It wasn't until our bedtime, though, that I realized why he hadn't punished me in front of the others. Climbing into my robe, long after I believed Bird had already fallen asleep, I felt the wetness before I smelled the sour stink of my own piss. He'd switched our sleeping robes.

And so this morning I lie in my own dampness, needing to piss again, Bird already up and out of the longhouse. I crawl out from his robe, squat over my own, and do it again.

SHE KNOWS I WATCH

The Crow is nowhere to be found, which worries me, not because of my concern for his safety but because the village elders have decided he will stay, that it's good for trade relations with his fellow Iron People to allow him to talk to us. And the elders have told me I'm to be his minder, and I'm not to let anything happen to him. It is as it appears, then. This malevolent spirit has already worked his magic on us. When not so long ago I laughed at him, pitied him even, now I have learned that he can't be trusted and I must watch him closely, and never leave him alone again with the girl. I caught him trying to work his magic on her, and I would have killed him then and there if it hadn't been for her words.

She has something special. She has a gift. Gosling verified this to me on our last visit. I know you had a gift, too, dear one. Yours was the ability to heal, and those of us who still remember you, we all miss it very much. There's talk among the wise ones that next year we'll move the village to new ground. This coming time of planting is the last that the earth around us will support our corn, and our scouts are out looking for suitable places. As you know, my love, we'll then hold the great feast and the great time of mourning when remembrance will commence, and I'll hold you in my arms once more for a little while. I look forward to that very much.

Dark will settle in soon and I've checked in every longhouse for the Crow. He's taken to walking outside the palisades. He strolls with his head lowered, holding the sparkling necklace in his hands, counting the beads on it, mumbling to himself. He's a strange one. And a stupid one, clearly, walking with his eyes cast down, not paying any attention to his surroundings. Now that the snow has left, the time of raiding parties approaches, and while it's still very early, I wouldn't be surprised to hear that some of their hungrier warriors have slipped onto our land and taken a scalp or two. It's a game we play with one another, a chance for the young men to prove themselves and collect a little bounty. I hope they take the Crow. Maybe I'll do it myself and blame it on them, though allowing him to be harmed will certainly diminish my stature. We'll see. But for now, I must find him before night falls.

Frustrated, I walk to Gosling's home. I've been spending more time with her lately, and each of us seems to be falling into that place of contentment with the other. I don't think you'd mind. I know you wanted my happiness as I would want yours.

I whistle low to let her know I'm here, and wait for a response. Nothing. And then I hear a low hum of voices inside and realize she must be deep in conversation with someone, a man, by his pitch. The snake of jealousy crawls into my guts and wraps itself around them, squeezing. I clench my fists. This is what happens when you get too comfortable with someone too quickly. I shouldn't have let my guard down so fast. Of course Gosling has other lovers. She's very special. But if I'm one of many, it's not a position I like. The snake, though, only tightens its coil when I imagine how I'll not visit her for a long time, how I'll ignore her, even when she beckons me with her mind.

When I turn away, her whistle, high and quavering, comes in response. I almost keep walking, but the desire to see who she's invited into her home overcomes me. Inside, I can smell her before I see her, the smell I wanted to believe she'd created just for me that makes me hard before I lie down.

And then I smell him, the sour, unwashed smell of him, and I don't want to believe that he's in her lodge. My eyes adjust to the low light, her fire just coals, the afternoon sun filtering in from the hole above, lighting the wisps of smoke that rise up and out.

"What's he doing here?" I ask.

"Sit," Gosling says, motioning to a place beside her and across from the Crow. "This charcoal, he's very entertaining."

I do as she says, and realize this is always the case. When I look through the smoke to the Crow, there's something like lovesickness on his face. Sweat dots his forehead, and he frowns, not happy that I've disturbed his reverie.

"What spell did you put on him?" I ask Gosling. I speak quickly, so the Crow won't be able to understand very much.

"He claims that he and the other charcoal don't have relations with women," Gosling says. "I want to see if this is true. If you hadn't come by just now, I'm pretty sure I'd be proving him a liar." She looks over to me and smiles, takes my hand and squeezes it. I'm not sure if this is to suggest she jokes. "Look at him," she says, laughing. "He hasn't felt like this for a long, long time." He must understand some of what she says, for he drops his eyes from hers and rests his hands uncomfortably in his lap.

"Me talk," the Crow mutters, "me talk to it." He points at Gosling. "You come here, in here. Me talk to you now." I stare at him, almost allowing myself to feel pity for this one, for how hard he struggles to communicate with us. But then I remember what he tries to say, and why he needs to say it, his wanting to change us, and I bristle in anger. "Great Voice, he loves you," he continues, pointing at me. "Great Voice is son child deer Christ. Christ kill for you to become him. Christ kill me. Die. Death for you. Christ." He wipes his forehead and looks, imploring, to Gosling.

"Your Christ sounds fascinating," she says in a quick, clipped tone. "Do tell me more, and explain everything that you can about him and about the place you come from." She smiles, licks her finger and touches it to her ear, then takes her thick braid and begins to stroke it. "Tell me everything you know."

The Crow, clearly not understanding her, looks confused. He dabs at his forehead with a cloth, then drops his hands back into his lap, seeming almost frightened. "Wood," he says. "Long wood. Two woods." I laugh, wondering if Gosling has damaged him. The Crow makes a chopping motion. "His hands are attached. His feet are attached," he says. "Hurt. He dies you." He points to me. "You die."

I feel rage flush my face. "If he says once more that I will die," I tell Gosling, "I'll kill him."

"Shhh," she says, and squeezes my hand again. "He struggles with the language. I've simply baffled him. He's told me how this Christ"—she pauses, as if the strange word is distasteful—"this Christ is the son of their most powerful oki. Supposedly, he was murdered by people this crow thinks were much like us." She stops and smiles at the Crow again, licking her upper lip. "He pleads with me," she continues, amusement in her words, "he pleads with me to pray to his okis, for it seems I will go to a bad place if I do not."

The Crow nods enthusiastically, and I wonder how much of what Gosling's said he understands.

"What do you think of all this?" she asks me.

"I think that I will kill him very soon," I say.

She pulls her hand from mine. "It seems we find ourselves at a place where the river splits," she says. "Important decisions to be made, Bird." I can't remember her ever saying my name out loud. "Decisions to be made." The Crow tries to speak again, but she waves her hand and he stops, looks back down at his hands folded in his lap. "He doesn't have the desired power over me," Gosling says. "I fear, though, that he will begin to have some over others once he learns the language better."

I scoff at this. "He's a sad joke for a man," I say. "He knows nothing of the land, nothing of us."

"He isn't stupid," she says after a pause. "Don't confuse his inability to speak well with his plans for us. You yourself challenged others to try to speak his language before laughing at him for trying to speak ours."

"Baah," I say. "That was before I understood his intentions. I caught him touching my child, trying to work something on her. I should've killed him then."

"You know you can't," Gosling says. "The elders won't condone it." She looks at the Crow and again strokes her braid slowly. He fidgets, and a small moan escapes his mouth.

"He's not a man," I say.

Gosling dabs a finger into her mouth. "I rather like his build," she says softly. "The colouring of his eyes intrigues me."

I get up to leave. "Have him, then."

As I walk for her door, she speaks. "I tease you. Do you really think I could be attracted to such a stinking and awkward creature? I chose you for a reason. I just want to test this one's strengths." She looks at the Crow and he looks away. "Make no mistake," she says. "His strength's building, and as much as I don't want to admit it, he will begin to win some of the weaker ones over." She turns her head up to the dying light pouring into the hole of her lodge and the sunlight strikes her face in the gloom.

Her eyes are closed, and her palms rest on her lap. "He'll gain power because someone you don't want to believe would ever help will assist him in spite of you."

I stand and watch her glowing face. I will her to tell me more.

"Your solution to all of this is simple. On your summer trading voyage, he'll want to go with you. Bring him. Bring the girl, too. Take the route along the Snake River."

I want to tell her this river is Haudenosaunee territory. I open my mouth, but she holds her hand up.

"Bring your strongest with you," she says. "Allow the Haudenosaunee to attack and let them kill the Crow for you." She pauses, opens her eyes and smiles at him. He stares at her, his mouth half-open. "Or better yet, allow them to take him prisoner so that he can be caressed by their coals before they take his life. Surely, then, news will get back to this village of his demise. Your problems will be solved."

I smile for the first time in a long while. I move, then, to leave, but think better of it. "I will be deeply upset if you prove him a liar," I say, but she's already turned her face up to the last of the day's light. If she hears me, she doesn't let me know.

———

HOW IS IT THAT I lose one family, a family that I love so much, only to be ensnared by these two demanding and difficult children, these two beings who drive me mad? I guess this is the way of our world. First it's the Crow, wandering around the village, talking like a damaged boy to anyone who'll listen, mostly those who need a good laugh. And now it's the girl, slipping out of the longhouse at odd times and disappearing through the palisades, where it's not safe for anyone to find herself alone. I've come to realize she's a wild animal, a wolf pup, perhaps, taken in by a human and too afraid of the darkness to run back into the forest, instead snapping at her feeder's hand out of anger and self-pity. I'll win her over. It's just a matter of time, sweet one. I know you'd balk at my comparing her to an animal, to a pet, but she really is like that. She won't bathe. She certainly isn't house-trained. She refuses to eat in front of me, instead taking her meal to a dark corner of the longhouse. She doesn't speak unless it's in a growl when I confront her or worse, when she whimpers and speaks out as she sleeps at night. I watch her, and she acts like a dreaming animal even then, her legs twitching as if she's running, her hands contracting into claws as she cries out. I do not yet understand her. But I'm patient. I will.

I haven't visited Gosling in a week so that she'll know I don't like her games. She can have her Crow. I'm thankful, though, that she's shown me a good path for what needs to be done. Something must be done. The others here, the elders included, are blinded by the promise of riches, and this makes me sad. This Crow doesn't bring that, although some claim he promises them everything they could ever want if only they just kneel down and reach their arms up to him. I won't be one of them.

———

THE WATCHMEN have told me that she sneaks out at a break in the palisades. They keep an eye on her for as long as they can but when she wanders into the forest by the river that leads to the big lake, they shrug their shoulders and say there's not much they can do about it.

Today, I decide to follow her. Leaving before she does, I get comfortable in a thick stand of cedar by the river's edge near where weirs have been set for the spring fishing. The clouds have finally given in to the sun this afternoon. To keep myself from boredom, I make a list of those I'd like to bring along on the summer paddle to the pale and hairy ones. Only special ones. Fox will certainly come. I've not asked him yet but I know. There are many eager young men in the village, and before making my decision I'll watch how hard they work at the clearing of fields and other duties that young men shy away from. So much is learned by seeing how well or how poorly someone accomplishes a job he dislikes.

When I think that she won't be escaping the village today, I hear footsteps and a low thrum of speech. I'd been examining the scratchings of turkeys in the dirt near me, vowing to come back here soon to hunt. Now I see who it is, walking slowly and mumbling to himself, wearing a strange wide-brimmed charcoal hat that shades him from the sun, his charcoal robes brushing the ground, his hands held behind his back, as if he's a prisoner of his own doing. Light glints off the Crow's necklace, and as he talks to himself I wonder what he's saying, if he's mad or really in conversation with someone I can't see. In this tall, gaunt creature I can see a power I don't want to acknowledge. He's absolutely unafraid of his surroundings, and yes, this is stupidity, but it also suggests what Gosling would say is his understanding that what will become of him will become of him, regardless of the little he can do to try and prevent it. He strides, I see, as if his path is already laid out for him. This one does have a power we don't yet understand. It's in his walk and in his mumbles.

The childish urge to jump screaming from the cedar and make him collapse in terror comes over me. But I won't do that. He walks by close enough that I can reach out and touch his foot from where I sit on the ground, cross-legged. He has no idea I'm even here. I know he's not long for our world, and Gosling's suggestion for his demise on the Snake River won't be difficult to make happen. Some little tug of sympathy for him is snuffed out by the knowledge that what I must do to him I do for my people.

I'm about to head home when I'm surprised to see Snow Falls walk up behind the Crow and call out to him with her strange voice. She must have somehow damaged it in all the turmoil she's endured before ending up in this place. It sounds scratchy with age or as if she'd once been strangled and the voice never healed. I don't like seeing her beckon him, something she's never once done to me. He stops his reverie and turns to her. I can see the white flash of smile in the shadow his wide hat throws.

She turns her face up to him and I see how she's pocked with old scars from some foreign sickness that came to our shores with the French and the Dutch and the English. It makes me wonder about her past, about what I erased forever that day in the snow. How different could her family have been from my own? We all share many traits, surely, including the desire for retribution, and for the return of those loved ones lost.

I watch these two stare at each other for a long time, and it takes everything in my power not to jump up and stop this. Did I not warn the Crow never to go near her again? Did I not warn him what will happen to him if he does? The girl holds her hand up and hesitatingly touches a finger to the necklace. The Crow tenses, not sure if he should let her, or maybe fearful that she'll yank it from his neck. She finally opens her mouth, asks him something in a quiet enough tone that I can't hear what she says. He takes a few moments to gather the words, to respond, his face working hard to find them.

When he does speak, I can make out some words. Fawn. Dead. Fish. Live. Eat. Dove. He seems stuck on many of these words, and I'd question his intelligence if I didn't know better. At least he's learning some new ones. He then turns to walk away. Smart Crow. Had he carried on any further, those in my longhouse having heard what I'd told him that day, I wouldn't have to plan the ruse of his demise. The elders know this girl is my daughter, and my longhouse would come to my aid if I were threatened with banishment for killing him. And so why don't I? Kill him for his behaviour with my daughter? I hear Gosling telling me to be patient, that to leave my fate up to anyone but myself is never wise. I am the hunter, not the prey. The Snake River idea is a good one, though I still don't know how I'll explain why I chose such a dangerous route. Gosling must see something in the future. She's told me it will work itself out.

It's time to talk to Fox about the summer's travel, so I'll sneak away. The girl is still staring at the Crow as he wanders back toward the palisades, his head bent and mouth mumbling once more. I can see in her posture that she's confused, and I'm surprised she doesn't realize it's because he dare not disobey me. When he should be treated like a prisoner, the elders have said he should be treated as a guest. So be it. And clearly he's a guest who understands his limits. The girl will just have to come to terms with this. Sometimes, it's not getting what we want that offers us the most important lessons.

As I smile to myself for being so wise, the girl calls out to the Crow again. It's not a word at all, but the plaintive call of a dove. He slows down but keeps walking. She calls in that tone once more and he stops. She runs the short distance to him. They stand face to face, each taking a turn speaking. She then extends her hand, palm open, to him. He hesitates before taking it. I clench dirt in my fists. He kneels down to her level and lifts his hand. She closes her eyes. With his thumb, he traces some sign on her forehead. When he's done, she opens them.

They stare at each other for what feels like a long time. He stands then, her hand still in his, and they walk a few steps.

That's when the girl turns her gaze to where I'm crouching and grins. My face flushes. She knows I've been here all along. She knows I watch.

IS ANYTHING IN THE WORLD THAT SIMPLE?

Fox raises his eyebrows when I tell him how many I want to come with us on our summer journey. We sit by his fire near the door of our long-house, dipping strips of smoked fish into our ottet. It's early spring, after all, and the fish, we pray as we consume them, will continue to be plentiful.

"That's a war party, friend, not a trading party," he says. "Do you realize how much that will cost you? You'll owe others and they won't owe you this summer."

I've never held anything back from him, but for the first time, I decide that I need to. I'm not quite sure I want to include him in my scheme, especially if it fails. Best not to let him know so if anything goes awry he can honestly tell the elders he's innocent of wrong-doing. I tell him something about how many furs the Anishnaabe have trapped this winter and traded to us that in turn we will paddle to the French. Fox just nods his head and looks into my eyes. I turn my head away, and in this motion I remember the Crow touching his thumb to the girl's forehead. In the flush of anger I feel even now in my face, I've never been more resolved.

"Given how life has been between us and the Haudenosaunee lately," I say, "there's no difference between a war party and a trading party anymore."

"Which route to take, then?" he asks. "Especially if we're really to travel with a hundred men?"

For the second time in moments, for only the second time in my life, I lie to my friend. "We'll see," I say. "When the time's right, we shall see."

We eat in silence then, and I once more convince myself that putting Fox in danger, never mind the young men who will come with us, is small payment for ridding our community of the scourge that has arrived and that won't stop coming. And to think I'm the one who brought him here. The elders asked me to do it when they heard last autumn that the French wanted us to accept him, but still. I should've tried harder to let our pursuers capture him on that day we were chased last winter. He somehow escaped them, I don't know how, even as he carried the girl.

"There's one more thing," I finally say. "A favour I need to ask of your wife."

Fox lifts his chin slightly, urging me to go on.

"Our summer paddles are never safe and"—I pause, searching for the right words—"given how dangerous it can be on our travels to the French, I don't think it wise to bring my new daughter." I tell him I know the girl is difficult and more trouble than most would think she's worth, and what I ask is an immense favour for a woman already burdened by the worry for her husband away on such a long and risky trip. "But will you ask your woman," I continue, "if the girl can stay back with her this summer? There's so much she can teach the child."

Fox smiles. "There's no denying that Snow Falls is a strange one." He realizes his words, and looks up to me, a little embarrassed. "I admit that my wife worries sometimes for the girl's head. And she certainly appears to cause you to sleep poorly." He shrugs. "I can't speak for my wife, but I can't imagine she would say no." Fox scrapes his ottet bowl with his fingers and licks them. "Of course," he says after a few moments. "We are all family, no? And now that it's been decided to move the village this summer, the extra hands will be good for my wife."

———

LIFE APPEARS NORMAL to me as spring grows warmer. I've asked another household to keep the Crow for a short while, as I secretly fear that I'll strike out and kill him if I see him touch my daughter again. The household, on the far side of the village, is happy to do it. They're patient and sit for days on end with him, trying to teach him our language. They hope this will attract more visitors who always come bearing gifts in order to watch and hear the spectacle. At first I remember what Gosling said about his learning our tongue and what it will hasten, but then I realize it's all fine. Soon enough, he'll be dead.

I send Snow Falls out planting most days, and she's good with a digging tool and carefully soaks and then counts out the kernels of corn for each hole in the dirt. I worry for the lack of rain, though. At this time last year there was almost too much, but the earth today is drier than I like it. And the air is noticeably warmer. When midday comes I find myself removing my clothes to the sun, something I don't normally do until summer. My usual job is to clear trees for more land, but now that we're moving the village, there's no need. Instead, I go back to the longhouse to decide what will be taken and what will be left behind.

Both in these fields and the new ones a day's walk from here, we plant the three sisters. The corn, if rains come, will be waist high when I leave in the summer, the beans showing off their lush leaves, and the squash blossoms blooming the colour of the setting sun. This is what I hope but would never dare speak out loud for fear of offending any of their okis.

———

FOR THREE WEEKS we catch barely any fish, and this, combined with the lack of spring rain, has all the houses worried. Normally at this time of year both are plentiful. Each house has asked the one who understands the fish the strongest to pray with all of us for it to return. Our man is Fox, and I listen intently each night as spring dwindles away, as he talks and sings to the fish, begging our brother to come back to us. How have we offended you? Let us know and we will correct our behaviour. Fox, a very good fisherman, has a special relationship to them, and even has a sturgeon on his stomach that his wife took a whole winter tattooing their first year of marriage. Each night he asks us to lie on our backs as he does, fifty of us in the longhouse, adult and child alike, to listen to what he has to say to the oki of the fish. And each night he begs of us never to burn the bones of fish but to bring them back to the water instead. Fox pleads with the fish that we respect it deeply and that we, the people, would never burn its bones.

Perhaps I'm getting used to the girl's odd behaviour. She's unhappy that the Crow no longer stays here. She's become sullen and even more quiet. This is certainly better, though, than her pissing in my bed. When she catches me looking at her, she sometimes puts her thumb to her forehead and makes the sign that the Crow showed her. I always turn away. Like a fever, this too will burn off. I continue taking her to the fields each day, and am always surprised when she doesn't refuse but instead throws herself, focused, into the work.

And despite the absence of rainfall and the fish having left us, I finally feel a sense of peace that I haven't known in a long time. The girl won't speak to me, but she stays by my side like a real daughter should, my darling, and I feel some of the hole that's so deep inside me begin to fill in, if only just a little. I also daydream that the girl will become whole as she gets used to living with our clan, that she's just going through the brutality of adolescence. I'm willing to wait the few years it will take before she's able to call me Father, before she's able to sit and talk and laugh with me, or to cry on my shoulder when she has her heart broken. I can wait, my love, because she'll take that place beside our dead daughters, the place they did not live long enough to inhabit. You, of all people, know that despite my hot head I'm the most patient of men.

———

FOX FINDS ME by the river this afternoon and tells me I'm requested at the council fire. He looks me in the eyes when he says it, searching, I think, to see if I've done something out of the ordinary. To be called to the fire carries much weight. It means that I'll be asked many of my opinions. Fox knows me almost as well as I do, and he certainly knows that I'm not being forthright with him. For the first time in my adult life, I feel like a child about to be called out in front of his peers.

At first I fear my plan to rid us of the Crow has been discovered, but only Gosling knows of it. Why would she dare speak of it? What, I wonder as we walk back through the palisades, would she gain by stabbing me in the heart this way?

To give myself a bit more time to breathe, I tell Fox I must go back to the longhouse and pick up some tobacco for the elders. He nods and follows me, and I wonder if they've asked him to stay with me and ensure that I arrive. I'm not used to this feeling, fearing that I've done something wrong and now will be punished.

As I climb up to my sleeping place, I tell myself that this isn't who I am, and even if Gosling has betrayed me, I'll argue that killing the Crow is the most important thing I can do for our nation. I feel my spine straighten as I imagine telling them they can punish me however they see fit, but I'll still die knowing I did the right thing. I grab my pouch from beside my sleeping mat and walk with Fox to the great longhouse.

The door on each side is open for the air to come through, and shafts of sunlight filter into the big room, illuminating the fish that float above me, saved for a future communal feast, tied drying to the beams alongside the special ears of corn reserved for future plantings. The smell here is different than in other longhouses. Each of this village's dozens of longhouses has a specific scent, the smell of mingling humans who've long lived together. Ask anyone to close his or her eyes and wander from home to home, and they'll all know immediately whose they're in. But this longhouse, much bigger than the others, is lived in only by okis. And okis, my love, don't have much need or care for scent, do they? The dust tickles my nose, the corn and fish make my stomach grumble, and the sight of the old ones sitting around the low fire makes me feel once again like a little boy caught doing wrong.

Taking my place, I sit cross-legged and listen as they talk and laugh. That the women sit alongside the men today rather than holding their own separate council means something very important has happened.

I take tobacco from my pouch and sprinkle some into the fire, whispering a short prayer, and then pass the pouch to old Earth Woman, who we call Ata, asking that she take a pinch as a sign of my respect and then pass it around to the dozen or so others who have now gone silent and glance at me before looking away.

"Has the spring planting gone to your liking, Tsawenhohi?" she asks, using my formal name, Osprey, as she takes her small clay pipe from its pouch and packs tobacco into it. Her hands are so dark and wrinkled that I wonder if the fallow fields might look like this if I were to fly like a raven above them.

"I fear for the lack of rain," I say. "This is my greatest concern."

She nods, taking a long hardwood stick from the fire and lighting her pipe. She puffs and puffs until her head disappears in the smoke.

For a long while we all sit and chat about everything and nothing. We talk of the impending move to a new village and I realize all that I must accomplish before the summer's travel. It'll be much work but everyone is excited for it. We smoke until the air around us is threaded with sunlight and so beautiful I can't stop looking at it, wanting to reach out and run my hand through it. My head's dizzy, and when my gut begins to sicken from it, I only barely puff on the odd pipe that's passed along to me.

Eventually, like a meandering river that begins to straighten and narrow, the discussion turns to the Iron People and our relations with them and why I would wish to take such a large party with me to their place this summer. They don't ask me to defend my thinking but instead speak openly about the good and the bad of it. Several of the elders observe that the trip might cause me to owe more than I am owed.

I nod then and speak. "Relations with our enemy have only grown worse in the last years, and I'm afraid that travelling safely in the future is impossible except in large parties. This is how I see it."

The others mull this over. "Our trade with the Iron People," the oldest, Aronhia, Sky Man, says, "has brought us oddities that have now become necessities." He reaches with his stick to the fire and taps the copper pot sitting there. "Our people just love this stuff. We can't get enough of it." The others laugh. Beside it squats a poorly made birch basket, and I wonder if it's been placed there to make a point. "If we are to remain the ones at the centre of the trade," Aronhia continues, "we'd better do whatever we can to keep those hairy creatures happy." Again, more laughter. Mine isn't nearly so loud because I know what's coming next. "And that means allowing the Crow to hop around the village and caw." There's a low growl of approval from the others, and I'm angry that no one cares to see the danger of this.

After a long silence, it's Yenrish, the Cougar, your mother's brother, my love, who finally speaks out. "Are we allowing our desire for profit to blind us? The people south of us who have lost so many to new illnesses, they know where the illnesses stem from."

"No one's fallen sick since the arrival of the Crow," Marten, the youngest of the circle, says. I know him only slightly, but his family's fearlessness in travelling through enemy lands to trade with the Iron People is legendary. They've become rich from it, though have lost many of their clan to the warfare and the worst of tortures. Marten himself was captured and escaped, but not before losing his right hand and most of the skin from his back.

"Maybe it's more than that, this idea that no one is sick yet," the oldest woman, Ata, says. The others wait for more, but she's wiser than that. I recognize how she attempts to lead the conversation. I want to speak but must purse my lips.

"Maybe it is more than that," Aronhia echoes.

The others around the circle begin to speak when it's their turn, some siding with Marten that if we are to maintain our dominance of trade over both our allies and our enemies, we have to move forward with these Iron People and their charcoal. "If they're all as powerful as the crow we keep now," Marten says, "I don't think we have much to worry about," and a few of the others laugh.

"So they are an evil that we have to absorb?" Yenrish asks. I take a pipe offered to me and puff lightly on it, wondering how Marten will answer this.

He simply nods.

"Is anything in the world that simple?" Yenrish asks.

Everyone around the circle sits without speaking for a long time. The light of dusk is already fading to night when Ata finally requests the fire to be stoked. There's still business to discuss. I want to stand and stretch but that will have to wait. A gourd of water is passed around, refilled, and passed around again.

"Let's talk about the most recent trouble," Aronhia says. No longer happy, he looks up at me, then, just as quickly, away. "Bring him in." He nods at the young guard squatting by the west door. The warrior stands and exits.

"One of our hunting parties was ambushed a few days ago," Ata says.

My stomach drops.

"The Haudenosaunee killed most on the spot, took a few home to caress with coals, and sent one back to us with their message."

I know this message can't be a good one. Impatient now, I mutter under my breath for the guard to hurry up and bring in his charge. No one speaks. We all just stare into the fire.

He returns with a second guard, the two of them supporting a heap of flesh, all but carrying him to the fire. They place him on a fur beside your mother's brother Yenrish, and that's when I realize he must be a relation of yours, dear one. He can barely raise himself to sit, and Yenrish leans over and helps hold him up.

I'm a war-bearer, but even I am taken aback by his injuries. He must be a very strong young man to have made it home alive at all. The strip of hair that once ran down the centre of his head has been removed with a sharpened clamshell or knife, which has caused the skin of his forehead and above what were once his ears but are now just bloody holes to sag and wrinkle. The hair was clearly replaced with hot resin from a pine to cauterize the wound so he wouldn't bleed to death, giving the young man forever the appearance of a pathetic baby bird with a thick and ugly scar splitting its head. They removed his left eye, obviously, for it is swollen nearly shut, a thin line of oozing red. The three longest fingers of his left hand have also been removed. He must be of that side and will never draw and sight a bow again. At least, I think, he could learn to do so with his right hand, but when he lifts it to his mouth to wipe away the drool, I see that his bow fingers have been removed from that hand as well. I don't want to see his back, for I can imagine it's been removed of much of its skin, as I'm sure his thighs have been.

"Can you repeat to us," Ata asks loudly so that he can hear, "what those who did this to you want you to share with us?"

The young man peers one-eyed into the fire, then mumbles that its heat hurts him too much and he wants to sit back in shadow. Yenrish stands and helps him up so the two warriors can move him into the dimness beyond the fire's light. The fire's too small and we sit too far back from it for him to feel any real pain, and I understand right now the true damage our enemies have done to him. He will go through the rest of his life being whispered about and pointed at by others. He will be shamed prematurely into his own death. The anger at those who created this blossoms, as it always does, in the deepest part of my belly.

When he's able, the young man speaks, his voice full of spit and blood. He tells us of how the enemy acted as though they knew his party, a dozen strong, had split into small groups, heading to different places within a day's travel of their home camp to pursue deer. He and his brother were captured a short walk from the land they'd tracked, and his brother was beaten to death in front of him with clubs. The Haudenosaunee then dragged this young man back to his camp and began torturing him with clamshells while waiting for the others to return.

"The rest of that day I tried to stay alive," he says. "I sang my death song and tried not to cry out when they cut or burned me." He stops to draw in his rasping breath. "The first thing they did when each of our hunters came back captured was cut both his ears off and place them in a birch basket." My eyes wander to the poorly made one placed beside the copper pot. "They told me when they left that this was to show you how important it is for you to listen to them."

He explains how he watched them kill each of his companions over the next few days in the most painful ways they could come up with. All had the flesh stripped from their chests and backs before being hanged by ropes over hot coals. When they passed out, cold water was poured over them to revive them and they were fed ottet to regain their strength before being roasted again. Some had their eyes carved out with burning sticks, others had hatchet heads reddened by the fire's heat seared into their armpits or between their legs. Five of the eleven gave in and began to scream for mercy, the young man reports, but six chanted their death songs and were able to smile into that place while staring their enemies in the eye.

"So tell us, brave one," Ata asks, "what did they ask you to share with us?"

The young warrior asks for water, and as I listen to him slurp at it with his damaged face, I realize I should do him the favour of finishing him if this is what he desires.

"We hold one of their own as a prisoner," he finally says. "Clearly she's special to them. They want her back." We can hear his strained breathing in the shadows. "I'd like to go now," he says. "Can I go now?"

"Of course, dear one," Ata says. "We will hold a feast to celebrate your bravery on the longest day of the year. You are an example to the young men coming up. The enemy chose you to be the messenger because of your fortitude."

The others respond with their Ah-ho!, and I lower my head when the young man is carried away because I know he's staring at me.

For a long time I listen as the elders confer. They talk about sending out another party to track down and kill the Haudenosaunee if they foolishly haven't left. They speak about how the land around us can no longer support a community this large. One proposes dividing ours into smaller entities spread out but not too far from one another, and this is rebutted by the fact that a very big village repels invasion by its sheer existence. They talk more of the French and the various tactics in dealing with them. They keep the fire stoked and speak of our enemies who've dared come this far into our country so early in the raiding season and talk around, I finally realize, the issue of why I am here.

The first of the morning birds have begun to call out, letting us know the sun is on its way, when finally my name is spoken.

The youngest, Marten, is the first to say it. "Tsawenhohi has clearly taken a girl who means much to them." I've been waiting to hear this. Now it's said. And so now it will be considered by all.

"What would Marten do?" Ata asks.

"I'd give her back," he says, "and expect them to pay me well for keeping her in such good strength."

It isn't that simple, but this night, and now this morning, is the time to listen and for me to bite my tongue.

They all take turns speaking again, revived despite the sun threatening. It's Ata who finally says it. "Their message is clear. They've travelled far into our country, early in the year, and will stand behind what they threaten if she isn't returned. Is she worth it?"

Again they all speak, each in his or her turn. Even Yenrish doesn't argue. Aronhia, the oldest man, looks to me when all are done and speaks just as a baby in a nearby longhouse wakes with morning cries of hunger. "We should consider," he says, "what is most sensible not just for the one but for the community." He reaches his stick into the coals and turns it. The tip burns the colour of a cranberry, then bursts into flame. When he stretches and slowly stands up, we all do the same.

———

I RUB THE SHORT NUB of stick against a carved-out piece of cedar, twisting it to mimic a turkey hen. Snow Falls kneels beside me, watching intently, as is her nature. The sound of the wood on wood as I twist my hand warbles like a bird who needs a mate, and the fresh scratchings of a male a short arrow flight from where we huddle is what has kept me here in this clearing since before daybreak. I'm surprised the girl joined me when I asked, out of courtesy, if she'd like to come.

She still hasn't said more than a few sentences in these last weeks, and I refuse to let her know she's winning this battle, that she's wearing me down. I twist the nub again and the call of the female echoes out from the cedar in my hand. I then place the wood beside my bow, an arrow already notched into place.

As I had hoped, the yawp of a male calls out from just inside the tree line across from us. His call is deep and the hunger for a mate is obvious in it. I pick up the cedar and stick and call out once more to tempt him out of cover. Then, as slow as I'm able, I pick up my bow. All I hear for a few moments is the gentle breath of the girl, now quickening some. I draw back and stare down the length of the arrow to where he will come.

A big male emerges, hesitant and alert. Despite what his instinct tells him, I know that his desire will get the most of him. He only needs to come halfway into the clearing and I'll have my shot. He puffs his chest and calls out again. As good as his meat will be, it's his feathers I need most. They are the only ones I will use for my fletching, and I plan on making many arrows for the summer journey.

He scratches at the ground and bobs his head, trying to entice the female he thinks is close by. Both confused and curious, he takes a few more steps, then thinks better of it and begins to retreat to where he came from. That's when an even larger male pops out from the bush, opening his wings wide to intimidate the other. I've never seen a turkey so large. He gobbles out coarsely as he approaches the other male, who makes only the slightest of challenges before scurrying off in the other direction, clucking in anger.

The huge bird, with the clearing all to himself, steps out in the middle and yawps once more for the female that he, too, had heard. He puffs out so big that I picture shouldering him back into the long-house to proudly show off to Fox. The fletching this bird will provide! My arm, tiring now, holds steady, and my fingers on the string hum for release. My aim is centred on the bird's chest, such a large target that I know I can't miss.

Just as I let go, I feel the girl's hand push my arm. I watch the arrow shoot hard to the left of the bird and thunk and splinter on a tree across the clearing. Quick as I can, I reach for another arrow and notch it, drawing back just in time to see the bird scuttle into the bush. I slowly release the tension on the bow and let the arrow drop.

When I stand, my knees shake. I fight the urge to slap her. I bend down and pick up my possessions, then start to walk away. Then I stop and turn. The girl stares at me dully. She smiles, but there's no light in it.

"In a few days, we will begin the move to a new village," I say, "and we'll leave this place, my home. It isn't your home. It can't ever be." I pause and search for the words. I want to tell her I've decided to trade her for peace. I want to tell her that along with her, I'll bring my most sacred possession as a gift, that I'll carry wampum from the Wendat people, crafted and sewn into one of the greatest story belts I've ever seen, that this is what I've been given to do. But all that comes out of my mouth is, "After the village is moved, I will paddle you to the designated place, and I will return you to your people."

I expect her to smile, but instead something like sadness flashes in her eyes.

THE KETTLE HAS BEGUN

I watch for days, for weeks, the preparations for what will take these Wendat, my people's enemy, beyond the summer to accomplish. I'm glad Bird will return me to my family. This village slowly pulls itself apart and is carried on the backs of the women and men and children to its new location a day's walk from here. It's difficult work, brutal work, but I won't have to help these ones much longer. Soon, I'll be carried in Bird's canoe to the land of my people, and there I'll be given back to them and hopefully be avenged.

He and Fox and the men of their longhouse focus on the construction of their new home, and I'm impressed by how quickly it's going up. Tomorrow before dawn we'll walk back to the old village and gather more of our possessions only to turn around the morning after that and drag them here. Some men dig holes and place the palisades while others build their new homes. By the looks of it, this village will be as large as the last one, maybe bigger. I work hard at remembering all the little details, anything that might help my father's war-bearers when they come to destroy it. I look for the entrances and the weaknesses in the palisades, and where the most important longhouses are. Bird won't send me away without paying for it.

He and the others who will be going on the voyage work especially hard, up before dawn and still building and chopping and dragging until well after dark. They need to do much before heading off, but instead of being short-tempered and exhausted, they seem very content, even happy. Maybe it's because of the new location that's been chosen, which I have to admit is beautiful. A river runs beside it into the Sweet Water Sea, and already fields are being carved out of the thick forest. There will be much firewood for a long time, and I can tell this place will be plentiful with deer and moose and smaller game.

This morning, as we leave the new village and head back to the old one, Bird and Fox stop at a large pit that's being dug. I wonder what it is. Men are already busy building scaffolding beside it.

"Word has gone out to all the other villages?" Fox asks.

Bird nods. "They're preparing the fire for the Kettle. I've been waiting for this day since I lost them."

"It might bring you a bit of peace," Fox says.

Instead of answering, Bird walks down the path and into the forest, the rest of us following.

———

EARLY SUMMER ARRIVES, and there is still much work to be done, I can see, but the old fields will grow through one last summer to supplement these new ones. I wake up hoping this day will be the day we leave. People seem anxious. They're planning some kind of ceremony, but no one speaks of it out loud and I'm too mad at Bird to ask him.

Men continue to dig the pit and it's now almost as long as a longhouse and as deep as one is high. The scaffold around it seems to be finished. Ladders go up to it, and so it must be some sort of stage. I hope to see whatever it is that's coming.

When I walk back to the new longhouse, Bird and Fox are wearing their tobacco pouches and each carries a small sack of ottet. They're clearly about to travel somewhere. Bird looks at me and actually smiles. "We have something important to do these next days," he says. He's about to walk out with Fox but then turns back to me. "The whole of our village is involved, and so if you'd like to join us, you are welcome to."

I shake my head. For a tiny moment it looks like he's been hurt by my response. He turns and walks with Fox out of the longhouse. I watch them from the doorway and, once they're far enough away, I follow.

All day long, so many people use the path that leads to the old village that I don't even have to hide from Bird. Clearly, there's one last important thing to do in that place. The day is warm and the light pours down through the trees as we near the Sweet Water Sea. I feel something I've never felt as I walk along with a greater number than I've ever walked with before, few of them even talking, just the sound of so many feet and so many people breathing. I feel like part of this group. When we break out of the forest and onto the trail on the cliffs above the great sparkling water, I tell myself that I'm not part of them. I'm not. But still, I want to know what it is that I'm now a part of. I want to know why we're walking back to the old village as one.

In the corner of my eye I see a woman who's stayed near me for the last while. It's Gosling. I turn away, but it's too late.

"I was wondering when you were going to notice me," she says.

I'm forced to look at her. "What is happening?" I ask.

"You're nothing if not direct," Gosling says. "The Kettle has begun. The Feast of the Dead has arrived. Now that they move their great village to a new place, they must invite their dead to come along with them. They can't leave the okis of their loved ones, just as we can't do that to the ones we love who still live." She looks over at me, and I glance back at her. "This isn't the tradition of my people," she says, "but those Wendat who decide on such matters allow me to bear witness."

We stay quiet for a long time as we walk high on the cliff overlooking the green-and-blue water below us, the waves rolling in and sending up spray when they hit the rocks. Finally, I ask Gosling to tell me more.

"Maybe if you just watch what happens over the next days," she says. "I could tell you what I have seen but that never truly lives up to the real thing, now, does it?"

FEAST OF THE DEAD

I share this with you, my dear Superior, and with any other readers my journals might find back in France, the most splendid thing I've yet to see in this heathen land. It is called the Feast of the Dead, and from what I'm told it happens every twelve years or so when the whole village must pick up and move to a new location once the fields around it have become exhausted.

While the moving of a community of two thousand or more souls is nothing short of a feat to witness, it's the community's ceremony, its reverence for its dead, that truly astounds me. As I have seen with my own eyes, it unfolds over the course of ten days. And it includes not just the one large village of the Attignawantan, the People of the Bear who are my hosts, but also the smaller villages that are of their nation. All these communities descend upon their respective cemeteries and unearth their deceased from the tombs in which they lie. Each family sees to its dead with such bereavement and care, their tears falling like raindrops, that one would assume the corpse had lately passed on. While this is sometimes the case, more often it is not, and the bodies are in various stages of decomposition. Some are simply bones, others have only a type of parchment over their bones, and other bodies appear as if they've been dried and smoked, showing little sign of putrefaction. Still others, the recently departed, crawl with worms.

Once the bodies have been unearthed, they are put on display so all the family members might grieve anew, and it's this that strikes me as especially powerful, this willingness of the sauvages to gaze down upon what they each will one day become. There's something in this particular practice that can teach us Christians a powerful lesson, that we may see more vividly our own wretched mortal state, that it's not this world we should cherish but the promise of the next. Yet this is only the beginning of the ceremony.

Once all the families have had sufficient time to see and to mourn over the bodies of their loved ones again, they then cover them with magnificent beaver robes. And when this stage of the mourning comes to a close, the families once again uncover the bodies and set to work stripping off the flesh and skin that might still be left, taking special care to burn this in the fire, along with any old furs and mats used in the original burial. Those bodies that have not yet putrefied enough are covered by a robe and left on a bark mat.

Now, it may seem barbaric and ghastly to hear of this practice of picking bones clean, but I must tell you, dear Superior, that I have never witnessed such absolute and pure love for a relative who has passed. One young mother cried so much as she cradled and cleaned her dead baby that her tears bathed the infant's bones. None showed any sign of repugnance at all as they removed the flesh from their relatives, and it is in this duty to the dead that all Christians might learn another valuable lesson. After undergoing such an obligation, what act of charity might seem remotely comparable? To look after the sick in hospital, to bow to and clean the feet of a sick man covered in sores, these would seem simple indeed.

After two or three days of mourning in their home, the families place the now clean bones of the dead into beautiful bags sewn of beaver fur and decorated with beads. Hoisting the bones onto their backs, the families place yet another beautiful robe onto their packages and leave their longhouses to begin the trek as one great community from their old village to the new one, families of other smaller communities meeting with them along the way in a display of timing that is startling. Like sparrows descending onto a mighty oak for an evening's rest, thousands of these sauvages congregate in and around the new village, and residents and visitors alike enter their own longhouses or the longhouses of their hosts, where each family makes a feast to its dead.

I have learned from one captain of the confederation that these Huron believe a body has two souls, or okis. One soul is more attached to the body and will stay with it in the cemetery, watching over it for eternity, unless someone bears it again as a child. When I asked the captain why he thought such a thing, he pointed out to me, as proof of this soul transferring from one body to another, the amazing resemblance some people have to a deceased person. Oh, these poor and simple heathens.

According to him, the second oki leaves the body and makes a harrowing journey to a "village of souls" that is very similar to those of the living. Travelling along the southern shore of what the Huron call the Sweet Water Sea, they must pass by a cliff painted with ancient animals, some human in form, others part man, part beast, and still others frightening sea creatures.

Beyond this, a malevolent spirit called Pierce Head draws out the brains of the departed, who then must cross over a river on an unsteady tree trunk guarded by a dog that will leap at them and frighten many off the log and into the wicked current below. God, give me the courage and resolve to enlighten those who walk in darkness.

But back to the ceremony at hand, dear Superior. Once all have arrived at the new village and have mourned for three days, the people carry the bags of bones, or spirit bags, to the largest cabins of their clans and put them on display, along with gifts for the dead that include beaded necklaces and kettles and robes. Another feast is held in each of these longhouses, and the songs of the deceased are sung as family members mingle and mourn. The guests are allowed to help themselves to any food they desire and even to take some home with them, which is typically forbidden. As they finally leave, they sing out as loud as they can, "Haeey! Haeey!" in order to appease and to comfort their dead relations in the spirit bags. It is truly something to hear, as frightening as wolves calling out to one another in the moonlight.

As the next couple of days pass, the mood changes to one of excitement as people of the different communities play games for prizes. With my own eyes I've seen women shooting their bows at distant targets, every bit as talented as any of the men as they try to win quillwork belts or necklaces or strings of beads. The young men battle one another in ferocious scrums to keep hold of a baton, while others throw spears to compete for axes and knives and beaver robes. These people are truly physical, as sleek and fit as any race I've ever encountered.

But then the mood changes to solemnity again. On the preordained day, families go to where their dead are displayed and once more unwrap them to say one last goodbye, the longhouses smelling a little stronger than musk. Tears flow anew, and it is startling to watch as women comb the hair of freshly dead relatives and mothers place beaded bracelets on the bones of their children and grown warriors cradle what is left of their wives. And then as one, each family stands, forms a line, and carries the remains of their loved ones to the pit that has been dug outside the palisades.

Let me describe this burial place. It is about the size of the inner courtyard at Versailles, and in the middle of it a pit has been dug at least two fathoms deep by fifteen fathoms wide. Around the circumference of the pit is an intricate and sturdy scaffold at least two fathoms high, with cross poles where the Huron, according to clan, will soon hang their bundles of souls. The bodies that remain whole, covered by their beaver robes, surround the burial pit underneath the scaffold, stretched out on their bark mats and fastened to stakes at about a fathom, or the height of a man. I'm told that they will go in first.

But before the spirit bags are hung on the scaffold, the sauvages, according to clan and village, lay their parcels of souls upon the ground, essentially once again putting them on display for curious visitors to stroll by and admire as if they are perusing wares at a village fair. For a distance of some three thousand feet these bags are laid out, poles planted beside them so that presents brought for the living may also go on display. All manner of beaver robes and quillwork belts and beaded necklaces and skinning knives and amulets are strung on these poles for everyone to see. I believe that the families and clans compete with one another to try and prove who has the most wealth. The spirit bags and gifts remain on display for several hours, as several thousand people have descended upon the new village to partake of the proceedings.

This is when the Feast of the Dead truly begins. The captain of each clan gives the signal and his people climb the scaffold at good speed and tie their bundles of souls to the crosspieces. Once all the bags have been hung, the captains, now that afternoon has arrived, announce and give away the presents, each made in the name of the dead, to different living friends and relations. I witness these sauvages approach to receive their gift, some crying, others smiling, and still others with moods upon their faces impossible to read.

Once all the presents have been handed out, the most extraordinary sight occurs when the sauvages line the entire pit with the finest beaver robes so that the robes extend out of the pit a few feet from its edge. Hundreds and hundreds of beaver furs line the ossuary in a stunning display of abundance. In European terms, the robes alone would be worth a king's small ransom, and this doesn't take into account all the furs used to bundle the corpses that will soon end up in the pit.

As evening has arrived, designated individuals take the whole bodies that hang below the scaffold to the bottom of the pit and arrange them in an orderly fashion, the din of the people all around growing. In the centre of it all, three kettles have been placed, apparently to feed the dead in the other world. Once all the whole bodies have been thus carefully placed and arranged, the people build many fires to cook their food and pass the rest of the night here.

At dawn the next morning, I awake to the louder murmurings of the Huron as the men of importance return to the top of the scaffold and begin to empty the bags of bones down to others waiting in the pit.

As the bones begin to fill the pit, the men below, using poles, continue to carefully mingle them in no order that I can understand. This is when the people begin to sing in such a lugubrious tone that one truly understands what utter despair is, hundreds and even thousands of voices rising up so that one can't help but weep for the living whose souls certainly head for damnation. It is a sound the likes of which I have never heard before and don't expect to again, one that filled my whole body with a great vibration of sadness.

There are so many bones that soon the pit is nearly filled, leaving only a few feet of space. And once the last bone has been placed, the beaver robes that still extend out of the pit are folded back over, and then mats and poles and eventually part of the scaffold, apparently to prevent animals from getting to the remains. After that, the excess dirt is mounded on, and women carrying dishes of corn sprinkle it onto the mound, doing so for a number of days following.

The rest of the day is passed in gift giving, and even I was offered ten beaver robes by an important captain. I turned this down, explaining that the only gift I desire is that he and his people begin to believe in Him, the Great Voice, the one who makes all things.

WASH YOU WITH MY TEARS

I hold you in my arms, my love. Since your passing to the land of Aataentsic and Iouskeha so many years ago, this is all I've ever wanted again. And I have wanted to cradle our daughters again, too, and now I finally do. We are all together once more.

The time for the Kettle has come, and the time for the village to move has arrived. I would never leave you behind. I sit here and cry and wash your bones with my tears. I hold you again as I hug you close to me. I watch over all of you this night.

The three of you aren't heavy on my shoulders as I carry you to the place of the Kettle. I stop at some of your favourite spots along the way. The place where the river splashes into the Sweet Water Sea. The cliff overlooking where the waves crash below it. The field that blossoms with berries in late summer. I remember our life together in the village we have now left for good. I didn't realize how sentimental I've grown over these last many seasons. I remember what it felt like to come home from a long journey, to walk into the longhouse and your arms, our girls hugging my legs. I've not been able to move on from you even though I know you want me to.

Many gifts are given in your names. Necklaces of polished beads, furs, quill tobacco bags, moccasins, and moose-hair barrettes dyed the colour of strawberries. In your death you still bring smiles to the faces of your friends, and they all tell me how they miss you, how they still dream of you, how they know for certain that you do well in the other world while you wait there for them and for me.

With my own two hands I place your bones into the ossuary and mingle them with the others so you will never be lonely. I sing your song as the tears flow down my face, my song weaving into those of the others until we are all one great voice. You are with me right now, my love. I can feel your hands upon my face and our daughters' arms wrapped around my waist. We are one again, at least for now, and as we cover you with the warmth of beaver furs, I whisper to you that it won't be too long now before we are finally together again.

THERE IS NO MIDDLE OUT HERE

It is with the lightest and most joyous of hearts that I write you today, dear Superior, to report on the many successes of my current mission. These people are obstinate and childlike. They live in a sinful world of heathen worship and are certainly under the sway of Satan, which makes my work all that more important.

And so it is the pleasure of your most humble of servants to report that I am on the verge of bringing this entire village of some two or three thousand souls to finally kneel at the feet of Christ and accept Him as the true Son of God.

I put down my pen and tear the page from my journal, rip it up into small pieces. I cannot lie, not to You, Lord. The girl, at least, has accepted You, or so I can only guess, but she is most probably mad, and the insane don't truly count as converts, do they?

At least this country is beautiful. We've completed our first day's paddle on what I've calculated is the summer solstice. A coincidence, or do they truly comprehend some rudimentary aspects of astronomy? I sit on a rocky escarpment sewn with windswept pine, looking out over a great turquoise sea. If I didn't know better on this day of bright sun and light breeze, I'd have guessed I was on a Mediterranean archipelago, my face warm with the day's heat. I've taken to calling this body of water the Sweet Water Sea just as the sauvages do. My companions have explained that this coast we paddle along is simply a bay on a string of massive lakes that stretch west of here for hundreds of leagues. I'm not sure if I should believe them. They seem prone to lying when they don't know the answer to something I ask.

Sixty-seven Huron, if my count is correct, currently accompany me back to New France. We left the village in a flotilla of canoes as the sun rose. It both impresses and confounds me that while I am, on the one hand, important enough to warrant such a large party for protection from the Iroquois, I also remain the constant focus of their derision and even outright anger.

Life did take a turn for the better in the spring when Bird sent me to live in another longhouse, whose members seemed intent on teaching me their language. I'm happy to report, dear Lord, that if those around me speak slowly enough, I can now understand much of what they say. And, most exciting, I am beginning to dream in their tongue, which I think is a sure sign of my progress. I've come to believe what I was taught before coming over, that to truly understand these people I must first learn their language. This is the only way I will ever be able to begin converting them to the true and righteous path and out of these dark days in which they reside. Satan might feel far away as I sit here on these rocks watching the sun set over the place they also call the glittering waters, though I must only remind myself that darkness is just a few hours away.

Making my way back from evening prayers, I see they've set up their shelters and have eaten, I assume, as most of them are already asleep. A handful of men sit by the fire and talk amongst themselves, stopping when I approach. Two of them mimic the sign of the cross and laugh. Another scowls at them and makes an eating gesture. When I nod and sit beside him, he hands me a birchbark plate with a small serving of sagamité mixed with smoked fish. Despite my fear that it's rancid, I scoop it up with my fingers.

"You like this place?" he asks me slowly so I can understand him. He's a very handsome young man, high cheekboned and with a frame like Michelangelo's David.

"Yes," I tell him. "I do."

He hesitates for a moment, not sure, apparently, how to say what he wants to. "You must make the decision," he begins, "either to paddle or not to paddle." He looks into the fire and I can sense he's being as genuine as he knows how. There's none of the joking in his tone that I've become accustomed to with so many of the others.

I nod for him to go on.

"You will be respected only if you make a firm choice," he says. "You can't choose in the middle. Paddle or don't paddle tomorrow. If you don't paddle"—he looks at me—"then maybe tell those in your canoe a story about your god. If you do paddle, don't talk, just paddle. Paddle until the rest of us stop paddling." He studies my face to see if I understand. "There is no middle out here." He lifts his arms, as if welcoming the world to him.

———

BUT NOTHING IN this world, their world, is idyllic for long. All morning the sky's gushed rain, and I've taken it upon myself to bail out the canoe with my birchbark plate. Shivering in the wind that gusts waves, rocking us and making me feel as sick as I was back on the ship that carried me to this continent, I try to be useful to them. Rather than being morose or angry to mimic the weather, the eight men in my canoe keep their heads down and paddle hard, as if they are in some magical trance, and, just as they do when the sun is shining, they bend to their task with a cadence that's both madly redundant and hypnotizing. I give up my weak attempt at helping for a short while, exhausted by their energy.

I listen to the rain hiss on water, the grunts of breath, the slosh of paddles dipping into the water in unison, the creaking of this canoe made, like my plate, of bark and resin and sinew, the scent of their bodies sharp, as musky and repellent as their food. I cannot comprehend how they live like this, an existence that to me is like hell. And yet, as the lightning flashes and I look to the canoe beside me full of frightening men, they are lit with such a dangerous beauty that I immediately know Satan must control this land. What am I doing here?

In the canoe ahead, now just a stone's throw from ours, the young girl rides with Bird. Two other canoes are far enough in front that I can't see them, acting as lookouts and guides. I know I am the fourth of ten canoes. As the rain turns to a steady and cold drizzle, I'm left here sitting in my soaked wool to contemplate. They have put me in a place where I'm considered precious cargo, squeezed in among the tightly bundled beaver and marten and rabbit furs. The canoes are so weighted with them that the gunwales dip dangerously close to each wave. These Huron have certainly mastered their universe in a way that keeps them alive. I want the rain to stop.

———

TODAY WE REACH what appears to be the mouth of a river pouring into this inland sea. The canoes, one by one, slow like great birds coming in to land. There's no discussion, or any other visible communication. It's as if these people act more like animals than humans. They seem to speak as if by some unseen communication.

Once the canoes have all beached, I ask the young man who spoke to me last night, the one named Tall Trees whom I've decided to call David, how it is they all know what the other is going to do before he does it. "How did everyone know to stop at this place?" I ask him.

He looks puzzled. "Did you not see the signs?" he asks.

I shake my head.

"Pay more attention, then," he says, lifting a heavy bundle from the canoe that he swings onto his back. He pulls a leather strap attached to the pack over his forehead to help support the weight. He turns and walks into the forest that crowds the banks of this river.

I bend over and attempt to lift a pack from the canoe but can barely get it over the gunwale. I drop it back in and search out a lighter one.

The sauvage beside me pushes me aside and throws the pack onto his back and the leather cord over his forehead. "Damage my canoe," he says, "and I'll kill you." I watch as he, too, slips into the forest.

Not knowing what else to do, I take out my rosary and pray while the men, like a line of worker ants, take pack after pack from the canoes and disappear into the darkness of the trees dripping with rain. Wandering over to Bird's canoe in hopes the girl might be somewhere close by, I realize that if I stand here much longer, I'll be left alone. The thought of huddling against the wind and staring out at this grey sea, the fear I still hold of an Iroquois war party emerging from around the bend in their own canoes or, worse, from the trees is a fear I cannot bear, and so I find a hide pack I recognize as Bird's that's quite manageable. Cradling it, I walk into the forest.

At first the path isn't hard to follow, but not very far in, the trees swallow the light until it's like dusk and I'm seized by panic, pushing through the thick forest without knowing if I should turn back or keep going. Stopping for a moment to look around, I realize that it will be impossible to retrace my steps. Thinking I hear voices just up ahead, I push deeper into the woods. Maybe the sauvages are teasing me, hiding and watching from behind the trees.

Now certain I can hear voices, I move as quickly as I can. Holding my arms and the hide pack up to protect my face from the branches that claw at me, I step out and into air, my feet scrambling to find some purchase. But it's too late, and I tumble and tumble, rolling down what must be a cliff until, my head spinning and my ribs bruised, I end up on the bank of a creek.

Sitting up, I look around and see the embankment is so steep I won't be able to climb back into the forest above. It wasn't their voices I was hearing but this burbling creek.

The rain's picked up since the beach, coming down hard enough that I have to squint my eyes. My cassock is slick with mud, and when I try to stand, its weight is too much for me. Racked by the stupidity of what I've done, I collapse into a heap and hold my head in my hands.

I know I'm crying because the water on my face is warmer than the rain. Curling up in a ball, weeping and shivering, I've finally reached my breaking point, and the voyage is only a few days old. Weeks more of this will follow, and that's if I ever manage to find them. What if they don't notice I'm missing and just paddle away? Or worse, what if they try to find me and can't? Who could find me here? Even if I scream as loud as I possibly can, in this wind and rain and down in this depression, no one will hear.

My breath comes in hitches as I consider my options. Should I climb the bank and somehow find the trail again? Or do I choose a direction and walk along this creek in the hopes of stumbling upon them? Or do I just simply sit and wait for someone to find me? Please, Lord, tell me what to do. I turn my face up to the sky and feel the rain, and I beg of You, dear Jesus, to please show me a sign.

Lightning cracks so close by that the hair on my body stands up and my skin prickles, making me jump as if I've been thumped in the chest, and before I know it I've slipped into the frigid creek, banging my knee hard against a submerged rock. The current tugs me downstream, and the mud from my clothing turns the clear water all around me brown. I can feel the weight of it slipping from me like clay. Standing, shivering, I splash handfuls of water over myself, rubbing my cassock. If I'm to die in this cruel land, I will not die like some dirty animal. I begin to scrub, violent in my actions, angry now that I've foolishly allowed myself to end up in such a dire place, and in the anger there's a bit of warmth.

I lift my heavy black robe up my body and struggle to pull it over my head. It makes a sucking sound as I finally wrench it free, so soaked and filth-encrusted that it weighs as much as a child. I swing it over my head with all my might and it smacks the water with a satisfying crack. I do it again, then again, releasing the frustration and miserable depression that these people have placed on my shoulders. I beat my cassock clean, so exhausting myself that my arms are too weak to lift it another time.

Holding on to the cassock, I allow myself to drift down the slow-moving creek, my body now warmer from the exertion as I bump into the occasional rock. I consider where I might be floating to and stare down at my pasty body encased in soaked cotton underclothing. I'm more gaunt than I've ever been. The length of my legs, of my torso, surprises me. I've not looked at myself for a long time. I'm too much a skeleton and make the decision here and now that, if I survive this day's stupidity, I'll force myself to eat more. Is that all right with You, Lord? My work of bringing these lost children to You might become a little less burdensome if I have the physical strength to do it.

It strikes me then as my cassock snags on a submerged bit of fallen tree that this creek must run somewhere, possibly to the big river I'm told we are to paddle up. It must. If I follow this creek I will, God willing, find the river they call the Snake, and hopefully find them as well.

I stand up shivering and wade to shore. There I squeeze what water I can from my cassock and pull it back over my head. Wool isn't the worst material for this land. The sauvages are fascinated by it and ask all the time what animal it comes from. I try to explain what a sheep is, what domestication and livestock are, and the best I can do is try and explain that where I come from we keep animals the likes of which they couldn't imagine in great numbers for our use. It is God's plan. They laugh at this, the idea that one might keep herds of friendly deer or elk that walk happily to their slaughter whenever it's time for the human to eat meat. Some ask openly if there aren't consequences of a life so easy to live. The question fascinates me.

At least the rain has slowed to a drizzle. My teeth chatter as I hug myself, the black wool heavy as I begin to wend through the bushes that line the shore. I imagine returning to New France, stepping at last through the threshold of a real house and heading straight for the hearth. I can see the cast-iron pot hanging over the flame, smell the scent of mutton stew. I hope, dear God, that this path is the right one. I am at Your mercy, but only say the word and I will accept that

I am to die alone and will do so, with happiness, here in this wild place.

The brambles tug at my robe like needy children as I push through the thick bushes, and I can see this must be the most glorious patch of raspberries on earth. But I am half a season too early. Instead of ripe fruit, I'm presented with thousands of tiny thorns. So be it. Today has become a test, and, while it's a day I didn't expect, I hope now to please You.

Moments of sheer panic slip into moments of exhilaration when I consider that today might be the day that marks my journey from the physical world to the realm of the everlasting. If this creek leads nowhere instead of back to Bird's party, then it will lead to You. In this way I console myself. Along the creek, I come across what must have recently been the bedding ground for some large animal, a deer or perhaps one of those beasts as big as a horse that they call a moose, the tall grass flattened in a circular fashion that, now with the sun peeking through cloud, seems like the perfect resting place. But no, I must push on.

I wade through the grass, fingering my rosary and hearing what might be faster water. Running through the last of the grass, I see the soil has become rocky, and the creek indeed runs into a river. I'm certain I smell the smoke of a fire.

Where the creek tumbles into the much bigger river, I turn to my left and I feel light-headed and so happy I have to hold in a scream when I see smoke rising from a fire and a few men resting by it. I'm about to shout out to them when it hits me like a slap. I realize I have no idea if these ones are Huron or Iroquois. What if I've stumbled across an enemy camp? I fall flat on the stones and bite my arm in the hope I haven't been spotted.

Peering up, I see that these ones sit by a stack of bundles. They must be my sauvages. I lie here and watch, shivering for the heat of their small fire. Soon, others come out of the forest, some carrying a canoe over their heads, a few with packs slung over their shoulders.

That's when the magnificent one I call David emerges. I stand, legs shaking, and move toward them.

They stare as I approach, their bodies steaming from exertion. The expression on their faces shows me they're confused. They must wonder how it is I managed to come from the opposite direction. I wonder the same thing myself.

"I became lost," I tell them. "In there." I point to the forest behind us. They don't answer. "My belongings," I say, "are back at the big water. Must get."

The men just shrug and sit back on their haunches by the fire. I stand behind them, trying to take in some of the heat as they talk amongst themselves. I don't know what to do. The idea of heading back into the dark forest alone again is so frightful that I'd rather lose my earthly possessions, my chalice, the Hosts baked from sagamité, my journal and quill, my spare cotton underclothes, the book on the lives of the saints the Superior gave to me before my departure. These all can be replaced, soon enough, God willing, upon my arrival in New France. My most valuable possession, irreplaceable in this harsh world, is the one I have around my neck, and that I carry inside my chest. So I will sit calmly and await the rest of the travellers before we begin paddling upstream. If one of them sees my bag and decides to bring it to me, so be it. If it is left behind, so be it. I won't go again into that forest alone.

When another group of men appears from the darkness of the bush, a canoe above their heads, I suddenly remember something horrible and my belly drops. What of Bird's hide pack I'd been carrying? Where is it? I've left it somewhere. Where, though? I look around me, despite knowing with certainty that I hadn't arrived here with it. It must be Bird's. I'd taken it from his canoe and recognized it as his possession. Where did I lose it?

Recalling my steps, I remember it in my possession when I first became lost. I remember having it even in the moment before I fell down the cliff. In fact, the bag shielded my face from the brambles and that is how I so blindly stepped out into thin air. I don't recall seeing it after that. This must be where I lost it, back where I fell. Another group appears, a canoe on their shoulders as well. They are almost finished with the portage. I had walked for at least an hour along the creek. If I go immediately, I might get there and back in the same amount of time now that I know the route. I fear, though, that they will have already repacked the canoes and paddled off by then.

It's best to just sit down with Bird and tell him what happened, that my intentions were honourable, that I was trying to be useful but then became lost. I can see his face turning red with anger when he realizes what I've done, that I'm slowing the voyage down. Can the bag's contents be so very important? Of course they are. These people don't travel with an ounce of unnecessary weight. Bird will be angry with me, though. I remember him almost killing me that morning. I can't tell him.

I make my decision. If Bird or another says that he misses his pack, I will confess and apologize profusely and hope they don't think I'm consorting with demons, something, I've realized as my language skills have grown, that I'm accused of quite often. If no one speaks out, then I won't say a word and will leave it to You, Lord, to prove that my mistake wasn't grievous. After all, in my desire to help I very well may have lost my own possessions, so is this not an even trade?

I watch as more and more of them come out of the darkness of the forest, gently placing the canoes in the water and reloading them, not talking now but set to the work. First one canoe pushes off, then another, the men bending deep at the waist with each stroke. Their progress is slow, and as they paddle in unison, I'm amazed by their strength and fortitude. How can we possibly make it all the way to New France, paddling for weeks against such a strong current? I will have to leave this up to them. The issue of this lost bag niggles, though. My stomach tells me I'm making an improper decision.

Then Bird appears from the forest, the girl at his heels. She has ignored me since this trip began, I assume on his orders. He carries a large bundle, the strap across his forehead as is their custom. He sweats and crouches when he's finally able to drop the burden. His age is near impossible for me to guess, but he's probably older than I imagined, his face thinner now that we've been travelling, the creases in it deep. Yet his hair is still mostly black, and he's as muscled in the shoulders and arms and back as a young man. But at last I glimpse his exhaustion.

The girl removes her own hide pack from her shoulders, staring as hard at me as I had at Bird. She then undoes the ties on her pack and pulls my black cloth satchel from it. Bird looks up, watching, the lines in his forehead deepening, as she leaves him and walks to me, smiling. She holds my satchel out to me, and when I take it, she asks that I bless her. My right hand rises up, instinctively.

THE OTHER FINGER IS MINE

Lying on my back and daring myself to stare into the sun for as long as I can, I drag my hand through the water. It's my way of slowing the canoe down, of making more work for the men who paddle and grunt around me. I like the smell of their sweat. I like watching the muscles in their arms and backs bulge with each stroke against the river's current. Lying here on this bundle of beaver furs, I imagine myself dead and lift my hand from the water and cross it over my other on my chest. The sun on my face darkens my skin and hides my scars so that in death I am the most beautiful woman in the world, and I am hard as a shell. My family who are still alive cry for me. The men beat their chests and the women tear the hair from their scalps. I am missed.

———

WE PADDLE FOR DAYS, and every moment of each day I think of ways to infuriate this old man, Bird. The easiest, I have found, is simply to spend time with the Crow, to ask him about his god, to have him make that strange gesture with his thumb on my forehead. I can feel Bird's blood heat up when I dare take the Crow's hand. I've won, but still, I think of ways to make Bird angry. I want to see him ignite. I want, I think, for him to get so mad that he kills the Crow. He has decided he doesn't want me, and I'm happy to be going back to my people, but I'm confused, Father and Mother, why I'm not wanted anymore. How dare he not want me anymore?

Each day as we struggle against the current, I watch the men turn leaner, more focused, more silent. From first light until night threatens we push up this wide, black river with birch and maple and poplar thick on the banks. So many good places for my father's brothers to ambush these canoes. I hope they've brought a hundred men, two hundred men. Enough to kill Bird and all of his war-bearers. The country here is beautiful. The rocks run right down into the water that's dark as the darkest night, and when the men stop to rest, I lie upon those rocks and let their heat soak into me. A wind from the east has brought good skies, and this kind wind blows away the flies and mosquitoes. These might be the most beautiful days of sun I've ever known after the rain of last week stopped. This is the perfect time, and the prettiest of country, in which to witness my father's brothers kill these enemies.

———

TODAY, AT THE END of an especially long portage, all the men gather at the head of a waterfall that splits a cliff in half. Each man in turn reaches for the pouch he wears on his back and takes from it a pinch of tobacco. Each then finds the appropriate crack or hole on the rock face of this great cliff and stuffs his offering in, the younger ones showing off how high they can scale the height, which makes me sick with fear that they'll fall. Others, in extra offering, lean toward the swirling waters that spin before gushing over the lip of the drop and sprinkle more of their tobacco there. Bird raises his arms and asks the spirit who lives here for a safe voyage. "You are Tsanhohi," he says, "and I beseech you to listen to my small voice, the small voices of my friends. We will speak as one so that our voice will be loud enough for you to hear as you fly above us on the drafts. Look down to us and protect us on this journey, and allow us to defeat our enemy if he chooses to fight." The men all answer "Ah-ho!" I can tell from how worn the cliff face is that Bird's people have come to this place for as long as there have been people to ask the eagle spirit who lives somewhere in the rocks here for help. Fox calls out and points up into the blue sky. I see the flash of Tsanhohi, a golden eagle, circling overhead. The men shout happily and reach for one another because their prayer is being answered. As they stare up into the sky I move to the cliff and begin to pull out tufts of their tobacco they'd just stuck in the rocks, as much as I can, and stuff it into my mouth. Although eating all of this tobacco will make me throw up, I ask Tsanhohi that these men not make it home again.

———

TONIGHT THE MEN are so tired they don't even bother to build a fire or raise their shelters, just cut down pine boughs for bedding and then lie atop them and fall fast asleep. The few lookouts fight to stay awake, their heads bobbing. One stands and paces, slapping his face. Another sits with his arms around his knees and his hands holding a knife below his chin so if it begins to sink he'll be wakened by the tip's pierce. Tonight I'll play a trick on Bird, one that he won't forget. I will not allow him to forget me.

The mosquitoes whine in my ears as I lie beside Bird, who breathes in sleep. I stare at his face, lit by an almost full moon. He's become even darker in the sun, and now that he relaxes I find him handsome without wanting to. Before we left, he had his hair carefully cut by the medicine woman called Gosling. She asked him to bring me along so I could learn how she groomed him and be able to do it myself on the journey. I watched her work on him, the animals tattooed on her arms moving as if by themselves. Afterward she gave me a thick clamshell, bigger than my palm, which narrows to an edge as thin and as sharp as any knife. She told me it came from a place beside the great sea where the French first appeared. She told me to take care of it, to use it with precision.

I've come to like how Bird wears his hair, down to his shoulder on one side and shaved to the skin on the other. This is the hair of the war-bearer, and Bird isn't afraid to let all know that he is one. He's kept it greased nicely with the oil of sunflower seeds, and the smell of it makes me hungry for something. He's a proud man, a strong man, and he's not shy to show it in his appearance. Who he is he shows to the world. The stubble on the bald side of his head looks sharp. All of the men have turned their attention to the work of travel and away from their grooming. I know that in the next few days when we approach the place where I'm to be given back to my family, they'll spend a long time grooming one another and making themselves fierce again with ochre. But before then, I'll groom Bird as he sleeps.

The guards are exhausted, though they're not asleep. I must be quiet. I must be focused. I crawl from the robe and look over at Bird. Despite his appearing to sleep deeper than dreams, I've learned he senses when I'm not near. Staying on my belly, I move slow, pulling myself along the ground a hand's width at a time. The urge to stand and bolt comes over me, but I tell myself I only need to get to the riverbank to find what I need. I have the whole night to accomplish this, after all.

One of the lookouts must have risen from a crouch not far from me. I can hear the bones in his knees crack and the low grunt of relief from his throat. The fire is just embers but the moon is bright enough to give me away if I don't lie still. The light snores of tired men surround me, so I pretend to be one of them and wait for the guard to move quietly away before I continue crawling toward the sound of the water.

When it seems safe enough to crouch, I do. I see the high wisps of summer cloud cross over the moon and in the moon's shadow I move closer to the black water. When it emerges again, I kneel and freeze. In this way I make my way to the bank where I sit with my hands on my knees and fight the desire to stand up and walk back to Bird, to stand up and pretend this dark idea never came to me. The moon continues to shine then disappear and I stare at the water moving by me, bright when the moon emerges, reflecting light in the black of it. In this light I stand and search out the rocks I'll need.

I see the flat one first and pick it up. The other is more difficult to find, and I walk along the bank. This stone I look for must be heavy but not too heavy for me to lift with one hand. Finally, after lifting many, I find the right one. With a rock in each hand, I slip back into camp and nestle next to Bird.

Staring into his face, I try to guess if he really sleeps. I reach gently as I can for his hand that he holds near his head. I do something I've never done before. I take it into mine. With my free hand, I slide the flat rock into place between us. Then I lift our holding hands to it, placing them upon the surface. Slowly, I pull my entwined fingers from his and reach into my dress and pull the clamshell out. If I'm to do this, if I'm to take some small revenge for what he did to you, my father, my mother, I can't think. I can only do. Rising to my knees, I pick up the bigger rock with my strong arm, and with my other hand I pin his little finger to the stone with the clamshell. I hold his hand in place with my own. He begins to stir, moving his head just a little bit, so I lift the rock high above my head, my whole body shaking now with the fear and effort. I swing the rock down, and I feel the scream coming out of my throat before I hear it. The crush of the rock smashing onto the clamshell, the clamshell slipping and shattering under my grip, vibrates up my arm. Bird wakes with a roar and has pulled away from me, rolled away from me, clutching his hand to his chest with the other.

So much blood, black in the moonlight, pools over the flat rock. I see as he stands that I must have done a very good job. Not one but two fingers lie on the stone. Shards of shattered clamshell glint beside them. I grab the largest sliver to defend myself against Bird, and that's when I notice that my own hand is smeared with blood. Bird reaches for me as men scramble and stand up all around us. I raise my hand to my face, and the understanding sinks in as blood pulses out. The other finger on the stone is mine.

LOST WAMPUM

Each stroke, my hand screams with pain. She's lost something important in her head. This is the only explanation. The others would lose respect for me if I refused to do my part of the work. It isn't in me to sit like a child or a crow and allow the others to carry my weight. Two days since the loss of my finger and still blood soaks the moss and hide tied tightly over my hand. At least she only removed the smallest finger, the most useless one. The stupid thing severed her own little finger in the process, but from the opposite hand. The clamshell must have slipped. I don't feel bad for her. She lies in front of me in the canoe with her hands and feet bound, as much to prevent harming herself as anyone else. The girl's pale but she won't die. The pain, as I can attest to, dear wife, is extraordinary. It allows neither of us to think of anything else. I wanted to ask her why she did this to me but all I need to do is remember what I did to her family. Maybe she hasn't lost her mind at all. Perhaps she's gifted. To be able to do this to me despite the fear of my response is impressive. I look to her and see that she looks back. I laugh as I stop paddling, dipping my screaming hand in the cold river.

Not only have I lost my finger, I've lost my kit containing the wampum meant as a peace offering for her family. This would seem like a joke if it weren't so serious. No one has it, and no one has seen it since the first portage onto this river. Blame has turned to the girl. Clearly, she wishes me more harm than even I imagined. Her people will see a great insult that I not offer them wampum when this is precisely what has been requested and is what custom must allow. So be it. She has caused me enough sorrow and I look forward to reaching the meeting place in the next few days and being rid of her. This is what I tell myself through the pain.

The Crow attempted to care for her yesterday, and once again I came very close to killing him, to taking out my anger in an irreparable way. Soon enough I will be rid of him, too. I can paddle with my group and spend the summer trading and my world will again feel almost normal.

—

TONIGHT WE STOP EARLY to begin preparing for our meeting with them. We are within a short paddle of the designated place where the Snake River is born from the big lake. No doubt the Haudenosaunee warriors have already arrived and do the same. Mine sit in groups of two or three, scraping one another's heads clean with shells, oiling their hair, applying ochre to faces and chests and arms. I watch how the young ones are nervous beneath their paint and bravado. Fox notes this as well as he shaves the one side of my head. "Their first taste of it soon if things go bad," he says. "That'll calm them down."

"No talk of it going poorly," I say. "I'm eager for the Crow to be gone." I hold up my wounded hand, suddenly light-headed with the thought that I've lost something I might never have needed. "And especially the girl."

He laughs. "I hope you won't wear such a ridiculous bandage on your hand tomorrow," he says. "And speaking of the Crow, how exactly are you going to get rid of him?"

"Simple," I say. "When they demand reparation for the ones we killed last winter, I'll give them the Crow. They've wanted one badly for a long time now." I pause to consider this. "You and I will tell the others that they wouldn't leave without the Crow and so I was forced to surrender him at the risk of bringing war upon us for not giving in."

"We can tell the elders there are other crows to be had," Fox says. "Maybe this will work. Maybe not. We'll see." He looks at me and I look back.

"Say it," I say.

"I've only known you to tell the truth." He stands then, and walks away.

When the time comes, we enter our canoes in the weakening light of the waning moon and paddle up the last stretch of river before the lake. Morning birds have begun to call as we beach where the current is too strong to go farther, and we hide in the bush onshore. I've sent Fox ahead to scout with a few of his chosen ones. The birds go quiet now, sensing our presence. We crouch and listen, more than fifty of us spread out on both banks, and I'm proud at how silent these men of mine are, these untested youth who I selected from only a gut feeling.

I have no idea if the girl's relations will act according to their word. I took lives without the knowledge they were so special, and this changes everything, dear one. You know this. They did the same to me.

Squatting and half-asleep on my haunches, my ears attuned to the early-morning world, I hear Fox approaching. He smiles at me, nods in the direction of the lake, and shows with his fingers how many of them and their location along it where it flows to river. A main body of them is indeed where they said they'd be, with smaller parties spread on either side. Unless they're very good at hiding, this party is only half the size of ours. I know they'll be perched in trees or lying in the thicker grass up the banks, ready for the eruption of violence if it's to come. They're not so different from us.

For now we wait, Fox beside me, his keen eyes and brain never relaxing, searching the mist on the river and lake for something the rest of us don't see. I try to go into that place in my head as I crouch, my knees beginning to sing with the pain that keeps me sharp. I remember leaving my home that morning a couple of weeks ago, the

Crow behind me in the canoe, trying to decide if he would pick up a paddle or not, when one old woman whose mind has become soft and who'd come to see us all off sang out to us, "Goodbye! Please take this drought with you! Bye-bye, and leave the Crow but bring back rain." I thought about her words all day. The crooked ones are so often right. I'd wanted to see Gosling before I left, to do more with her than let her groom me, but she's been quite distant with me since we moved the village.

The sun now at its place that gives no advantage to either party, I whisper last words to Fox to make sure he remains hidden but close enough to watch my back. I stand slow, stretching up to another bright day, a beautiful day, another day where no rain will fall in my village to nourish the three sisters. My knees pop. Not too many more seasons of what I'm doing. This is a young man's game, after all, and I'm surrounded by those who want, one day, what I already have.

I tread to the shore with the Crow and seven men, all carefully selected by age for that combination of wisdom and strength. The girl will wait here until I call for her. As the enemy demanded, wampum and the girl will be exchanged for my life being spared. I can't wait to see the reaction of the enemy when they see the Crow. As for the wampum, I'll have to admit the tragedy of its loss. There's no doubt that my enemy will demand seven of my people to replace the seven whose lives we took that day last winter, and this will be a heated debate that I'm not willing to bow to. I'll simply then explain that the death of you, dear wife, and of our daughters has never been recognized, and my voice will tremor with the anger that makes them realize how many unseen debts are unpaid. They'll understand, or they'll not. I can only hope now that I've hidden my warriors on the banks and in the trees well enough to outwit them. We will soon see.

We spot each other at the same time. He's my equal, a leader, a man of a certain age and importance, and we have the same height and build. But he wears his hair down the middle and my first impression is I can't wait to cut it from his head. It strikes me then why I feel so strongly against him. He must be a relation of the girl.

We walk to them, taking our time as the last wisps of morning mist burn away in the sun.

"I told you only seven men," he calls out.

I stop, look around me as if surprised, and call back, "But we are seven."

"What of the charcoal with you, then?" he asks.

"Oh, him," I say. "I've never considered counting him as a man." My warriors laugh behind me. I clutch my club in my good hand and smile at him.

"No games," he barks.

I raise my club and sweep it across my view. "You're on my land," I say. "No, there will be no games."

We both stare at one another. Yes, he looks fierce, his hair shining in the light, his arms ropy with the muscle of paddling so far, his shoulders and chest full. He's younger than me. The ochre on his face can't conceal that he hasn't yet seen or done what I have. I picture launching myself at him, club raised high, stone and sharp wood thudding into his skull.

"You should remove the animal from our presence, then," he says.

I look at the Crow. "I'd thought to give him to you as a gift." The Crow's eyes widen. Clearly, his language has improved.

"I don't see my relation," he says. "And if you've allowed that"— he points with his chin to the Crow—"to have come even within breathing distance of her, the death sentence will be yours."

"He's harmless," I say. "Let's talk about what's really important." I pause so that the next words come out right. "There will be no wampum for you." I lower my club. "It was lost on our paddle here, and for this, I deeply regret."

I can see by his face that he doesn't know how to answer. The wampum we were to present him took our most talented artisans weeks of intense work, the weaving of our stories and of our hopes and wishes and especially of our promises, each single, hand-polished bead cut and shaped from foreign shells, drilled for the thread to pass through, each bead glittering and weighing almost nothing but immeasurable in price when it's chosen and sewn next to the other so that our hopes and our history emerge into something that can be held, that can be weighed in the hands, to be passed around and explained. This, I realize, this wampum, our story meant for these people who are our enemy, has been lost. And I'm the one responsible for losing it. It's my fault, I see, staring at this man. I have lost my people's story, my gift to the ones who are our enemy, in the hope of changing that course. I now know that the course we are on, this other leader and me, is a course of warfare. And that now that I've told him I lost the wampum, only one of us will see tomorrow.

"That's not what we agreed upon," he says.

I want to tell him that if he were to grow older, more and more it would seem that much he's agreed upon, much he's accepted as fair and good and right, will suddenly no longer appear as such. Instead, I say, "Shame." As soon as that simple word leaves my mouth, I know where this will go, and go quickly. I can sense from how his shoulders tense that he does, too. The others around us, listening close, also see what cannot be avoided, and I know they size one another up.

"Bring me my brother's child," the Haudenosaunee says. "Now."

"In due time," I say.

"You've got this all wrong," he says. "It's you who owe us."

"No," I say, stepping toward him. "That isn't true."

He stares at me, clearly convinced that I'm doomed if I continue moving forward. He knows my people don't want to go to war and will take it out directly on me if I cause it.

I turn to my most physically imposing warrior, Tall Trees. "Alert Fox and the others," I say. "It is on." And as I turn back to the younger warrior in front of me, his eyes open wide with the realization that I will not play by the rules. Low and from the hip, my club arcs across me and catches him below the jaw, snapping his head up. He falls back as others move forward, and, indeed, it is on. Men become dogs, growling and barking and biting with their knives and clubs. I hear Fox call to our men that it's time to fight as I stand over their leader, on the ground and twitching in pain. His equal to my Fox screams and darts toward me but Fox leaps high and drives his knife into the warrior's chest and the two fall onto the sand and rock. I watch as Fox straddles his man, pulling out the knife with both hands before running it across the dying man's neck.

The leader remains on his back, eyes rolled into his sockets. I lift my club and swing, crushing his forehead. His body convulses, and I move on.

As our men rush along both banks to engage the enemy, Fox shouts that their archers are taking aim. Arrows whistle by as those of us in the open run for cover in the trees. I see the Crow, bent toward one of their dying, talking to him, the man lifting his arms as if to ward him off. The Crow lowers his hand and runs his thumb along the man's forehead.

Gathering with the larger party of our own just inside the forest, Fox and I speak our wishes. We assume the enemy's number is smaller than ours given their reaction to my initial violence. I killed their leader, after all, and the response was much lighter than expected. My men killed or wounded all of the leader's party of warriors, and only two of my men suffered and by the looks of it should survive. Fox and I divide our men into groups of four and five and send them to seek out the enemy, and he sends others to the far side of the river to let them know of our plans. Today, with our superior numbers, we shall hunt them. I'm almost saddened this will be the case. It seems they underestimated our strength, and especially our resolve.

For the next while we fight pitched battles, my archers taking some from a distance, the majority of us moving slow through the trees and trying to outsmart the other. The cries of two or three men meeting one another echo out from the forest every little while, and all of us tense for the outcome. Fox and I stay close. The girl is safe with two young braves. I've told them to kill her if they are overrun but only if they're absolutely sure they will lose her to the enemy. She and I, our connection is too strong, I now realize as I run my good fingers over the severed one. Our connection is too weighted in blood now for me to allow her to be taken away. As for the Crow, last I heard and last I saw, he walks among the dead and wounded like the bird that he is, pecking at those poor men's foreheads, trying to gain something for himself from their dying bodies.

By afternoon, the forest is quiet. Fox comes for me where a creek runs into the lake, a good walk from where I began this violence earlier. "We've found their canoes," he says into my ear.

"How many," I ask. "And what size?"

He holds up five fingers, then explains with his hands that one is large, one is medium, and three are small and quick. Fox himself slit the throat of the sentry left to protect them. The ones we scuffle with aren't foolish, have at least as many canoes at another location. The five canoes we have found carry maybe twenty men. From the fight they've put up today, this must be half their fleet.

"Collect as many as you can without making undue noise, and we'll gather in wait," I whisper. Fox smiles, then sneaks away. From my estimates, we've been presented the opportunity to finish the rest. It will be a statement that can't be ignored by them, that if they come to the border of our territory again, they'll suffer the same consequences. And wiping out this warrior party of such esteem will certainly erase any concerns of my elders about whether or not I'm a leader in good standing. Any of my decisions regarding the Crow, and especially the girl, will hopefully be respected. Still, I feel a flutter in my belly at the thought of doing the opposite of what was expected of me. I can picture the looks upon their faces when I return home with the girl rather than the Crow.

With a handful of my men acting as dogs, chasing any of their stragglers away from our own canoes, I lie with Fox and twelve others he's managed to gather. More slip in every little while. I can't hear them but I can sense it. As far as I can tell, we've not given up our surprise. Birds sing in the late-afternoon forest as we lie above the creek where their canoes sit high on the bank, hidden in the tall grass. Soon, as dusk settles, probably, they'll begin to congregate and try to make their night escape from us. And so we wait.

I wonder about the girl, how she will respond now that I'm on the verge of changing her future forever. I want to laugh out loud with the realization that by killing her uncle, I've tied her to me with a rope that can't be cut. This girl who has disfigured me, today, with my actions, I have made my own. I acted without thinking about what I was doing for the long term. And that action, that changing the course of events without thought, is as powerful as dreams. All this must be listened to.

Or am I lying to myself? Can I convince myself I haven't wanted exactly what has happened from the time we set out on this journey? Hopefully, at least, the Crow is dead by now.

My eyes grow heavy as clouds swallow the last of the sun. Rain comes soon. As a younger man, I'd be near mad with the tension of the battle looming. But I'm older now, my love, and realize acutely that each day is one day closer to you.

Fox wakes me from my reverie by resting a hand on my back. He hears something. I open my eyes and focus. There it is, the swish of tall grass against thigh, the crunch of pebbles and sand underfoot, the low moan of a wounded man before his mouth is covered. We will not use bows tonight. Tonight we will go in with knives, clubs, and spears. In this way we'll finish them.

Waiting, the night close enough now that the enemy is just shadows, I can feel the air cool and the rain that approaches. The storm will be heavy and should pass quickly. We'll have to act fast when we are sure that they've all gathered so as not to let any of them escape in the rain.

I watch in the dusk as the enemy, in ones and twos, slips out of the forest and down to their canoes, picking them up and carrying them to the creek. We have our warriors on both sides of this small river, and when I stand and make the initial move the rest will follow.

The beginning cold drops of rain hit my naked back and cause me to shiver. The first of their canoes is in the water and the few men in it start to paddle. The others, nervous now, come out of the forest for fear of waiting too long. This must be all of them. It's time.

Just as I stand, the sky opens and the rain begins in earnest. Through sheets of it I see a sight that makes me feel something like envy. The last couple of their warriors have my Crow, bound and gagged, and they drag him down to the creek and shove him like a bundle of furs into their canoe and then climb in themselves.

Five canoes on the creek, the first one, the large one, already reaching the lake, the last just ahead of me as I bolt down the bank with a knife in one hand. The rain sings on the water of the creek and I'm crashing into it and launching myself upon the man in the stern before he even knows I'm there. Jumping up from the shallows and wrapping my arms around his chest and neck, I pull him from his vessel and into the water with me. The canoe tips over, dumping the bound Crow into the creek as Fox grabs the warrior paddling in front.

I can't hear my warriors descend on the other canoes, but in the steady drum of rain in the growing dark, I know my men are eviscerating the enemy. I take a large breath and pull my paddler under the surface and he struggles against me fiercely. I reach for his neck with my right hand and shove my knife into it, and this causes him to struggle harder. I can feel ribbons of his warm blood in the cold water and as I stay under with him, each of his kicks, each of his swings pump more blood from his neck until, in the dark, I imagine the creek is red all around us. His fight slows to spasms, and when I'm sure he's dead, I burst up and take a deep breath. Fox has already smashed in the head of his enemy, and in a flash of lightning I see that he stands ready to help me if I need it.

Their canoe floats capsized a short distance downstream and we make our way to it. The rain continues to pound and lightning punctuates the gloom of the night. I don't worry about the others. Our numbers are overwhelming and my young men hungry for the glory, the bragging rights of battle. I'm glad not to be our enemy tonight.

As we reach the canoe and turn it back over, lifting it from the shallow creek to rid it of the water, Fox points to the Crow still farther down, lit briefly by lightning, fighting to keep his head above water, his mouth, for those brief seconds we can see him, frozen in a scream.

"Your problems are solved," Fox shouts over the hissing water. The Crow will drown, and I won't be blamed for his loss in the heat of battle.

This canoe we've taken is a fine one. I can see that it was either stolen or bartered from an Anishnaabe. I run my hand along the birch-bark, note how carefully each long strip has been sewn and rosined against leaking. It's very light and will be very quick. Haudenosaunee don't have access to birch like this where they come from and travel in much lesser elm-bark canoes that rarely last a whole summer. "This one is yours," I shout to Fox. "It's perfect for your size and strength." He grins. "I'll stay here on the bank. Check on the others and let me know what you find out." Fox nods and disappears into the rain.

I sit on the bank and allow my hands to stop shaking from the rush of the fight. It's cold here, but a good fire isn't too far away. As lightning flashes again, I look to where I saw the Crow last struggle, but he isn't there anymore. He must have slipped under.

Curiosity gets the better of me and I stand, telling myself I'm simply moving to get warm. I walk down the bank and search for where the Crow might be. In another flash, I see his dark robe billowing in the water. I walk into the creek, the water chest high here, and turn him over. He appears dead. I lift him from behind and drag him to the bank, laying him out on his back. I consider cutting the leather straps from his bound wrists. I'm not sure why. Instead, I reach down and place my hand under his neck, lifting so that his mouth opens. Both hands on his chest, I kneel above him and push down. Nothing. I push again. Still nothing. I tell myself I do this to make sure this demon is dead. And then I push down on his chest again. With each push,

I begin to tell myself that if he comes back to life, he will prove me right, that he is a sorcerer and I will then slit his throat. With each push, I begin to tell myself that if I am to bring him back to life, maybe I can control his power, that it might become mine.

When I'm about to stop my attempts to revive him, he sputters and water erupts from his throat. I knew it was too good to be true. He takes great gasps and spits up more water. His body quakes. He sucks in air and some heat begins to return to him. The rain has stopped and a partial moon throws faint light that makes him appear blue. He really is a demon.

Something in me, though, as he breathes deeper and stops gagging, feels relieved. What have I done now? What have I done to my people and to myself?

I SAW YOU, LORD

I saw You, Lord, when I drowned that night. I saw You come down to me and felt Your hand take mine. It was then I realized it for certain. I no longer need to be afraid in this land of savagery. You guided me here, after all, and the lightning I saw flashing in the sky was Your light. I am a changed man. And I'm no longer fearful in this troubled world.

We've paddled for many days since the battle on the lake, and the men around me are even more watchful now that we've entered the Iroquois country. Surely, vengeance will be on the minds of the vanquished. I ministered to at least a dozen enemy warriors and offered them last rites before they died. Since there are four fewer men in our canoes, I've taken to paddling, remembering the words of the one I call David that I must be fully dedicated if I am to accept this work. Certainly, the hard work keeps my mind focused and I sleep the last nights without dreams, even the muttering of the wounded men in our party not waking me.

———

THIS IS THE COUNTRY that haunts me still. I'm sure of it. Back when I first came to this land, when the Algonquin tribe promised me safe passage to the Huron and then left me alone on the shore and paddled away like cowards, this is where I huddled and prayed and feared for my life for almost a week. I even think I recognize the island I hid upon as we now canoe past it, the same island where I contemplated my approaching death. I begged You there, Lord, to do with me as You saw fit, and when I ran out of my meagre supplies and could no longer see with clear vision, I smelled the smoke of a fire one evening. It was the Iroquois war party that had scared off my Algonquin companions. I was sure of it.

And that is when I made my decision. Rather than starve to death even as the mosquitoes feasted on me, I decided that martyrdom was the better option. Taking my chalice in my left hand and my crucifix in the other, I marched straight into the midst of their small camp, saying the Lord's Prayer in Latin with as steady a voice as I could muster. The men shouted and scurried back when they saw me.

It was then I realized they wore their hair long and braided in the Kichesipirini fashion. I knew that these were allies of the Huron, and I collapsed in relief, my body near spent from starvation and fear. Given my condition, those Kichesipirini must have thought I was a madman, or possibly a magician of some sort. They debated all evening as to what to do with me, I am sure, for their language is nothing like the Huron's. They talked and pointed and talked some more.

The next morning they made a place for me in one of their canoes and took me to their autumn hunting camp, where I bided my time until they eventually, that winter, brought me by snowshoe to Bird and his small hunting party. Despite this not even happening a year ago, it feels, Lord, as if a lifetime has passed.

———

TODAY, THE CANOES serving as advance scouts come racing back toward us at full speed. My stomach drops as I wait to see the pursuing Iroquois, gleaming heads and painted faces, the muscles of their bodies straining in chase. Instead, a great cry rises from the men around me as they take their paddles and drum them on the sides of their vessels.

The two scouting canoes then turn and disappear once more around the crook in the wide river. The men in our boats dig paddles into the water and turn ferocious with their strokes. It's only when we make the bend do I understand. First I see the smoke before I smell what I haven't in a long time. A scent I can only describe as Christian man, the scent of civilization, comes on the wind. A tannery, the butcher's shed, the wool and cotton and leather of the tailor, the manure of the stable, all of it comes at once on the breeze and I breathe deeply, my eyes welling with tears now that I've returned to a place I thought I might never see again, this island of humanity in the wilderness.

Habitation. New France. My salvation rises up sharply from the banks of this wide river. Champlain chose the place wisely. A clear view of the water and land on all sides, a cliff steep enough to prevent frontal attacks, the palisades thick and well maintained, with stone buildings like anchors behind them. This sprawling bit of the old world in the new is our foothold, the womb that will birth the next great civilization. I scramble from the canoe, nearly tipping it over in my rush to the gates.

Guards in their helmets and shining breastplates stare down at me from the palisades, pikes in their hands glistening in the afternoon sun. One turns his head to call to others. I hear the clatter as more make their way up the steps and heads begin to appear all along the length of the fort. My legs feel weak as I stare up at the men. They stare back down at me, looking confused, some of them even a little frightened.

"Will you let me in, then?" I finally ask, and my voice, gravelly with the journey and unaccustomed to my own language, breaks the spell.

A young soldier, no more than a boy, startles and mutters, "Of course, Father," before his dirty blond head disappears. I listen to the shout of orders and the feet of men in the dirt as logs are lifted and the gates are opened to me. My Huron have stayed on the river by their canoes, and I realize now that of course the sight of me, a lone and dishevelled Jesuit appearing out of the wilderness, would fascinate these ragtag soldiers.

I'm taken to the priests' residence, my knees shaking in anticipation. So much to tell! So much to share! I fear I'll cry when I open my mouth. The young blond soldier covers his face with a filthy rag before knocking on the thick door, then he slips away, muttering something under his breath. I look to see where he's gone but already he's disappeared down the dirt path that leads back to the palisades.

Nothing stirs. No one comes. I lift my hand and knock on the door myself, my fist light on the wood, then heavier when still I hear nothing behind it. Then comes coughing and the slow scuffle of feet. I want to shout that it's Christophe, and I've returned from the wilderness with stories to tell and God's word in my heart. When the door finally opens, I don't at first recognize the old man who stands there, a handkerchief in his hand, his skin so papery it's near translucent in the light. He squints, and as he raises up a hand to ask me in, his body convulses in hacking coughs. It's only when he looks at me, the handkerchief bloody with his sickness, that I recognize him, a priest not much older, healthy as a donkey when I left this place, now crooked and dying.

"I thought you were one of them," he says.

I wait for him to say more, but he turns and walks back into the shadows. I follow.

"Others are to arrive any day now to take my place," he says. "This is God's will."

We sit and talk in the pantry by a fire, Xavier shivering in a blanket beside it despite the summer day's heat.

"Many sick now," he says.

"You should be outside in the fresh air and sun," I admonish.

"Too painful on the eyes," he says, lifting his hand to cover them, as if even the idea of the sun is too much. I know from this it's the epidemic.

I want to cover my mouth, my face. I want to leave this place now. But where would I go? God, you are telling me to be strong. I will be strong for You.

"How are the others?" I ask. I think of François, of young Joseph, of the others I left behind.

He shakes his head. "The sickness has been bad," he says. "This last winter especially. A boat with the ones who were to join you arrived just before the freeze." He wipes his nose with the bloody rag. "They must have brought it with them. No greens all winter on top of it, and half of us are sick now. Or dead."

I keep my head bowed and listen. "Word is of another ship coming soon?" I finally ask.

He nods. "If it doesn't arrive before this year's freeze, then we're all doomed."

I want to tell him that we are only into the height of summer now, that months stretch out luxuriously before us. But then I remember how fast the cold comes in this land, that one afternoon I might sweat with just the idea of movement, and the next I shiver and freeze. "Today is a good day," I say instead. "Today is a blessed day."

He wants to nod, I think, but instead coughs blood into his handkerchief.

———

SIEUR DE CHAMPLAIN has sent a courier with the news that he'd like me to join him for dinner tonight. He's asked that some of my Huron companions join me, especially the one called Bird. He wants to meet the warrior chief whose reputation certainly seems to precede him. I leave the safety of the palisades, the same blue-eyed waif allowing me departure through the heavy gates. I can feel his eyes on my back as I walk down toward the river and the encampment of the Huron, wondering why he's so fascinated with me. I ask the warrior David where Bird might be. He shrugs and goes back to whittling down a straight branch that I imagine will become an arrow.

I walk through the camp, searching, asking different warriors if they know where Bird is, and I receive the same cold reception from all of them. Finally, I see Fox. He sits on his haunches, staring out at the wide river in front of us. Despite his diminutive size, he is incredibly strong. I saw with my own eyes the speed and agility of his murderous ways, and my revulsion, my terror of this little man, causes my hands to shake. But all I need to do to calm down is remember the light, the warmth that I know awaits me when I'm called by You.

"Why do your men treat me so coldly?" I ask. These Huron don't like pointed questions like this, I've learned, the questions that force them to give me either the desired answer or none at all. They never, I've learned, ask one another questions such as this. They consider it the height of rudeness. I know etiquette dictates that I ask more gently, something along the lines of "Have I done something to hurt or offend you, my cousin?" But asking Fox in so pointed a way helps to conquer my fear of him. These people talk around the issues, but now I refuse.

When he doesn't answer, I try a different approach. "My Great Chief gives a feast tonight," I say. "Bird comes. You come." I can sense the slight change in his countenance with my words. After all, his pride, all of these people's pride, is everything to them.

"Where is this feast?" he asks.

I point up the hill. "At Great Chief's longhouse," I say.

"I will tell Bird," Fox answers. "We will come."

His words stop the conversation. I search for more phrases, wanting to tell him what time is appropriate, what he should expect, what he should bring, and how he should act, but the language escapes me. I've learned much these last months, but I still have so far to go.

———

AT THE RESIDENCE, I find a new robe that nearly fits and heat water for a bath. I'm shocked to see my reflection in the mirror for the first time in almost a year. My face is so drawn it gives the appearance that I am a skull, and when I remove all my clothes and pour water over my body, I resemble a cadaver. In the short time I have here in New France, I must replenish my physical body as well as my soul. Due to the lack of proper nutrition, I imagine, my hairline has receded almost entirely, and the ring of hair that I do have left is long and matted. I look freakish, I now see, and understand why the soldiers stared at me so. If I were vain, I'd be ashamed, but I've learned there is no room for physical vanity in this wilderness. I leave that to the sauvages. Finding a pair of scissors, I cut the hair from my head and as close to the scalp as I can. I then trim my scraggly beard into a sharp V on my chin. I stare at myself hard in the mirror, and my eyes, Lord, they burn with Your intensity still. With a fresh cotton shirt beneath my cassock, I already feel human, a Christian man once again.

Xavier's impressed that I am to have dinner with Champlain. "He's warming to us Jesuits," he says. The two of us sit in the chapel, having just finished taking the other's confession. "He understands that our role in this country is vital to his own interests."

"But aren't our interests the same?" I ask.

Xavier tries to speak but falls into a coughing fit. I place my hand on his thin back and feel the strain of his heated body. When he can catch his breath, he says, "Don't be so naïve. Champlain's sole interest is the conquest of this land, damn the Dutch and the English."

Xavier is wrong. The illness has affected his brain. "And ours," I say, "is the conquest of souls. Sometimes the brutality of man needs to show itself so that we may understand the stakes."

"Spoken like a true believer," Xavier says.

I want to tell him that what I've seen in this last year has taught me life is simply a preparation for the afterlife. I look over at him and understand he isn't long for this world and stop myself from speaking.

"Go on your way now," Xavier says. "Don't keep a man like Champlain waiting."

———

I'VE NEVER SEEN such a table of guests. Champlain sits at the head, his hair long and carefully coiffed, his shoulders, despite the heat, covered in his finest robe, his golden medallions of conquest around his neck. He looks like a king. Despite his regal appearance and despite my not wanting to admit it, he's pale, frail looking, and puffy. It isn't the sickness of consumption that afflicts the others, I can see. It's another one, the one that comes when a man doesn't want to admit he'll soon die yet knows this is what pursues him, baying like a hound. Champlain will pass on to you, Lord, before the year is out. And then what will happen to this desperate mission in the wilderness without its noble head?

Still, though, he puts on a good face, greeting those who come to sit around him in a big voice. His confessor, Father Lalemant, sits on his left, and behind them stand a coterie of guards in leather breast-plates, most holding pikes, but two with muskets at their sides, no doubt to awe and restrain the Huron guests from behaving rashly. But having seen these sauvages fight, I know the guards would have no chance to even cock their guns before their throats were slit or their heads bashed in.

The worn wooden table, long enough to sit a dozen guests, is full, most of them Bird's party. A second table, shorter though, had to be added to ours. It sits four others. Our governor knows these people and their habits, after all, and he knows the greatest offence is to invite them to a feast and then turn away part of their party. For the Huron, he is as close to a chief as a European can be. For short stretches he lived with them as a younger man, and he's fought and killed Iroquois alongside them. He champions the Huron, for he knows they are adept businessmen. He's even learned some of their language.

I sit to his left, four seats down, a place of minor importance but still within range of his direct questions. Bird sits to his immediate right. Bird, like the others, has come in full regalia. His face, like the rest, is painted in strips of sharp colour. Some of the men have chosen yellow and some red or black. Some have chosen more than one colour, and others have added ochre to their lips or beneath their eyes, the effect at once frightening and beautiful. The black hair of these warriors, cut and styled so intricately, shines in the early-evening sun that pours through the windows. Champlain, when I glance at him, seems happy and at home.

He raises his crystal glass, and the light glitters on it, around it, through it like a lit jewel. He must have chosen the seating, the angle of the sun. I watch how Bird is literally struck by the green and yellow and red bands of colour that project through the crystal. The brightness makes Bird squint. His face lights up with the hues, the refraction of it dancing across his features. A few of his warriors gasp. When Champlain smiles and twists his chalice, I see that it's empty.

After a time, Champlain stands, asking Father Lalemant to pray for our souls. I stand with them, and in the long, awkward silence that follows, the sauvages look to one another before the scraping of chairs and jostle of cutlery and porcelain settles to silence. As Father Lalemant murmurs in Latin, I glance up to see the Indians watching him. When I look at Bird, I see he watches me. I drop my head and close my eyes.

When Father finishes, we bless ourselves. Only a few of the younger warriors attempt to mimic. As I'm about to sit, Bird lifts his arms to Champlain and calls out like a falcon, high and haunting. It's loud enough that the soldiers begin to lift their weapons, shocked. Champlain smiles broadly, happy for the attention.

"You come to us," Bird says in his tongue, lifting his head high and speaking directly to Champlain. "You come to us and so we come to you. We come to you with gifts and we come to you with furs from our animals, and all of this is in our desire to become a great family with you." He pauses for a moment and watches as Father Lalemant leans to Champlain and translates what the governor doesn't fully understand. "I come to you," Bird continues, opening his arms wide, "we come to you with a message from our elders. Our elders wish you to become family, to aid us in our troubles with the Haudenosaunee, to accept our furs in exchange for your weapons." He pauses, looking at the men around him. "We want you to be our brothers, we want you to join us and become one great village with us, a village that is strong enough to sustain the coming attacks from our common enemy. This day, I beg of you to acknowledge, this day approaches faster than you might believe."

Again, Bird pauses, allowing Lalemant to translate his words for us. A good heat washes over me when I realize I understand even more than the crux.

Now Champlain stands, adjusting his long fur robe, his forehead beaded with sweat. Bird sits to listen. "I hear you, my brother," he says, lifting his arms to Bird and his party. "We are brothers, yes?" He waits for Lalemant to translate to the warriors. They agree with a loud "Ah-ho!"

"We have friends in common," Champlain continues, "and we have common troubles. The Dutch to the south care nothing for you, and the English would be happy to see you wiped from this world." Champlain pauses for the translation. I listen carefully to Lalemant's words and am impressed at how good he is. One day, I will be so sure of mouth, too. "But we French have proved ourselves strongest. The evidence is that we are still here, despite the British doing everything they could to dislodge us from this place and you people that we love." Again he pauses so that the father may capture and translate all his words. He sits so that Bird may speak.

"The English and the Dutch give our common enemy their weapons, and their weapons put a great fear into our bodies," Bird says. "If our nation of the Wendat is one body, then the weapons the Haudenosaunee have been given by their friends from over the sea put fear into the centre of our great body, into our heart." Bird pauses for what we all suddenly know comes next. "You are our brothers, and so we ask you to gift us those." He points to a musket being held by a soldier behind Champlain. "The only way to battle our common enemy and win is to be allowed to fight that enemy on common ground."

Lalemant leans to Champlain to translate but Champlain brushes him away with his hand. It's Champlain's turn to stand, and as he does, he takes the musket from the soldier. The soldier looks shocked. Then, holding the gun in both hands, Champlain walks to Bird. "You are a great warrior," he says, handing the musket over. "I can see that you have suffered in battle." He points to Bird's missing finger. "And great warriors need great weapons. So I give you this as a sign of my friendship and as your brother. Tomorrow I will have my greatest warrior show you how to use it." Champlain returns to his chair and sits. Bird remains standing, the long gun in his hands. He stares down at it, then looks up, then down again. The other Huron whisper amongst themselves, and I overhear the one I've named David asking Fox when they'll receive theirs as well.

"Now let us eat!" Champlain announces, clapping his hands. Servants arrive carrying platters of lamb and beef and whole roasted chickens, goose and duck and a large kettle of fish stew. Steaming loaves of bread arrive, alongside heaps of fresh vegetables. Champlain has planned this well, and he spends greatly from his storehouse. He understands the importance of this alliance, the importance of rejuvenating it with a feast, of sowing seeds that will certainly blossom, this food something the sauvages in their simplicity understand fully. The servants, I can see, are frightened to the point their hands shake as they dole out mounds of food to the hungry warriors.

A younger Huron grabs a leg of duck and begins to eat it before he's admonished by an older one beside him. The young one places the leg back on his plate, his mouth grease smeared so that he looks like a child caught doing wrong. All of the warriors' eyes watch Champlain, waiting to see what he will do. He picks up his napkin and tucks it into his collar under his chin. The others try to mimic, some who wear their breastplates finding a purchase for the serviette. But most are shirtless and try to rest the white cloth across their chests, willing it to stay perched there. Champlain then picks up his fork with his left hand and his knife with his right. All the warriors do the same.

Pinning a large piece of beef with the fork, Champlain daintily saws into the meat, cutting a small chunk. A clatter and scrape of forks and knives on porcelain ensues as the sauvages attempt the small feat. Champlain raises the chunk of meat on his fork to his mouth and chews slowly, the look on his face announcing how he relishes it. The others do the same, some struggling to keep the meat on their forks, others with so large a piece that they can't fit it into their mouths.

This mimicry goes on for minutes, the warriors struggling, dropping food and napkins, growing frustrated in their louder murmurings. But none of them dare eat in their normal fashion, quickly, and with their hands.

After a time, Champlain looks up and smiles. "We are all brothers, yes?" he asks. "Well, then, let us eat properly like brothers!" He places his fork and knife down, takes a large goose leg in his hands, and bites into it with abandon. I can almost hear the warriors gasp with relief and the room erupts with the feed, men devouring flesh and waving for more, the servants sweating to keep up with the doling. I look about me, unable to feel anymore what it was like out there in the wilderness, so far away, and yet just feet away on the other side of the palisades. Will I be able to return there, Lord? I don't think I can.

I note that only Bird doesn't feast. He sits, holding the gun's barrel with the hand that now misses its little finger, the gun's stock on the floor in front of him. He stares at it, mesmerized. Father Lalemant has noticed, too. He leans to Champlain. "With all due respect, I think you misunderstood what their chief was asking of you," he says.

Champlain waves to a servant and tells him to bring the wine. "You underestimate me, I think." Champlain places his meat down and looks to Lalemant. "This one named Bird would certainly like more than one musket, I am sure." The servant returns and fills Champlain's goblet. The servant then fills Lalemant's. He is about to fill mine but I place a hand over my glass. As the servant walks away, Champlain calls him back gruffly. "What of the rest of our guests?" he asks.

Lalemant raises his eyebrows. "Are you sure that's a good idea?" he asks. "These sauvages, they respond poorly to the grape."

"No more poorly than the peasants who have built Habitation with their own callused hands," Champlain says. He waves to the servant, who goes about filling the glasses of the warriors. "As for handing out weapons," he continues, "I've handed out just one. Maybe one or two more next year. The British are fools for being so easy with their gifts of destruction. Mark my words. Their allies, the Iroquois, when they are in the position of power to do so, will turn against their friends." He spits out this last word and looks at Lalemant. Then he looks at me, which catches me by surprise. I've felt invisible all night. The focus in Champlain's eyes forces me to look to my hands on my lap. "For the French to crack this great continent and all of its wealth—and I include the wealth of souls, Fathers—we must crack the Huron Confederacy. They are the ones, clearly, who control the trade in this savage land. And so we must control them." His eyes burn into me. "That's where you come in, dear Fathers. It is your job to bring them to Christ. We will then leave it to Christ to bring them to us." Champlain claps his hands and stands. "Listen carefully, Lalemant, and be prepared to translate it all."

Champlain lifts his crystal glass of wine and raises it in the air. "This drink," he says, "is the colour of blood. It is the blood of our God. And these ones here," he says, lifting his glass to Father Lalemant and then to me, "are our Fathers. And they are the sons of our God. We love our Fathers more than our children or ourselves. Our Fathers are held in great esteem in France. It is neither hunger nor want that brings them to this country. They do not want your land or your furs. If you love the French people, as you say you do, then love these Fathers. Honour them, and they will teach you the way to Heaven."

Champlain then drinks deeply. I watch as the others follow suit, wincing at what must be a very bitter taste for them. Some keep gulping, until their glass is emptied. Father Lalemant carefully translates Champlain's words. When he is finished, the sauvages, in one great voice, call out "Ah-ho! Ah-ho!" Champlain smiles.

"Very soon, one of our great canoes will arrive," Champlain says. "If you are willing to wait for it, you will find that when it arrives, it will be filled with gifts for you to take back home to your wives and your brothers and your uncles and aunts and children." He pauses so that Lalemant can translate. The sauvages smile and nod. I can see that already the wine affects some of them.

"But the greatest gift that our great canoe brings to you is more of our Fathers." Again, Champlain pauses. "Our Fathers leave their loved ones and a good life back home to bring you important messages. And so I ask you to bring these fathers back with you so that they may teach you, and especially your children, a knowledge so great and so necessary." Once Lalemant translates, the servant makes another round, filling glasses. I look around the room at these men who are becoming drunk for the first time. Some are glassy eyed, others talk excitedly amongst themselves, no longer caring about etiquette, and a few, including Bird, sit silently, a stony look on their faces, impossible to read.

An hour later, I am ashamed and embarrassed for my sauvages, and more so for my countrymen, who have given them this poison. The Huron pass a long pipe around the table, smoking and making speeches, slurring their words as Bird watches with that same stony look on his face, his hand still on the barrel of the musket. The pipe comes to Champlain, and he puffs it contemplatively before passing it to the one beside him. Another sauvage stands and, waving his arms, speaks so unclearly I can't understand much.

An hour later Champlain slips away, no one but Bird seeming to notice. Outside, a large bonfire is set, and like moths, the sauvages are drawn to it, one by one, until the room is empty, the table and floor scattered with bones.

I let the candles burn out as I stand at the window and stare down below me to them dancing and singing around the fire, most of them stumbling drunk, others passed out on the periphery. The singing and shouting and shrill cries of anguish, the souls below me cast in the bright light of the flame, their painted faces twisted and ghastly, remind me of something I have seen before, back home. A painting, maybe? A woodcut from my youth in Brittany?

Behind me, the scrape of a chair. I turn and peer into the darkness. As my eyes adjust, I make out a form in the corner, shoulders rounded in a slump, the posture of an old man. His voice comes out of the darkness, just above the singing and screaming of those around the fire below.

"The world tonight has changed," he says. "The world tonight, it has changed forever."

I recognize his voice now. It is the voice of Bird.

SHINING WOOD

Bird no longer cares for me. I'm allowed to wander at will but my hand aches so miserably that I don't go far from the camp and the river. I've taken to holding my fist in the cool water to help ease the pain a little. I crouch by it on a flat stone and when the fist unclenches, I wiggle my fingers below the clear surface. It sometimes looks like I still have five of them on that hand. The warriors tend to stay away from me. There's talk that I'm a witch. Let them think what they want. I plan to be left here with these hairy men from another world and in this way I'll find my way back to my family. Today, when I flex my hand, a ribbon of blood weaves up and reddens the water. It's stubborn in healing.

Since none of them will come near me, I dress my wound each day myself, finding moss to pack around the nub of finger that's left and then wrapping it tight with a long thin strip of deer hide. The Crow often comes looking for me but I'm good at hiding from him. Today, though, the pain is great enough that I decide I'll look for him and ask if he might be able to help. I noticed this morning when I cleaned it that it weeps yellow, and this makes me scared.

Yesterday, I tried moaning out loud when I knew Bird was near, but something has come over him. He walks around with what one of the warriors calls the thunder stick, muttering to himself. He looks like he carries a great weight. I think he might be possessed by some-thing, an oki we passed over canoeing the river, or maybe one from the forest.

Walking the perimeter of this strange village, I look for an opening, a break in the palisades big enough to squeeze through. It's well made, and their warriors walk along up top, their faces frightening beneath their shining headdresses. I have no other choice than to go to the main gate and see if they'll let me in. A huge man with so much hair on his face that he looks like a bear stands there with a long spear in his hand. His eyes are bright in the blackness of his face and I don't like the way he stares at me. His lips are pink beneath his beard. He won't stop staring at me. I point inside and then cradle my wounded hand. I look up at him again. He licks his thick pink lips. He waves me in.

I scurry past and walk along the fence. I'll find the Crow this way, by staying in the shadows and watching. Fifty or a hundred steps from the gate and I come to some kind of structure made of wood that reminds me of a giant box trap for snaring lynx. With my ear pressed right up to it, I hear nothing. Peering inside, I see that it's a dark room, a place maybe for the warriors on watch to rest out of the sun. As my eyes adjust, I see a table at the far end, what might be food on it. My stomach grumbles. I place a foot inside. Grasshoppers buzz close by. The whir echoes in my ears. I take another step. Slow. Another. I peer over my shoulder and the sun is bright enough to shut my eyes. Something scratches in the corner. I freeze, then look toward the sound. A mouse darts through the shadow. The round shapes of crabapples sit on the table. I picture myself picking one up and biting into it, the cold of its inside making me shiver. I'll rush now and be gone with one or two of them and no one will know.

I run to the table, take an apple in each hand. As I turn to run out, the light from the door darkens and I smell something sour. What stands in front of me, blocking my way out, is backlit by sun. I see the legs first, and then the thick body, and finally the hairy face of the bear man.

I wonder if I can squeeze past him, maybe pretend to go to one side and jump to the other. He says something I don't understand. I stare up at him. I'm frozen. He says it again, and this time waves his hand for me to come to him. I don't know what else to do, and so I take steps forward and raise the apples in my hands to him. His head looks the size of a boulder. He stands with his legs apart. I can hear him lick his lips again. When I'm close I can see that he'll hurt me. His eyes tell me all of this now that I'm close enough that his stink chokes me.

"I am sorry for taking these," I tell him, knowing he won't understand my words. "It's just that I'm hungry." I lift one of the apples higher, the one in my good hand, and with all my might I throw it at him and jump forward to leap out. He growls and swings at the apple just as I dive onto my stomach and slip between his legs. Sun and dust burn my eyes as I stand and begin to run but I'm pulled back by the hair. He drags me into the darkness of the room and I begin to shout because I know that this will be the end of me. I scream and scream until his heavy hand slaps over my mouth.

I taste blood and the huge man throws me on the table, his hand not leaving my mouth. The apples under me crush as they dig into my ribs and back. I want to breathe but the hand won't let me. His other hand feels for my robe and begins to tug it off and he runs his hand up and down my chest, so rough that I think he tries to burn me with it. I reach out with my good hand and hit him hard across the ear but this only causes him to remove his hand from my mouth and slap me. He presses his face into mine just as I try to gasp for air but all I suck in is the stinking breath and spit of him and this makes me begin to cough. His hand now pulls at my legs and he puts his hand lower and tries to wiggle a finger into me, and as he does this he lifts his mouth from mine and moans and that's when I scream again, so loud in this room that I think it will split the ceiling so the light can get in and free me.

He stands and pulls down his leggings, then spits in his hand and reaches back to me and so I begin kicking at him, wiggling so that he can't touch me there. I scream again but this time it goes the other way and makes me choke so that I begin to retch. He places his hand over my mouth and nose again and begins to push forward, the heat of him burning me between the legs. I can't breathe. I want to breathe. I can't.

The little bit of light in the room fades before it explodes white, so bright that I must close my eyes, and just as I do I see he closes his eyes to the light, too, and suddenly looks frightened.

When I can open my eyes again, the crushing weight of him is off me. I gulp air and try to sit up to run but I can't. I crane my neck and see the door of this trap has been flung wide open and the Crow, tall and skinny and shaking, stands there. His mouth's open. He's shouting so hard that his whole body shakes but all I can hear is the ringing in my ears. The one who attacked me stands with his head down and his hands covering that part of him as the Crow approaches, swinging his hands in open slaps across the bear's face. Each time the Crow screams at the bear, I swear I can see the Crow puff bigger. Then the bear falls to his knees and the Crow stands over him, his voice now beginning to sound in my ears, hollow at first, but louder and louder as he slaps at the bear's head over and over and the bear cowers lower.

Other men pour into the room now, some glancing at me, others stopping at the door, trying to make sense of what the Crow calls out. A couple of the men take the bear by the arms, yank him up so that he's on his feet, and lead him out into the sun. He doesn't look at me.

The Crow comes to me, his hands outstretched. He reaches for my robe and covers me. I lie there, flat and still as I did last winter, wanting all of these men to think I am frozen or I am dead and just leave me alone forever. I burn down there and reach under my robe to feel. Lifting my hand, I see that it's dry. He's not taken that from me. The Crow offers his hand to help me, and as he does so, I jump up, fast as a hare, and run out of the room and back to my people and the river.

———

WHEN BIRD HEARS of what's happened, I hide. I feel like it's my fault and I don't know why. For the rest of the afternoon I lie in the forest on a bed of moss, hidden under ferns, drifting to sleep and then waking to the light step of warriors searching for me or to mosquitoes in my ears.

I'm too frightened to stay when the dark begins creeping closer, and so I slip down to a large fire on the shore. There, in the shadows outside the ring of flame, I listen to Bird ask the others what compensation is deserved for an affront of this severity. Some of the angrier warriors call for his death.

"And so what shall we do?" Fox asks. "Do we demand that their chief hand the perpetrator over to us?"

A dozen warriors hoot their desire.

Bird raises his hand. "If he's serious about being our friend, our brother"—he almost spits out the last word—"then we should give him the opportunity to prove this."

Warriors call out in disapproval. I can hear the blood in their voices.

"Hear me," Bird says, lifting his hand higher. "This is their great leader's opportunity to show that he understands us, that he is indeed in line with our notions. Let us wait now and see what he decides. Let us wait to see what compensation he offers." He pauses and looks down before looking up at the men massed around him. "Then we shall decide if he's truly our brother."

Many of the warriors nod. But many of them are clearly not happy.

"And if we as one agree that the compensation is fair, we have avoided conflict." Again Bird pauses. "But if we as one agree that it is not, I will demand something more." The men quiet at this, and I can hear what they now hear. Bird has left them little room for disagreement. He's made sure his men in their anger don't decide to act on their own in order to seek revenge tonight. This man who killed you, my father, is so much like you.

———

THE BEAR MAN IS STRAPPED, shirtless and on his chest, to a large piece of wood. His arms are stretched so hard I can tell it must hurt. Men pound on drums with sticks in a quick rhythm, and the one who's their chief speaks in words I can't understand. The chief sweats in his fur collar and he looks very ill, like he won't make it to next spring if the winter is a tough one. A man then walks up carrying a length of leather that splits into many pieces at its end, each tipped with sharp, glinting metal. All of us who've travelled here by canoe stand in a group to watch, asked by Bird to witness. He wouldn't want me here, so close to that man, so close I can see the thick coat of fur on his back. But the idea of being by myself down on the river is too much. I crouch between the legs of the warriors and watch as the man with the leather lifts it high into the air and makes it crack.

The bear roars out each time the sharp pieces glint in the sun. His fur darkens and his shoulders begin to pour blood. The one who swings the leather at him sweats and groans with each stroke, and each stroke the bear's roars become closer to screams. I look over to the others who are like him. Some watch with open mouths, and others must turn their heads with each swing. Finally, the one with the leather stops. The bear man slumps, and I can hear him begin to sob. The warriors around me mumble and kick dirt, embarrassed by him, by his weakness. The bear cries out something that makes the men who understand his words turn to one another and whisper. The man with the leather, once their chief looks at him and raises his hand, begins to swing again. Again, the bear roars and the Wendat around me shake their heads and point to his weakness and the bear's back turns to ribbons of flesh and blood.

Again and again the man swings and the bear cries out before it all stops. And then their chief begins it all over again with the raising of his hand until the bear no longer moves, even when the glinting leather cuts into the fresh skin of his legs. A warrior near me comments to his friend that it seems unfair they don't revive the bear, now clearly in another world. "What is the point of this torture," the warrior asks, "if he isn't present to understand its point?"

When the sun has sunk low enough to cross the palisades and throw its shadow spears on us, I watch as the Crow pushes his way through the crowd and reaches for the man with the leather who no longer works with much desire. This causes the tired witnesses to reawaken and some even shout out what sounds like approval. Our warriors wake up too, lifting their heads high to see what will happen. The man with the leather looks confused and my Crow calls out to his chief and I want to know the words he says but can't hear them over the restless crowd. Even the chief finally looks like he wakes from where he has gone.

The Crow lifts his arms and shouts out more words. I don't know what they mean. I look to their chief and see he holds himself tall. The Crow keeps calling out and then points to Bird's warriors. The French look at us and begin talking. When the Crow finally stops his shouting, their chief raises his hand and a group of war-bearers cut the straps from the bear's hands and drop him onto the ground. He looks dead. I don't feel sad.

Only then do I realize Bird stands beside me. "That was rather brutal, wasn't it?" he says. He snorts and spits on the ground like he wants to rid himself of what he's just seen. "Did you watch how the Crow tells them they behave worse than us?" Bird looks down to me, and I see something like kindness in his eyes, something like a look you'd give me when you hoped for me to understand, Father. I want Bird to take my hand and lead me away from here, from this place that frightens me. Instead, he walks away.

———

TODAY BIRD LOOKS SCARED, although he tries to hide it. He holds the shining wood in both hands and peers down its length, a French war-bearer beside him. The war-bearer tells Bird to squeeze. A boom like thunder despite the high blue sky of summer and gulls scream and take wing and Bird stumbles back, his face disappearing in smoke. The French laugh at Bird's warriors who watch wide-eyed with hands over their ears. I watch as well from the tree line, holding my aching hand. The French warrior slaps Bird on the back, and Bird stares down at the carved wood in his hands, at the smoke pouring from its mouth. I saw it, how it breathes flame. I've now seen the shining branch from across the water where the others live. This is the weapon they say can kill two or even three men at a time with just its roar. Bird possesses it.

Again and again, the French war-bearer teaches Bird how to make the shining wood boom. And now he stands away from Bird, having shown him how to pour black sand and a shining rock down its throat. I wait and watch for Bird to make the thing bark. I watch how all the warriors wait, too, their hands close to their faces for the coming noise. Bird looks determined now as he hugs the wood to his cheek. I try to keep my eyes open so I may witness it.

Just as Bird is about to do it, the greatest thunder I've ever heard splits the sky so loud that the leaves in the trees around me shake and flutter to the trembling ground. The men, all the war-bearers from all the places they come, dive to the ground and cover their heads and I do the same for fear my ears won't ever work again.

When I dare, I lift my head from the earth and look up at the wide river, to the sight of it. A monster floats before us, so big that the men on its back look tiny. They shout and wave and smoke pours from a hole in the side of the beast. Rather than running away, the French jump to their feet and begin hollering at it, waving their hands in joy. Our warriors are tensed to run but see how the French are so excited. Our people, they stand up straight and watch.

Up in their great village, men begin to shout, too, and it isn't long before what must be all of them are running down and lining the bank of the big river, waving and howling. A gang of them run to their heavy canoes and pile in, some almost falling out as they push hard against the current, sitting backward and pulling on their paddles so I realize that these people must really be backward and maybe don't want to look forward.

My eyes turn again to the monster on the river. No one will notice me. I sneak through the legs of men shouting and pointing and laughing. Some of them cry. This thing brings something important. I'll find out what it is. All I can see now as I stand on the bank, close enough to Bird that I won't be pushed down or grabbed by one of the French, are the few straight trees growing up from the back of the beast with great white robes flapping from them in the breeze that men wrestle to secure.

Bird calls to Fox, and seeing me beside him, smiles and lowers his wounded hand to mine. Without wanting to, I reach up and take it, and together we walk to Fox who holds the canoe steady as we climb in. I sit in the middle as we glide out fast into the river, cutting across the current, easily passing the big, clumsy canoes of the French. I stare as the monster grows larger and larger the closer we get to it, am amazed that the water of the wide river can support its weight and I wonder how this can be, wonder if the hairy ones really are sorcerers. As we pull up to it now, the men above us on its back go silent and stare down, their eyes wide. I suddenly recognize that they're as scared of us as I am of them. They're thin faced and hairy, some with yellow-tinged skin. I can smell them from here and want to hold my nose but force myself from doing it.

Then Bird stands up in the bow of the canoe and reaches his arms out wide. He tells these men above him that he's honoured they've travelled such a great distance to visit, that he hopes their stay in this land will be a good one but not very long. Fox laughs. Their faces tell me that these men don't understand any of the words. But Bird's gesture of open arms tells them everything that needs to be said.

One lowers a rope so that Bird can take a hold and Fox may stop paddling. More and more French are staring down at us, and for the first time I see what we must look like to them. Broad-shouldered Bird with his hair carefully shaved on one side, his cheekbones taut, the muscles of his shoulders and arms and chest enough to make a man think twice about arguing with him, and Fox behind, small and powerful, his ropy arms laced with veins and his eyes sharp and black as a raven's. We are the people birthed from this land. For the first time I can see something I've not fully understood before, not until now as these pale creatures from somewhere far away stare down at us in wonder, trying to make sense of what they see. We are this place. This place is us.

IT WILL NOT PREPARE YOU

For the first time in over a year, dear Lord, I am able to celebrate Mass with my peers and for Your greater good, speaking it in Latin with no fear that my words will be misunderstood. The new arrivals beseeched me to perform this Mass and I do it with a warmth in my heart I've not felt since leaving Brittany. I can tell the new arrivals near burst to hear of my adventures and of this new world. But I will be coy in my sharing. I can tell them of what this dark world of sauvages is like until the breath leaves my chest for good. The only true way for them to understand, though, is to experience it for themselves. I plan to request of Champlain that I stay behind here in New France for the next year in order to complete my relations and send them back home while the new entourage travels out to the land of the Huron to gain experience. I need the rest, Lord, as I need to regain my physical and especially my spiritual strength. The idea of heading back into that wilderness makes me want to weep. You understand, don't You?

———

I'M QUITE TAKEN by the zeal of these new arrivals. Two brother Jesuits have come, as well as four laymen to help assist them in their travels, teaching, and eventual conversions. All of them are so young, though. Still, I'm impressed and a little envious, as I was never offered such support. Clearly, some word of the importance of this mission is getting through to those who hold the purse strings back in France. But I must admit that in these last days, I wake before dawn and wrestle with the grave worry that our work is being exploited by those who wish not for the souls of the sauvages but for the riches of the land, and that they are using us as the tip of the spear for their earthly gains. I have found some solace, though, in recognizing that we Jesuits are indeed the sharpened spear tip. We are Your soldiers, Lord. We are the soldiers of Christ. And the folly of those who wish to make profit not from souls but from the furs of animals will certainly meet with Your anger. I trust, Lord, that Your divine plan has long been engraved in something far denser than stone.

———

THIS MORNING AFTER MASS, I take the two new Jesuits, Gabriel and Isaac, up to the ramparts to look down upon them. Again this morning, even before first light, I awoke with a start. I realize it will be unfair to send these brave men out with no knowledge of those who will try to devour them.

We peer out to the shore of the wide river below us, to the encampment of Huron who laze by smoking fires that keep the hordes of insects at bay, even from this distance the bright smiles of the men flashing in the sun as they talk and laugh.

"It's a rather idyllic scene, no?" Isaac says. "They're not so different from the accounts I've read of them." Isaac smiles his very white smile. He's a handsome young man, but I already see that his blond hair is beginning to thin. Give him his year in hell and, like me, there won't be much of it left.

"Are the heathens always so relaxed?" Gabriel asks. He appears a little older than Isaac, and unlike Isaac, he's not ready with his smiles. The unruly black hair of his head and on his face only helps to magnify his intensity. His eyes flash with it whenever he looks at me.

"They are amazingly lazy," I say, "for the most part. But when it comes time to canoe or to hunt or to plant corn, they work with an intensity I've never witnessed before. You'll soon see this yourselves when you paddle out to their land with them."

"I'm glad you'll be there to share your knowledge with us along the journey," Isaac says, smiling wide. Poor Isaac. It won't be so long till he no longer smiles.

I shake my head. "No, my young one," I tell him. "I've requested of Father Lalemant that I stay back here for a year to recuperate and to finish my reports."

"No!" Isaac says, his eyes brimming with tears. Gabriel simply flashes his serious dark eyes at me.

"I'm afraid it is so," I say.

"Well, then," Gabriel says. "You mustn't waste any time in telling us everything we need to know for our mission to be a success."

I hold his gaze before looking down to the lazing sauvages on the beach. "First of all," I say, stroking my beard to a point, "you should understand fully and completely that there will be no success for a long time. Maybe never."

Isaac gasps. I can see Gabriel's hands grip the rail of the rampart till his knuckles turn white. He shakes his head.

"You don't want to believe me?" I ask. "I speak to you honestly, for I do not want you going into that dark place ruled by Satan with the same naïveté I did." I pause again. The image of that sorceress, Gosling, flashes through my head, and despite myself I feel a stirring deep below my belly. "You must be prepared to go in as if for battle. Believe me. I can speak all day as to what I've witnessed, but it will not prepare you for what you will soon discover for yourselves."

"Is there nothing else you can share that might enlighten us?" Isaac asks. He looks like he really might cry. Just as he says it, the girl appears on the riverbank, not far from Bird and Fox. She must have been squatting on the shore. She cradles her hand. You speak to me then, Lord, the light of the sky shifting and brightening, the sun coming out from behind a cloud. As if scales fall from my eyes, I can see so much more clearly now, can see that the hand the girl cradles is infected, that it's tobacco Bird passes to Fox for the pipe that lies next to them, that a deer stands still on the far shore of the river, so still that not even the sauvages have noticed it.

"This, then," I say to them, my voice quavering, "will be the key to our mission." Isaac smiles. Gabriel turns his dark eyes to mine. I look at them both. "Do you see that girl there?" I ask, pointing to her standing on the beach. They squint and then nod. "On a night not so long ago, she ambushed their chieftain and cut off his finger with a rock and a sharpened shell." Isaac gasps again as I point now to Bird, laughing at something Fox has said to him. "Now she misses a piece of her own finger as well." I let this information settle with the two young Jesuits.

"As punishment for her crime?" Gabriel asks. "An eye for an eye?"

I smile sadly and shake my head. "No. As she cut off his finger, she slipped and severed hers as well."

"She's disturbed in the head?" Isaac asks.

"She's ..." I pause. "Different." I gather myself. "But she's also the first to show real interest in the faith. So much so that I know in my heart she will be my first true convert."

The two young Jesuits nod their approval. They might as well scream for me to tell them more for the way they lean to me.

"Do you know what her punishment was," I ask, "for disfiguring this man who has become her adoptive father?"

They shake their heads.

"Nothing," I say. Again I pause to let this sink in. "Absolutely nothing," I repeat. "Never mind corporal punishment, there was not even so much as a chastisement." The young men shake their heads some more. "These Indian nations are all the same. They neither punish nor even scold their children." I hold Gabriel's stare. "And this is the great conundrum. Their children are the door to their conversion. But without our ability to use the rod, imagine how much trouble this will give us in our plans to bring these young ones to the Lord."

I look back down to Bird on the shore. The girl sits close beside him now, and he cradles her wounded hand in his, rubs something into it that he's taken from his hide bag. "They have their potions for every ill," I tell the two Jesuits. "It's witchcraft. I've even witnessed a sorcerer pretend to suck a sickness from an old man's belly. The sorcerer leaned to the man and made loud slurping noises, then spat what appeared to be tobacco juice onto the dirt beside him." Both Isaac and Gabriel listen with wide eyes. "Those watching went into a small frenzy, acted madly enough that the old man was forced to sit up on his own, smiling like an idiot. None of them were wise enough to recognize that this was simply trickery on the part of the sorcerer, who'd obviously hidden tobacco in his mouth before arriving. You'll be confronted by this type of foolery on a daily basis."

Bird must have said something funny to the girl, for she smiles brightly, looking up at him. She allows her hand to stay in his. A pang of jealousy roots about in my gut.

QUICKENING CURRENT

The Crow certainly doesn't seem happy. And neither am I. He'd apparently hoped to stay with his kind in that fortress of nightmares they've created on the cliffs above the wide river. But their great chief Champlain had other ideas for him, and told me himself they needed the Crow to help their new ones understand us. I watch him in the canoe ahead, listless in his paddling. Somehow, my love, my great plan has fallen to pieces. Not so long ago I thought I'd figured it all out. The Crow would be dead or a captive of the Haudenosaunee, who would have the girl back with them. Instead, I still have both, and six more of these creatures to drag back home. Fox calls the new ones charcoal. "They are as heavy and as dumb," he says as we watch two of them ahead of us in their hosts' canoe lamely attempt to paddle. With their fresh robes, so black they absorb the late-summer sunshine, I think Fox's name for them is very good. But I will still call them all crows for the way they hop around and peck at dead or dying things.

"If we were to burn them," I ask, "do you think they would give the same heat as charcoal?"

Fox laughs. "We could soon find out," he says, digging deep and pulling ahead of me in his fast new canoe.

Four days travelling with the river's current from that place of the hairy ones and we are in a good but wary mood. Autumn already presents itself in the mornings that make me shiver to get out of my blanket, the first wisps of winter's beard not so far away. We set our nets each evening for fish and keep a close eye out for deer and moose. The approaching moon of turning leaves will tell us much about what to expect this winter. And we are not so far from Haudenosaunee land now. None of us sleep well in the short time allotted, listening, even in our dreams, for the hide-covered feet of our enemy.

Fox knows something feels amiss these last couple of days. His canoe stays close to mine, and our most observant scouts lead us. As soon as this great river of the Ottawa People splits, we will have to make an important decision. To return home on the Snake where we slaughtered their envoys would be the quickest and the most obvious route. But the Haudenosaunee, badly stung by us, have by now been given enough time to raise a response. Every bend in the river I wait for their arrows to sing near my head. My new gift from the hairy ones rests on a hide pack in front of me. I can make it roar now, and if given a handful of breaths to stuff another piece of lead down its throat, make it roar again. I know, my love, that once more I will be tested.

MY BLOOD

My blood. I can feel it. I drag my hand in the water, the hand Bird has begun to mend with his roots. I didn't need that finger. I know it now. For each day that we paddle, for each time that we portage another rapid, I can feel my blood, my family closer to me.

———

THE LAST OF THE SUMMER loons call when it's time for exhausted travellers to sleep. I'm not sleeping anymore because I know that my father's brothers are close.

———

I'VE BEGUN TO LIKE Bird much as I would one of them, maybe even you, my father. Is that wrong? I must, then, remember what he did to you all, Father, Mother, Sister, dear Brother. I know we paddle through the place where they found us last winter. This is the place where they took you away from me. And they dare return to it so soon? It makes me turn away in disgust, and to hate the man I'd started to trust.

TONIGHT WE CAMP without a fire. The men eat their ottet quickly, but none seem able to sleep. They can sense as surely as I can that my blood is close. I close my eyes. I'm the only one who does sleep soundly tonight beside the sighing river. I dream of my family around me, am held in the arms of my mother, tickled by my brother, caressed by my sister, fed by my father. He smiles down at me and places a warm piece of deer meat in my mouth. The blood of the meat is strong. It is fresh. *Tomorrow*, he whispers as he fades like morning fog on the river. *Tomorrow*. I open my eyes to the first light of the day, remove the stump of my wounded finger, and wipe the blood from my mouth.

THE HORROR OF IT

I don't quite believe what begins to unfold. From both shores of this wide river that the Huron call the Snake, Iroquois, dozens and dozens of them, pour into canoes hidden carefully in the tall grasses. Some are already in the water and closing in on a few of our stragglers. I watch as their archers in front pull back on their bows and release, the arrows cutting through the air and striking some of the closer Huron paddlers. Within moments, the Iroquois surround the canoes slowed by the wounded and begin hacking at them with hatchets. Screams echo across the water.

That is when I see the canoe of four young donnés, their blond hair flashing in the sunlight. Their canoe has been hit by Iroquois arrows and is sinking. Most of the sauvage paddlers are dead or flailing, and the donnés desperately try to paddle away from the approaching demons. I shout to them to push harder, and hearing my voice, they look up. One holds out his paddle as if I can somehow reach him and pull him to safety just as an Iroquois canoe draws alongside and a warrior grabs him by the hair and drags him aboard screaming as the others hack and smash those still alive until the canoe finally sinks, the dead men floating away downstream.

I feel a blow on my shoulder and fear I've been struck by an arrow. Turning, I see it's David hitting me with his paddle and growling at me to help them go faster or we'll all die. Glancing to the nearest shore, I see more and more Iroquois canoes emerging from the tall grass.

There must be hundreds of men. They will kill us all.

Bending at the waist with the stroke as I've witnessed my sauvages do, I grunt with each effort, try to keep the quick rhythm and realize I'm holding my breath. Is this the day, Lord? I know as I take a deep breath that I don't want to die today. The sun above us is warm and cool river water splashes in my face, kicked up by the man desperately paddling in front of me. A volley of arrows hisses into the water all around us, and David moans behind me. I look and see an arrow sticking from his shoulder. He shouts at me to paddle for my life.

Bird and the girl's canoe is only a stone's throw away from us off to the left. Bird shouts at Fox in his own canoe. Fox shouts back. He tells Bird that it's time. Bird places his paddle down, reaches in front of him, and picks up his musket. He leans with it over the gunwale of his canoe. The other men continue to paddle hard. As if this is something he's done all his life, Bird stares down the barrel and fires the weapon. A cloud of smoke envelops his head and the canoe rocks with such ferocity that I fear it will tip over. I immediately look in the direction he's fired and see a panicked group of Iroquois stop paddling, the side of their canoe ripped open and several of them screaming in pain. Bird busies himself reloading.

I know the Iroquois have caught up to the canoes behind us when the sounds of mortal conflict cross the water. But half of our canoes are still ahead, and Bird has reloaded and takes aim again. He doesn't fire, though. Our pursuers have slowed and, like a swarm of bees, attack those in our group who weren't speedy enough. The poor men will face a brutal death tonight. Looking away, the rest of us continue to push ahead. Exhausted, I stop paddling to catch my breath and look back.

To my horror, a flotilla of Iroquois canoes breaks from their carnage and begins pursuit of us again.

TWO

Success is measured in different ways. The success of the hunt. The success of the harvest. For some, the success of harvesting souls. We watched all of this, fascinated and frightened. Yes, we saw all that happened and, yes, we sometimes smiled, but more often we filled with fret. The world must change, though. This is no secret. Things cannot stay the same for long. With each baby girl born into her longhouse and her clan, with each old man's death feast and burial in the ossuary, new worlds are built as old ones fall apart. And sometimes, this change we speak of happens right under our noses, in tiny increments, without our noticing. By then, though, oh, by then it's simply too late.

Yes, the crows continued to caw as crows are prone to do, and after a while we got used to their voices even when they berated us for how we chose to live. Some of us allowed them their cackling because we found it entertaining, others because we believed our only choice was to learn how to caw ourselves. And still others kept them close for the worldly treasure their masters promised.

It's unfair, though, to blame only the crows, yes? It's our obligation to accept our responsibility in the whole affair. And so we watched as the adventure unfolded, and we prayed to Aataentsic, Sky Woman, who sits by the fire right beside us, to intervene if what we believed was coming indeed coalesced. But Aataentsic only need remind us that humans, in all their many forms, are an unruly bunch, prone to fits of great generosity and even greater meting out of pain.

THEY COME

They come to me. I have learned their voice, Lord. And they begin to listen.

A dozen of them sit or sprawl in the longhouse as I hold up a Host to the light pouring in from the chimney hole above. Brooding Gabriel stands beside me with a dented tin chalice in his hands. Sweet Isaac has been forced to a lesser role because of his missing fingers. He has difficulty holding much of anything, must pinch the Communion wafers he offers to the gaping mouths of the converted between the nub of his left thumb and the fingerless palm of his right hand.

Most of those in front of me are old enough to be near death. The few younger ones show the affliction that has decimated the village in recent years, their faces pocked with it or, if they still fight it, their skin dotted with welts of oozing pus. I sometimes awake in the early morning, dear Lord, jolted by the fear that we've brought this upon them, but You calm me back to sleep by reminding me that they need persuasion, just as Egypt's Pharaoh had.

With the language of the Huron that I've learned over the years, I speak for You.

"The Great Voice is one body," I declare as the poor things watch me from their mangy beaver blankets. "And He is three bodies together." I wrap two fingers of one hand around one finger of the other. "But He is not simply three gathered together." I look down at them as I pull my fingers apart, seeing the confusion in their eyes, the ache for understanding. I make a fist with one hand. "He is what you call an oki, what we call a *spirit*." I say the word slowly so that those who choose to try to imitate it may do so. "He is the most true of okis, of spirits. The most powerful by far. He is the only being that can be at once the father, and the child, and the very true spirit. He is three, but he is one."

An old woman, one who questions me incessantly, lifts her bony finger. I've named her Delilah since she loves to tempt me into debate. "I have seen many of the oki in my life." She pauses as if deciding whether she will say more or not. "When I was young a powerful oki entered me. It hurt. It took my virginity." Delilah smiles. "It hurt, but it felt good, too." A couple of the others laugh.

I try to ignore her. She reminds me of that one, Gosling. These old Huron women are so often jugglers and tricksters.

"How old is your Jesus oki?" a serious young man asks, his face and chest ravaged by disease. This one I've named Aaron, for Moses' older brother, the one so persuasive with his arguments. Aaron is close to being swayed, but like a bird that I try to tame, the slightest jerky motion on my part sends him flitting away.

I think about how best to answer. "This cannot be known. What can be known is all of the many things He has made. Remember that when He existed, the sky, the earth, all kinds of things did not yet exist."

"And he made those things?" Aaron asks.

I nod.

"What tools, then, did he use to make all these things?" he asks. "And where did he get these tools? If he is the first oki, he couldn't trade some other oki for them, could he."

I see the trap being set. "He had nothing to make things with," I answer. "He just spoke, and then something happened. This is how powerful He is."

The Huron in front of me turn to one another and begin debating amongst themselves. I must hold their attention a little longer. Lifting my arms, I raise my voice. "The Great Voice made all kinds of things, too many to be counted. He made the things we see when we move our eyes side to side. But many other things He made we do not see."

They stop their talking and look up to where Gabriel stands beside me, his arms crossed. Isaac, weak since the Iroquois returned his damaged body back to us, can't stand for long periods and sits on the floor at my feet. "Some of the things He made, like stone and sand and metal, do not live," I say. "But trees and animals and humans and spirits do live."

I must decide which course to take. I want them to understand and accept, but I can't go on too long or they'll begin debating again and then I've lost them. "Listen carefully," I say. "There are three lineages among those who live. The trees and the grasses and the bushes are one lineage. The fish and the animals are another family. And humans and spirits are the other kind of life."

Serious young Aaron speaks up once more. "Are you saying that stones and water and trees and animals have no oki? Only humans possess this spi-rit?" He says the last word haltingly, almost comically.

I nod.

"But we," Aaron says, sweeping his arm to those around him, "all of us, all of our lives, have been taught that everything has its own spirit. Everything contains the ability to live."

I keep my gaze upon the young man until he looks down. "Do you see a tree fleeing when you approach it with an axe to cut it down?" I ask. "Do you hear a deer beg for mercy before you shoot it with your arrow?"

An old man I've not yet named speaks up. "When I kill an animal, I thank its oki for allowing me to eat, to live." The others nod. "When I use a rock for a fire circle, I thank its oki for the heat it will give."

I lift my hand for silence. "I agree that there are dark powers in our world," I say. "And these dark powers are masterful at presenting themselves as something they're not. An animal or a tree or a rock cannot possess an oki—"

"How do you know?" Delilah asks.

"Because a tree or a deer or a stone cannot pass from this life to the other. To the world after death that exists high above us."

She shakes her head. "Again," she asks, "how do you know?"

"Because the Great Voice, the most powerful voice, says so," I answer. "His voice is in this." I nod to Isaac, who struggles to pick up my Bible with the stumps of his hands. I hold it up in front of me, my brain humming as it once did when I played chess so many years ago, plotting a number of moves ahead. I open the tattered book, and when I find the passage, begin to read from Genesis in my own tongue. "'And He said,'" I speak loudly, "'Let us make man to our image and likeness: and let him have dominion over the fishes of the sea, and the fowls of the air, and the beasts, and the whole earth, and every creeping creature that moveth upon the earth.'" I hand the Bible back to Isaac.

"What did you say?" Aaron asks.

"This wampum that I run my eyes across," I say, nodding at the Bible, "is the one true wampum, so you must listen to me carefully if I am to share it with you." I pause, noting they grow restless for me to share more. "No. You are not ready yet." They groan in unison.

"Tell us what you said," Delilah demands, reaching her arm up to me.

"Yes," the old man echoes, "you must tell us."

"But I don't think you are ready to hear what this wampum says," I tell them again.

"Baah," Delilah says, some of the others laughing quietly at how agitated she and the old man are. "Stop treating us like children. If you wish for us to wander away, that's the surest way to do so." She makes as if she is going to get up and leave, struggling to stand so that Aaron must rise to help her.

"I do not wish to treat you like children," I answer, raising my hand to her, palm out. "But the Great Voice says that you must give up praying to your okis, for they are false. They will lead only to harm. I cannot share my wampum until you are able to promise me that you will listen only to the Great Voice." I'm rarely so direct with them, so demanding. In the past it has proven useless, pushing them away rather than bringing them closer. But I admit, dear Lord, that even I sometimes grow frustrated.

The congregation begins to stir, growing more restless, and I again realize that I'm losing them, but I've been talking for hours and we all need a break. From experience, I know they won't go anywhere until I hand out their meal. But my practice of keeping them with me in the longhouse all of Sunday won't last much longer, either. This spring is the first in three years with enough rain for the crops to begin taking root. The summer, it appears, will be the first plentiful one in the several years that Gabriel and Isaac have been here. With the good harvest, I fear my flock will scatter back to their clans.

"It's maddening," Gabriel says, leaning over to me, "how even after all this time they still frighten like deer."

"I told you long ago, dear Gabriel," I say, "to prepare yourself for the greatest test of your life. Our patience is paying off, is it not? How many have we baptized?"

"Thirty-eight," Isaac says, looking up to me and smiling. When the Iroquois tortured him, I fear something in his mind broke. But he's a good young man still. I take note that I should soon cut what's left of his long, matted hair. He looks like a madman.

"Yes," Gabriel says, "but the majority were on their deathbeds."

"This isn't what's important," I say sternly. "What's important is how many accept Christ before their eyes close for eternity. And it's also important to report this news so the Church understands we don't toil in utter darkness."

Gabriel's glance suggests to me that he thinks we do. With Champlain's death so shortly after we left New France, our small mission, I fear, has been forgotten.

"Well, then," I say, clapping my hands together. "Shall we get started once more?"

Like a classroom full of children, the ones in front chatter and laugh, not paying attention for my call to sit. Now that the warmth of spring has come, most of them don't wear much. The handful of men in the longhouse wear deer leggings up to their thighs, breechclouts covering their lower extremities, deer or beaver robes slung over one shoulder so that sometimes I'm struck by how they resemble Greek senators from ancient times, regally standing and smoking their long pipes as they talk with one another. The women before me, even Delilah, think nothing of allowing me to peer up their loosely worn robes at their bare legs. Sometimes, as if they test me, I see much more.

"Do you accept my wampum?" I ask now that they begin to settle.

"Perhaps," young, argumentative Aaron responds. "But we do not believe your claim that okis exist only in humans. All of us have seen them in other beings at different times."

"Let me explain more clearly, then," I respond. "There are indeed okis everywhere. But the only one to be trusted is the Great Oki, the Great Voice."

"But now you contradict yourself," the old man speaks up. "You yourself said on this very day that only humans have okis, and now you say that there are okis everywhere."

I realize the complexity of my argument cannot be boiled down any more simply. "We humans have okis in us," I explain. "And these okis are given to us by the Great Voice. It is up to us whether or not we allow our okis to grow strong and straight like a beautiful oak, or bent and gnarled like a thorn bush. The Great Voice wants us to be as the oak tree. But there is an enemy to the Great Voice, far stronger even than your hated Iroquois." I pause. They listen intently. I've found a track that they might follow.

"In my tongue, this great enemy's name is Satan." I speak the name slowly. "Satan is the worst of the okis. I fear for you that when you pray to what you think is the oki of an animal, you are praying to Satan."

"But how can I tell if the oki I ask for aid is not corrupt, will not enter me to harm me?" the old man asks, seeming suddenly deflated. "Did I ask the wrong one, the oki that caused the sickness to enter me?"

"There's only one oki powerful enough to protect you, and that oki is the Great Voice," I answer. "If you are to ever ask an oki for anything again, know this. If you ask the Great Voice for help, He will never bring harm to you."

"But I tried that!" Delilah says, excited. "I asked your Great Voice to allow my husband to live through the illness. But he died anyway." She makes a low wail in her throat and wrings her shaking hands. She is such the actor. She looks up. "And so I see no need for your great oki."

I hear Gabriel grumbling beside me. I know that he wants to ask her, "Then why are you here?" He's done this before, and it caused great mirth in the longhouse when Delilah answered, "Because I was bored."

"The Great Voice," I say, "often makes decisions that we can't understand. But the Great Voice always has a purpose in doing so. And the Great Voice has told me," I say, looking straight into Delilah's eyes, "that you will see your husband again in the afterlife if you accept my wampum as he did on his deathbed."

"And if she doesn't?" The voice comes from right below me. I look down and see Gosling sitting behind a smiling Isaac, his eyes closed in bliss as she strokes his hair, untangling the knots. I look at Gabriel, whose face mirrors my own shocked expression. "Did you see her arrive?" I ask him quickly in French. He shakes his head.

"And if she doesn't?" Gosling asks again.

"How did you get in here?" I ask her.

"Why, through the door, like everyone else," she says. The ones on the ground around her laugh.

"But you weren't here a moment ago," I tell her.

"I'm quite small," Gosling says demurely. "I often go unnoticed."

"You are a sorcerer," I say, trying to find my balance again. "She," I say to the crowd, pointing my finger at her, "is what I speak about when I tell you that the world contains bad okis."

"Don't be so cruel," she says, feigning hurt.

Others begin to speak up, old men and women who've never said a single word these past months.

"But Gosling has only ever helped us!"

"She saw the enemy coming in dreams and warned our warriors."

"She can cure many illnesses."

"There are those," Gosling says, "who believe you and these other Black Gowns are the malevolent okis and have brought the famine and the disease and the drought to us."

"We come only with goodness in our hearts and with the words of the Great Voice on our tongues," I say. "You are not welcome here."

Isaac, as if in a trance while Gosling continues to stroke his hair, shakes his head and whispers, "I'd like her to stay."

"If she isn't welcome here," the old man says, beginning to stand, "then we do not wish to be here."

"Do you," I say, looking at Gosling, "believe that we are responsible for the troubles that have fallen over the land these last years?"

"You expect a simple answer, a simple yes," Gosling says, "for this will vindicate you, as you clearly believe you're not the cause. Rather, you see your arrival so long ago as an unfortunate coincidence." She smiles and begins twisting Isaac's long wisps of hair into a braid. "Myself, I think that where we find ourselves is more important, more grave, than any simple question or answer."

The others in the longhouse listen intently. Gosling licks her fingers and brings the tip of Isaac's braid to a point. I feel that same feeling in my lower stomach as she gazes into my eyes, smiling.

"Leave him alone!" I say as forcefully as I can.

"No," Isaac answers.

"She has him in a spell," Gabriel says.

"You are trying to convince them," Gosling says, "that what they know so surely is in fact wrong."

"I simply bring them a better way, a chance to live differently."

"You're upsetting a balance generations in the making," she says. "What you seek to do will split this village, will weaken all of the

Wendat. And when this happens, the Haudenosaunee will take note and take action."

"You give me too much credit," I answer. "I do not have the power to divide a nation."

"Your wampum speaks quite the opposite of our beliefs," Gosling says, as if she hadn't heard me.

"What do you mean?"

"Your wampum declares that everything in the world was put here for man's benefit. Your wampum says that man is the master and that all the animals are born to serve him."

"Is this not true?" I ask.

She smiles, shaking her head. "Our world is different from yours. The animals of the forest will give themselves to us only if they deem it worthy to do so."

"So you claim that animals have reason, then? A consciousness?"

"I say that humans are the only ones in this world that need everything within it." She stops stroking Isaac's braid. "But there is nothing in this world that needs us for its survival. We aren't the masters of the earth. We're the servants."

"And I am here to be a servant to them." I raise my arms to those in front of me. There will be no winning this debate with her, I see. It will take cunning and time to beat the devil. "Let us all say a prayer before our meal."

I DON'T WANT IT

So many longhouses left abandoned, so many fires that will never burn again.

When Bird brought me back here once again three summers ago, the illness struck and it struck brutally. Hundreds dead that winter. Every family was visited. Not enough healers, not enough orenda, not enough strength to save the dying, never mind to bury the dead. Many unhappy okis haunt this place now. Too many. They keep me up at night.

When I returned that summer so long ago, I was still a child. And for the third time that year, I watched Bird and his men kill my family. That's when something inside me broke. That's when I made the decision that I couldn't return home again. Bird had won. He'd won me. Now, when strangers come to trade in our village, I tell them I am Bird's daughter. But this doesn't mean that a daughter can't hate her father, does it? I think you can still hear me, my real parents. I can accept him as a substitute, but this doesn't mean I won't one day end his life, as he did yours.

———

THE OLD WOMEN have been screeching like seagulls, telling me it's time to prepare for womanhood. The old women assume my moons have begun coming to me, and though they haven't I lie and say they have, and so I'm taken out past the palisades to where the thickest moss grows in the dark ravines, swarms of tiny, biting flies enveloping us in black robes as we walk along the river that runs into the great bay. I'm shown how to choose the freshest of the moss. The sweet scent of new life growing from rot fills my nose. But this isn't all. This is just one small part of what all those old birds want me to learn. We wander near the river's bank, spread out from one another with downcast eyes to look for baby ferns, still curled tight so that I run my finger along the stem up to where I pinch free the head, my finger tracing around and around and around to where the tip nestles into itself. We lean and pick with one hand, our deer robes pulled up to our thighs and acting as baskets. I want to complain that I'm unhappy. But I'm not. The sun is warm on my back.

Back on the river again, this time with knives, we walk through the new shoots of tamarack, cutting off the tops that we will boil as tea. I'm shown once again how to create a rock weir to lure the spawning pike along the shore, the channel running narrower and narrower until it's thin enough for us to straddle it with sharpened maple spears, patiently waiting for the long flash of scales before we strike fast as snakes, wrestling the large fish to the land before they can shake themselves off and dart upriver, their gouged bodies leaving blood ribbons in the stream.

The old women take me to the fields to help prepare them for the coming of the three sisters. We tie our robes high to let the air cool us as we build up dirt mounds and dig holes in them, scatter a handful of corn kernels into each one, the kernels gorged from their soaking in water in the hopes the earth we pat back on top will accept them. These new fields are still small, and the smell of burning tree stumps comes sharp on the air as the men work hard now to make up for lost time, to make up for sickness and the death of so many, the fields each day growing a few feet bigger as forest succumbs to rows of squash and beans and mother corn. This is the first spring in three or four where the people of the village come out in full numbers. I'm worried to see how many have been swept away to the other world. But still, these people smile for the work.

———

TODAY I'VE BEEN SENT by the old women to wander the village in search of something that I'm told will catch only my eye. No one knows what it is, but when I see it, the old ladies say, I'll know. When I find it, I'm to take this object to the women's longhouse out in the fields, and then the ceremony will begin. For the next weeks, I'll be expected to sit with them as they talk to me about what life can bring. I won't be allowed to leave their special longhouse, they say, unless it's to work the fields with them, and I will only be given certain foods to eat, the foods we've harvested together that they claim will bring me the strength and the wisdom a woman will need to survive in this world. As I wander aimlessly through the village, I tell myself that it's mornings like this I wish I were a boy.

The middens at the edge where the women dump the refuse of the longhouses is the first place I head to. I walk around the large piles of fire ash and old, torn birch buckets and bits of rotting hide and smashed pottery hoping that someone might have dropped a few glass trading beads or a special amulet or a wood or stone carving in her haste to finish her chore. Kicking my feet through the dust, I want to uncover something, anything I can bring back to the women so that I might begin this rite and just be done with it. I find nothing but my nostrils filled with the acrid scent of the houses' many fires.

I wander the perimeter of the village next, dragging my hand along the palisades, noting how many places it would be simple for a Haudenosaunee warrior to slip in. Now that spring is here and we've begun the planting, we'll tend to this as well. These last weeks it's as if the people here are awaking from a long nightmare. So many died the last winters that some days the wailing seemed to come from every direction. I've listened to Bird and Fox talk all night at the fire for a long time now. The first year, their talking was filled with the worry that my people would hear of the sickness and swoop in to destroy the Wendat. The second year's talk turned to how the Haudenosaunee were just as deeply struck by the illness and this is why they hadn't come to take us. Over this last year the talk has come down to how whichever of the two enemies heals fastest will decide who wins the trade and, in this way, the war.

I cut down a path, listening for signs of life in this row of long-houses. Most of the community is out in the fields today. As I walk, though, touching my hand to the walls, trying to sense something from them, I hear a baby crying, its mother quietly shushing it. Farther down I hear voices through wood, and as I sneak up, I begin to make out words. *You will be mine.* A laugh. *You will.* A moan. *Not here.* Something in my belly tightens, and I want to sit and listen for a while longer, but the voices of young men walking by on the other side of the long-house make me move.

I circle around and head toward the path where I heard them. Peering around the corner, I recognize them as the ones who speak so loudly of becoming Bird's next great warriors. These are the same ones who, when asked to collect water or weed the fields or bring firewood, spit and say it's women's work. They're soon to be young men, and they're disdainful of almost everyone. And lazy. Little do they know that Bird would never tolerate such behaviour on his travels.

There are three of them, their hair shining bright with sunflower oil, the sides of their scalps freshly plucked. All of them wear only breechcloths and moccasins. The middle one's breechcloth is deco-rated with porcupine quills, and despite my not liking these boys, the muscles of their backs and legs are very pretty. The middle one with the porcupine quills carries a bow. The one on his left, a club, and the one on his right, a spear. Their faces are painted as if they're going off to war, I see, as they turn to one another to talk and laugh. These are no warriors, though. They have no idea that I follow them.

A raven sits atop a longhouse in front of us, looking down at the boys with its black eyes, its head turned to them as if it wonders what they might be. It's a big raven, its feathers shining blue-black in the sun. The boy with the spear points at it. The porcupine-quill boy pulls an arrow from his quiver and strings it, draws back his bow. He takes aim at the raven, his taut arms tense. He releases the arrow, its flight so quick it's just a streak through the air. I watch as it sings by the raven, inches from its chest, arcing up and out, over the palisades and toward the fields. The one with the club shoves his friend, laughing that his arrow might strike an old woman bent over weeding in the ass. The boy with the bow ignores him, draws another arrow and begins to pull back. But the raven, cawing loudly, pushes up and takes flight, catching an air current and riding up high above them within seconds. Laughing, it swings down and lands again on another longhouse. Watching the boy with the bow, I see in the slump of his shoulders that he deems the shot too far. The three of them soon move on, and I follow.

They come to an abandoned longhouse and stop by its door, daring each other to enter. The one with the spear makes a move to open the door but then pauses. They don't want to enflame the dead owners. Instead, he bends and picks at slim green shoots of tobacco that have begun to sprout where, sometime last year, the residents scattered the seeds.

The one with the spear says, "I'll bet you there's dried tobacco in the rafters."

"Well, go in and find out," the one with the bow says.

"You first," the one with the club says.

The young man with the bow pushes the door open. He's hesitant but I can see now he must go through with what he's started. A plan forms quickly in my head. I sneak the long way around the house I spy from and make it to the other side of the empty longhouse. I can hear that they still hesitate at the front threshold. I know I shouldn't do it for risk of offending the dead occupants, but I ease this end's door open and, like a lynx, dart inside and under the closest bed platform.

The dust is so thick that I must pinch my nose hard and hold my breath to keep from sneezing. My eyes take time adjusting to the darkness, but soon I can see the silhouettes of the three boys in the beams of light and dust floating in the air. They stand alert, tensed to run out. I follow their tilted heads to the roof, but the rafters are bare. From what I can see, the place is empty.

Porcupine Quills begins to walk in. What am I doing? What if they see me? I swallow that fear and decide I will act when the moment presents itself.

"Where are you going?" the one with the spear asks.

"There's nothing here," the one with the club hisses. "Let's go. I don't want okis haunting me in my sleep."

Porcupine Quills looks back at them and spits on the ground. "What kind of war-bearers are you two?"

He moves forward more boldly now, his eyes obviously adjusted. He taps his bow on the sleeping planks on either side of him, as if he's counting them.

"Do you remember the one named Leaps Water?" he asks the boys behind him. They don't answer. "You remember her, the one with the big tits." He laughs, but the others stay as still as the walls around them. "She used to sleep here," he says, tapping a platform. "She liked to kiss me here." He turns to his friends and lifts his breechcloth.

"Don't speak of the dead that way," the one with the spear says. "I'm leaving before something bad comes to us."

Porcupine Quills turns back toward me and takes a few steps forward. "What do we have here?" he says, and I know he's seen me, despite my having squeezed up against the wall as tight as I can. I can see his moccasins now. They're well made. But then he walks away and lifts something from the opposite platform.

"Don't touch that," the one with the club says. "Are you crazy?"

"What is it?" the one with the spear asks.

I watch Porcupine Quills' feet turn toward them. His calves are strong. "Just a broken arrow," he says. "I'd hoped it would replace the one I lost shooting at that raven."

His feet turn around again and step straight toward me. I take as large a breath as I can and then, just as he's about to tap the platform I'm hiding under, I release the loudest screech I've ever made, my throat tight. I'm amazed that it sounds like a giant, angry raven.

The boy falls on his ass and skitters backward, his hands and feet frantically kicking up dust. When I take another deep breath and make the same piercing cry, he jumps up and runs to the door as fast as he can. I peer out from under the platform and see him disappear through it, his friends already gone. The broken arrow lies in the dust beside me.

Outside, the sun bright in my eyes, I continue my search, laughing whenever I think of the frightened boys. I hope the okis of the house forgive me for what I did. I hope they understand my intentions.

A few people have come in from the fields to take a rest and drink some water. The men stand in circles in front of longhouses, smoking pipes and talking among themselves, their robes draped over their shoulders. I can hear women and small children inside their homes laughing and talking and playing. A few people nod to me as I walk by, but I keep my eyes straight ahead. While most of these people still seem put off by me, because I am Bird's they offer a quiet greeting.

I sometimes feel, dear Father and Mother, as diseased as the three crows who hop around the village. I suppose I'm kept for the same reason they are. The desires of a few have outweighed the desires of the many. Even I know this. After all, I'm within earshot of Bird's evening discussions with his followers. He's become more powerful now that many elders have passed on to the other world from disease or age. He and his man Fox. It's Fox who made the winning argument that if the village banishes the crows, another village will take them without hesitation, despite the dangers. And when this happens, the trade with the Iron People will leave us and flow to where the crows land. But their continued presence here, and their actually beginning to win over some Wendat to their ways, well, something will come of it. There was a balance here that seems upset, and so something must come of that. And when it does, I want to witness it.

Walking down the main path of the village toward Gosling's lodge, I can see how the dust rises from the walkways, humans and dogs kicking it up into the air. We need rain again. The early spring was wet and promising but now the sky has dried up. And now that the illnesses have subsided, the threat of drought approaches. There's much grumbling from all corners. We can't afford a dry summer. The three sisters will wilt and die, and after them, so will we. A summer of drought promises to be the end of us. The special ones of the village have been working hard, urging all of us to do what's necessary. We give one another our most important possessions, we hold dances that last for days, and some even, when it is dreamed, throw a feast and empty their pantries of everything. The sun above us, though, burns as hot as it ever has this late into spring and shows no signs of abating. We all pray for the storm clouds to rush over the great bay and to us.

Up ahead, I see dogs circling in front of a longhouse, barking and yipping, trying to get at something I can't make out for their number. Fearing they're trying to pull apart a smaller dog, I run up, picking a stick off the ground and swinging it at them, and the first ones I hit yelp and slink away with tails between their legs. When I've waded through them and sent most of them off to a safer distance, I come face to face with a bear cub, as big as the biggest dog here but much thicker, tethered to the longhouse. It froths at the mouth and bares its teeth at the closest dogs who still jump and strain at it. I hit the closest dog on the nose and it cries out, scattering the other dogs away.

I see the spit of dogs on the bear's neck and back. It looks up to me with red-rimmed eyes and growls, but begins to calm when I sit down just out of its reach, showing it I mean no harm. The bear paces back and forth on its short leash, then sits on its hindquarters, looking past me to what I imagine must be its home. I'm tempted to untie the tether and let it free, but I'm too afraid to reach near the animal's mouth. The people who live here are known for their ability to find orphaned animals. They've had baby skunks and fawns, rabbits and raccoons and foxes and even hawks all living with their families at different times. Eventually, we don't see the different animals anymore, once they've grown enough to become too wild. I assume that they end up freed into the forest or into the families' cook pots.

The bear looks past me again, growling frothy spit. I turn to see the three boys have sneaked up behind me, close enough for the one with the spear to reach out and tap my shoulder. I'm surprised they were able to do this. I take pride in my senses.

"Is this your bear?" Porcupine Quills asks.

"Does it look like my bear?" I respond.

He holds a long arrow over his shoulder, and when he pivots to whisper something to his companions, I see the big raven pierced upon it, its body glistening black in the sun, the beak half open and pointing to the ground. Its wings spread out in death, the animal's span is near my own height.

"That will bring you bad luck," I say, pursing my lips and nodding to the bird.

"How do you know?" he asks, looking down at me, his hips thrust toward my face.

"Because I'm a witch," I say.

"You have the marks of a sorcerer on your face and shoulders," the one with the club says. "You were sick with the illness, but clearly it didn't take your life."

"I'm too strong for the illness," I say. "It ran from me screaming when I was still a young child."

"You'd be pretty," Porcupine Quills says, "if you weren't scarred."

I stand up now, angry.

One of his friends notices my hand. "Look," he says. "She's missing a finger."

"Were you tortured by the Haudenosaunee?" Porcupine Quills asks.

"I was," I say. I laugh to myself. "But I lived to tell about it."

"You have a nice body," Porcupine Quills says. "Look, you two," he says to his friends. "She's already starting to grow tits."

I give him a push. "Do you want to play with me?" I ask.

His smile surprises me. I'd wanted anger. "Yes, I do," he says. "But I'm willing to wait one more year until you're the right age."

The bear behind us huffs, as if it's amused by our exchange. All three boys laugh.

"Killing that raven is as bad a curse as entering the threshold of a dead family's home without their permission," I say.

The boys stop laughing. Porcupine Quills looks a touch paler suddenly.

"Did you—?" the one with the spear begins to ask, but his friend hushes him.

"This is for you," Porcupine Quills says, lifting the arrow and the raven from his shoulder and holding it out to me.

"I don't want it," I tell him.

He holds it closer. "Maybe I won't be cursed," he says, "if I give it to you."

"And pass the curse on to me?"

"You've already admitted you're a sorcerer. You can't be harmed by this."

I look down at the raven. Its eyes have turned a milky white. This makes me sad. They were so black they bounced back the light not long ago. Its claws have begun to contract in death. Without wanting to, I take the animal. Despite its size, it isn't as heavy as I imagined.

"The great war-bearer Bird is your father," Porcupine Quills says.

I nod.

"Make sure to tell him that I'm good with my bow, that I can take care of myself. Let him know I'm a fine hunter."

"Killing a defenceless raven makes you a fine hunter?" I mock. "I can tell you this. He will not be impressed."

"He will," the boy says. I'm about to say again that Bird won't, but the boy cuts me off. "And tell him that I plan for you and me to get to know each other very soon."

I want to tell him that this will never happen but he's already walking away, his friends following like dogs. I want to shout at him. I want to scream. I do. Instead, I'm left holding this dead raven, a young bear huffing behind me, and my face flushed hot.

THE CREATOR'S GAME

Fox signals for me to look up from the tall grass in which we hide. Five of their warriors have snuck out of the edge of the forest across from where we lie in wait, at the very place Fox said they would. They're big and strong, and it looks like the four who flank the one who holds his netted stick more carefully than the others has what we want. They've skirted around our much larger group without detection and left them in the forest behind. All that's preventing them from crossing this field and claiming their victory is our own group of five.

The sounds of fighting erupt in the forest behind our enemy as they crouch and scan the field. They know we're here, that we'd never leave this last stretch undefended. A noisy hive of people from our village who've travelled all this distance to watch shout and laugh behind us, jeering at the five, urging them to dash across and claim their prize. Our people know where we are but would never give our position away.

The first two warriors begin weaving through the field, trying to draw us out of cover. But we wait. When they've made it halfway across, the shouts of our crowd growing louder with the tension, the other three stand and begin to make their way across as well, the front two protecting the one with the hide-wrapped sacred stone. Fox and I know that once they meet up with the lead two, the five will make a desperate charge to the tall post placed in the ground. And once they touch it with the stone, they will have won.

The five now squat in the field, the one with the stone whispering directions. They sense we're close but I don't think they know how close. Just as they begin to stand, Fox and I jump up from the tall grass and run directly at them, our three younger, stronger warriors quickly gaining on and then passing us, swinging their sticks above their heads, the other five standing and tensing to meet the approach. Our front three clash with the five, the shouting and clacking of sticks as they swing for each other's arms and legs and torsos, mixed with the roar of the spectators a few hundred paces behind us, filling my ears with the noise of a waterfall. Two of their five break away from the fight, Fox and I breaking with them. Fox pounces upon the one with the stone in his netted stick as I duck the swing of the warrior who leads him, swinging hard with my own stick to crack it across his shins, causing him to fall. In that second, the air filling my chest, the blood pounding in my skull, I feel young again, young like this one whose eyes widen below me as my mouth opens in a wail and I jab the butt of my stick into his belly so that the wind leaves him and he can't get up.

Glancing to our three young warriors, I see they struggle with their opponents. I'm disheartened to see one of my men, the one named Tall Trees, apparently unconscious on the ground. He towers even over me. His size and build alone sow fear into our enemies. Clearly, our other two will soon fall to their three so I must act quickly. Fox's much larger man kneels on top of him, hitting him in the face with his free hand. I swing hard enough to send him tumbling, the hide-covered stone rolling from his netted stick. I scoop it up, the power of the prize pulsating through my arms. Lightning striking water buzzes in my head. Fox stands unsurely, bleeding from his nose and eye, which has already begun puffing shut. I gesture with the stick toward the forest and he understands, sprinting for it.

I begin to trot backward, away from the forest and toward my own crowd who stand just behind the pole in the ground. Two enemies who are left standing advance on me, slowing as they wonder what

I'm doing. Cradling the stone, gently rocking it back and forth in my netted stick, I taunt them to come get me. I glance back for a second to see the open mouths of my people screaming for me to run to where Fox is at the edge of the forest, waiting.

The two advancing warriors speed up, running toward me, and as they draw within ten paces, I lift my stick above my head, cock it back, and whip it forward with all my might, sending the hide-covered stone sailing high above their heads and toward Fox. Both of them stop, realizing their foolishness and growling at me just as Fox jumps up and catches the stone in the net of his stick. He raises the prize high to me before disappearing into the safety of the forest. My people roar behind me.

———

A GREAT THRONG overflows the big longhouse, my villagers on one side, our hosts on the other, a row of fires burning between us and warming kettles filled with different stews. Injured warriors are given places of honour on the ground near the fires. I can see Tall Trees stretched out, resting his head on his arm. He came to shortly after Fox disappeared with the sacred stone into the forest, and I sent him back to our host's village despite his wanting to continue the Creator's Game. He's too valuable to me. I will need him in a few weeks when we travel back to the place of the Iron People. This will be the first big trading mission in many summers, my love. It's vital for the commerce, but more importantly to show our enemies that we remain in control. The Haudenosaunee, from every report I've heard, remain weakened by the sicknesses. We must go this summer, despite my worries about leaving so few of the strongest men back home to protect the village. The sicknesses were especially cruel to the ones who appeared strongest, and they were the most painful to lose. Many boys wanting to become men will have to prove themselves this summer, for they'll act as our home guard.

The elder who speaks for our hosts is good, but he's gone on too long. The stews will soon be burnt in their kettles. This is the third time now that he's circled back to thanking us for bringing the Crow so that he might be studied and understood. I worry that the old man has become soft in the head as I can almost repeat, word for word, what he says yet once again.

I glance over at the Crow, who watches intently as the elder speaks, acutely aware of his being the centre of attention. How did it happen, my love? It seems like I'd loosened my attention for only the briefest time, but when I focused back on the visitor again, he'd nearly mastered our tongue. But what's most frightening is how many he won over to his strange views at the depth of the sicknesses. Those who didn't think that the Crow himself had brought this sorrow to us suddenly began listening to his lies about how we'll find ourselves in paradise when we pass from this place. I can see why this would appeal to the simple-minded, and maybe it's best that he take our weak ones to his side. No, that isn't right. Forgive me, my love. I'm hungry and cranky. My thoughts wander and I need to eat.

"We welcome the Attignawantan, the Bear People, to our home," the elder says again as he paces between fires. "You are our big brothers, and we look up to your wisdom and physical prowess. On the battlefield you vanquish your enemies, and you make pathways to those from over the great waters so we may in turn live in comfort and with bounty. You bring this charcoal so that he may teach us how his people see the earth and the sky, and by allowing him among you, despite the grumbling of some that he is a dangerous oki in the disguise of an ugly, diseased, and hairy beast, you allow him to walk freely among you and enable us to exchange our animal furs for their goods. We thank you for this."

The old man squats on the ground as if to examine the dirt, and I think that finally he is done. The crowd is revived by the promise of feasting. But then he stands up again.

"You Attignawantan have travelled a great distance to challenge us in the Creator's Game. And Sky Woman smiled down on us today.

Aataentsic has watched us suffer much these last years and I dreamed that she's sad for us and is ready to take pity on us and so this is why I called you here to partake of her game. She told me in my dream that we're to play in her honour for two more days and treat our brothers as fiercely as if we were true enemies so the blood pouring from our wounds will nurture the fields for the three sisters to grow strong this year. But Sky Woman wishes that when we end the game and when you Bear People depart, we'll not be like cousins but like brothers. And the wounds that our young men suffer will serve as a sign of our fierce devotion to one another."

"Ah-ho! Ah-ho!" the people respond as the old man's talk crests up higher than it has all evening, as if he's finally found his head. Even I, despite my hungry belly, begin to feel caught up in his words.

"I dreamed, too, that the Haudenosaunee, still feeble from the coughing plague, will not interfere in your trade this summer. I dreamed that in the coming years, though, they will grow even angrier with your refusal to stop crossing their country in order to trade with the hairy ones, that they seethe that you allow their charcoal into your village, and so we must all continue to act not just as cousins but as brothers, for we can't defeat the enemy alone but only as a group. And so I encourage you, you young warriors before me, to play as hard as you can for the next two days, to try and wound one another for the next two days, for your wounds will bind well and make you stronger instead of fearful when you hear the screams of your enemy in battle. The Creator's Game will teach you this and make our two communities as close as family. Only in this way will we be strong enough to resist our common enemy."

With that, the old man finally sits and raises his arms to the women across from him, who stand with ladles in their hands as we guests are urged to partake of the kettles.

Our hosts have spared no expense with this feast and fill our birchbark plates with steaming mounds of trout and sturgeon and pike stew, with deer and bear and moose meat, with corn flavoured with berries and the syrup from maple and birch. When one plate is finished, our hosts urge us to stand for more, for we must all eat until the kettles have been scraped empty. My belly that was groaning for food now moans from fullness as the quiet talking of neighbours and the sighs of the sated and the pop of dry wood being consumed by the fire blanket the great longhouse. Indeed, our cousins have been good to us, and tomorrow on the field we will fight hard again as if we're hated enemies, for the old man is right in saying that this game will teach our young men to think clearly in battle, toughening their bodies and their minds for what they'll soon face.

My head has dipped down to my chest, my plate resting on my thighs, when a hand on my shoulder wakes me. Fox, his one eye swelled shut, he's smiling the smile he saves for news I don't want to hear. "Get up, Bird," he whispers coarsely. "Awake. Their great chief asks you to speak now."

I wipe away the drool that's slipped onto my chin with the back of my hand, hoping no one has seen it.

"Get up!" Fox says again, pushing on my arm. "Say something. Say something good."

I lurch to my feet, my exhaustion falling away just enough that I stand with some semblance of authority once I see how many wait for me to speak.

"Arendahronnon, yes, you, people of this great rock upon which you decided to eke out your existence," I begin, trying to be funny but now worried it sounds more like an insult. "Arendahronnon, you People of the Rock," I begin again, "you've found an idyllic world in which to spend your days, close to our friends and great hunters and medicine people, the Anishnaabek to the north, and you are surrounded and protected on the three other sides by water. Yet your fields are as large and plentiful as any in the country of the Wendat. But do not assume this will prevent your Bear brothers, we Attignawantan, from crushing you tomorrow and the day after, as we crushed you today, in the Creator's Game."

The crowd, listening intently, laughs just enough to free my tongue.

"My cousins, you Arendahronnon, no, my brothers, we all indeed become closer by participating in this little brother of war with each other."

People nod and exclaim, "Ah-ho!"

"As your elder so rightly says, we must band together as one if we are to continue dominating the Haudenosaunee." I wonder what else to say, something that will impress them, and before I can think better of it, I open my mouth. "I offer you this, my brothers. Travel with us to the land of the hairy ones this summer. We will go as a single force, an unbeatable force. We will go as one in order to show the Haudenosaunee that we can't be defeated."

I can feel Fox's eyes on me, even as our hosts respond with enthusiasm. He knows that a group this size travelling through Haudenosaunee land will be taken as more than a great insult. It will be a declaration of war. Not only that, the Iron People will certainly drive down prices when they see the large volumes of furs that arrive with such a large contingent. I look at Fox, who shakes his head at me. But I've certainly won our hosts over as they stand and call out my name. They've wanted this offer from us for a long time and I've just given it away.

When they quiet, I realize there's one more thing to say, one more issue I must address. "It's no secret that there's a stranger in our presence, one who can't hide among us for a number of reasons, not least because he's the colour of a fish belly." The people laugh good-heartedly. I look at the Crow, who smiles tight-lipped. "He is a strange creature indeed," I continue. "You cannot miss who I speak of, for he is the one whose hair slips from his head and comes to rest on his face." The people laugh more. "He's a big man, though, and I've watched him slowly get stronger these last years. He's found followers in my village, and they say he can shoulder a great weight." The longhouse now studies him, talking among themselves, weighing him as if he were something to be traded or not.

"But beware of this charcoal, my brothers," I warn them. "Despite his strange appearance, he is very bright and has become attuned to our ways. He especially likes to prey on those who are infirm in body or mind." The crowd leans toward me. "He waits until one is on his deathbed before whispering his incantations. He promises great riches in the afterlife if you accept his oki as your own. But he doesn't explain that the cost is your forever being separated from the loved ones who've gone before you."

"Why do you keep him around?" someone asks. "Wouldn't it be better to caress him with the coals?"

I thoughtfully reach my hand to my chin. I'd planned on having to defend my actions, as indeed I've been doing in my own village for some time. "Because he is only the first of many who have started coming to our land," I say. "And despite the very real threat he poses—for is it coincidence that the diseases afflict us when he arrives?—despite the great threat of him and his kind, he must be studied so that he can be understood. We Attignawantan have taken this upon ourselves, despite the dire consequences, so that we may all learn how to protect the Wendat nation from their advances." The people nod in contemplation, some even in appreciation. "And I promise that we will share with you, my brothers, what we discover."

I sit then, and lean back. The longhouse buzzes with discussion and debate. I feel I've spoken well, despite foolishly inviting them with us. As if to emphasize this, Fox leans to me and whispers, "You certainly ruined my trade year. I hope you offer your war-bearers a cut of your profits to make up for what you just allowed to come out of your mouth."

"If you think you're upset," I say. "Imagine when the Haudenosaunee hear how many of us plan to travel through their country this coming summer."

Fox smiles. "It certainly will be seen as us sharpening the axe. Perhaps it's time that we strike first."

"Don't fool yourself," I answer. "We've been at war since long before

I took the girl. If the illnesses hadn't befallen us all, we'd already be near the end of it."

Fox looks at me. His eyes glow in the firelight. "For once, I think you're right," he jokes.

Their old one stands again and the longhouse settles to quiet. "I've heard this charcoal has mastered the Wendat tongue," he says. "I, for one, would enjoy hearing him speak." The people shout their approval. The old one holds out his hand to the Crow, who after a moment stands and clears his throat.

I stare at him as hard as I can, trying to get him to look at me. He'd better speak very carefully.

He makes the movement with his right hand that I've grown accustomed to watching him do, touching his forehead, then his chest, and then his left and right shoulders. People used to speculate that he was casting a curse, but as far as I can tell, despite his claim that this action protects him, I think it's more of a nervous tic.

"I've come from very far away," he begins, "to bring you a message from the most powerful oki, the Great Voice, the creator of the world. If you accept him into your heart, you will live forever."

"Then why do so many who listen to you die?" a young warrior asks.

"The life I offer you begins after death," the Crow continues, barely having to consider the question.

I'm constantly amazed by his willingness to make absurd statements that so often anger or offend without any concern for his own safety.

"The gift I offer you lasts forever."

"And what do you want in return?" the same warrior asks. I start to like him.

"The Great Voice tells you that the medicine in your body, the oki in your body, when it leaves your body behind does not dwell in one place. The medicine in your body, the same medicine that each of us has in our body, once our body stops breathing, that medicine needs to go somewhere. Now," he says, holding his hands together, "the medicine in your body has the chance to go up into the sky." He lifts both hands in the air, pointing them at the chimney hole. "I offer you the chance to become Sky People." There's much mumbling when he speaks this, but he ignores it. "I offer you a chance for riches after your physical body stops and your medicine leaves it, a chance for you to have all you desire, worth more than all the beautiful cloth and fur and wampum you can imagine." The Crow pauses in order for us to absorb his words.

"If you listen carefully, you can hear the Great Voice say it. 'Never will the day arrive when I abandon you. Always you will see my face. Always, I will love you. Always, as well, you will love me. You will never weary when I prepare a palisade for you. All the pain you felt while you still lived on earth you will no longer feel. In winter you were cold. Every summer you sweated. You will never go hungry or thirsty, for I will send that all away.'

"This is what he says," the Crow almost whispers so that we must lean closer to hear him. "He says that you will never need to ask for anything else if you accept Him, if you allow your oki to go up to the sky to Him, for all the things you can possibly desire are furnished where He lives."

The Crow stops, breathes in deeply, and looks around at the faces studying him. I'm uncomfortable with his talk, with the way so many listen.

As if taking up my challenge, the same young warrior speaks out again. "Really. It is that easy to gain everything we can possibly desire? Where do I offer my services so that I may be given everything I desire when my body stops breathing?" His friends chuckle. "In fact, it sounds so good that I request you stop my body from breathing right now. I want to get on with the pleasure." Many others laugh at his words, breaking the Crow's spell.

"The only ones," the Crow speaks over the noise, "who will make it to the country in the sky are those who restrained themselves from being bad while they still lived."

"And how do you judge if I am bad?" the young warrior asks.

I lean to Fox. "Make sure that we learn who this young one is," I whisper. "He will go far."

"You must ask yourself," the Crow answers, "Did I take pity on the poor? Did I not steal, kill, commit adultery, or get angry? Did I?"

"What you ask is impossible," the young one says. "Every one of us, including you, I'm sure, has done one of these things. In fact, many here have, just today, done all of these things multiple times!" Again, people laugh.

The Crow looks unfazed. "The Great Voice offers us much more than what I've already spoken about. Listen to Him, what He offers. 'You were afraid,' He says, 'while you walked on the earth. You feared those you killed.'"

I can feel the young men all around me bristle at the words. I breathe easier and remind myself to just let the Crow keep talking next time I'm concerned he might win some of us over.

"The Great Voice says, 'Never again touch your scalp in fear, for those who wish to harm you can never find you here. In this place in the sky there are no quarrels. There is no envy. There is no anger. If you do good here on earth and become a sky-dweller, you will continue to be beautiful in body, and other great things will happen to you. You will have a beautiful house, beautiful possessions, good-tasting food.'"

Indeed, the Crow's words are full of promise. But as I look around me at the people, I can tell most are not feeling tempted by him. Voices rise up while he still stands there, his arms raised to us, clearly having more to say. Now, though, the people talk, weighing what he's said, debating the possibilities, the ease of his promises, the question of what we must do to become sky-dwellers.

"Well," Fox says, "he certainly makes it all sound like summer evenings."

"All of it so perfect," I say. "But to gain so much, imagine what we must give up." I raise my own arms to those around me, to the fire and the kettles and the women and the children. "There's something he's not telling us." We both laugh.

I look up and the Crow stands there patiently, his arms now at his sides. He knows we'll eventually quiet and allow him to finish. The talk grows quieter, and soon to near silence, the fires crackling, a few people snoring. It's getting late, and if he doesn't finish talking soon we'll all be too exhausted to play the game tomorrow.

"I know you question me, that you think what I offer comes too easily. I know you think I'm trying to trick you or use sorcery on you. You may even think I've made up this story. But why would I travel so far, across the great water, at such peril to myself? Why would I leave my beautiful home and my loved ones and the food I'm used to and clean clothes for my body? Why would I give that up if it were all a made-up story?" The Crow smiles. He says, "Ask me this. Why would I accept the Great Voice's command that I separate myself from physical relationships with a woman if what I tell you isn't the truth?"

Someone in the crowd shouts, "Because you like men instead!" and the longhouse breaks into laughter.

The Crow ignores them. "We charcoal have given up everything from our world, all that we know, all of our comforts, so that we may bring you the message that the world after this one is the true world, the world you must live to strive for every day." He acts as if he's deciding whether to continue or not, though the throng listens intently. "The charcoal have travelled this far to tell you that what you now do, the way you now live, will prevent you from reaching the good land I speak of, that perfect place in the sky."

The Crow knows how to offend without trying. At these last words, people erupt into talking, some of the young warriors bristling like porcupines, ready to fill him full of quills. No doubt that if there weren't elders here, they'd do it.

Fox and I listen until the chatter dies down. We're content to watch this talk go the course we're sure it will. The same course it has done in the past in our own village.

"And if we decide not to accept the life you tell us to?" a bent old woman asks as she adds wood to the fire.

The Crow is invigorated by this attention. His listeners in our own village often grow bored with him and their numbers shrink or swell depending on the amount of food he's able to offer on any particular day.

"There is a fire that burns," he now says, "deep in the earth. But it is very strong, even more powerful than the fire you know, the fire you sometimes use to caress your prisoners." He looks to the hearths then, his clean head sweating and his eyes flashing in the light. His face is still thin, but not gaunt like it used to be. The hair on it is the colour of snow at the edges, and in his long dark robe he seems now to be a part of the ground on which he stands and the shadows that surround him. He has been learning the tricks of the sorcerers, I think. He has gained some power from somewhere around us, from someone among us, these last seasons. I was once sure he'd have wilted by now like a drought-stricken cornstalk.

"Your fires burn the skin first, so that it tears from the flesh with ease. Your fires make you pull your hand away, your foot away, when they are too close to it. Your fires cause great pain, and within a day or two, your fires will end the prisoner's life." He holds his long white fingers out to the flames dancing in front of him, gazing as if he contemplates each bony one. "But the fire inside the earth is of a different kind. The fire that awaits those who don't wish to live for the sky has a different heat. And even water cannot put out this fire. The fire tells you, 'Give up hope. Even snow will burn here. Even lakes will burn.'"

I look around me at the people listening to him. There's no denying we love our fire, that we understand its subtle and not so subtle strengths.

"But the fire inside the earth," the Crow says, "will not consume humans." He pauses. "Think of it as when an axe head is placed in the fire. Leave it in the fire for as long as you want and it will turn red and then white from the heat, but it will not lose its form. Think of the fire in the earth as doing this to the bodies of those who live badly when they are alive."

Once more, voices rise up to debate this point before quieting again.

The Crow speaks louder now. "Do you admire the frightening fire that burns inside the earth? Your medicine, the way I watch you use it, is at the point of going there."

At this, even the older ones voice their disdain. A few young men go so far as to stand before the old man quells them. "Let him speak," I hear him say to the war-bearers. "He is our guest, after all."

The Crow continues as if he hasn't noticed the anger rippling through the longhouse. "Do you think the many damaging things you do will be forgotten?" he asks. "The Great Voice forgets nothing. Who hates himself so much he says, 'I want forever for the flame to eat my body'? Would you continue to be brave, to not cry out if it burned you? You can be brave when your enemy burns you. I've seen it. If you don't cry out, your name will be honoured forever. Maybe over one or two or three days your body will burn before your tormentors tire of caressing you. But you will have to lose hope inside the earth, for the fire will never stop."

At this, the Crow stops, and I hope for his own safety he is finished. The heat of our young ones' anger is hotter than he apparently knows. They're feeding from a strong source the Crow can't ever understand, one that allows them to participate in the Creator's Game so that they learn not to fear but to flourish. All his talk serves only to incite them.

The Crow raises his face again to the audience. "If you continue your path, no one will love you any longer. The Great Voice will hate you. All will be angry with your badness. 'Oh,' the ones who you leave behind will say, 'oh, he is frightening. Go away. His corruption is bad.' And the okis will rejoice in tying you up. They will reproach you when you suffer. You can't escape them inside the earth. They will tie you up and mistreat you forever." The Crow's voice rises higher as he says this, until now he is almost shouting. "Fear it! Fear that which burns inside the earth."

He steps back into the shadows, his clothing allowing his body to all but disappear, his pale head glowing like a moon. He knows what he does, I suddenly recognize. He knows he pushes us to get angry, because he knows that when we get angry we'll pull that anger apart in order to inspect it. He wants his words to offend so we're forced to consider them for a long time.

If people were sleeping earlier, they're awake now, talking and gesticulating, the Crow's having ignored the custom here of visitors not offending with harsh words the graciousness of the host.

"But maybe he knows no better," a man says to his woman. "After all, he comes from a place we can't imagine."

"He knows," I hear the woman answer. "He's lived among us for a long time now."

The Crow emerges from the shadows once more and everyone falls silent. "I have just a very little bit more to say. No one made me come here. I knew already before I travelled across the great water your practice of burning, of eating flesh. That doesn't cause fear in me, this custom of killing other humans. I already knew your nature, your custom of covering each other with fire. I knew all this. Still, when I left my home, I thought, 'Those who cover me with fire, those who eat me, I do not fear them.' Because I know it won't be long I would feel the pain. But inside the earth I fear very much. I would not ever lose consciousness."

Then he raises his arms to us. "And I am afraid for you," he whispers. "I come to warn you about the fire."

A log in one of the cooking pits pops, sending a small shower of embers into the air as if in emphasis, startling a few children nearby.

"I come all this way," the Crow says, "to warn you of this danger. I do not wish for you to be consumed."

With that he recedes into the shadows again, finished his speaking for the night. I don't like that he's been given the last word, that we'll all go to sleep soon with those words in our heads. The same creature I once laughed at and even pitied, I see, has grown into something I hadn't imagined.

GLITTERING EYES

The raven has begun to stink. I don't care so much, but the women of the longhouse complain now. They don't understand why I wanted to keep him whole. Eventually, Father, wouldn't his brain and entrails refuse to rot anymore? I study his eyes carefully for the first days here after we return from preparing the fields for planting as the women teach me their songs and how to sew. The eyes, they've already changed to the colour of clouds before rain and have sunk into the skull, flies buzzing about. I sprinkle ash from the fire into the sockets and see how the claws clench like fists as the muscles dry by the fire the old women keep burning for me. I keep the bird stretched out as in flight, and he's as long as my arms reach wide. His beak's bigger than my finger, slightly curved and black. The feathers of his neck are thick and blue-black when the light from the smoke holes strikes them. He sleeps by my bed. He is all I found when the women asked me to go out and find that which only I will recognize, and I think I surprised them with my discovery. This raven, he certainly surprised me.

A week's gone by now, though, and I'm told I must act. The women, on some days just a few, on others a bigger group, I think they found it strange I brought home a raven pierced through by an arrow. They've gathered in this longhouse to lead me into womanhood, but I don't feel ready for it. I can see they want to ask me where the raven came from, if I'd shot it or it was pierced by somebody else, but I won't tell. Images of that boy's back, of his strong legs, wake me up the first nights. Porcupine Quills. I don't know his name, but this is what I'll call him. I hate him for his assuredness, for his pride. I want to touch his body with the tips of my fingers, the nine I have left. I want to taste his skin.

I use a sharpened clamshell and run it from the chest to the tail, parting the feathers as I go, opening the raven to the light. I gag when I reach my hand in with the shell to cut out the lungs and the heart and the stomach. The old women are right. This should have been done already.

I collect the stinking entrails in a pile, and when the raven's cavity is empty, scraped clean of what it once held, I take more ash and rub it inside my bird, feeling the heat still despite his death, and then I lay him on his back, his body open to the world so it may cure. I scoop the guts in my hands and decide now they need to become ash, stoking the fire until it burns hot, then casting the guts in, the heart, the lungs, the fire eating them all as I whisper prayers to the orenda of this creature, asking it to protect me and to teach me as part of it roasts, then blackens, then turns to ash. I can feel the eyes of the women watching me. They can teach me some things but they can't teach me all of it.

———

TODAY AFTER WORKING in the fields we make sleeping mats out of corn-husks, the women showing me how to weave them tight, tying off the ends every length so they won't unravel. They've also shown me how to peel and roll hemp on my thighs, creating twine the men will use for snares and fishing nets, and how to grind the surplus corn that we'll trade with the Anishnaabe this autumn for furs and meat. I've watched them carefully and learned how to fashion bone awls, and sinew from the muscles of deer and moose. With these tools, they show me how to stitch birchbark drinking and eating bowls.

One woman, Sleeps Long, the one closest in age to me but who's probably twice as old, the beautiful one with the pretty blue and grey tattoos around each wrist, I watch how she uses a thin needle made from a marten's cock, how she works it with careful patience to sew porcupine quills into patterns that blossom over the days into flowers that she says will be a gift for her husband. It isn't until the afternoon she holds the breechcloth up to me, her long neck proud, that I recognize the designs and realize where I've seen them before.

That night I lie awake on my sleeping mat, the women around me snoring gently, and I picture the boy who killed the raven, Porcupine Quills. He's hiding in a tall cornfield, and, as if part of me is a bird, I see myself from above looking for him in the field. I watch myself open my arms and this makes the wind pick up, a wind that grows strong enough to flatten the cornstalks so that Porcupine Quills has nowhere to hide, a wind so strong it erases the pockmarks from my face and body, a wind that somehow replaces my missing finger. And that is when Porcupine Quills stands from hiding and walks out to me, opening his arms as he approaches.

———

THIS MORNING I TAKE Sleeps Long's hands in my own and admire her tattooed wrists. Two snakes, intertwined, wrap around one, and on the other a songbird clutches a branch.

"I dreamed both of these," Sleeps Long says. "I think the snakes are meant to be my husband and me. The bird, I believe, is my son."

"You have a child?" I ask her.

She nods.

"How old is he?" I ask.

"He's in his fifteenth spring," she says.

"You must have been very young," I offer. She smiles at the compliment. "And what's his name?" But before she can answer, I blurt, "I'd like a tattoo."

"And what would the tattoo be?"

"I'd like a tattoo of the porcupine quill patterns that you sew," I say.

She laughs. "Yes, you are a strange girl indeed."

I take no offence to this. She doesn't mean it as an insult. I'm used to it. "And where would you like this tattoo?" she asks.

I point at my throat, but thinking better of it, I drop my finger so it hovers over my chest.

She laughs again. "Well, maybe when you're a little older," she says. "I suggest you wait until after your first moon, at the very least." She glances at me. "It will be soon, I think. But for now, how about, instead of decorating you, we decorate your raven."

Sleeps Long suggests we use cornhusks to stuff the raven's cavity. She likes my idea of keeping it whole rather than separating it out to use the wings as fans, as some of the other women have suggested. "What will be the point of a complete dead bird?" one of the old women asked. "Why not make it useful by using its parts?" But something in me wants my raven as I first saw him, a bird that sits complete and watches me while I sleep, that holds my place in the longhouse when I'm away, that causes strangers to step back and stare. There's power in that.

With the cornhusks stuffed into it, Sleeps Long carefully sews the bird back up with her sinew and marten's cock, joking to me as she does that she once knew a boy whose own wasn't much bigger. "All I felt was this pricking. Not pleasant at all." For the first time I can remember, I laugh. She looks at me then as if I am some new animal she's never seen before. Then her eyes crinkle and we laugh together.

"We have to remove the brain," she says once the raven is sewn shut. She pinches her nose and points at the head and sunken eyes. "Can't you smell it?"

I shake my head. "I don't smell death anymore."

Sleeps Long's eyes are no longer crinkled. "You're not the only one who's suffered loss," she says. She lifts the raven off her lap and places it beside her. "The people who were once your own killed my father and brother when I was your age."

I shrug my shoulders. I want to ask her if she witnessed it with her own eyes.

"What the men do, what we do, it's a circle," she says. "It's been a circle for a long time." I watch her with my eyes turned to the side. "We were once all the same people, but we're not anymore."

"I'm not the same as you," I say, now looking directly at her. I feel your anger, Father and Mother, burning in my guts. You were taken away from me, not allowed to be with me anymore, when I most needed you.

"How is this grief explained?" Sleeps Long asks. "How is it digested? I have never figured that out." She looks around her to see if any of the old women are near. "We hurt one another because we've been hurt," she whispers. "We kill one another because we have been killed. We will continue to eat one another until one of us is completely consumed."

She straightens her spine and lifts the raven back onto her lap. "Let's remove the brain now," she says, "and replace the eyes with something special."

She slits the neck open and, using an awl, pulls until its long black tongue hangs out. She then carefully works the awl into the head from below, scraping and cutting as she goes, until the tongue and the muscles that held it in place, and then the eyes and their tendons, and finally the yellow mush that was once the animal's brain lie in a small pile beside me.

"Do you wish to bury it or burn it?" she asks, obviously having noticed what I'd done earlier with the other entrails.

I lift the pile in my hand and again step to the fire, throwing it all in. It's done. That which will rot is gone. The rest of the animal, its tendons and muscle, will simply harden. I've been careful to keep the shape of the animal so that it stands, wings stretched out and up, its neck and head arched defiantly.

"Do you think we can dry it so its mouth is open, like it's calling out?" I ask Sleeps Long.

She nods as she strings her awl with thin sinew. "You're going to have to keep a close eye on it as the tendons shrink," she says. "You'll be very careful for days to try and make it how you want it, and then you'll begin to get forgetful, and then before you know it, you'll wake up one morning and the bird will be a shrunken old woman with one wing pointed up and the other straight out with its claws curled up into balls and you'll never get it to stand."

"I won't get lazy," I say. "I already see how I know it will be."

Sleeps Long picks up the raven with both hands and holds it above her head. "It's very big," she says. "I'm not sure I've seen a bigger one. How'd you come about it?"

Instead of telling her that her son gave it to me, I say, "You mentioned something about eyes." I point to the sockets, black holes now that make the raven look frightening in a way I don't want it to. "Look at how scary that is," I say.

Sleeps Long digs around in her sewing pouch and pulls out pieces of tanned hide and quills and finally shiny, polished pieces of shell. I didn't know she was a wampum maker. She sorts through the shells until she finds two that are a bit bigger than my thumbnail. "What do you think of these?" she asks, holding them up to the light of the smoke hole. The shells, polished to a high shine, appear as if something glows from within them, like the colour of the sky just before the sun comes up, and as Sleeps Long twists them, the light hitting them in different ways, they change colour all the way to the sky just after sunset. I don't know what to say. She knows it, smiling as she bends to the work of slipping one into the slit of the raven's throat and pushing her fingers up into its head until the shell flashes, streaked with a bit of blood, from the raven's eye socket, winking at me.

"But how will it stay there?" I ask. It's too beautiful, more beautiful than I could have dreamed. It needs to be just like that.

"I'll stuff the head with something, maybe corn silk. That will keep them from shifting, and as the blood dries, it'll secure them even better."

I clap my hands in happiness as she works to slip the other shell in and then sends me to look for corn silk. When I return with a handful, Sleeps Long holds the raven so it stares back at me, its eyes sparkling as if they're on fire, making me feel like I'm on fire, too.

"I've come up with an idea for how to make it keep the shape you desire," Sleeps Long says. She explains how we'll hang the raven upside down and from its claws above my sleeping place so the wings will spread, how this will allow the neck to arch just right. Sleeps Long holds the raven in her hands, her breath ruffling the feathers of its head as it watches me so that it looks alive, my bird watching me with its shining eyes so that I can barely make sense of what the beautiful woman says.

———

FOR THE NEXT many days I wake in the morning, opening my eyes to my raven who hangs upside down above, watching me. I check him carefully to make sure he holds the shape that he must and that his claws, big as my hands, still hold the stones I found, talons gripping them to keep their shape. When I first entered this longhouse, a couple of the old women sat me down and explained the coming days wouldn't be easy since they knew I didn't want to be here, but that I'd end up liking it. One of the old women said she'd dreamed just that. In my head, I called them crazy, dried-up witches. I won't show them, though, that they were right.

———

SOMETHING'S DIFFERENT TODAY. The women chatter with one another as they eat their morning meal and don't pay any attention to me as they usually do, explaining exactly where each bit of food came from, how it was prepared, how, due to proper prayers and burnt tobacco to the Sky Woman Aataentsic and her good son Iouskeha, this is all made possible. There's no teaching me today how to place squash seeds late in winter in bark trays filled with powdered wood and kept close to the fire until they sprout and can be planted by the corn. There's no talking today of how Aataentsic fell through a hole in the sky and the turtle surfaced and the world was born on its back, or discussion of how the different curing societies perform their rituals according to clan. When we're done eating, Sleeps Long walks to the door where the planting tools are kept. She takes one and the other women stand, following suit. I watch them all, some gathering tools, others the baskets of corn kernels they've been soaking for days and will now use for seeding. Only when they begin shuffling outside do I realize that I'm to do the same.

The sun's so bright that as I walk through the fields kicking at dust I hold my hand over my eyes. There's been no rain. It's normally plentiful during the planting moon. There'll be much fretting over this today. I keep my eye out for Porcupine Quills. Most of the men are off to another village to challenge their cousins to the Creator's Game and I wonder if he's gone with them. I can picture him running so fast no one can catch him and he wins everything for us.

In the forest all around, the men who've been left to guard against invaders chop at trees, slowly, painfully, clearing more land. As we work each mound, digging into it and planting kernels, the women do just what I knew they would, chirping like birds around and around the lack of rain, wondering aloud if someone they know might be responsible for cursing us all, if the ones from over the great water are responsible for this, too, just as they're responsible for the sicknesses that descended and killed so many and then left. As I dig and plant, standing then bending only to stand again, my mind wanders to the Crow, how he seems to have lost interest in me now that others are becoming close to him. As the morning wears on into afternoon and the sun begins burning my neck and back, this idea that he's decided to slight me makes me begin to think I shouldn't be so easily forgotten. No, he won't be able to forget me that easily.

THE DAYS NOW are spent with the women working the fields, the men out in the forest clearing it, or on the water fishing, or in their heads preparing for their first journey to the hairy ones in a long time. Bird and the rest of them returned in very good spirits and with many gifts and even more promises. They'd beaten our cousins, the Arendahronnon, and once again proved themselves dominant. Everyone gossips the same thing, that Bird, victorious, made a promise to allow our cousins to travel with his men to trade with the Crow's people, and how their numbers crossing into Haudenosaunee country will surely inflame their great enemy, how it's akin to declaring war so soon after the illnesses seem to have left. Some think that Bird is great for doing this. Others say he thinks only of power now and it's gone to his head and he wishes to speak for too many. As we tend to the fields, the women around me say there'll be discussion of this by the council fires. A few words used lazily might very well promise to ignite a fire no rainstorm can put out. My adopted father, Bird. Is he like you once were, my real one? I remember you were considered great by our people. I remember you were loved very much. You were like Bird, were you not?

At home, Bird and Fox stay up late every night, planning their summer journey. Now that I've come home, I listen from my sleeping place above them as they make decisions as to which young men are most worthy of accompanying them, which route is not just most expedient but safest, how such a large group will have to travel as many smaller ones in order for the world around them to accept their numbers. I listen carefully as they speak names, wondering if one, which one, will be Porcupine Quills'. Now I regret not letting Sleeps Long tell me what she named him. Will he go with Bird? I want him to stay back with those who protect us, the ones Fox says are most important for the well-being of his family, of all the families.

I note, too, how Bird once again awakes very early, a good sleep still left before dawn, and sneaks down the ladder and out of the longhouse.

I know what he does. I know he goes to visit Gosling so they can make each other whisper out like they do. He doesn't realize I follow him. I do worry Gosling might, though. I tell myself that despite her being a seer, I don't think she sees much other than Bird when she's in his embrace. Still, I stay back a good distance as he enters Gosling's home. I'm tempted to slip closer to hear what they talk about, to hear how they come together, but I can't take that chance.

I WANT

I keep an eye out for the boy I like, the son of Sleeps Long, the one I've named Porcupine Quills. All of us stand on the shore and watch as the men load their canoes. The sun's out, bright and hot, too hot for this early in the summer. Still no rain, and I know this worries Bird. People are grumbling that the Crow and his helpers have brought this drought to us, are casting another curse. The mumbling is getting so loud that Bird told Fox last night that when they return from their trade mission, he's worried the crows won't still be alive. "We should bring back some more from that place, just in case," Fox joked.

"That's all we need," Bird said, "more charcoal in the village." They went quiet for a while before he added, "Maybe it's not a bad idea after all. Having a replacement might prove good insurance."

The men are wearing their breechcloths and moccasins and their skin glistens with sunflower oil, their heads plucked clean except for the plumes of hair down the centre, the hair glistening with the oil, too. They've painted themselves for this trip, for their meeting the Arendahronnon at the river that runs from the great bay and to the Iron People. Blood or squash-blossom ochre lines many of the men's eyes or stands out in stripes on their cheeks, and some of them had their women paint their sacred animals upon their bodies, or stamped their women's or children's handprints upon their chests so that they remain close to the travellers' hearts.

I've never seen so many canoes prepared for one journey. Almost all the men of the appropriate ages wanted to go. It has been a number of difficult seasons, and the village is the domain of us women. The men's domain is the forest, where they can act without fear of upsetting the women, where they are in control of their fates—to some degree, anyway—and where they can be free. Eventually, many places on the mission were settled by a lottery. Most of the men who didn't win are out clearing forest. But some, Porcupine Quills and his two friends among them, I now see, stand close to the canoes and watch everything, no doubt hoping Bird might change his mind at the last moment and invite them. In the throng of people, I can't even get the boy to notice me.

Bird's in his canoe with Fox and six others from our longhouse. They're the first to push off. No goodbyes or displays of affection, for that would only attract the attention of any malevolent oki that might be nearby, an oki who wishes to cause pain by stealing the lives of loved ones. In groups of two or three, the other canoes follow, and it isn't until the last of them disappears around a bend in the river leading to the big water that people silently begin walking back to the village. Something's descended that can't be seen but only felt, as surely as if the air has cooled. The chill of knowing we're vulnerable to those who wish us harm now that the strongest of us have left. Not only are the travellers' lives in danger, but so are ours.

I keep a close eye on Porcupine Quills, who, along with his two friends, is among the last to leave. They talk and gesture toward the Crow and his two helpers, one of them pale and white and sickly looking, missing most of his fingers from his time in Haudenosaunee captivity, the other with black hair covering his face, his black eyes like an osprey's, seeing everything. All three stand with a few Wendat who listen to them, two old women, an old man, and a boy who mustn't be much older than Porcupine Quills. They make the sign on their bodies that the Crow taught me so long ago, touching their heads and then chests and then each shoulder, before bending their heads and whispering to one another.

Porcupine Quills shouts at the charcoal to stop placing curses. They ignore him, but I can tell by the way their bodies tense that they're scared. Porcupine Quills shouts again, and still they pay no attention. He clenches the club he's carrying and runs at them, lifting it and glancing it off the head of the sickly one, who crumples to the ground. The old people cower, but the young Wendat who's Porcupine Quills' size charges at him, only to be pulled up short by the Crow. Porcupine Quills again raises his club and swings now at the Crow, who stands and appears willing to accept it. The club stops just shy of his forehead, his eyes cast down and closed. Porcupine Quills screams into the Crow's face, loud enough that he stumbles back. Turning then, Porcupine Quills walks, laughing, to his friends.

"You!" I shout to him. "Tell me your name."

He stops and looks at me. His friends watch with fascination. "You have no need to know my name," he says. "With your father gone, you're useless to me. Worse still, your scars make you ugly and you're missing parts." He and his friends laugh loudly as they stroll away.

I'm so dizzy that I sit down hard, the ground feeling unsure. Looking up to the sun, I see many of them and realize I'm crying. I haven't cried in a very long time.

A voice behind me asks if I'm all right. I won't turn my head to him. "That boy's rotten inside," he says. "If you wish to know his name, it's Carries an Axe, and he's the son of Sleeps Long."

A voice I recognize as the Crow's then says, "Come, Aaron. Help me with the brother."

I hear them all walking away. Looking around, I see this boy is the one who wanted to fight Porcupine Quills. He assists the Crow and his dark helper in carrying the injured one up the hill, his feet dragging and blood dripping onto the dry ground.

———

ONCE I'M HOME, Fox's wife comes toward me, cradling something in her hands. In the darkness of the longhouse I can't make out what it is. Not until she's next to me do I see the furry face, the black-ringed eyes.

"Bird asked me to give this to you," she says, holding out the raccoon. "He said it will keep you company until he returns, and by the time he comes home, the raccoon will be ready to be released into the forest again."

She places the tiny, warm body in my hands. The animal opens its mouth and begins to cry.

"You'll have to feed him often or he will not live," she says. "Take your finger and dip it in warm ottet, then let the baby lick it off."

"I don't know if I can do this," I tell her.

"It's easy," she says. "All you need to do is keep him out of harm's way until he's old enough to fend for himself."

I sleep fitfully that night, worried I'll roll over and crush the animal that snuggles into my armpit. The raven above me hovers upside down, his tendons hardened and his body in the form that it'll now hold forever. Tomorrow I'll cut him from his rope and find a new place to hang him so he can watch over me and the new little baby.

Finally, I feel myself slip into the dark, deep place, the place where I feel safest, sleep wrapped around me and through me. I dream flashes of sunlight penetrating the forest, hear water splashing down rocks, children laughing. The raccoon is now grown and follows me like a dog wherever I walk, my raven with the glittering eyes swooping from branch to branch above us, our protector calling out, talking to us.

"You sleep deeply," the raven says, but I disagree. I've learned to sleep light to keep my ears alert. "But you didn't hear me approach," the raven says, and I tell him that's because he's got wings and knows the magic of silence. "Open your eyes and look at me," the raven says.

I jolt, wide awake in my bed. My body is frozen in sudden terror, sure that someone lies beside me, but I'm unable to move my head to see who it is. The raccoon makes a yawning sound and I feel his little feet push against me as he stretches in sleep. Yes, there is somebody lying beside me. I can make out the light breathing. My body, though, refuses to respond to my asking it to move, to do something.

"That's a lovely bird," a woman's voice whispers right next to me. It's her. I know that she lies on her back right beside me, both of us staring up into the black. I can smell her. It's her. Has she come to kill me now that Bird's gone? I want to ask her how she got into the long-house without making the dogs bark, why she lies beside me, but my throat won't work.

"You don't need to speak at this moment," Gosling says. "Too many speak too much without ever really saying anything, yes?"

I want to nod, to do something. I can't.

"A bad storm's coming," she whispers. "It comes. Most, I think, know it, though they don't want to recognize it. But it's coming." I hear her scratch her skin, maybe at a mosquito bite on her arm. "They don't want to know this because they don't think they can change the route they're travelling. They think the river is far straighter than it is."

She laughs as if there are others here with us, as if they agree and laugh with her. "No river is straight. And sometimes we have to picture what's ahead so we can take the landscape into account." Again she scratches. "You seem confused. Let me be clear. We're all in such a rush to get through our lives, aren't we? Let's say that we make our way down the river, a river we've not travelled before. If the signs of faster water appear, isn't it wise to pull the canoe out, to listen for a bit, to walk down the bank to see if rapids are around the bend?" I hear her scratching again. "Or is it wise to just keep paddling, despite the quickening water and the likelihood of danger ahead? Really, it's very simple."

Gosling laughs lightly again, again as if she's talking with more than just me, as if we're with others. "What's beautiful," she says, "is there are certain of us who can see what comes." My eyes adjusted now, I can make out the broad outline of my raven, the wispy feathers, the curve of beak. "Certain of us know what comes because we can see through the darkness that's the future as if we have a little fire. You," she says. "You have something special. You might just have the gift of the medicine woman. But it's something you need to learn to nurture as one nurtures the three sisters. And once it grows, then you'll need to learn how to control it." We lie on our backs beside each other, the raven above. Finally she says, "You can speak now."

I feel the muscles in my body relax, the fear, just a little, draining from me. My jaw, clenched since she woke me up, suddenly releases. "I don't want power," I manage to say.

"You don't want that boy who hurt you today to want you?"

The question stops me. Eventually I say, "He doesn't deserve me."

"That's a fine answer," Gosling says. "But it doesn't stop you from wanting him."

She lifts her finger in the light that's just starting to sift in from the smoke hole above. She slowly turns it in a circle, and the raven, as if a wind has entered, begins to follow her movement. "That's not so hard to do, you know, once you learn how."

Gosling raises her other hand, and with both in the air above her, she joins her thumbs together and begins to open and close her hands like a child mimicking the flight of a bird. Above us, the raven makes me open my mouth in surprise and fear as it opens and then closes its wings over and over again. Gosling quickens her pace, and the raven soon lifts up and rights itself to fly above us in circles, tethered by the length of rope attached to its feet.

"He has such lovely eyes," Gosling says. "Did you make them?"

I shake my head.

She continues to work her hands, steering the raven around and around, the wind from its wings causing the tears that come out of me to slide down my cheeks. It's so scary, so beautiful. I know, right now, that I want this power, too.

ALL THINGS TO ALL MEN

They force Gabriel, Isaac, and me to work the fields with the women, something considered a great insult. Poor Isaac who's already suffered so long and so hard in this cruel world, now recently concussed and making little sense when he speaks. We toil in the heat with the women who avoid us, our backs bent and the sun beating against our black robes until we swoon from thirst. For hours every day we pull at weeds, the only things that seem to grow in these desolate fields. They spring up overnight and choke the meagre crops if the pulling goes unattended for even a few days. The three of us have taken to kneeling a number of times through the mornings and afternoons to pray for rain that refuses to come, the cornstalks now shrivelled and dying like starving children. Every day, the dirt pushes farther under our nails so that our fingers swell with pain each night as the nails separate from them.

When we kneel, the women stop their own toiling to watch, not with curiosity but with something close to hatred. I feel the heat of their anger, Lord, and I ask that You soften their hearts so they can understand we wish for rain for their sake more than for our own. I've accepted that I will die a brutal death in this heathen and hostile land, and I accept this with humiliation and with joy, for I'll die for You in my attempts to harvest even a few souls.

Isaac, too, senses that our time here probably grows short. With so few fingers left, he's useless at working the weeds. Often, he just sits and speaks mindlessly. "That boy with the club hit me because he wants me dead," Isaac often says. "They all want me dead. They'll kill the three of us this summer because they believe we've cursed this land. Have we cursed this place, Père Christophe?"

Hot-tempered Gabriel grows short with him, and many times I have to calm Gabriel, his eyes blazing with something that frightens even me. I must calm Isaac and Gabriel both, soothe them with reminders that we're not here for ourselves but for our sauvages, yet just one more burden for my back that only grows stronger with each challenge. I've found something in recent years that nourishes me not just spiritually but physically. I've grown stronger with each new punishment. Even the Huron comment positively when we travel and I pick up the early-morning paddle, not putting it down until the end of the day with the others, lifting my fair share of the load as we portage long distances up rocky slopes. I thank You for this, Lord, for this flush of power that courses through my body. I bend down to pluck weeds in the field and consider this not an insult but a great blessing.

Each evening that we return to our small and simple residence, I must climb onto the roof and remove the arrows that young, angry warriors have fired into the cross atop the entrance, welcoming all who enter. Each evening as I struggle to pull arrows from the wood, I await the one that will pierce my back. Clearly, we're no longer welcome here. The drought has become so bad we now ignore the weeds and instead march back and forth all day like ants, hauling birchbark buckets and hide skins of water, trying desperately to keep the dying crops alive. From morning till night we struggle across the fields and to the river, a mission that seems akin to trying to put out a tremendous blaze with thimblefuls of water. There's nothing else we can do.

———

A RUMOUR'S BEEN circulating that an Iroquois war party has entered our country and is about to attack. A young man from a neighbouring village was caught loitering near our own and was accused by some of the younger, more volatile warriors of spying for the enemy. He's since disappeared and is now presumed murdered. This has become a summer of deep and frightening discontent, anarchy lurking behind every tree, horrid violence creeping closer in the late-evening shadows. The sun is at its full height for the year, staying strong till long past last prayers and attempted sleep, and the anxious young men patrol the palisades until dawn comes, stoking large fires and crying out all night in frightening shrieks to show any potential enemy who might huddle in the nearby forest that the Huron remain awake and strong. Everyone in the village is on edge, the women fearful to travel out into the fields alone, the men exhausted and short-tempered. Their mood's grown so frayed that Gabriel and Isaac and I can no longer show our faces for fear of being killed on the spot. Even the converts avoid us now for fear of being struck down. We huddle in our small house alone, awaiting our fate, praying for the souls of those around us, begging You, Lord, for rain. I'm left with nothing to do but pick up my quill again and scratch out words that might somehow make sense of the madness descending all around.

———

TODAY I AWAKE to Isaac screaming. Gabriel and I burst out of our blankets to soothe what I imagine is a nightmare, only to find him sitting up in the early-morning light, cradling something and rocking.

"Have you hurt yourself?" I ask. "What is it?"

Gabriel kneels to force Isaac to show him, then scuttles back like a crab. Isaac raises a severed human hand, still dripping blood.

"This is a sign," Isaac says. "Someone must have slipped in here in the night and left it upon my chest as I slept."

"It isn't a sign of anything but the devil's work," I say. "A grotesque and simple attempt to intimidate us, that's all."

With all the calm nerve I have, I walk to poor Isaac and hold my hand out. He just stares at me. I gesture for him to give it to me. He looks down at the bones and flesh and then back up to me before placing it in my palm.

I take the hand to near where we keep our vestments and chalice and altar. I put it on the ground, then pick up a wooden spade and begin digging a hole. I can feel Gabriel and Isaac watching me. When the hole is deep enough, I sort through my scant possessions and find a length of old cloth, wrap the hand in it, lay it in the hole, then fill the dirt back in.

Standing up, I call Isaac and Gabriel over to me. "Let us pray," I say, "for this young man who was accused of spying and then disappeared. We can assume this limb belongs to him. And so we shall bury him here in our residence because he died a martyr to the madness closing in all around us. If only we'd had the chance to offer him salvation, to have saved his soul before his grisly death. But we have this small part of him that we can claim for God." I bow my head, as do the others. "He's one more victim of Lucifer in this unforgiving land," I say. "He's not the first, and he'll certainly not be the last. But let his death strengthen us and our mission. Allow this attempt to frighten us to only stiffen our spines. Allow his death to help bring eternal life to the sauvages around us."

———

I URGE GABRIEL to pick up the quill as well and write for not only himself but also poor Isaac. Regardless of our situation, our promise to our superiors is that we'd keep journals, our recollections which might be shared with those who wish to fund our mission, and for the public in France, whom I've heard are fascinated with our exploits in this dark land. Most important, these accounts will remind our superiors of the importance of what they've sent us here to do. They are our living journals, our prayers and reflections, our examination and scientific mapping of these tribes and their customs, a growing dictionary of their language, and, ultimately, my living will and testament. I realize this is all I have to show the outside world of my work, my life. Is it vanity, then, dear Lord, that consumes me like a fever as I stay up writing late into the night, the words pouring from me in an endless stream?

This morning, when I look up from my work and ask if Gabriel will not do the same, he snaps, no doubt driven by his insomnia and the unceasing tension of the village.

"You're a fool," he spits, his eyes glaring. "Do you truly believe this drivel you write all night will ever find its way back to France?"

I drop my eyes in the hope that he'll continue to rant, to empty himself of the poison that fills him.

"When's the last time we received correspondence from our superiors? What, now, two years? Two years! For all we know, the Church thinks we're dead. Or worse, we're still alive but they don't care. They've forgotten us, Père Christophe. We're dead to them, and soon we'll truly be dead at the hands of these heathens." He points at our thin walls. "It won't be long before the warriors come in here and begin their slow torture."

Isaac, huddled in a corner, moans. "If they come for us, dear Brothers, promise me that you will kill me quickly," he says from the shadows. "I have been through their torture once, and I can't suffer it again. Please, I beg you. Kill me quickly."

"And do you remember what they promised in their last correspondence," Gabriel continues, "the one that arrived with those Algonquin traders? More priests, more donnés, our own mission here in Ihonitiria, our own fortress complete with soldiers to protect us, a place where the sauvages come to us prostrated rather than this, this ...," his voice trailing off as he holds his arms up in defeat. "Who is it you think you're writing to?" he asks me, his voice quieter now. "Who do you think will ever read the words you scribble all night long? Is this not a daily act of madness? Are you not like Nero fiddling as your savage empire around you burns?"

I say nothing for a long while. Isaac weeps quietly on his thin blanket.

"I write for you, dear Brother," I finally tell him. "I write for Isaac. I write for myself in the belief these words aren't wasted. I write in the hope we've not been forgotten by our Church or by our nation. I write to please God, for I treat these relations as my prayers."

Gabriel's hot eyes seem they might cool.

"All we have is hope," I whisper. "All we have is our ability to communicate in a way the sauvages cannot. It is the simple act of writing that lifts us above these poor devils. That alone is reason enough to do it, is it not?" And as I say this, an idea begins to form in my head. "It is time for us to stop cowering. It's time for us to truly put our physical lives and, more important, our souls on the line. We must stand up and be soldiers of Christ. It's time to stop hiding in this stinking house. Let the three of us go out into the light bravely," I say. "We will perform a Mass, a Mass that will bring rain. Or else it will be a Mass that brings our martyrdom. Either way, it's better to act than to sit back and be acted upon."

With these last words, Gabriel kneels before me, rests his head on my lap, and begs my forgiveness.

"Hush," I say, stroking his head. "We're but mere mortals and have been sent to a place that would break even our most hallowed saints and warriors. Our time has come, sweet Gabriel, to take up the cross and move forward bravely."

———

WITH THE FEAR removed from our hearts, the three of us walk the village again, no longer afraid of the violence that's hung over our heads this summer. We speak to everyone who will listen, explaining that we'll offer Mass each day in the hopes rain will follow. Delilah, one of my earliest converts, isn't afraid to stand in front of her longhouse with us, listening and asking questions.

"Why don't you just ask your great oki for rain to fall? This won't only save yourselves but surely will bring many of us over to your way of seeing." The old woman smiles then, as children poke their heads from the doorway behind her, watching. "There's no quicker way to make a believer than to offer a person something at the exact time she desperately needs it."

"The Great Voice works mysteriously," I tell her. "He listens when we bow our heads and touch our head, our chest, our shoulders with our right hand." I make the sign of the cross for her. "If you will admit your sins and ask Him to accept you into His heart, if you resolve once and for all to serve Him, we will pray to Him for nine days. And if you truly believe, on the tenth day the rain will come."

"You realize," Delilah says, "that if you make us this promise and fail to deliver, you'll seal your own fate."

"It's not up to me, or to you, for that matter," I say, "to seal our own fates. The Great Voice has already decided how the rest of my life will go, and when I will join Him in the place called Heaven. But you and the ones in your longhouse ..." I point to the children behind her, who, like gophers, quickly draw their heads back into the darkness. "It's up to you and the ones who you are responsible for to accept His word, to follow it, and to give up your evil ways. Only then will you all be saved. Maybe, if the Great Voice sees fit, your physical bodies will be saved by rain. And even if they aren't, you should rejoice, for the part of you that's most important, your oki, that part of you we call the soul, will go directly to Him and you will live in paradise forever."

I watch Delilah contemplate this, and for a long time neither of us speaks.

"I will take it upon myself," she finally says, "to try and do what you do, to try and live the way you tell me to live." She glances back at her longhouse where the children's faces have emerged into the light again. "I'll do it because we're suffering and face starvation. I'll do it for my family." She seems on the verge of tears. "I'm sad to do it, though, because I will be alone in death, separated forever from everyone I love. But that's a small price to pay, I think, if I can help save those I love."

I want to correct her, to explain that if she persuades the others to be baptized, they will join her in Heaven. But Delilah's already disappeared into her longhouse.

———

GABRIEL, ISAAC, AND I begin our nine days of novena, saying a Mass each morning, petitioning the Virgin Mary for rain, our prayers fervent as we look through the smoke hole of our cabin at the high blue sky. Each day, Delilah joins us, watching closely, kneeling when we kneel, standing when we stand, blessing herself when we do. Each day, I offer her a piece of the body of Christ, and she accepts it on her tongue. For five days, Delilah is our sole apostle.

Gabriel grumbles about this but I tell him to be patient, that Delilah is a well-respected elder and it doesn't go unnoticed that she joins us in prayer. "Can't you feel the power of what we are doing?" I ask. "It's as if the air itself is changing all around us. Have you even felt a sliver of fear since those dark days have lifted?"

Gabriel nods. "Yes, Brother," he says. "I do feel the difference."

We bow our heads together, Isaac joining us, with Delilah watching, trying to repeat our Latin words of praise, a child exploring the garden for the first time.

On the seventh day, I can feel a presence enter our cabin as the four of us whisper our novenas. I do everything I can to stay focused, to complete the prayer before looking up. I fear, though, that when I do, the petulant face of Gosling will be looking back at me, mocking. The sky remains as blue and as high as it has all summer.

When we finish, we stand as one and turn to the new arrival. My heart swells when I see that instead it is young Aaron, whom I thought we'd lost to the darkness once again. He stands in front of us for a long time. No one speaks.

Finally, I break the silence. "What do you wish from us?" I ask.

"There's talk throughout the village that you're working your magic in the hopes of rain." He pauses, realizing that I bristle at the word *magic*. "They say you neither sleep nor eat nor drink for nine days. That on the tenth day you promise rain." He stops. I gesture for him to get on with it. "The young warriors say that if the rain doesn't come, your power is so weak they can kill you without fear of reprisal."

"These brazen young ones say all sorts of things against me when Bird isn't nearby."

"They mean what they say," Aaron continues. "Some among us who know the spirit world speak loudly that the magic you work is meant only to bring death to us."

"What we work isn't *magic*," Gabriel spits. "And the diseases that have plagued you aren't our doing, either. Just look at the filthy ways in which you all live."

I raise my hand to him. "Now is not the time for anger," I counsel him. "Let's not undo now what we've worked so hard to achieve." I turn back to Aaron. "The great wampum we call the Bible speaks of plagues descending on faraway lands when the people refuse to accept the Great Voice. Go back and tell your warriors this is no different."

Aaron thinks about this for a moment. "They didn't send me to talk to you," he says. "They'd be very angry to know I've come to warn you of their intentions. There are only two days left after this one. There's no sign in the sky at all of what you hope for. Some of the old ones are already preparing their own death feasts. Most of the village believes it's not simple coincidence that since your arrival we've suffered both sickness and drought. It's too much for them to accept."

"So if we don't bring rain," Gabriel says, "we'll be killed for having lost our powers. And if we do bring rain, we'll be viewed as witches?"

Aaron's lack of a response speaks for him.

"And what do you believe, Aaron?" I ask.

"My name is He Finds Villages," he answers.

"You no longer accept your Christian name?" I ask, and I see he hesitates.

"I'm here," Delilah interrupts us, "because I hope to save my children and grandchildren from starvation this winter. I don't like being here, and I'll miss my people in the afterworld, but I've decided it's in everyone's best interests that I take this chance." I think she's done, but then she continues. "If you were to join me, He Finds Villages, it might not be so lonely in the world beyond this one."

Before I can correct her, Aaron says, "I'm not happy to be forced to make such a decision without proper reflection. You know if I'm to bow my head with you now, I'll very likely be killed along with you in a few days when the rains don't come."

"This is the decision you alone have to make," Gabriel says.

Isaac looks at him, at us, as if he needs to say something.

"I will join you if ..." Aaron pauses. "If Bird's daughter, Snow Falls, joins us as well."

"Your decision," I say, taken aback by his request, "must be based upon your own heart."

"That is my heart," he says. Delilah smiles.

"You must do this for yourself," I say.

"I wish to do this for her as well," Aaron says. "Isn't this what you teach? That we must live for others?"

"He's right," Isaac says.

I hush him. "I can't make the girl join us in prayer. Like yours, her decision must come from her own heart."

"Will you promise to try, to ask her to join us?" Aaron asks.

Isaac nods. "Of course!"

Gabriel shakes his head at this madness.

"You must make the decision for yourself, for your own soul," I tell him again, my voice firm.

I can see, though, that Isaac nods his head vigorously. "We all must do it for love! You must do this for love. What other reason is there?" The poor brother has gone mad.

Aaron looks at Delilah, then at Isaac, both of them smiling, nodding at him. "I will do it, then," Aaron says. "Tell me, what do I need to do?"

I bow my head, partly in frustration. A soul saved, I tell myself, is not always a flawless undertaking. There's no time to consider the means, just the end.

"Let us pray," I say out loud.

———

TODAY, I WRITE in my relations, is the tenth day, the Feast of Corpus Christi. I didn't sleep last night, not out of fear but out of wonderment at Your ways, dear Lord. You have already decided this day's outcome, and Your will shall be done. I accept it with open arms.

An hour before first light and the others around me rest fitfully, no doubt anxious even in sleep to witness this day, this day that may be their last on this physical earth. I bend to the weak flame of the dying fire and continue recording my thoughts.

Near first light, the footfalls of an approaching crowd make me dart up on my feet. "Awake!" I call to the others, and my brothers and Aaron and Delilah climb from their sleeping mats to stand beside me. The mob, a large one by the voices, makes no attempt to approach quietly. I can hear the seething, the thirst in it. They've come for their payment.

"Let us join hands and bow our heads in prayer," I say. "Dear Lord, let those who wish us harm find us serene and in prayer. Let us face this day and its travails with grace and humility."

Gabriel's hand is sweaty, but his grip firm. I hold Isaac's mangled stub as he shakes in fear and whines like a dog. "Please, please, please," he whispers, "please kill me now."

"Shhh," I whisper to him, to all of us. "Have faith in the Lord. Trust in His goodness."

The crowd now surrounds our cabin, the voices urgent, some shouting angrily. I can feel their heat through the thin walls. Then they enter in a wave, their bodies upon us. A high-pitched wail fills my ears. I lift my head and see Delilah, her mouth open and her head back, singing her death chant. The bodies surround us, press into us, pull us roughly apart from one another. The hands grab me, pull at my cassock. Gabriel and Isaac and Aaron and Delilah disappear in the roar. And then I am pulled outside as well, dragged through the mob.

HOUSE OF CROWS

Opening my eyes, I hear the rush of feet outside and people shouting for their friends to follow them. My raven swings lazily on his string, watching me with his shining eyes. For weeks I've been trying to make him fly of his own accord, fixing him with my gaze, willing him silently to move, or begging him in whispers. Gosling has promised that if she finds me worthy she'll teach me how, and much, much more. But first, she says, she needs to see if I'm worthy. How will she decide this? I have no idea.

More shouting. More running feet. My raccoon nestles in my hair, pulling it with his little hands. "Not so hard," I tell him. "Let's get up and see what goes on."

I pick him up and rise from my sleeping mat. He's grown quickly in the last few weeks and has begun to get into mischief, stealing food and being a nuisance to the old women. I look around me. Once again, everyone has already left the longhouse. The others tease me about sleeping so deeply but I've never cared about that. When more feet rush by, I too rush.

As soon as I'm outside I can feel something in the air, something that feels like happiness, as if a weight's been shed. Many people have gathered near the palisades by the crows' home. Immediately, I fear the talk has come to this, to doing. This last while, the anger directed at the three strange men has grown so intense I can't go near them. I quicken my pace, the raccoon on my shoulder, holding on to my hair for balance. Swarms of people move in circles around the house of the crows, and then I see them in the crowd, their charcoal robes standing out.

The mood isn't violent at all, though. Everyone's pointing and shouting and clapping hands at the horizon where a bank of cloud rises on a cool, stiff wind. Coming from that direction, the wind promises only one thing. The people surrounding the crows are celebrating their magic, not preparing to kill them for it. I can see that this isn't apparent to the crows. As I push deeper into the people I see that the one called Isaac shakes and cries like a little child. Christophe and Gabriel have their heads bowed and pray to their great voice. The old woman, Dawning of Day, who's been with them the last days, seems to understand the mood and begins to laugh and clap. She pushes through the people to Christophe and shakes him, points at the horizon. He looks at her, then looks up, and then his face is like the sun rising. He lifts both arms in the air and clutches his hands together, shaking them at the coming rain.

I lift my face, too, to the first drops. We all do. The sky opens itself to us and I thank the okis, Aataentsic the Sky Woman, even the crows' great voice, for saving us. Even though the rain is beginning to fall hard, the women go out to the fields after the short rejoicing to tend to the shrivelled three sisters, to beg their forgiveness for abandoning them this last while, to ask if they'll grow strong now that rain has come back. I follow the women from a distance and take in all that I see and hear just as the ground takes in rain.

———

WITH THE RAIN PLENTIFUL, the tempers of the young men cool. I've taken to following the crows around the village as they try hard to get the people to come to them. Dawning of Day and the young one called He Finds Villages follow them again. I know the names that Christophe Crow gave to them. He calls Dawning of Day a name

I find hard to say. Delilah. I like the way pronouncing it makes my tongue click. Delilah. I don't think, though, that I have learned how to say it right. He Finds Villages' crow name is Aaron, and that isn't so hard. It sounds solid and weighted like a Wendat word. I've caught this one staring at me when I allow them to see me. His eyes make me uncomfortable, like I must glance away. Something inside him is strong. Too strong, like he's burning from the inside. Despite the same scars of sickness as mine, he's not bad to look at, though.

———

FOR THE PAST WEEK, the sun shines in the morning and the rain comes every afternoon. I work with the others in the fields, weeding and watching the three sisters grow bigger. The harvest will be a good one if the sky stays like this. But no one will speak this desire out loud for fear of ruining it. I keep my raccoon tucked in the folds of my dress that I tie about my waist in the heat of the sun. He likes to sleep there, tired from his excursions. He's a creature of the night, like me. My breasts burn in the sun. I'm sore there, and when I feel each nipple, it's like a small pebble grows under the skin.

Afternoons leave me free to wander. Sometimes I follow Carries an Axe and his two friends, careful they don't see me. My new name for him, Raccoon Shit, suits him much better. I will not call him by his real name ever now that he has made it clear what he thinks of me.

It's obvious he and his friends are horribly bored, and the crows have become the focus of their torment. I watch the boys shoot arrows into the crossed pieces of wood that stand above the door of the crows' house, and each evening I watch Christophe Crow come home and lift his robe like a woman and climb up onto his roof where he struggles to remove them. I plan and plot and dream at night about how to find my revenge. I will show that boy what it means to hurt your child, Father and Mother. I will find my revenge, dear parents, in a way that would please you. I hate this boy with the pretty body and the stupid friends.

Tired of watching them, I go to visit Sleeps Long and show her how my raccoon has grown. As soon as I enter the longhouse this day, I can tell something's amiss. It's the odour in the air, the hushed tone of the adults, the absence of children and dogs playing loudly. I creep in and head to Sleeps Long's family fire only to find her on her sleeping mat, shivering under a beaver blanket despite the heat of the day. I kneel by her. Her eyes are closed, but when I speak her name she opens them. Her skin's grey, and her beautiful face looks so much older than it is.

"Sleeps Long," I say, "what's wrong?" My raccoon chatters as if he, too, worries for her.

She smiles at his small face sticking out from the nest of my hair.

"There are those who wish you harm," she says from nowhere, her face no longer smiling. "I've been dreaming much lately."

"You're suffering from a fever," I answer, stating the obvious, but puzzled by what she's said.

"There are those who wish you harm because they sense you have power and they're jealous of it. People you don't even know, and some you do."

"Don't speak in riddles, Sleeps Long," I say. "Has someone been looking after you?"

"You know my husband Tall Trees has gone off trading with Bird. My mother does what she can for me."

"You need a healer," I say.

"None have offered to come," she tells me. "And I don't have much to give even if one came."

"I know someone," I say. "She's very powerful. I'll find her for you." I stand. "I'll be back as soon as I can."

I run through the village, weaving through all the children and adults and dogs coming in from the fields. The rain's started again. At Gosling's small home, round in the Anishnaabe fashion, I call for her. No answer comes back. I circle it, speaking her name. Nothing. Without thinking, I go inside.

The fire is cold, and by the lack of scent it hasn't burned for days. I go closer and see rain puddles in the pit below the smoke hole. She didn't bother sealing it and so maybe didn't plan on being away for long. I think back to when I last saw her and realize it hasn't been in many days, since not long after she brought my raven to life. I sit on her sleeping mat to think. Herbs and roots hang drying from scaffolding above my head. A pile of kindling rests near the fire circle. A beautiful pair of moccasins, stitched in a way different from ours, puckered instead of smooth at the toes, lies by my hand. I pick them up and trace my fingers over the beautiful beadwork. I've never seen anything like it, with flowers across the top and a snake wrapping itself around the sides from one edge to the other, the work as delicate and time-consuming as a wampum belt. I know they were made by Gosling, and an overwhelming desire to take them floods over me. Instead, I force myself to gently place them back exactly where I found them.

Standing again, I wonder how I might find her. Sometimes she disappears back into the forest for so many days people begin to doubt if she'll ever return. If she's gone for a long time, she'll not have left many of her possessions behind. I use this as my excuse to look around her home. Gosling's a woman who doesn't live with much. A few bowls and smoking pipes are lined up against one wall, along with some empty leather pouches. Across from where I stand, a large birchbark box sits by the wall. I hesitate before opening it. It has hide straps so it can be carried as a pack. Slowly, I lift the lid of this box that comes up to my waist and is as wide as my arms stretch. The scent of cedar and of tobacco and sage and sweetgrass wafts out, something stronger below it. The scent of smoked moose hide.

I glance at the door. The smells draw me back. I can't resist and reach my hands in. The box has been carefully constructed with thick birchbark on the outside and lined with thinly cut cedar to keep out the moths and insects. This, I can tell, is where she keeps her winter clothes. I pull out a moose-hide robe that's soft as skin and heavy with the scent of woodsmoke. It's tightly stitched and has flowers beaded onto the front. Though the day is warm, I pull it on. Below it are mittens and leggings and tall moccasins, all of which I can't help but try on, too. Before I know it, I'm dressed for the coldest winter day, sweating and inhaling the smoke and hide in my nostrils.

Children run nearby, laughing, and I jump. The rain outside has stopped and I don't know how long I've been in here wearing Gosling's clothes. I pull them off and am about to put them back when I see a porcupine-quill box peeking out at me from the bottom of the container, partially covered by a rush mat. As I pull back the mat, I see that more boxes are nestled there, lining the bottom. They're beautiful, decorated with dyed quill flowers, or with patterns of stars or deer or birds.

I run my fingers over the quills of one that would fit in my palm. Feeling the power pulsing out of these boxes, I'm sure they contain Gosling's special medicines. I'm sure of it. One day I'll have my own quill boxes. I will ask her to teach me how to sew and bead moccasins her way and how to make these beautiful boxes out of porcupine quills. I'll ask her to show me what magic to place in each of them and how to use this magic. I must show her I'm worthy of her knowledge. But first I must find her so she can make Sleeps Long better.

I sneak out of her lodge. I don't know where else to look, so I go back to Sleeps Long's longhouse. I find her still collapsed on her sleeping mat. I'm worried I'm too late, but as I kneel down she opens her eyes.

"I looked for the healer," I tell her, "but she wasn't there. She's not been home for a long while." For the first time I want to say out loud that I wish Bird were here. He'd know what to do. He'd know how to find Gosling. "What can I do?" I ask.

Sleeps Long smiles weakly at me. "Maybe if you think hard of her, maybe if you dream of her tonight, she'll receive your dream. Whisper what you need to tell her to your raven and ask him to fly to her." With that, she closes her eyes.

Tonight, I lie in my bed and do as she suggested. I beg the raven over and over to fly away and find Gosling and tell her that she must come now to help Sleeps Long get better. His eyes, catching the light of the fire, look alive. I whisper to him until my eyelids grow heavy and then I jolt awake and ask him again to fly. I even tell him that if he does me this favour, he shouldn't feel obligated to come back, that if he'll do this for me, I'm willing to let him go.

All night I see flashes behind my eyelids. I see all of it from above, as bright as daylight, a waterfall at dusk pouring over sharp rocks, dark forest with herds of deer weaving through the trees, a great stretch of water the colour of a robin's egg, so clear I can see big fish swimming just under the surface. I am the raven, flying over the land of rock and pine that separates her people from ours, searching for Gosling.

In the morning I sit by her home, hoping she's received my message. I should be working in the fields, but Sleeps Long needs me. My raccoon chatters, telling me he's bored as we stretch out in the sun. He begins to wander off, and I tell him not to go far.

I open my eyes to laughter nearby. It's not nice laughter. My raccoon. I jump up and see Carries an Axe holding him by the tail, swinging him at his two friends, who try to swat him with their open palms.

I run at him, screaming. "Put him down! Give him to me now!" I slap his face as hard as I can. He stumbles, dropping the raccoon, and I watch my pet dart into Gosling's doorway.

The boy stands up, his friends now quiet and watching me. He rushes at me and my body tenses for his to slam into mine. I close my eyes.

Nothing.

"Open your eyes," he says. I do. He's smiling, his face so close to mine I can smell his breath. "Did you think I would hurt you?"

"You should be ashamed of how you act," I tell him, "with your mother so sick she might be dying."

"I'm sorry if I scared you or hurt the animal," he says. "I didn't know he was yours."

He wants me to forgive him, to tell him I'm sorry. He smiles like a little boy. "I don't believe you," I say.

"And I'm sorry for the cruel words I spoke to you when your father left that day," he says. "I was hurt he didn't choose me to travel with him, and I took it out on you."

I look at his friends to see if he's lying. They turn away from us and talk in whispers to each other. "Don't speak to me," I say. "And if you ever touch my animal or me, my father will kill you."

I turn away then, and not knowing where else to go, I stride into Gosling's home. I can hear laughing but not what the three of them say. I hate him, I hate them. I will find my revenge.

Clicking my tongue for my raccoon in the dim light, I sense another presence in the room, and I'm suddenly afraid that Carries an Axe has somehow sneaked in. But a woman says, "He's here, safe with me." I see her now in the light filtering in from the smoke hole, her small frame hunched near the dead fire. "I travelled long and fast to get back," Gosling says. "I'm tired."

Knowing she wants me to, I walk to her. The raccoon sits in her lap, nuzzling her hand. She feeds him something, acorns, maybe.

"He likes ottet," I tell her, not sure of what else to say.

"Ottet is fine for Wendat," she says. "But wild animals need to eat from the wild." She looks up and smiles. It doesn't feel warm. "Soon, he'll be too much for you to keep, you know. When his sex comes, he'll turn angry and mean. Prepare for that."

"Did a raven come to you last night?" I ask.

She looks up at me with a puzzled expression on her face. "What do you mean?"

Suddenly, I feel foolish. "I dreamed I sent a raven to find you. I ..." And no other words come.

"You're a strange one, aren't you," she says. I look down at my feet. "And apparently you like to sneak around where you don't belong." I can feel my face grow hot. "It's all right. There's nothing in my home I'm afraid to lose."

I want to ask her about the quill boxes but I don't dare. "I came looking for you to help me," I say. "I'm sorry I came into your home without permission. I was just trying to find you." She doesn't look at me, instead looks down at my raccoon, who's still eating from her fingers. "How did you know it was me who came in here?" I ask.

"The spiders that live here told me you disturbed their webs. Is this now your new secret place to visit?"

I shake my head. "I've only been here once. Can you really communicate with spiders?"

Gosling laughs. "You'll believe anything I say, won't you? You need to learn to relax when you're near me. That's your first lesson."

"How, then, did you know I'd come into your home?" I ask.

"It was simple," she says. "The way you just walked in, it was more than apparent you'd been here before. You just didn't know I was home, did you?" Before I can answer, she continues. "My moccasins were disturbed. I can easily tell that."

I glance down at where I remember them being yesterday, but they're not there.

"And if I needed any more proof," Gosling says, "I just follow your eyes." She laughs as my face flushes. "And it's obvious that you opened my bark trunk. Your footprints are small and very distinctive."

"Are you upset with me?" I ask.

Gosling holds the raccoon out to me. When I take him, she stands. "Help me start a fire," she says. "The mosquitoes will come soon and I need to get rid of the damp."

I step outside to collect dry grasses and when I come back in we arrange the kindling. She removes her flints from her bag and begins striking them. Gosling leans down to blow, speaking between breaths. "You must watch," she says. Tendrils of smoke rise near her lips. "That is the gift the animals taught us, and it's the gift that links us to them." She blows some more. "The animals always watch. Look at your raccoon."

I glance over to him. He follows what we do as if fascinated.

"Why do they watch?" she asks. "Why does the hawk stare from his perch or from the sky? Why does a deer stand absolutely still and focus so hard it doesn't blink?"

I think about this for a moment. "In order to catch their prey?" I answer, thinking of the hawk. "Or maybe to avoid it?" I add, thinking of the deer.

Gosling laughs. "You're learning," she says. "If you watch carefully enough, you'll survive. And if you learn from everything you see, you'll gain power from it all."

I'm confused. She can sense it, for she adds, "There's a lesson in everything you'll witness today. In what you witness every day. That bold boy wishes to make amends because he realized what he said when your father left was foolish and won't get him what he wants."

I nod.

"So watch everything. You need to notice what people usually miss even when it's right in front of them." She looks up at me standing above her and cocks her head like a bird. "A person can't just become a healer. One is born with that gift, just as a good hunter is born with that gift."

I guess at what she wants me to say. "I have that gift. You're here today when I begged you to come."

She laughs and waves her hand as if at a fly. "There is much involving chance and luck in this world."

"My friend needs help," I say. "She's very sick. She needs to live."

Gosling reaches out, and it takes me a few moments to realize she wants the raccoon back. It chatters as she cuddles him in her hands. "That Crow was born with something. I could tell it when I first saw him. He's good at watching but he doesn't like to. How he manages among us will all depend on how much watching he manages to do." She laughs to herself. "He's become very good at speaking, but how much does he actually see?"

Gosling stands and places the raccoon on her shoulder as she picks up her hide bag. "We'd better visit Sleeps Long and talk to her."

As we walk out she pauses by her birch trunk. "My winter clothing's quite warm." She doesn't turn to me to see me blush once more. She doesn't need to. "I keep quill boxes that I've made over the years," she says. "They're not as good as my mother's. My mother was truly gifted." Gosling faces me. "She tried to teach me but still I feel I'll never be nearly as talented as she was." Gosling smiles. "When I finally believe I've made a porcupine-quill box that rivals my mother's, that will be the day I feel it'll be worthy of holding something special. For now," she says, shrugging, "they just sit empty."

———

I WATCH AS GOSLING kneels beside Sleeps Long, who appears unconscious. A couple of old women sit in the shadows on the other side, watching as well. Gosling lifts a hand over Sleeps Long's belly. Her hand drifts down, over one leg and up the other. Gosling runs her hand back over her stomach and up to her chest, where it wavers for a moment before going on to Sleeps Long's head. She does this three times.

Gosling gets up and walks past me and out the door. I expect her to come back, but when so much time passes that I feel sleepy, I stand and stretch and head out to find her. Outside of her home, I call her name. She tells me to come in.

Her fire burns hot and she sweats by it, peeling bark from tamarack branches and dropping it in her boiling kettle. "There are three types of illness," she says, not looking up. "There is the illness that comes from natural causes. There is the illness that is born of someone with power wishing harm upon you. And there is the illness that comes when strong desires go unfulfilled."

"Which one does Sleeps Long suffer from?" I ask.

"Which do you think?" Gosling responds.

I consider this for a while. "I fear she suffers the curse of someone powerful who wishes her harm," I finally say.

"Why do you assume this?"

"Because Sleeps Long told me that she dreamed of those who wish harm."

"Who wish harm to *you*," Gosling corrects. "Sleeps Long is beautiful, and there are many men who desire her, but all she desires is for the safe return of her husband, and she knows in her heart that he will return soon. So what does that leave us with?"

"That she's sick from natural causes," I say.

Gosling scoops tamarack bark from the kettle with her ladle and places it on a flat stone to cool. She looks up at me. "Go out into the community and announce I will hold a curing ceremony this evening. Make sure the Crow and his followers are invited."

Gosling turns back to her work. I too turn, and then walk out into the afternoon, the news ready to pour from me.

———

SLEEPS LONG'S HOUSE is crowded with onlookers trying to secure a good vantage. She lies in her same spot beside her fire, smiling weakly at those who surround her and whisper their wishes for her to get better. "You have Gosling looking after you now," one says. "Take heart! She will cure you, indeed!"

Everyone hushes when Christophe Crow and his followers come in, holding their heads high and making their touching sign to those around them. A couple of people laugh. Others move away or just watch. The two Wendat with the charcoal names Aaron and Delilah don't look so proud, though. They keep their heads down and refuse eye contact. I don't believe they wish to be here where people are torn as to what to think of them. Since the rains have come back, Christophe Crow's house has been full of Wendat interested in his magic, but still Aaron and Delilah are the only two who kneel with him every day.

Christophe Crow walks up to Sleeps Long and crouches by her. As he raises his hand, she turns her head away. "If you accept the Great Voice now, you will live forever in happiness," he says. The crowd falls silent.

"I would rather live in the fires you speak of," she whispers, "if this means my husband will be beside me."

He then speaks words in the language no one but his helpers can understand. They join in with him, and when they're done they once again touch head and chest and shoulders. I look around me to see the whole room watching closely.

When Christophe Crow stands, a voice speaks out. "Are you done yet?" Gosling asks. Laughter breaks out. Gosling steps from the shadows right beside the Crow and makes him jump. People laugh even harder. "Did you not realize I was right next to you?" she asks.

He again touches his head and chest and shoulders. "You are of the devil," he says.

Gosling smiles. "I'm not sure I'm acquainted with the friend you speak of."

"He is no friend," Christophe says.

Waving her hand as if to shoo him away, Gosling kneels by Sleeps Long and takes a turtle-shell rattle from the hide bag strapped over her shoulder. She shakes it all along Sleeps Long's body and begins singing a song in her language. When she stops, she looks straight at me, her eyes beckoning me forward.

"Feed your friend this sacred drink," she says. "Help your friend to get stronger." Without wanting to, I walk to Gosling and reach into her hide bag, take out a skin filled with warm liquid. I can feel Christophe Crow's eyes on me. They burn into me. I refuse to look up. Kneeling, I untie the top of the skin and lift it to my friend's lips. The liquid that pours out smells strongly of the forest, of wet grass and moss and dark loam. She takes in what she can, and I wait as she swallows, then give her more.

Gosling begins shaking her rattle again and singing in her strange, high voice. The room is so quiet it's as if no one is here with us. Gosling, still singing, places her ear to Sleeps Long's chest, now shaking the rattle slower.

She lowers her ear near the sick woman's stomach and hovers over it for a long time, her voice going softer and softer until all of us lean forward to hear her better. She lifts her head and shakes the rattle beside Sleeps Long's hipbone so fast that it's only a blur. When it stops, the only sound in the house is the crackling of the fire. Gosling lowers the turtle shell onto Sleeps Long's body and moves it in circles. Sleeps Long moans out, not in pain but as if she's being released from it.

Gosling drops her head to Sleeps Long, places her mouth onto my friend's skin. I stare, fascinated, as she begins to suck with all her might, Sleeps Long crying out. Gosling drops her rattle and pins Sleeps Long's arms down as both continue to shake with the effort. Her legs kick in spasms and then Sleeps Long screams louder and goes slack. Gosling continues to suck, less intensely now, and finally raises her bloodied mouth from Sleeps Long's hip. I can hear the murmuring of people all around me, and the muttering of the crows.

After wiping the blood from her lips with the side of her hand, Gosling opens her palm and spits what look like small pebbles into it. She holds them out to the fire, her palm open and covered in spit and blood, the pebbles like wampum beads glowing in the firelight. People lean in to get a glimpse and many cry out "Ah-ho! Ah-ho!" when they see what she holds.

"These stones were part of what causes her illness," Gosling tells them. "They were encased in her organs and caused great pain. Her body couldn't pass them."

"Baaah!" someone cries out. I see it's Christophe Crow.

Ignoring him, Gosling holds out her hand. "Pass them around," she says. I look at Sleeps Long who rests, finally looking peaceful. The skin by her hipbone is blotched, turning from the colour of blood to the colour of a bellflower. "Study those stones closely," Gosling says. "But make sure to throw them into the fire when you're done. Dispose of the evil properly."

"Evil, indeed," Christophe says loudly, and the crowd turns to him. "You're nothing but a juggler, a magician. Yes, dispose of the pebbles properly, the same stones you placed in your mouth when no one was looking."

I expect Gosling to spin on him in anger, but instead she smiles and lifts her shoulders. "I've been caught," she says. People around us laugh nervously. "At least this one can rest now." Gosling picks up her turtle-shell rattle and shakes it over Sleeps Long's body. Sleeps Long moans out. "And does what you offer suggest trickery or something more?"

"I offer truth," the Crow says. "I don't offer trickery or sorcery."

"We shall see," Gosling says. "Sorcery is a word used loosely by you. And you use that word as a weapon when you wish to strike out."

Finally I sneak a look at Christophe, whose eyes flash at me. The frightening charcoal named Gabriel seems ready to jump forward and strike Gosling. He's a dog on a tether. But the other one, Isaac, only blinks and smiles at her, holding his hand out as if he, too, wants to hold the pebbles being passed around.

"There's more healing to be done," Gosling says, standing up. "Oh, my knees ache now that I'm growing old. I will need your help, child." She holds her hand out to me. The crows stare at me. I'm torn.

I raise my hand and she takes it. For the first time, I notice that we're the same height. I look to her.

"Help me pick this woman up," she says, bending to turn Sleeps Long on her side. I'm surprised by how light she is as we lift her, barely awake, to her feet. Gosling slips behind and cradles her in her arms. "Give your friend more drink," she says, and when I place the skin to Sleeps Long's lips, her eyes open a little and she smiles when she recognizes me. I smile back and pour some into her mouth.

Gosling begins to sing again, at first low but rising in intensity with each breath. The longhouse has gone silent and I know the crows look at us, at me. Gosling begins to bounce Sleeps Long as she stands behind her by lifting her up and down as if they're a mother and child playing a favourite game. In part to escape all the eyes on me, in part out of fear, I step back from them. Gosling's voice rises as she bounces this beautiful woman as easily as she would a baby, and I wonder where Gosling's strength comes from. It's as if she grows bigger as we all watch, the bouncing becoming a shaking, Sleeps Long's face turning red, her mouth open, her arms flapping like a baby bird's trying to fly as Gosling's singing becomes a wail that grows so loud it sounds like many.

And then all of us in the room step back at the same time, women moaning and men holding out their hands as something like sand begins falling out of Sleeps Long's hair. Gosling's in a frenzy now, shaking her with a power that I fear will snap her neck. And as I watch, the sand begins to fly from Sleeps Long's nose and then her mouth and then her ears so I can feel the grains of it pelting my face and arms just as if I were by the big water during a windstorm. People gasp and some call out Ah-ho! once more and others begin to wail, and then I begin to shake just like Sleeps Long. All of us do, I'm sure, until, exhausted, we fall to the ground as one, Gosling on top of my friend, holding her and wiping her eyes and nose and mouth with her hands.

I sneak a look over to the crows and they're as pale as I've ever seen them. Gosling cradles Sleeps Long in her arms as if she's her own child, and when I see the colour come back to both of their faces, I know to reach for the skin and offer it to them. My friend opens her eyes when I speak her name and smiles weakly at me and takes the bag from my hand, drinking deeply. Gosling stares into the fire, and me, all I can do is stare at Gosling.

SOMETHING MUST BE DONE

Base trickery. That is all it is. Sleight of hand is the magician's first lesson. But Gabriel and Isaac won't listen to me.

"Père Gabriel, Père Isaac, I beseech you," I tell them today after morning vigil. We sit at our rough-hewn table that both impresses the Huron who visit and makes them laugh. They far prefer to sit on their haunches or on the ground when they eat. "That wretched witch Gosling is nothing but a charlatan. The other night was a good show. I'll give her that. But that's all it is. A show."

"The bloody pebbles she extracted from the stomach of the girl," Gabriel says. "Maybe this was sleight of hand. But I'm not even sure of that. Did you see the wound the witch left on her skin, and did you touch what came out of the girl? Those were no stones. That was human refuse."

"What of the sand storm that flew out of her?" Isaac adds. "How could one possibly stage such a thing?"

I'm left unable to explain any of this, I realize, for I myself don't know the answers. "Let's look at this as we should, then," I say. "We're in a dark land, securely in Satan's clutch. If indeed that sorcerer has demonic powers, we represent the light. It's our mission to banish all that which is evil." I won't give in to her, Lord. To it. To him, the evil one. "I must re-emphasize that she's a truly talented magician, and nothing more. But if it makes things easier for you, dear Brothers, to believe she possesses something darker, then gird yourselves for a battle we have no other choice but to win."

———

THE MORNING IS SPENT walking about the village trying to gauge that night's damage. Just as I begin to make headway, it seems, I'm pushed to my knees again. That sorcerer has taken the upper hand with the community. It's clear to see by the way people on this morning either ignore me or openly taunt me. Only a few evenings ago, so many of the sauvages still straggled about our home, expecting food and gifts, we were forced to shoo them away so that we could sleep. And now even Aaron and Delilah are embarrassed to be seen with me. Only a month ago, our prayers delivered the rain and saved these ingrates from starvation, and yet today those three boys who have been the bane of my existence this summer openly stalk me, hurling insults and rocks.

The leader, the one with the fine build, directly approaches me, the same wicked club he used to assault poor Isaac in his hand. I stop and look back at him. I can't let fear overwhelm me now.

"Gosling's power is just as strong as yours," he says. "In fact, Gosling's power is far superior."

"Then why was she unable to bring the rains?" I ask, and this throws him off balance.

"How do I know it wasn't she who did that?" he asks.

It's a weak answer, and I tell him as much.

He scowls, the anger rising up red from his neck and into his cheeks. The hand with the club twitches.

"Think twice," I say, "before striking down someone with power such as mine." I turn then, head bowed, my large hat covering my scalp from the sun, and head toward the fields, trying not to give away the tension in my back as I await the shattering blow.

The women in the fields ignore me. Bent to the weeding and the trimming and the deep care of each of the plants they treat as graciously as their own children, they talk amongst themselves and refuse to look at me. The plants have grown tremendously this last month, are already past waist high, and with one more month's passing they'll have grown taller than the tallest Huron. That's when the harvest will begin and the men will return only for a short while before heading out once again, this time for the autumn fishing and hunt. The Huron man feels complete only when he's away from the village. Here in this place, the women rule.

Delilah's working with a group of her sisters, and I approach with a smile on my face. "Will you join me in speaking to the Great Voice this evening?" I ask.

She pretends I'm not there.

"Delilah," I say, "what has changed?"

She stands from her crouch, her breasts bare in the hot sun. I avert my eyes. "I felt shame that night," she says. "I shouldn't feel shame in front of my family."

I'm confused. "Shame?" I ask. "What makes you feel shame?"

She turns back to her work. The women around her act as if I'm not there at all. For long, uncomfortable minutes I stand useless, not knowing what else to do, but then a desperate idea comes to me. I think of the supplies meant to get us through next winter.

I straighten my back. "I will hold a great feast," I announce to Delilah and her sisters. "A feast of many kettles." These Huron can't refuse such generosity, which they consider the greatest of traits. "This feast will spare nothing," I declare. "All of my stores will be used." With that I walk away, excited at the prospect of putting my life back into Your hands, but a little fearful of the reaction I know will come from Gabriel and Isaac when I share the news.

———

"WHAT WERE YOU thinking?" Gabriel asks.

I've already prepared my answer. "You know, dear Brother Gabriel, they will never refuse a chance to gorge themselves. We'll win back their hearts through their stomachs."

We stand in front of the little tabernacle we painstakingly built by hand from small sheets of copper and scraps of wood. The cross atop it is stout and gilded.

"Well, that's the most short-sighted thing I've ever heard you say," he spits.

I'm tempted to remind him that I'm his superior, that his admonition's unacceptable. Instead, I allow him to go on, to vent his frustration and tire himself.

"And what are we to do," he continues, "when winter is upon us and we have no supplies?"

"We were promised," I counter, "that Bird and his party will bring more when they return."

"Ha! Just as we were the last three years running. It's as if our *brothers*," Gabriel says, baring his white teeth at the word, "have decided we no longer exist. But there's no need to revisit that concern, is there?"

I reach a hand out to him. "Trust in Him, and He will give you all that you need and more. Don't forget the most fundamental of our lessons, dear Brother."

Gabriel shrugs in defeat. "You are the superior here," he says. "I will find Père Isaac and help him with collecting the firewood."

I follow him. "I will help you," I say.

He walks quickly as if to lose me, but my stride is far longer. Gabriel, though not tall, is lean and hungry, and his fire is something to behold. In our haste we've left our hats behind, and the sun beats down on our heads. The rain has disappeared the last days, and I await the tension another week of its absence will bring.

Once we are beyond the stockades, the same feeling of vulnerability, the same feeling that someone or something watches from the shadows of the trees, is almost unbearable until I am forced to swallow it down. We head toward our designated wood-gathering lot. The Huron, I've noted, though so generous in every other respect, protect their woodlots. Sweating even in the shade of the forest, I understand why. The work of supplying fuel for cooking and for heat throughout the year is of such magnitude that it would make the sturdiest French peasant blanch.

Isaac doesn't hear us coming, and he cries out when Gabriel touches his shoulder. "Please, Brother, warn me of your approach," he says to Gabriel, trying to catch his breath. I've considered sending Isaac back to New France, fearing for his mental and physical health. Even now I see that his last hours' toil, trying to collect dry brush and branches and snapping and gathering them into bundles with his mangled hands, is pathetic. But I know if I were to ask if he'd like to go home he'd refuse. After the Iroquois captured and tortured him, after they told him to never return to this country again, God whispered loudly enough into his ear. You've come back to this land of your own volition, sweet Isaac, and it's here where you'll fish for souls the rest of your days.

"We are to offer a feast, Isaac," Gabriel says glumly, "so don't stop collecting the firewood. We'll need much of it, probably more than we'd burn on the coldest winter week."

Gabriel glances at me, but I smile at how Isaac's face lights up. "A feast!" he says. "Yes, this is just what we should do for the dear people." He claps the nubs of his hands together. "What shall we prepare?"

"Everything," Gabriel mutters.

I cut in. "It's time to play to their, how shall I put it, their weaknesses," I say. "Their willingness to squander all they have just to impress the others is something we can exploit." I choose my words carefully. "Yes, their spirit of generosity parallels Christ's. We've all witnessed that. But we must question for what reason, to what end, they hope their generosity might benefit themselves."

I glance at Gabriel, whose sour demeanour softens as what I say begins to sink in.

Isaac simply appears confused. "Look," he says, still excited. "I've found a wonderful ingredient for the feast." He bends to pick up his wide hat, filled to the brim with mushrooms that he must have been picking all day. "I've not had these since we left beloved France," he says. "Won't they make a wonderful addition?"

Of course," I say, distracted. "You've done very well, Brother Isaac." I turn back to Gabriel. "We haven't left our homes, our families, the simple comforts of our former lives that now seem kingly in order to enjoy the scorn and torture and yes, the misguided generosity, of these sauvages. We've travelled so far at great peril to our physical and spiritual selves to bring these lambs into the fold." I stop then, searching for more. But I think it might be enough. We will hold a feast, and the people will come, and we will begin once more to guide them toward their salvation.

———

RUMOUR HAS IT that the juggler Gosling will attend, and this is fine. I've got a few of my own tricks planned, if need be, to counter her tonight if she decides to show off. As I look around our residence, I too late realize it might not be big enough. Already, long before the sun has set, dozens of Huron have arrived in full regalia, their faces painted in red and blue and yellow ochre, the men's hair fierce and shining with oil, the women's long and plaited, all of them wearing their finest deer skins decorated with beadwork. There's no denying, Lord, that they're a beautiful people, the most beautiful people I've ever laid eyes on. The men alone would put our greatest athletes to shame, and the women are as supple and ample and alluring as any of the European royalty. If only they understood and repudiated the darkness of their ways. But this is my mission, isn't it, to turn them toward the light?

As promised, we have opened our stores completely, and I've given direction that nothing is to be saved. Isaac has taken it upon himself to bake loaves of bread in our small stone oven and already has a group of fascinated wretches standing around him, watching intently. Children and dogs run around without care, rolling in the dirt with one another. If there is one thing I will never grow accustomed to, it's the sauvages' inability to chastise their children. In all my years here I've never seen an adult even raise a hand in anger toward a child. Indeed, this should be one of the first behaviours we must try to modify. This will not happen, dear Lord, until converts are won, yes? Tell me, give me a sign, that one day this will be the case.

Rather than turn glum at my own party, I walk over to the women who help us prepare the feast. There's no chance that Gabriel and Isaac and I could have done this on our own. The house is nearly too unbearably hot with the fires they've started, and the smoke is atrocious, but at least it keeps the mosquitoes away. And even I must admit that the smells emanating from the kettles are quite glorious. As I look into one that Delilah stirs, I can't begin to guess what might be in the dark roux of it. I've become used to their way of apparently not caring what meats they mix in their pots, and have eaten soups that contain bear and beaver, fish and fowl. Beyond that corn paste, ottet, which tastes like glue and is their staple on long trips, I've been strongly impressed by their kettle feasts. One thing I can promise You, dear Lord, is that by the end of the night, every kettle will be scraped bare, leaving little for even the dogs that will inevitably lick the pots clean.

I'd like to ask Delilah about the feeling of shame she'd admitted to a few days ago, but she's bent to her work and doesn't look up.

Isaac approaches, carrying a birchbark pail filled with the mushrooms he picked. "Here, Delilah," he says, offering it to her. "For your kettle."

Delilah turns to him, a smile lighting her face. His simplicity never fails to win these people over. She takes the pail and glances inside. "Either you joke with me," she says, "or you're ignorant of these."

Isaac looks as confused as I must. "Did I do something wrong?" he asks.

"These fungi will kill a person within a short while of eating them," she says. "Where did you find them?"

"Growing in our woodlot," he says.

"I wonder if that is simply chance," Delilah says, handing the bucket back to him. "You will show me where tomorrow. But for now, get rid of these. Don't be lazy and burn them in the longhouse fire, either," she adds. "The fumes will make you vomit for days. Build a fire outside of the gates and away from us. Burn them there, but be careful not to inhale the smoke."

Isaac stares down at the mushrooms, and then up to Delilah, a strange look on his face, as if he understands something I don't. "I won't be long," he tells her. "I'll be careful but quick. I don't want to miss the feast."

Delilah turns her attention back to her kettle, obviously not wanting to speak anymore. I'll leave her alone for now and try to lead her back to the fold later tonight with generous action rather than words. Maybe this could be a pathway into their hearts.

Hearing a commotion by the door, I look and see the three reprehensible boys who've so thoroughly terrorized me this summer walk in, looking fearsome in their dress and manner and paint. A few older women call out to them as if in a swoon, and the younger girls, including my near apostle, Snow Falls, do the same, but genuinely. Something must be done. The overt sexuality of these people is beyond embarrassing. It's grotesque. I have the urge to tell them to leave but am reluctant to cause a scene. Besides, this feast is for one and all and I can't be selective about which souls enter through the door.

The feast begins as they always do, with long speeches and a raining down of compliments and thanks upon the hosts' heads. I sit with Gabriel and Isaac near the centre fire, listening intently. Gabriel's getting better with the Huron language, and Isaac mastered it long ago. Tonight, I feel little need to translate. The speechmakers, the most important men who aren't on the trading expedition, compare us to osprey and our hospitality to the great inland sea. Wonderful orators, they recall even the tiniest facts about us Jesuits and our history with them. By the time they've finished, my years amongst the Huron have been celebrated and explained down to the most mundane detail. As always, I'm amazed, even more so by the complete lack of anger or alienation toward us tonight. Maybe I have finally found a pathway to them.

When I stand to speak in return, I see that Gosling has once again slipped in without my noticing. She sits near the three troublemakers, and it makes me wonder if she isn't the agent behind their devilry. Her presence takes the wind out of my magnanimity, and I find myself searching for words. It's obvious that my attempts to strike fear into them aren't working. Maybe it's time to take another tack. I jump in, not sure where I'll go.

"I thank you for coming to us tonight," I begin. "I have opened up our cache of food in the hope you will understand I wish to share with you. I'm not here to take." I pause to try and find a stronger direction.

"We came here not to take from you but to give to you. It's your choice whether or not to accept what we freely give. I will not go on long tonight because we are all hungry. My stores are now gone, but that they are used to nourish you makes me happy."

I sit down, then, ashamed at my inability to take this opportunity to preach and to convert. But then, hearing their appreciation, their grunting what sounds like "Ho, ho," I raise my head. The people stare at me as one, and only then do I realize that, maybe, this is working.

Neither Isaac nor Gabriel nor I am used to eating more than just enough to keep us from starving, but tonight we are like our sauvages, and having waited until everyone else has been fed, we gorge ourselves, partaking until our stomachs feel as if they'll burst. All around us are in a joyful mood, and there's none of the antagonism I've carried like a heavy burden for so long with just brief respite. On an evening such as this with all of us like one great family, with even Gosling smiling and laughing with the rest, I can truly see, Lord, a future for these ones that isn't damnation.

We hosts are urged to stand once more after we've eaten and rested and eaten again. The guests call on us to speak, to tell them something interesting or to teach them something from where we come from. One of the three awful boys shouts out to Isaac to tell him what it was like to be tortured by the Iroquois. I fear this will send him into another fit, but it does quite the opposite. For the first time since meeting him in New France, I see him straighten his back and become solid again.

He lifts his arms in the air. "See these?" he asks, nodding at his stumps. "This happened to me when I went on my journey to meet the Neutrals not long after I came here to you." The crowd hushes, ready for the story. "I was new to your country, and I believed in the salvation of Christ."

I am about to stop him from doing irreparable harm to our mission, but he continues before I'm able.

"And I still do," he says, "even though your enemy captured me and the party that accompanied me. They killed most of us with arrows and clubs near a waterfall where we couldn't hear them approach." His audience listens, intent. "They killed everyone but me and a young girl you'd sent with us whose family had married into the Neutral."

Isaac stops here and I expect him to cry but instead he smiles. "I feared more for the girl's safety than my own," he says. "I swear. But as we were bundled off to the enemy camp, I watched one of their warriors barter with the others to allow him to adopt her, for, as it turns out, he'd lost his own daughter to one of you." They nod at this, transfixed.

"When we entered their camp, men were lined up on either side, and as I walked between them they rained down blows with fists and clubs until I thought it was time for me to die. But this was just the beginning of it."

Isaac takes a breath, the room silent but for the crackling fire. "Two of them each took one of my hands, and while the others held me down, they brought my fingers to their mouths and chewed until they spit them out. This took over an hour." His stumps shake now. "But they were not yet done."

Isaac lowers his stumps and struggles to lift his robe from his body. "Your words will suffice," I whisper to him. I can hear those nearby tsk-tsk me.

"All that night they took sharpened sticks of fire and poked and prodded and penetrated me until I passed out. And then they revived me with cold water and began again. When it seemed I would bleed to death from the wounds on my hands, they cauterized them with red-hot axe heads."

I want Isaac to stop now, but still he continues. I peer over to Gabriel, who stands stoically.

"After two days of torture they let me rest for a whole day, feeding me by hand and pouring cold water into my mouth and binding my wounds with salves as tenderly as if I were their child. I expected the worst was still to come, but this is when they told me I would live if I desired, if I made them a promise."

The crowd leans toward him.

"They made me promise that if I were to leave this country forever and return to my home, if I were to carry the message back that my kind were not welcome here, then I could go free."

With this, the air seems to deflate from Isaac, and he sits back down. The audience remains silent. Confused, I look at Gabriel, wondering if we, too, should sit down. Judging from his reaction, he has no idea either.

"It is either very brave or very foolish," an old lady then says, "to break your promise to a Haudenosaunee."

"Which are you?" someone else asks. People laugh at this, and after the intensity of his confession, I'm shocked. I look down at Isaac. Again I'm surprised by the smile on his face. Like that, the tension is broken.

"It is time for you, tall charcoal, to entertain us," someone then shouts, pointing at me. Others join in the harangue, laughing and calling on me to do something.

Gabriel leans to me and whispers, "Why not give them a little of their own trickery?"

I lean closer to him. "What do you have in mind?"

"I've been thinking about this since that witch caused such a stir," Gabriel says. "A donné back in New France used to win favours among the Montagnais with a simple trick that always amazed them."

"Tell me more."

"We will need a quill and some parchment." He then whispers instructions in my ear.

"Brilliant," I say in French. "Retrieve them." I turn to the guests and clap my hands. "The one you call Gosling is not the only trickster in the room." Everyone goes silent. I was hoping to make them laugh. "The Great Voice has given us Black Gowns special gifts as well." I look out over the guests covering the floor, watching me. I need to build this up and truly impress them.

"When the Great Voice beckoned us to speak His words for Him, we had no choice but to obey. And we obey with all our hearts. Doing what is requested of us, though, is no easy task. To become a Black Gown, we must swear off all temptations, temptations of the heart and of the soul and of the flesh."

"He means he won't be with a woman," someone shouts. "Or a man, for that matter." People laugh.

"But to give up these temptations means that we are given other gifts." I see from the corner of my eye that Gabriel's returned. "One of these powers," I say, "is the ability to share what is in our heads without speaking to one another."

I can tell from their reaction that I've piqued their interest.

"What am I thinking?" a young woman asks.

"I could tell you," I reply. "But you'd be ashamed of yourself." People do find this funny, so I grow bolder. "I need someone to come forward who wishes to have their thoughts exposed."

No one makes a move. This is not the time for them to act coy. "I promise it won't hurt," I say. "All I ask is for one person to come forward and tell Gabriel something about themselves, a secret, for example, or any bit of information I couldn't already know."

Finally, an old woman stands. She approaches Gabriel, hesitant.

"Tell me something," I hear him ask her. She glances at me, looking embarrassed, then leans and whispers in his ear.

Gabriel listens intently. His eyes widen. The woman finishes speaking and he hesitates before jotting her words down. "This thin bark I hold will carry her thoughts to Christophe," he tells our audience, then hands me the parchment.

I read the words quickly before lowering the paper. Looking up to the expectant crowd, I speak. "You're not able to enjoy intercourse anymore because your sex fell out of your body." I look at the woman, my face, I'm sure, flushed red from the words. She nods solemnly, and I can hear some of the people gasp. "Is there anything else you wish Gabriel and me to pass between each other?"

She shakes her head but reaches her hand out for the parchment. "There are strange markings on it," she declares to the crowd after studying it. "They look like the drawing of rapids in a river. That is all. Yes, they must have some kind of magic."

She goes back and sits down, looking proud for having been so brave.

"Does anyone else," I ask, "wish to have their thoughts travel soundlessly between the Black Gowns?"

A young man stands and whispers to Gabriel. When the writing is handed to me, I announce that he hopes to travel on next summer's trading party to New France. He nods solemnly and sits. A woman shares that her first child died at childbirth. An old man admits he no longer wakes hard in the morning, and people laugh. Before I know it, the Huron are jostling to have their thoughts told. In French, I call out to Gabriel and Isaac, "I think we have found a sure way to make them come to confession!" They laugh, and we continue to perform until I realize we shouldn't squander this new gift.

"The Black Gowns have grown tired," I announce. "We must rest now." Our sauvages groan out loud as one, clearly disappointed. "But you are welcome to visit us any time you like in order to have your thoughts carried on the thin bark between us."

When the people settle back in their places, some yawning now with the sun long set, the rumble of thunder emanates through the house. Several of them turn to one another, surprised. None of us saw any signs of rain this evening.

Lightning flashes brightly enough to make me blink even though the windows of our cabin are shuttered. People gasp. Everyone's awake now, sitting up. A few of the young men hurry to the door and pull it open. Outside, it's as still and hot as any of the other dry summer nights we've experienced the last week.

"Look at the stars! There's not a single cloud in the sky," one of them reports. The mumbling rises.

"Close the door," someone says, "but stay by it." The young man obeys. The room goes quiet.

Again, distant thunder rumbles and lightning flashes through the room. When instructed to, the young man flings open the door, and outside remains the same. When he closes the door again, it's immediately followed by the sound of rain tapping the roof, the rain growing in intensity to a ferocious pounding. People shove closer to one another as a cold draft enters. Over the roar of it, a man shouts, "Open the door!" He's barely audible over the pounding, but as soon as the young man swings the door open, the storm stops, the world quiet outside except for the sound of crickets singing. People gasp and chatter.

"Keep the door open!" an old woman commands. "We're being haunted by sorcerers!" Rather than these words calming them, people become more animated.

"It's the Black Gowns!" somebody shouts. "The charcoal are terrorizing us!" Faces turn to the three of us.

I shake my head and raise my arms. "We are not sorcerers! The Great Voice frowns upon magicians! This evil is not of our doing!" I scan the panicked faces for Gosling but can't find her. "If you wish to place blame for this sick magic," I shout, "point your finger at the sorcerer Gosling!"

More faces turn to me, some questioning, others confused, a few angered by my words.

"Where is she?" I shout. "Why does she disappear at the most opportune moment? This is not the doing of the Black Gowns. We come only to help you."

"Shall we close the door again?" someone shouts.

"Where's Gosling?" Gabriel cries.

"I am here," she whispers into my ear, her breath hot.

Gosling stands arched up to me, her face close enough that I can see the crinkles around her eyes. "I am here." She smiles wider. "Don't you forget," she says, "whose country you are in."

I can feel her hand stroke the small of my back, and I find myself fighting an erection so immediate I must place my hands in front of me.

"Don't ever forget where power comes from," she says, stroking my belly with her other hand. I grow even harder. "It isn't just from here," she says as people's eyes dart around the room and they wait for the next flash of lightning, debating whether it's safer to leave this haunted place or to stay.

She reaches the hand on my belly lower, and I try to stop her but moan instead. "Don't ever again think that our energy only comes from here," she whispers, slipping her tongue into my ear as she strokes her hand down the length of me and I start shuddering in spasms, my knees buckling. Lightning flashes and people all around me cry out and I cry out, too, falling to the ground.

When my convulsions stop, I see young and old Huron staring down at me. Gosling's nowhere in sight. The night has gone quiet enough that we can once again hear the crickets. One by one, the faces pull away, the crowd walking out of my house, some quiet, others muttering.

"He's a sorcerer, a witch."

"We've always known that about them, haven't we?"

"I'm afraid of them."

I listen to them all as if I have the hearing of an owl or a deer, the mumblings of these people I've travelled so far to save who are now frightened of me.

Gabriel's and Isaac's faces appear above and they pick me off the ground. I stand there, shaking, wiping my brow with my right hand, Your hand. I look into their eyes. "I'm sorry," I tell them. I am truly sorry, my dear Lord.

BE STRONG FOR YOUR OWN

Now that we're near home, I've sent Fox and a couple of others ahead to carry the news of our arrival. My own canoe is too heavy with the summer's bounty. After so long, my love, I've stumbled upon a chance to avenge your death and the deaths of our daughters in a way I never imagined possible.

I pulled out my three prisoners' fingernails myself, then cut slits in their necks and shoulders so they can't struggle against the leather thongs that bind them. As our pack of canoes wends along the high, rocky banks of the Sweet Water Sea, the wind in our favour, the sun hot on our chests, I daydream not of the next few days caressing our enemies with fire, my love, but of the fishing and the hunting that I will finally do when the leaves fall, the fishing and hunting that I will finally do without the torture of knowing your life might have passed without being truly avenged.

My prisoners have been taking turns singing their heart songs. Two of them I find very good, full of images of their lives, songs of their families and their women and their accomplishments and their hopes for where they're now heading. These two men are older, one nearly my age, and their voices are strong despite what they know comes, and they sing up into the sky with cries that are as pretty as any bird's. We've found our drumbeat, our prisoners and us, and any canoes within earshot paddle to the rhythm of their voices.

It's no surprise that the one whose song is weak is also the youngest.

The other two have been urging him to show resolve. He's not much older than a boy, though, and so doesn't have the experience yet to sing from his heart. He doesn't have the experience that creates his song. For a moment the other day, I caught myself trying to imagine what he now feels, so young, without the living necessary to navigate in his head what his body will soon go through. I had to stop myself from doing this, as there is no place for emotion of this kind in the next days.

Tomorrow will be our last day, and this evening we decide to stop earlier than usual. The sun hangs on the horizon of the big water, and its light, combined with the breeze, causes the poplar leaves along the shore to shimmer and dance. There's no rush to empty the canoes and set up camp. We're almost there. We pack and light our pipes and do the same for our prisoners, eight in all, for they deserve this much. All of us squat on our haunches on the shore and puff, no one talking as we watch the sun sink lower.

I will allow the younger warriors to do tonight's work as they rise one by one to their duties. This is my favourite spot, my sacred place where I came to do my fast and my quest for a name when I was not much younger than the boy prisoner. Do you remember that, my love? Even then we knew we were destined for each other. I remember paddling here alone, that when I left our old village I could feel your eyes on my back. I hugged the shoreline of the Sweet Water Sea, where sandy beaches gave way to rock walls. I didn't know my destination, only that I was told I'd recognize it once I saw it. Close to here is where I found those ancient drawings on the cliffs that rose up, drawings made with paints I couldn't grasp for their resilience. The old ones in the village had told me to watch for them, explained they'd been made by an ancient people who lived on this land long before us and knew far more than we did. Some argued they were the Anishnaabe, Gosling's people, others that they were related to us Wendat. Maybe tomorrow I'll slow my canoe for a time and find them again, point them out to my prisoners. I can still picture the outlines the colour of blood of a sea creature hovering below men paddling big canoes, a horned beast frightening me to my core. Yes, tomorrow I'll stop and show something important to the ones who will soon head to the place of dreams.

So close to home, the men are restless tonight. They build great bonfires and begin to dance around them, urging the prisoners, arms bound tightly behind their backs, to stand and dance, too. There's no meanness in this gesture. Our prisoners know as well as we do that if the situation were in their favour, they'd ask us to do the same. We celebrate the closing in on home, and allow them to celebrate their passage into the next world.

After the dancing, my three prisoners sit by my side. The oldest one leans to me. "We're not so different," he says. "And our nations aren't so different. We are all peoples of the longhouse, yes?"

I don't respond.

"All that the five nations of the Haudenosaunee wish is for peace," he says. "We don't hate you. It's the charcoal you've allowed into your homes that we despise." He then tells me that if we were to rid ourselves of them, the world might become a better place for all of us.

"And if we were to ask for peace with your five nations," I say, "what would the conditions entail?"

"We would take your women and children as our own," he answers. "We've suffered as wickedly as you and have lost too many to the sicknesses."

"And what of the Wendat men?"

"Well," he says, "those who can become Haudenosaunee will. And those who can't?" He shrugs. "I think you know."

"And so the Wendat will cease to exist?" I ask him.

He nods.

"This," I say, "is a peace we can't afford."

With a clear night and no threat of rain, we fall exhausted onto our sleeping mats with the stars shining down on us. We've camped close enough on a sandy spit of ground that the waves washing on shore fill my head with the promise of the coming dreams. I keep my three prisoners beside me and tell myself I will sleep lightly and remain vigilant. This night will be the last good chance for escape, and some of my cruellest war-bearers have been tormenting them about this all day.

As I sink into sleep, I awake to the moaning of the youngest one. I open my eyes and sit up, look down at him cast in the light of the fire. He's of a good build, thin but strong through the shoulders and chest and tall for his age. If he hadn't been caught, he might have made something of himself. I was particularly careful when removing his fingernails and slitting his shoulders. He's still so young as to be particularly adept at snaking himself out of his bondage. I'm worried I might have been too focused in my cutting. He cries out in pain once more.

Others around us begin to stir awake. I can tell my two older prisoners haven't closed their eyes all night.

"It's your fingers that hurt the most, yes?" I ask the young man.

He looks up to me, his eyes pleading. "Yes," he says.

"Be strong, you!" his relation hisses.

"Yes," the boy says.

"Do you know it's your very own clan who murdered my wife and daughters?" I ask the young one. He doesn't reply. "Do you know your two relations who lie here beside you have already admitted to taking part in that killing?" Again he won't respond. "The pain you feel now," I say, "is nothing compared to what you will begin to feel tomorrow when our people greet you at our palisades."

"I had nothing to do with killing your family," the boy says.

"Be strong for your own!" his relation spits.

"But I have nothing to do with that history," the boy whines.

"Be strong for your own," I, too, whisper. "Tomorrow, when you arrive at my home, you'll be greeted by a line of people who wish to meet you. It will just begin then. You won't sleep tonight," I say, "but you should rest and breathe in this fine air while you can."

The boy grits his teeth. "If you freed me from these binds," he whispers, "I would kill you now."

"You would try," I say. That's the spirit, young one! The heat of anger, I hope you soon learn, diminishes all the other hurts. At least, young one, for a short while, long enough, hopefully, to dampen the ferocity of what approaches.

AN ABOMINATION IN GOD'S EYES

I note the quiet departure of the women from the fields as they lift all at once, a flock of sparrows, from their duties. Gabriel and Isaac, bent to their weeding, haven't even noticed the exodus. At this very moment, my Lord, I realize I've begun thinking like one of them, like one of my sauvages, noticing immediately that the birds have stopped singing on this bright and sunny day, that the sounds of the grasshoppers have halted, that the women have left without so much as a whisper.

Fighting the urge to speak, I motion for my brothers' attention, the corn so high and dense all around me I suddenly feel smothered. The enemy who'd threatened to swoop in for the last months has finally arrived, ready for slaughter. I sense them through the green stalks, watching.

"Something's awry," I whisper to Gabriel and Isaac. "I fear an Iroquois war party is nearby. We must get out of the fields."

Gathering our few tools, we wind through the corn single file, my body tensed to run into a scowling warrior any moment, his thorn club raised to strike me down. Finally we emerge out of the fields, and it takes everything in my power not to run the last stretch of open ground to the gates of the palisades. It's on a day like this that I'm thankful the Huron are such master craftsmen, having protected the entire community with three walls of tall, sharpened stakes, a rampart built high from which sentries see everything around them.

Inside, rather than a sense of panic, though, people chatter and smile. A large group gathers near the central longhouse. My brothers and I deposit our tools by our door and go to find out what's happened. We see a face we haven't in a long time, surrounded by men and women alike, his hands raised in the air, gesticulating. Fox has returned at last from the summer trade mission, and I move closer to hear what news he brings.

He's come back a day ahead of the others, he says, and the mission was extremely successful. Someone mentions Iroquois captives, and I realize the Huron are bringing back prisoners and will soon partake of their brutal ceremony, one I've heard stories of.

That evening, after prayers and a simple meal of bread and thin soup, Gabriel asks me what he should expect. We sit out of range of poor Isaac, who doesn't need to hear this.

"These people are extremely imaginative in their torturing," I tell Gabriel. "As imaginative as any inquisitor ever was. Maybe more so."

Gabriel listens intently, his eyes urging me to go on.

"There's nothing random in their practice. Everything is intentional. This is one of their highest ceremonies."

"But why?" Gabriel asks. "Why do they wish to cause such pain to another human?"

"Why does the Spanish Inquisition do what it does?" I ask. "Why does our own Church burn witches at the stake? Why did our own crusaders punish the Moors so exquisitely?"

Gabriel thinks about this. He knows I don't beg answers for these questions.

"Of course it's easy to say that we mete out punishment to those who are an abomination in God's eyes," I say. "But it's more than that, isn't it? I think we don't just allow torturers but condone them as a way to excise the fear we all have of death. To torture someone is to take control of death, to be the master of it, even for a short time."

I think Gabriel wants to debate this further, but Isaac approaches, asking what we so intently discuss.

"Nothing of importance," I say. "I was simply expelling hot air." I pause for a moment before speaking my next words. "Dear Isaac," I say, "the Huron will apparently be bringing Iroquois captives home in the next days, and you know what they'll do with them. I understand if you don't wish to bear witness and try to save the souls of those poor wretches before they die. Gabriel and I, though, will need to be there for this very reason. Please do not feel obligated."

Isaac looks paler than usual in the dim light of the hearth. "I," he says, his voice shaking, "I prefer not to be present."

———

THAT NIGHT I SLEEP poorly, tossing on my reed mat with visions of Huron dancing around the fire and peeling the skin from their enemies. The tortured Iroquois beg me to help them, but when they open their mouths no sound comes out, their long hair, their faces becoming those of young European women, the fires growing brighter as they envelop the women's feet. I want to stand up and release them from their ropes but my body refuses to obey and soon I can feel the heat of the fires begin to make me sweat. In my tossing I can smell flesh burning, hear the screams for mercy as inquisitors gnaw the fingers from the charred hands of the women, as soldiers in chainmail slice new victims' breasts off with their knives and roast them over the same pyre they'll soon use to immolate them. This is when I grow angry with these soldiers, ordering them to be tied and burned at the stake in their armour so their bodies cook in the ovens of their own chainmail. I become the one who makes the decisions now. In these troubled half dreams I imagine the sweat that pours from me is blood when I realize I'm no longer a spectator but an accomplice, helping to hold down a young English soldier no older than a boy as he's burned with red-hot axe heads heated in the fire. And then it's my turn. I'm tied to a post and a woman with long black hair gapes me open below my chest bone. Reaching her hand in, she removes my heart, and, horrified, I watch her take a bite out of the still-beating organ. I jerk awake.

Someone has stoked the fire and I sweat through my nightshirt. I go outside and let the cool air calm me down. I know now that I must attempt to talk Bird out of what he plans to do.

SERPENT WITH A LYNX'S HEAD

We are up long before the sun, and I'm quite sure that no one's really slept at all. We're ready for the final push. With the canoes loaded with axe heads and kettles, glass beads, sewing awls, fishing hooks and strong rope, a few muskets and lots of powder and shot, our smartest dogs, and all the other bounty of a good trading summer, we put the prisoners in last, making sure their weight is distributed properly so that the canoes remain stable.

I also make sure they're tightly bound. I don't put it beyond my three to try and flip the canoe once we're out in the open water, as I would certainly do the same. Drowning is far preferable to the alternative. But they're calm, docile even as first one and then the others take turns singing their songs.

The sun will soon make its appearance over the trees on the eastern shore, but until it does we stay close to it, just far enough away to avoid the swells that wash onto the rocky beaches. The old ones tell stories of foolish young men overloading their canoes and paddling out in the hopes of crossing this big water, never to be seen again. The Anishnaabe tell us this water opens in turn to even bigger waters and then to a great inland sea. The world amazes me with all that it holds. I keep looking for the rock wall and drawings, hoping we won't miss them in the darkness that soon will break.

As if it's been destined, just as the sun hits the water and the sky lightens, the cliffs come into view. I turn my canoe to them, the other men adjusting their strokes to mine. There's no need to speak out loud. As the nose of the canoe heads for shore, they understand what it is I want to do.

We have to come in through the sharp rocks carefully as it only takes a nick to puncture the bark keeping us afloat. I have a young warrior hold the canoe steady and off the rocks while I take my other men and the prisoners up to see the drawings. The rest of our party's kept going, but for now I don't worry about catching up with them.

"This is where I found my secret name," I tell them on a thin outcrop that leads us above the water. For a few moments I worry this isn't the location as we continue up the cliff. I fear looking weak and foolish. But then ahead we see the first drawings, just a few etched into the rock in blood-coloured ochre, one a scene of a canoe full of paddling men, another of a moose, and another of a strange human with a deer's head. I lift my finger and trace the outlines. When I place my palm flat upon the rock, it feels as if my hand sinks into the stone, as if I enter another world through its hard shell. My hand glows hot with the touching, and as I close my eyes I see the old ones paddling and singing, followed by a water snake, one longer than their canoe, the paddlers unaware of it. The world my body's entered is as real as this one, bathed in light.

When I finally take my hand from the rock, I urge the others to do the same to see if they, too, experience what I do, if they, too, enter into another world when they touch the cliff. My young warriors awkwardly explore the paintings with their fingers, covering up their embarrassed laughs with coughs when I ask if they feel light or heat or cold on their hands or in their bodies. But Tall Trees, he's different. It's clear he understands what I experienced, that he experiences it too when it's his turn. I watch his face go slack as he drifts into the other place. I'm happy for this, happy to know I have someone who might one day be close to a son, someone I'll be able to entrust with my life. I'll tell Fox about this when we have some time to ourselves. I nearly remove one of my prisoner's bindings but then think better of it. As much as I'd like to see if they feel what we do, I realize it's best not to.

Instead, I lead the group farther along up the rocky bank to bigger life-sized drawings of more men in more canoes, and there, below them, the water creature that has haunted me all these years. It's slightly different than I remembered it, still a snake, but horned, and not a water snake at all for he has the head and teeth of a lynx. We stop and gaze at this drawing above us. No one speaks. These figures are older than we can imagine and yet remain so sharp and clear. I look to the prisoners and they all look as well.

Breaking the silence, I tell everyone we must paddle hard to catch up to the others. I let all of them start back down but pause for a moment to look once more at these pictures. Knowing for certain I'll not ever see them again, I burn the images into myself.

———

BEFORE WE CAN SEE THEM, we know they're there. We can hear the chattering of excitement through the trees.

"Be strong," the older ones say to the boy. "It'll get difficult now."

I've been asked to lead our trading party to the palisades and can feel the desire of the men following me to be home. This is the largest group I've ever known to make the journey. We gifted our neighbours, the Arendahronnon, who travelled so far with us, five of the Haudenosaunee prisoners, and I imagine they're at their village by now and in the midst of their ceremony. With these three who walk just behind me, we'll soon partake of our own important ceremony, love, one that will dry our tears and remind us of where we all must journey.

As I break out of the trees, I can see the men we left behind have made good progress in clearing more fields, and the women have planted them well, the corn so high it blocks my view. I weave through the three sisters in their mounds as the din of those awaiting our arrival grows stronger and stronger.

Nervous my three captives might try to make a desperate last escape, I've tethered each of them to a trusted war-bearer. The voices grow louder as we weave through the field, me following the sound of them, my people, for guidance. To show those behind me that I'm not overcome by emotion, I stop by a stalk of corn and pull one to me. I peel back the green husk and inspect it for insects and then sniff it. Finally I take a nibble from its tip before gently slipping the husk back in place.

And then the palisades of my home scratching the sky just ahead of me appear through the fields. My people know we're here and they've obviously been teased by dear Fox that we bring many gifts for them, and the voices are so close through the three sisters that I speed my walk just a little, breaking through the last of the crops before the sight of all my relations. All of my people stretch out before me, their voices roaring like big rapids pulling me to them.

I try to keep a face of stone as I walk toward my people, who begin crying out now that they see what I have with me. They've already formed their rows, and I walk through them, the captives being held back until I reach the gates of the village.

Turning to my war-bearers, I raise my arms and wait for the din to quiet. "We've travelled very far this summer and it's been a good one. The Iron People from over the great water have renewed their ties to us and have promised this friendship is now permanent. Soon, you'll all see with your own eyes the riches we've brought back. This is a good friendship, and both parties have made many promises to keep it strong."

I look around me at my people. I smile. "But trade is not the only activity we partook of," I say. The people around me begin to murmur, some laughing, others growing restless and pushing to get closer to the front. "A group of Haudenosaunee foolishly believed our advance canoes were its own party." I pause. "Let me assure you of their surprise."

People laugh. I can feel them ready themselves for the release that I know has built up for so long. They'll have the opportunity shortly to rid themselves of the frustration of fear that's gripped them. And many will have the chance now to avenge the loved ones they've lost at the enemy's hands.

"We were generous with our cousins, the Arendahronnon, who accompanied us," I continue. "Many Haudenosaunee were captured alive, and we took our revenge as we saw fit. We also made sure to give our brothers a prisoner for each finger of the hand as a sign that our bond with them is strong. But we have kept these three," I say, motioning to the two men and the boy who stand silent and listening, their heads held high, "so an old but very deep wound might begin to heal. We've been engaged in this mourning warfare with our enemy for a long time. And this warfare says we can only begin to dry our eyes through their sacrifice.

"The oldest one of these three," I say, pointing to him, "has already admitted to being in the party that took the lives of my wife and daughters, as well as the lives of a number of your own." The people gaze upon him. "And so we will pay special attention to this one. We'll caress him as gently and for as long as he can stand."

The captive begins singing his song, his voice steady and beautiful. He raises his head to the sky and sings in a perfect quaver so that we all listen. I lift my arm to Tall Trees, who holds this one's tether. Tall Trees unties it, shoves the man toward the waiting throng. He walks toward us, his arms bound tightly behind his back, singing.

The first ones on either side are women, many of them old, some with sewing awls, others with flint or bone scraping knives. They close in and stick him in his legs and stomach and chest, slash at his back. He continues to walk with his head held up, singing evenly. Already I'm impressed.

Young boys dart through the women's legs with burning sticks they jab into the prisoner's thighs and buttocks. One of the braver boys lifts the man's breechcloth and tries to stab him there but he keeps walking as if the boy isn't even present, eyes focused as he fixates on something on the skyline.

The next group he walks through are young men, a few of whom wanted to join me on the trading party but I'd deemed them too young and inexperienced. As if to make up for that slight, they're especially cruel, so much so that as I watch them rain down blows on his head and shoulders with sharp stones and clubs I fear I might have to intervene quickly to keep them from killing him. But still he keeps his voice high and steady despite his legs buckling a number of times as he almost falls but somehow holds on to his step. He emerges from them with the blood pouring from him and filling his eyes so that he's blinded. Now he can only keep his direction from the jostling and the noise.

"This is for my brother who died at your hands!" a beautiful young woman shouts, emerging from the crowd and slicing deeply into his chest with a sharpened clamshell. I can see how the skin opens like a smiling mouth and the blood spurts out. The captive can barely keep his gait and his voice is no longer audible in the shouting, but still he finds his way to keep going, singing his death chant despite those who swing their fists.

Finally, as he stumbles close to me, I make the decision not to caress him yet. I will allow him to catch his breath and his fortitude before his next day or two unfold. As others approach and beat him, I see the Crow through the throng, watching all of this happen, fingering the glinting necklace of the splayed and tortured man he always wears on his neck, the very same necklace I remember coveting so long ago when I first led him to my home. The Crow's face remains thin but it's darker and he is taller than the others around him, his shoulders strong.

His expression isn't one of fear or pity or disgust but something almost like distraction, as if he'd witnessed this many times before and it holds no interest for him. He must sense I'm looking, for his eyes meet mine through the roaring people. We stare at each other for what feels like a long time. I'm impressed he looks so well, even though the hair of his head's mostly gone and the charcoal hair of his face begins to show the colour of snow. His eyes remain attentive. Sharp. Just before he turns away, he makes the strange sign that's his custom, and I realize I feel as if I'm looking into the eyes of an old friend.

MOURNING WARFARE

I watch Bird emerge from the corn as if born from it, his face painted and his head shorn on one side, the hair long on the other and shining in the sun. He walks with a slow, sure stride, wearing only his breech-clout. He's as dark as I've ever seen him from his summer voyage under the blazing sun, and the weeks of hard paddling and portaging have left him with the physique of a Roman god. He's an entity I've struggled to describe when I write back to France. He's as much a wild animal as he is a man. His eyes miss nothing and he speaks with the finesse and gravity of a philosopher. There's no wonder he seems to have gained such prominence in this place. At first I was left confused by the politics of these people, but Bird's growing importance has clarified for me that there are two types of leader here, civil and martial. As three Iroquois warriors appear behind him, each tethered to a captor, it's clear which sort of leader Bird has become.

The throng jostles and roars as the returning travellers come into view. The first two prisoners are men, similarly dressed in just their breechclouts but with unadorned faces. Their hair bristles in a high strip down the centre of their heads as is their fashion, and they walk proudly despite their arms being tied tightly behind their backs. I'm fascinated to see how they act as if their predicament is nothing new. But the third captive is little more than a boy, and despite his obvious attempts to appear brave, his eyes are wide with fear and even from here I can see him shaking.

While the others hold back, Bird walks slowly through the throngs of villagers, who part neatly for him. I am near the gates to the palisades and he stops and raises his arms not far from where I stand. Hundreds and hundreds of Huron crowd the gates on either side. The din hushes. Bird speaks.

He tells the village that the summer's trade was especially good and how happy he is that everyone will benefit, and he speaks of how he has made stronger bonds with the French. For this I am pleased. And then he turns his attention to the prisoners, explaining how they foolishly mistook his advance party for their own force and how these Iroquois were so easily overrun. Bird mentions the celebration afterward in which many Iroquois prisoners were tortured and killed. He then shares the shocking news that one of the captives, the oldest one, if I understand correctly, had a direct hand in killing Bird's family.

The prisoners are then released, one by one, into the seething crowd that has formed a gauntlet. Everyone is involved in the ferocious beatings that ensue, old women, children, all ages of men. Some simply use their fists and feet while others reach out with sharpened clamshells and burning sticks or knives. Throughout the whole ordeal each of the prisoners sings and chants in voices high and wailing, and to each of their credits, their voices remain strong until they're overwhelmed with what must be tremendous pain. I want to believe that the boy will be treated a little less violently, but the mob seems particularly focused on him. And yet this is only the beginning.

Once inside the village gates, the people quiet, and a few old women go to the prisoners, now lying on the ground and covered in blood. I expect the women to resume the torture but instead they revive the men with water and attend to their wounds, treating them as gently as they would their own sons. Evening is still hours away, and the ceremony is one of the night. People take turns visiting with the prisoners, and I'm shocked to see a couple of people actually laughing with one of them. I assume that inside Bird's longhouse, the preparations are being made. I approach the three men and kneel to them. They gaze at me impassively.

"Do you wish to live eternally?" I ask the oldest of them.

He simply shakes his head.

"Do you?" I ask the next one. He, too, shakes his head.

"And you, young one, do you wish for your soul to live forever?"

He turns to the older ones but they refuse to look at him. "Stay strong," one says.

The boy turns his head back to me, his eyes pleading.

———

WHEN THE MOMENT presents itself, I approach Bird, who stands in front of his longhouse. He's finally alone.

He looks at me. "I take it your summer was productive?"

I nod. "There are those who listen to me now," I tell him.

"I guess that's good," he says.

"What do you plan to do with your prisoners?" I ask.

Bird just looks at me as if to say he doesn't believe I'm that naïve.

"There are other options," I tell him.

"Careful where you tread," Bird says.

"Let them live," I say.

"Is that what your people do with your prisoners?" Bird asks. "You used to preach about how you wanted us to eat the body of your saviour, but I notice you don't speak of that anymore. I don't think it's your place to tell us what we should do. We've been given the opportunity to dry our eyes after such loss at their hands, and you would take that away from us?"

"What you plan to do is simple and utter brutality," I say. "And yes, my people practise their own form of it too, but that makes none of it right."

"You cannot change what will soon happen," Bird says. "We are at war. And what my people will go through tonight is mourning warfare. It isn't your place to try and change it."

With that, Bird turns and walks into his longhouse.

I DIDN'T WANT TO BE

When the crowd around the three captives has thinned, I sneak up as close as I can. They've been moved inside our longhouse for now, as Bird wishes them to be left alone. The late-afternoon light is fading, and it won't be long before the ceremony begins in the largest of the houses. I wonder if they'll all be tortured together or one by one. I hope it is together, for I don't want to go through days of this. I secretly believe no one else does, either.

I look at the men carefully to see if any are my relations. I don't recognize them, and as I am about to leave them, I notice the boy watches me. His eyes are desperate. He knows there's nothing I can do for him. I only hope he goes quickly but I imagine this won't be the case. I'm tempted to go closer to him, but then I see Bird looking at me from across the room. I head to him instead.

When I heard he was close to home, I didn't want to be excited. I simply didn't. But then I realized how much I had missed him, how much we all missed him during this summer of fear and anger. He's the calm one, the steady voice, the one with great strength. It's hard for me to admit I love him as I do you, real father.

He holds his hands out to me and I take them. He smiles down at me. "You've grown taller," he says. "You're growing up."

"Did you bring me back any presents?" I ask.

He smiles wider. "Now is that the only reason you seem happy I'm home?"

I nod.

He laughs. "You are a very funny girl." He looks around him. "Don't you still have that pet I left with you?"

"I do," I say. "But more and more he wants to be alone."

"You'll soon have to let him go back into the forest," he says.

"I know. Gosling told me this as well."

He looks surprised to hear her name.

"We've spent time together this summer." I hesitate before going on. "She's teaching me."

He raises his hand to his chin, then nods in approval. "She will be a good teacher for you." Looking over my shoulder, he says, "Now there's a strange sight."

My raccoon has approached the prisoners and, standing on his hind legs, stares at them as if transfixed.

I walk over and pick him up. "Leave them alone," I scold. I can feel the boy's eyes on me.

I go back to my father and hand him my pet. He weighs it in his hands. "He's grown as fast as you. Indeed, he'll have to go back to the forest," he says, lifting him up and looking at his sex.

"Why are you treating the prisoners so well?" I ask, looking over to them being given sips of water as their wounds are dressed again.

"They are the incarnation of my beloved dead family," Bird says, gazing at them.

He can see by my eyes I don't understand.

"Each of those three represent, for me, a family member I have lost," Bird says. "Aataentsic the Sky Woman enabled me to capture them and she allowed that their lives would be given to me as payment for what I've lost."

"Will your heart hurt less once you kill them?"

Bird thinks about this, and hands me back the raccoon. "A little, I think," he says.

———

THE FEAST IS THE biggest I've ever seen. The longhouse, despite its size, isn't nearly big enough for everyone who wants in. Because I'm Bird's daughter, I have a place close to the prisoners. They've been unbound and I glance at their hands, fascinated with fingers swollen twice their size lifting food to their mouths. I wonder what's happened to cause this but then remember someone mentioning their fingernails had been pulled out as soon as they were captured. It makes it far harder to try to do much of anything with your hands, never mind attempting to untie the leather knots holding you.

"Eat well," Fox's wife says to them, she and Fox on the other side of the prisoners, "for you will need your strength tonight."

They nod to her, and the oldest man smiles. "The food's very good," he says. One of his eyes is swollen shut. "It is much appreciated." The others nod in agreement, and the boy looks at me. His cheek bleeds from a deep gash, and Fox's woman reaches over to pat it with some moss. I can see that, despite his efforts, the boy's hands shake. Glancing to his plate, I see he's eaten very little. All I can do is look away. I'm not hungry, either.

Different people stand to speak, and they all praise these Haudenosaunee for their bravery thus far and for their excellent singing. Some, like Bird, speak of their loss at the hands of the enemy, and in particular at the hands of the oldest one, who holds his back straight and his head high, listening intently to every word. The warrior is called exceptional, and people take turns praising his great skills. Some speak of what they'll do to him tonight. I know that my own people, you, my real father, you yourself had done this to Wendat prisoners while you lived. But I was too young to witness it. Tonight, it seems Bird wants me to witness everything. I'm his adopted daughter, and to watch him do this to the people who were once my own is the final act of my truly becoming Wendat.

The whole time I feel the eyes of the boy constantly glancing at me. It makes me feel sick to my stomach that there's nothing to do for him. I don't want to watch him die. I don't want to watch any of them die. I don't like this at all and I think that when it begins I'll go away, far enough away I don't hear any of it.

People have stopped giving speeches, and the kettles are near empty. Looking at a smoke hole above, I see night's finally fallen.

Men begin to stand around the different hearths, clearing their voices, stretching up to the sky, waking themselves from their full bellies. A few start into a song I recognize, a good song about summer corn and Aataentsic trying to outsmart her good son Iouskeha but how in the end he wins and the harvest for the Wendat is good. They begin to dance around the fires once their voices find their pitch, their feet rhythmic, the women watching intently with faces that give no emotion. Others have picked up the drum and beat out the rhythm.

It isn't long before the three captives are asked to join in the dance. The crowd pays special attention now as different men pass by, offering their hands, urging the prisoners with hoots to stand up with them and partake.

The three rise as one and begin to pound their feet around the central hearth in time with the others, looking down at the ground and raising their arms like wings as they swoop and spin, joining in the song like it's their own. The boy loses his awkwardness and his fear, it seems, now that he dances. He moves gracefully, like a hawk drifting in slow spirals above me. Every time he dances by me, I do everything in my power not to reach out and touch his skin. The song builds in intensity, and all the men dance or sing or drum, the women keeping witness. I don't want this to end. The feeling in this place is that we are all of the same woman, Aataentsic, the flawed one, and that we have all tried to do as well as we could, but some have failed, and some have been unlucky, and some now control their destiny, at least for a short while, and some no longer do.

I watch the boy swoop and spin and sing, and as I sit mesmerized, an idea begins to form in my head, an idea so simple I begin to believe it might very well be pure enough to save him.

CARESSING

The two eldest take turns walking the length of the longhouse. They've been stripped naked and their hands are bound in front of them. The oldest one urges those who reach out to stab his legs with burning sticks to do a good job, to make sure they amuse themselves as they take their time killing him. The other continues to sing his death song and stares up into the darkness of the top of the longhouse. I've let the boy sit, bound tightly, at my daughter's request while I consider what she's asked.

I've made it clear to all that the prisoners must live until morning light so the sun bears witness to their death, as is the custom. First we will torture their legs only, before the caresses become more exquisite. These ones are tough, though, and we must make them cry out for mercy during the night or else we'll certainly face misfortune in any future battles with the Haudenosaunee. The eldest passes by me, and he requests I pay special attention to him tonight. He smiles. His eyes are blank. He's putting himself in a trance. I push him into the hearth so that he's forced to walk right through the fire. I can hear the skin of his legs sizzling. As the second man passes, I take my pointed, burning stick, and thinking about how you, my love, were tortured and scalped, I jam the stick deep into his thigh so his song stumbles from his throat.

When they've made enough passes that they're having real trouble walking, I ask them to lie down on hot ashes that have been spread at either end of the longhouse. Those who've come to participate and to bear witness act in a calm and orderly fashion. There'll be no drama or inappropriate behaviour. We'll continue to practise restraint all night, and word's gone out throughout the village that no one shall partake of sexual intercourse as a sign of respect for all involved.

Fox and I walk over to the younger of the two who continues to sing his death chant, the skin of his back stinking from the heat of the ashes upon which he lies. His chant has allowed him, too, to enter his trance, and it becomes my mission now to break him from it so that he begs. After untying the prisoner's hands, Fox takes one in his while I take the other, and we proceed to break each of his fingers and then, using a rock, the bones of his hands. When still he makes no sign of crying out, I take a burning stick again and insert it in his ear. I stand and ask a few women close by to take their turn. They wrap each of his wrists with leather cords that they rapidly pull back and forth until the skin beneath them ruptures. His song's barely audible now, but still he won't cry out. When the women are done they revive him with some cold water.

Fox and I head over to the other side of the longhouse and perform the same ritual on the older prisoner. Rather than sing, though, he remains silent, and we are particularly cruel in our breaking of his hands. When he doesn't react to the burning stick I've poked in his ear, I request a clamshell and cut off two of his fingers. So he doesn't bleed out, I coat the bloody nubs with burning pitch. Still he remains quiet. He's very good. They both are.

Once they've rested sufficiently, I tell the people to take their turns caressing the prisoners. People line up to cut the men's arms, their legs, their chests and stomachs. One extremely focused woman burns the genitals of the quiet man with a red-hot brand. But still, neither one will shout out.

While they still have the strength left in them, I have the captives stand again and do another pass through the middle of the longhouse. Their fortitude is extraordinary as people reach out to burn or stab them with thorns or bone knives or burning sticks. I can tell, though, with much of the night still to pass, they'll soon quickly wear out. Again they sit and this time are fed a little and given more cold water to drink.

Many of us use this time to go outside into the cool night air to rest and prepare ourselves for the next stage. The Crow and his dark-eyed helper approach me then, asking that they now be allowed to come inside. I'd refused their entry earlier as they had no valid reason and might interrupt or cause a scene. This Crow's been with us a long time but this doesn't make him one of us. I shake my head.

"Allow me this just once," he says. "Remember the words of the great leader Champlain when he asked that you treat us as if we were your own."

"Why do you wish to witness this?" I ask.

"I cannot lie to you, Bird," he says. "I wish for the opportunity to ask your captives if they'd prefer to come to the Great Voice."

I think about the strength of the captives, and how we still haven't been able to make them beg. "If you can convince them to come to your power," I say, "then it might very well change what I think of you."

Fox listens intently, understands my tone and allows the two crows to come inside.

Once the Haudenosaunee have steadied, we begin again. The eldest asks to walk the length of the longhouse once more, and amazed, we allow him to. Rather than remaining silent this time, he begins to sing his death song in a high and steady voice. Each of us in turn reaches out and hits or cuts or burns him. His body's beginning to swell, and he's losing much blood.

"I see that your canoe is leaking," Tall Trees says, towering above him. "Let me caulk it for you." He pours burning pitch onto the captive's chest wounds to stop the bleeding. Still, the man doesn't cry out. Instead he thanks Tall Trees through clenched teeth.

Walking on, his feet dragging now, he resumes his song. Near my hearth he doubles over, and I fear that with the last punishment he'll pass out or die, his head hanging close to the fire. He tries to straighten himself but then doubles over once more, his hands falling into the coals.

Too late, I realize what he's doing. He scoops up handfuls of coals and flings them toward the walls. The calm that's enveloped us erupts into panic as one dry wooden wall of the longhouse catches fire quickly. Fox shouts for water. The captive tries to rush out in the madness, but Tall Trees tackles him before he can get outside. He'd have had such little chance in the condition he's in, never mind his hands are tightly bound and badly burnt, but I continue to be impressed by his strength and now his cunning. People quickly put out the flames.

The other one's gone silent, and I worry he's already slipped away. I ask a few young warriors to douse him with cold water, and through the crowd they assure me he still lives.

"Make him sing his death song," I say, and the young men bend to their prodding with knives and thorns. The night has almost passed, and soon it will be time to bring them out to the sun. The captive's low wail echoes through the longhouse.

He's too weak to walk on his own, and so while the older one is allowed to rest, my young warriors carry this one around, pausing to give others the chance to take more vengeance on him. Your mother's sister, my love, removes a sewing awl from her bag and beckons the men over. They lower him to her, and she begins to stitch a gaping wound across his stomach.

"You are responsible for killing my favoured child," she says as she pushes the needle through his skin, looping the gut thread and piercing him again. "I don't want you to bleed to death just yet."

Everyone watches as the Crow kneels by him and makes the sign that is his custom. The brooding young charcoal with the face covered in hair hovers above. The Crow whispers to the prisoner, and I see that the Crow holds his sparkling necklace in his hand. He raises it to his mouth and kisses it, then lifts it to the Haudenosaunee's lips. His death chant grows desperate, and it's as close to his begging for mercy we've managed all night. It's obvious. He's truly afraid and he's maybe even remorseful, and in not very long he'll pass into peace. But still I'm amazed once more by this Crow, by the power he's learned to grasp.

We revive the older captive and he too is carried around to be caressed once again, his most painful wound also sewn shut by one of your own, my love. Both of them are tiring now, but despite our efforts, neither has begged for mercy. Our resolve is weakening, I can see, so I ask Fox to take a few men outside to prepare the scaffold and build the fires around it. Night will soon leave and the sun must be the witness.

The captives look more like skinned bears than men when I decide it's time to carry them outside to the fires burning in the fields not far from the crops. Morning won't be far away, and we have to ensure that fine line between pain and their death. To allow them to die before the sun's face witnesses it is especially poor behaviour and will only invite bad luck upon our heads.

The scaffold's as tall as a man and built underneath a tree. The young warriors lift the captives onto it and tie the tortured men's hands onto the limbs above so both are forced to stand for the final caresses and so the village can witness their final moments. Hundreds if not more have already gathered in the fields. A young warrior shows off by climbing the scaffold with a birch bucket and tells the prisoners they look cold before pouring scalding water over their heads.

With the sun imminent, I ask my warriors to take their burning brands and try to make the prisoners beg for mercy. Both have gone silent now and there isn't much life left to drain from them. The warriors insert the brands into the two men's orifices and when they still don't cry out, the warriors pierce the men's eyes. Still nothing. The sun's first rays begin to peek over the horizon. I nod, and my warriors use their sharpest knives to scalp the hair from the captives' heads, then pour burning pitch onto them.

"These two are the bravest men I have ever had the pleasure of meeting," I declare as the sun rises fully into the sky. "End it now."

Tall Trees picks up his club, climbs the scaffold, and proceeds to smash the captives' heads in. I watch young warriors make cuts in their own necks and line up below to allow some of the dead men's blood to drip into their bodies. In this way, they know the Haudenosaunee will never catch them by surprise. Others cut open the captives' chests and remove the hearts. They will roast and eat these, thus acquiring their courage. The people watch all of this silently. But tonight, when the sun sets, we'll all make the most terrible noises we can manage, to drive our enemy's spirits away from our village.

Fox leans to me. "That's over now," he says, trying to judge my mood.

"It is," I answer. I only wish it had brought me more comfort now that the sun's risen. "How do you feel?" I ask him.

He shrugs. "Tired. It isn't something I've ever enjoyed much."

"We weren't able to make them beg for mercy," I say. "This worries me deeply."

"There's still the boy," Fox says.

I'd forgotten that. "My daughter asked that we adopt him," I say.

"Will you?" Fox asks.

"You know I can't deny her anything," I tell him.

A NEW MISSION

Gabriel and I approach the scaffold once the mob's thinned. The sun shines on the two men who've been pummelled and cut and burned to the point they're hardly recognizable as human. I had so wanted one last chance to ask if they'd denounce the devil and accept the crucifix. Children run about with sticks to which strips of the prisoners' intestines have apparently been tied, brandishing them like flags. Groups of young warriors huddle around two fires, roasting what I assume are the men's organs. These are a ragged and brutal group, and I'm deeply confused how they at one moment can treat each other so gently and with unconditional love and then the next torture their enemy so horrifically.

I take a deep breath and then climb the scaffold, Gabriel behind me. I can feel the warriors watching, and I don't know if I'm breaking some unspoken law, but I refuse to let them stop us.

With Gabriel as my witness, I bless the eviscerated corpses and then pray over them. It's too late for baptism, and so sadly they can never enter Heaven. Given the stories of what they did to Bird's family, I imagine they've already passed through the fiery gates of Hell, a place that will make the last night's torture seem like nothing. Finishing my prayers, I take my crucifix in my hand and kiss it, reflecting on the tortures of Your only son.

Once we climb down, several young men surround us.

"What were you whispering to them up there?" one asks.

"I was speaking to the Great Voice," I say. "I asked Him to forgive these men their sins."

The warriors become upset with these words. "It's not up to you, charcoal," another says, "to beg forgiveness for our enemy."

"If we were in their place," another says, "they would've been just as careful. Probably more so. The Haudenosaunee like to take days with their tortures of us."

"An eye for an eye," I say to Gabriel in French. This further infuriates the men around us.

"What did you say?" one asks as they begin to jostle us.

"He must have just cursed us," another says.

Before I know it, we're on the ground, the men beating us. But as soon as it has started, it stops. The warriors bend down and pick Gabriel and me up, brush us off, and present us to Bird.

"They fell down," one of the warriors says to him. "We were just helping them stand."

"What did they do now?" Bird asks, looking amused. "Don't even tell me." He motions for Gabriel and me to walk with him. He leads us into the cornfields.

"I have news for you," he says. "I think it's good news. Our people have reached an agreement with your people. We've agreed to allow a large contingency of you to come to our lands on the promise you'll trade solely with the Wendat."

I see Gabriel smiles broadly. I can't remember the last time I've seen him do this. I realize I'm smiling, too.

"This is tremendous news!" I say. "When will they come?"

"Before the first snows fall," Bird says. "We made a deal with the Kichesipirini to guide them here, and if they're wise, they'll be leaving soon so as to arrive in time to prepare for the winter."

"We'll have to make room for them," Gabriel says. "I'm certain our small residence won't do."

"You don't understand," Bird says. "Enough of your people will be coming to form a small village. You'll have your own village."

I'm stunned. It's as if I've been living under a death sentence and now Bird has announced I'm to go free. I hug Gabriel. Bird stares at us flatly.

"This is incredible" is all I can mutter.

"Come to my house," Bird says. "Your people have sent packages for you."

———

ISAAC CAN'T CONTAIN HIMSELF when we tell him. Bundles lie upon the table and on the floor. Soon we'll open all our gifts.

"Do you see what happens when we place ourselves in the hands of the Lord?" I ask. "Throwing that feast and emptying our pantry was the right thing to do."

"Our own mission," Isaac says, his eyes glistening. "This means we'll be free of having to live like the Huron, doesn't it?"

"We'll build a mission that reflects our beliefs and our values," Gabriel says. "We'll lead through example, and the Huron will come to our ways. It's inevitable."

"Let's not get ahead of ourselves," I say. "Let's open the packages and see what's been promised before we make too many plans."

Our gifts, in part, consist of new robes and underclothes. This is a very welcome gift. Our old ones, full of mending stitches, are so threadbare, the coming winter was a daunting thought. Years ago I'd requested a new Bible, as mine has been soaked so often it's now twice its original size, and this, too, has arrived, along with a tin chalice, sheaves of writing paper, and pots of ink, all of it miraculously unscathed in the journey.

I've placed the letter I assume is from the governor of New France on the table and save it for last. Gabriel and Isaac look at it so often I finally give in to their silent wishes. It's indeed from him. I read it aloud:

"'I write in the hope that your health is good and that your mission of saving souls goes well. There's been much upheaval on the continent that I imagine you've heard little about, but I will spare the details. Suffice to say that God has smiled upon the great woman that is France as well as all of her dominions, and the powers that be have finally come to the understanding of the importance of our mission in the new world, especially the mission that you brave and loyal Jesuits have agreed to accept.'"

I read on to Gabriel and Isaac. The governor speaks of how Europe has become hungry for all things in this new world: the furs, the fish, the adventure and stories. I slow down when he explains that our journals that have made it back are being shared beyond the Church with the public, and these journals have captured the fancy of the aristocracy and even the common man, that our reflections on life amongst the sauvages have driven the public imagination. It's hard to absorb. I must stop reading for a few moments and take a deep breath. My eyes burn with pride and with joy.

"Our cry from the wilderness has not just been heard," I tell Gabriel and Isaac, "it has been answered."

The governor explains that benefactors in France have opened their purse strings now that we and England are at least at a temporary peace, and the furs and timber and fish continue to stream home from the new world. He proclaims us Jesuits the leaders in a new, important era and verifies what Bird told us this morning. A large group of men, all of them sworn as donnés who will abide by our laws and our beliefs, men who will live like priests but who have yet to be ordained, are travelling toward us as we read this. We are to build a small mission that will serve as a fortress of the faith in this dark wilderness, and we are to grow our flock from the surrounding Huron, for this will help guarantee the French continue to be masters of this land.

"Your courage and your fortitude," the governor finishes, "do not go unnoticed. We commend you for your undying duty. May the light of the Lord soon shine brighter upon New France."

SEASON OF WITCHES

I've already heard the stories of this passing summer, of how the Crow performed rites that brought rain and saved the crops and then he threw a big feast that ended with a frightening display of magic. His medicine's only been growing.

To further complicate things, I now find myself with a new child, one who probably wishes me dead after what we did to his family last night, this one who's not a child at all but a young man. When my daughter tugged at my arm, though, her eyes full of tears, and begged that we adopt rather than dispatch him, some small memory I thought was long gone awoke in me and I agreed. Now I'll have to work at making sure he becomes a family member. It shouldn't be too hard, as he knows what will happen to him if he doesn't ingratiate himself.

———

"A DECISION WAS REACHED between us and our brothers the Arendahronnon," I say to the crowd gathered before me, "to allow the charcoal their own village." The sun is high and bright. Far too many have gathered to fit into a longhouse. "I know we've been having this discussion for many seasons." People listen intently, but it's hard to tell what they're thinking. "The village will be small, and removed enough from our own so as not to interfere with our crops and our hunting and fishing grounds and our woodlots."

"And who made this decision without our counsel?" an older man asks, one who I recognize as a distant cousin and who once desired more power than he was ever granted.

"Please remember, cousin," I say to him, "the sheer size of our trading party this year. I chose it carefully, and virtually every family in the community was represented, and they agreed to this idea. And also, cousin, don't forget that our brothers the Arendahronnon were with us on this voyage, and they too found it a good decision."

I can tell he wants to say more, but he struggles for the words.

"Will Wendat be allowed to live there?" the young man called He Finds Villages asks.

"What Wendat would want to live there?" a woman answers, making many laugh.

"If one wishes to move to the village of the charcoal, I don't think anyone will try to stop them," I say. "It seems to me that only the very infirm or the very young or old tend to go to them."

"What I'm most afraid of," one of the elders says, "is they bring more of their diseases with them." People nod.

"Never mind their magic bringing drought and famine," another says.

"They'll be far enough away that this won't be an issue," Fox says. I'm glad for his quick thinking.

"And we must remember the reason behind their coming here," I add. "Their great chief has promised he'll deal only with us in trade and will take up arms against the Haudenosaunee if they call for a bigger war." I don't mention that after our latest skirmish, this is sure to come. "As I see it, this is a good agreement, and the benefits outweigh the risks."

Far more heads nod in approval, and some people even call out "Ah-ho!" I'd never wanted or thought, my love, that I'd be standing in front of my people arguing such important decisions, but it seems this is what I'm meant to do.

———

INSIDE THE LONGHOUSE, still blinded by the bright light outside, I hear a voice I don't recognize and one that I do. They speak in the Haudenosaunee language, not terribly different from ours, though I'm surprised my daughter still remembers it. She speaks to my new son. They don't know I've come in, and I feel guilty for listening in on a private conversation, but I need to learn.

"My father," she says, "is the bravest of men. He's a great warrior, and everyone who knows him loves him."

I'm taken aback by this and bow my head to listen more.

"He's the same one," the boy says. "I'm sure of it."

"How can you know this?" my daughter asks. She scolds her raccoon for pulling on her hair.

"Your father was a relation of mine," the boy says, and suddenly, I'm deeply confused. "The stories of his life and his death are everywhere back home."

She talks of her dead family as if they're still alive. At first, I don't know what to do, but as they discuss their possible kinship, I grow calm. It's simple. My child has been a complicated one from the start, and now that we've brought this boy into the longhouse, these complications grow like a summer thunderhead. I can't allow this to go on.

———

MAYBE IT'S THE COMMUNAL worry of what we're about to give the charcoal, maybe it's the season of witches, but as summer begins its slow turn to autumn and despite the crops' abundance and the promise of a gentle winter for it, episodes of unhappiness abound. A number of women whose men journeyed with me on the summer's trade have left them for others, more than a few of us have fallen sick, and now many claim they're the victims of the crows' sorcery. The elders watch this unhappiness persist, and I know they worry. The time of harvest is close, and it will clearly be a good one, so this general sense of unhappiness is a bad sign. The happiness of our village must be addressed.

The council summons Fox, and when he returns we sit and talk. He's been asked to venture to our cousins' land, the land of the Tahontaenrat, the Deer people.

"Take Tall Trees and a few other good ones with you," I suggest. "Haudenosaunee war parties might very well be wandering about and looking for revenge."

"If we move quick," Fox says, "we can get there and back in three days."

"Do the elders wish you to take news of the coming charcoal village?"

Fox shakes his head. "The one called Spirit of Thoughts has become very ill. She wishes the Deer's medicine and for them to put out word to the atirenda from all the communities to come to our aid. She dreamed that hers is the affliction of unfulfilled desires and this is what causes such unhappiness in the community."

That makes sense to me. She must feel the illness can become much more serious for all of us if she wishes the society of the atirenda to visit.

"I'd come with you," I say, "but I have to deal with my new son." I don't mention that Gosling has been calling to me since my arrival home. I need to pay her a visit.

"What's wrong with him?" Fox asks.

"I fear I made a big mistake. I sense great trouble in him and believe I'll have to break it to my daughter that he's not a good fit."

"Another sacrifice ceremony, then?" Fox asks.

"At first I thought we could trade him back to his people," I say. But Fox knows as well as I do that things are so bad between us all that even attempting to begin a barter with them seems impossible.

"That would be far too dangerous," Fox adds. "With our killing that war party on our travels, they'll be in no mood for trading."

He's right, of course. Although I don't want to go through with it again so soon, I will have to announce my intentions. Snow Falls isn't going to like it. I'll wait until after the curing ceremony to break the news to her.

———

TWO DAYS AFTER Fox's return, I hear drumming and rattling out in the fields. And then the singing starts, many, many voices raised high and strong. People in the village head to the gates of the palisades to answer the song. The atirenda, the practitioners of the medicine dance society, have come in full force, carefully painted and coiffed. Some wear masks of straw or carved wood, and others have created the appearance of physical deformity by stuffing bark or straw under their clothes so that they look like hunchbacks. These medicine people, the atirenda, they don't just come from the Deer people. They've come together from all our villages at the behest of the Deer.

We all sing, so many of us that it's a startling sound to hear, the village answering the atirenda's calls in a roar. If any malevolent beings are nearby, they've been fully warned.

The atirenda soon come in through the palisades, and the welcoming throng leads them to Spirit of Thoughts' longhouse. Those who are invited step inside, and I'm surprised to see the Crow there. I don't understand how he was offered such an honour.

For half the day the atirenda surround her, dancing and singing and shaking their turtle rattles, trying to figure out the source of her illness. They've been informed of her dream of an unfulfilled desire, one that she can't quite make out yet. These atirenda will help her find what it is. This is what they do.

I can tell from their growing pace that the dancers will soon begin their ritual. A group of them surrounds one of their own as if they're wolves and he is prey. One of the dancers throws something at him and he catches it, holding up in his hand what appears to be a bear claw. Another throws something else that he deftly catches. When he holds it up, we see it's the large wolf tooth. Someone else throws dog sinew at him, another a handful of stones, all of which the dancer in the middle catches.

And then he begins to go into convulsions as if he's been poisoned. The ones surrounding him step back to allow him to flop and squirm on the ground, grasping his stomach and his neck. Blood trickles from his mouth and nose, and soon begins to pour so that it splatters all around him. I look at the Crow. He's gone very pale. The rest of the crowd, including Spirit of Thoughts beside him on her reed mat, watches with silent fascination. When the bleeding man on the ground goes still, a few of the atirenda shake their turtle rattles and begin to dance again, slowly picking up the pace. The man on the ground is now silent, his head in a pool of blood. Others bend to the nearest hearth and pick up pieces of red-hot charcoal, holding them out to us. Three or four of them then place the charcoal in their mouths, chewing slowly before swallowing. They pick up more and this time after they've chewed they bend to Spirit of Thoughts and blow the powder from their mouths onto her body, another dancer following them and sprinkling water on her while still another fans her with the wing of a turkey.

As the dancing slows and Spirit of Thoughts closes her eyes, I look once more at the Crow, who makes the sign on his head and chest and shoulders with one hand, grasping his sparkling charm in the other.

The dancers and singers finally go silent and attend to the man on the ground, reviving him with some powder and forcing water down his throat. Groggy, he opens his eyes and moves his arms. They've taken him to that other place and now brought him back. In the morning, Spirit of Thoughts will hopefully see what the desire is that needs to be fulfilled.

WHAT'S RIGHT FOR YOU

I sit today in the fields with my new brother. He told me his name is Hot Cinder, but lately I've come to suspect he can't be trusted. I think his head went wrong when he watched his relations being tortured to death. I can't blame him for this. He says that whenever he closes his eyes, he dreams about his own torture and he can't stand it. He constantly puts his swollen fingers in his mouth and claims we're cousins but I know we come from different clans. He is Turtle and I am Wolf. We're from distant villages. He has nothing to prove we're related beyond his words. He swears, though, that he'll find a way to prove it to me. I think he's simply trying to ingratiate himself and become a part of this family. It's a survival instinct. I'm sure of it.

"I'll protect you," I tell him. "You need to find a way to sleep without dreaming. You need rest." I could tell him how I behaved when I first arrived here, contrary to everything and acting like a wild animal and pissing in my father's bed. He wouldn't understand, though.

Sleeps Long, now that she's recovered and her husband, Tall Trees, is home, spends time with us. Her son, Carries an Axe, has decided to ignore me. Sleeps Long freely admits Bird has asked her to watch over me in order to keep an eye on this new boy. I'm fine with it. I saved his life, but I don't think I like him. He seems weak in the head, and beyond that, is needier than my raccoon. In our first conversations a few days ago I wanted to believe he knew who you were, Father. I wanted to believe that you're still alive in the memories of our people. But the more Hot Cinder talks, the less I trust him.

"I come from a family of hereditary chiefs," he says as Sleeps Long busies herself grinding corn, but I can tell she's listening. He leans to me and whispers, "I fear they'll want to take revenge."

"Of course they will," I say. "This is the cycle."

"But it will be against my new father," he says. "Your father."

Sleeps Long puts down her pestle and turns to us. "This talk only invites unhappiness," she says, looking at Hot Cinder. "Maybe it's best if you listen for a while instead of talking."

He looks down at his feet. "I'm sorry," he says, and places some of his fingers back in his mouth.

———

SINCE THE ATIRENDA came to visit, the people's mood has become more peaceful. Even Hot Cinder is calmer and doesn't talk all the time. He's become fascinated by the raven hanging above my sleeping place and constantly asks about it. "It's my charm," I say. He tells me he wants one as well, and though he's a few seasons older than me, I have to explain that he'll need to find his own charm.

———

IN THE LONGHOUSE, my raccoon has gotten into Fox's pouch and pulled out his tobacco while looking for food. I stuff it back in his hide bag as my raccoon climbs down from the rafters and onto my shoulder. Hearing footsteps and fearing that they're Fox's, I turn to see my father in the doorway.

"Come walk with me," he says. He looks serious, and I worry that he knows I followed him the other night when he awoke very late and stole over to Gosling's lodge. I wish the two of them would stop sneaking around and act like a normal couple. I don't understand why they don't.

"Daughter," he says as we stroll through the village, my raccoon playing with my hair, "you know there's been much unhappiness in the village this last while."

I nod.

"I think the root of it lies with our bringing the crows here." We keep walking, heading toward the palisades. "The visit of the atirenda was good for everyone, I think. Spirit of Thoughts is well enough that she can sit up and talk, but she's still weak."

We go through the gates toward the three sisters. I can tell there's something he needs to say, so I stop walking. "Tell me," I say.

He looks down at me with his head cocked and his eyes narrowed, as if he wants to ask how I know what he's thinking. Men are so easy to see into.

"Spirit of Thoughts dreamed that in order for the healing to begin," he says, "she must have a feast."

I like feasts and tell him as much.

"Her dream told her," Father continues, "what needs to be consumed at the feast."

I'm excited to hear.

"Her dream told her that all the animals of the village except the dogs will be consumed."

The raccoon chatters as if he finds this funny. "I'm letting him go tomorrow," I say, lying.

"We have to listen to her dream," he says. "We can't lie. It won't do any good."

"But he ..." I look for the word. "He's my friend." The raccoon, as if agreeing, pulls my earlobe.

"I'm sorry," Father says, taking him from my shoulder.

———

SLEEPS LONG EXPLAINS once more that sometimes the needs of the group are more important than those of the individual. I don't want to hear it. She rubs sunflower oil into my hair and I cry into my hands as we prepare for tonight's feast.

"I hate feasts!" I say. "I hate people!" They've killed my raccoon and now they expect me to join them in eating him to fulfill the dream of an old woman who clearly hates me.

"Don't cry, Snow Falls," she says. "You were soon going to have to release it into the forest anyway." She hesitates. "I imagine it wouldn't have lasted long once you'd done that."

This only makes me cry harder.

THE BOY NAMED He Finds Villages who sits beside Christophe Crow and now goes by the charcoal name Aaron keeps glancing at me as we all sit in Spirit of Thoughts' longhouse. I refuse to eat. I don't care. I want to scream at He Finds Villages to stop looking at me. He smiles. I curse him in my head and look away.

The stews, the old woman announces, contain bear and blue jay, snake and squirrel and goose, rabbit and frog and dove, and raccoon. I wish, when she says this, that she'd not gotten better.

"My dream told me," she says, "that we needed to rid ourselves of our pets. And just look at how many of them we kept!" She points at the many full kettles.

People all around me laugh at this.

"We, in our home, need to rid ourselves of our pets," she repeats. "This was my dream. We are sick and we need to allow our houses to become clean again. We need to rid ourselves of those guests we once thought were welcome additions to our homes but that have soiled it with their ways that are not ours."

I look over to He Finds Villages because I know his eyes are still on me. He tries to tell me something with them but I look away, turning to the face of Christophe Crow instead. Christophe Crow's face is the colour of blood beneath his charcoal beard as he himself watches Spirit of Thoughts.

My father nods to my untouched bowl. Sleeps Long whispers to me that I need to at least make the effort of pretending. No one else seems to notice, but I imagine they do.

"I can assure you," Sleeps Long says, "the kettle from which your bowl was served doesn't contain your raccoon. It's clearly a bear stew."

I look at her. "Do you promise?"

She nods. "Have you ever known me to tell an untruth?"

I will trust her, then. I lift my fingers to my mouth and eat a little. Father seems to breathe easier. I eat from my bowl very slowly, so slow that I'm just finishing it by the time the kettles are scraped clean.

Father stands to talk. He thanks Spirit of Thoughts for her hospitality and then says that he has a very important announcement to make. He looks down at Hot Cinder, who immediately places a couple of fingers in his mouth. The swelling has gone down but the nails haven't started growing back in yet.

"I've thought hard about this," Father says. "And I've made a decision about my new son. I've decided that more sacrifice is necessary."

Hot Cinder begs me with wide eyes to once more save him.

"To show the generosity of our people, I'll send Hot Cinder to live with the charcoal in their new village. I hope he helps lead them to a good place."

I'm relieved. Clearly, so is Hot Cinder. People turn to each other and discuss this, many of them calling out Ah-ho! Christophe Crow looks pleased. He smiles at the boy, and the boy looks back at him. I'm happy about this decision. The idea of keeping him around had begun to bother me. I much prefer being alone. Fox leans to my father, and I can hear him whisper this was a wise and good decision.

Once the feast has broken, I walk out into the night, lonely for my raccoon. People will be up early tomorrow, as word has come that if the weather holds, the Iron People from far away will be arriving. Soon we'll begin harvesting the three sisters and the men will head out into the forests and to the lakes for their hunting and fishing. Christophe Crow and the others will leave us very soon to build their new village before the seasons turn. I realize then I will miss him.

I'm nearly at the palisades when I sense someone following me. I stop and turn, half expecting to see Gosling. Instead, I come face to face with the boy.

"What do you want of me, He Finds Villages?"

"Call me Aaron," he says.

"What do you want, Aaron?" I like the way the name sounds on my tongue.

He holds a large hide bag out to me. "I brought you a gift before I leave," he says, and only then do I realize both he and Hot Cinder will be going with the crows.

"I don't want anything from you," I tell him.

"I think you'll like it," he says. "I promise."

Hesitant, I take the bag from him. It squirms and I almost drop it.

"Open it," he says. "Don't be afraid."

With one hand I loosen the tie and slowly pull it open. My raccoon pops his head out and chatters to me, climbing out of the bag and onto my shoulder.

"How?" is all I can ask, for fear of crying.

"I was put in charge of killing and skinning the animals for the feast," Aaron says. "Spirit of Thoughts hoped this task would encourage me to stay with my family instead of leaving with the charcoal. I recognized your raccoon and hid him away for you."

I want to hug him. "You've made me very happy," I say.

He moves closer, as if to touch me, but instead says, "I should go now." He walks away.

"I'll come to visit you in your new village," I call after him.

———

OUT IN THE DARKNESS of the forest, I sit with my raccoon as we say our goodbyes. "Be strong out there," I tell him. "Protect yourself and find a good woman. Have a family."

We sit together for a long time and I think he understands what's happening. "I can't keep you in the village anymore or people will know and you'll be eaten. This is what's right for you." The raccoon pulls my hair, then reaches a paw to my face. "It's time for me to go now," I say. "Father will be worried, and soon the sun will come up. You need to find a good place to hide for the day."

Standing, I hug him one last time, smelling the wild in his fur, stroking him. I bend down and set him on the ground, and then, as an owl hoots not far away, I leave him and head back for home.

CAPTAIN OF THE DAY

In these seventeen months that have passed, dear Superior, life here in the new world has become something quite different, startlingly different now that we live by our rules and laws and customs in our own village. The donnés have truly been a godsend. Two dozen good-natured and hard-working men who live by the Gospel and require little have begun for us what promises to be a well-fortified and complete home. The dozen lay brothers who have arrived have proven themselves more than up for the task of helping to plan excursions out into the land of the Huron, and we even have a group of ten soldiers wintering with us before they make the journey back to New France in the spring. And so we feel very protected and, if not exactly comfortable, at least like civilized Frenchmen again.

There is talk of more arrivals in the coming summer, including the much-anticipated blacksmith and livestock. I find it amusing to picture chickens and pigs making the treacherous and trying trip in sauvage canoes.

On a separate note, we three Jesuit brothers, when not working to help carve a community of light out of the darkness here, have continued to go out on missions to preach the word of God. While the Huron of the Bear nation, the people who kept us in their community for so long, seem satisfied to see us again when we visit, the people of the other nations, with names such as Deer, Rock, and Cord, seem far less hospitable. Apparently, outbreaks of influenza have come to them and they blame us for their troubles. But still, we soldier on despite the very real physical danger to us. Threats against our lives have been numerous, and poor Père Isaac, already having suffered so cruelly, was beaten yet again by people who claim to be our allies. Thus far, Père Gabriel has avoided physical violence but has said many times that he welcomes it if this is what the Lord desires. I can't imagine having better friends and brothers to help me bear this particular cross.

I put down my quill and rest my hand. Looking around me at this room, a fire burning in the hearth and sitting in a proper chair at a table built by the hands of a carpenter, I can almost imagine I'm back in the French countryside at a peasant's home.

Despite the snow blowing outside, I feel the need for air. Another blizzard seems to be coming. The snow's already drifted as high as the palisades, but at least this offers a windbreak. The sun at this time of year lies low on the horizon, and the light filtered through cloud makes me melancholy. My feet crunch on the icy surface that is my new home, and I bend my head to the bitter wind that comes off the Sweet Water Sea.

We're close to the water here, and just a day's walk from Bird's village, which is even less by canoe. I trudge along the path that will soon disappear in the whiteness and try to imagine in my mind's eye what this place will become. Already we have built permanent stone-and-wood structures. A chapel, a carpenter's shop, a refectory for the donnés and laymen that serves both as a kitchen and communal eating place, and even a granary for the farmers. We've allowed our sauvages their own separate residences on the other side of the community, and here they've built longhouses and a few smaller round residences for visitors. We've attracted not only Huron but also Algonquin and Anishnaabe as well. We've made the rule that there be a Christian longhouse and a non-Christian longhouse separated by a fence, and intentionally the Christian longhouse is larger and sturdier. Many families have come to us this last year, and our converts now number two dozen. But just as many non-Christians have come to our door asking for handouts. We cannot turn them away and daily appeal to them to accept our faith.

When the weather allows, I'll head out into the wilderness to collect more souls. I've debated this with Isaac and Gabriel, who are content to stay here in the safety of our new home and wait for the sauvages to come to us. I argue that we must continually make forays into Huron country in order to show them we aren't afraid of the physical or demonic dangers of their world.

I walk to the refectory to see who might be about. After stamping my feet at the door, I'm greeted by a large fire in the hearth and men sitting around the table. The laymen are a bit of a rough group, and they don't like to mix with the sauvages.

"Good day, Father," one says. Others nod and greet me as well.

"Have you seen Isaac or Gabriel?" I ask.

They shake their heads and look away. While on the surface they are respectful, I often sense some bitterness, possibly anger toward me. I'm not sure where this stems from, as I've only treated them well. I must assume this unhappiness is born from suffering a long winter cooped up like livestock in a barn. That, and the hard reality of having landed in such a desolate place with only a slim chance of ever seeing home again. So be it. You have a plan for all of us, Lord, and we're here to fulfill it.

As I walk outside, the young Iroquois once called Hot Cinder and whom we've baptized Joseph frightens me by jumping out from behind the wall of the refectory, grinning foolishly. I think he lost something that horrible night he witnessed his relatives tortured so cruelly.

"What will we have for supper, Father?" he asks.

"We will eat sparingly, Joseph," I say, "for there is still much winter to survive before we can grow crops again."

"Aaron has been treating me poorly," the boy says. He pronounces Aaron's name with the guttural inflection of his people. "He says my mind is weak and I need to leave him alone."

"Where is he?" I ask. Aaron has become my first true victory.

Joseph looks away, his sign to me he doesn't know or won't tell.

"Well, then, do you know where Delilah is?"

"She was in the longhouse sewing when I last saw her," Joseph says. He puts a few fingers in his mouth, a habit, I assume, from when Bird pulled out his fingernails. It clearly gives him comfort. Despite the bitter cold, he wears only a hide tunic and leggings. I've asked him before how he can stand such cold in so little and all he says is that he can feel the fire that burned his relatives.

"I must go to see Delilah," I say, walking toward the longhouse.

"I will come with you," Joseph says.

"I'd prefer if you stay here." Though it's not his fault, with this boy my patience reaches the breaking point after only a few short minutes. I must strengthen it, dear Lord, and promise to start practising tomorrow. "Why don't you go to the eating place and visit with Captain of the Day?" I say.

His eyes light up, but then he frowns. "The hairy men will send me away. And if I don't listen, they'll hit me."

"Tell them you're there on my instruction," I say. I head to Delilah's longhouse.

To our communal surprise, she journeyed with us to this new place based on her promise so long ago to convert if that might save her family. But Delilah is unreliable at best and misses her family so much that she's sunk into a relentless sadness. Even my promise to bring her along on our next expedition to her home does little to lift her spirits.

Again, today, once I've entered her longhouse, she cries as she speaks. "I will die and never see them again," she says.

"You will," I explain, "if we can win them over to our side." This tactic hasn't worked yet, though. I look around at the other Huron huddling by their fires. They look frightened and hungry. A few children cry.

"There's been much stomach illness," Delilah says. "The children soil themselves numerous times a day, and I fear it's spreading to the adults as well."

"We'll make sure you have the medicine we have," I say. "But the most important thing I can give you is to tell you that you must continue to put your belief in the Great Voice. He knows all. And He will not let you suffer if you put your trust in Him."

Delilah stares at me. She wants to tell me something but won't.

"Tell me," I say.

"I want to go home," she says. "But now I can't. Even if I could I would only bring back the sickness we've begun to suffer and kill those I love." She holds in a sob.

I want to scold her for the silliness of her thinking but instead allow her to go on.

"And now because I made a promise to you, I feel like I'm being caressed with hot coals. I've made a great promise to you and I won't break it. I worry, though, that my promise to you has not only doomed me but also doomed the ones I wish to be with forever."

I open my mouth to speak, but she stands up from the fire.

"I don't request a discussion," she says. "I only wish to do what you ask of me." She's about to walk away but hesitates. "Something very bad is coming," she says. "I fear it's already here. What comes will be the end of us, and of you. But my dreams tell me this is what you hope for."

I'm stunned by her words. I stand up, feeling light-headed in the smoky longhouse. My stomach suddenly feels sick. Before I throw up, I claw my way through the haze and burst out the door.

———

"THE SAUVAGES," Gabriel says at the dinner table, "have no under-standing of manners, but I'm convinced my experiment with them will work."

Isaac and I, along with several laymen and donnés, listen intently. It's indeed true that no matter how often we tell them they can't just barge, as is their custom, into our residence at any time of the day or night, they ignore us. The donnés are growing short-tempered.

"Have you noticed their fascination with that clock?" Gabriel asks.

A gift from a sponsor so far away to remind us that our time in this world is short, it's a simple enough piece with an unadorned face, sitting squat on the mantel, ticking out its rhythm. I'm amazed it made the near-impossible journey at all, never mind in working order.

"They think it's magical," Gabriel says. "Their simple minds believe it's possessed of a spirit. They say it has a soul, a magic like none they've ever seen before."

The men laugh at this.

"They have more faith in that clock than they do in God. And so I've been using it as an experiment."

"Tell us, please," one of the donnés says.

"I've been experimenting with Joseph. He's probably the worst of the lot, coming in at all hours to disturb us with his chattering."

Several men nod.

"But he's especially fascinated by the clock. I've told him its name is Captain of the Day and he must obey it. When the clock's about to strike the hour, I pretend to command it by shouting, 'Speak to me, Captain of the Day!' and when it does, Joseph nearly falls over in fear and amazement. And depending on the hour, right before the clock sounds out its last note, I command it to stop." Gabriel smiles. "And then I tell Joseph that the clock says it's time for him to leave."

"And does he?" another donné asks.

"With great speed," Gabriel says to a burst of laughter.

"But this must serve as more than simple trickery for our amuse-ment," I speak up. "Why not use it to teach them about God?"

When one of the donnés groans loudly, I give him a stern look.

"We will use the clock," I say, "to bring them to Mass in the morning and the evening, and also to call them to supper. But if they don't obey when it's time to go to Mass, then the Captain of the Day will tell them that they don't get any supper."

The men seem to like this idea.

"And when it's time for them to leave and give us some peace," Gabriel adds, "we'll tell them the Captain of the Day is commanding them to go home."

"We shall put this experiment into effect immediately," I say.

———

THE WINTER CRAWLS, its brutal cold growing through the month of February. The illness that so many of our sauvages suffer shows its ugly face to us as well. I worry it's influenza with its high fever and vomiting and diarrhea. Whereas the donnés suffer it for a week or two and then tend to get better quite quickly, a number of the Huron end up dying. I'm losing my flock just when it was showing signs of growing. Isaac and Gabriel and I perform eight last rites over a two-week period, all of us suffering the fever now as well. The earth is frozen too hard for us to bury the corpses, so we store them in one of the temporary shelters built for visitors.

Despite this setback, those who remain well enough to walk continue to visit the Captain of the Day, their only amusement in an otherwise bleak winter.

These beleaguered people, especially the children, wait patiently, often for a full hour, to hear it chime out to their wonderment. Gabriel has devised a system in which the clock will speak when it's time to go to Mass, or heat the kettle, or go home. For now, it works brilliantly.

Today, I watch the flock await the chime that announces the evening prayers, many of them sweating and coughing. I've person-ally taken stock of our storehouse and must put my faith back in

You, my Lord, to provide what we need. Spring seems as far away as sweet France, the wind howling and snow battering the shutters of the refectory.

Aaron wonders aloud if he might have permission to ask the Captain of the Day a question when he next speaks. Gabriel looks at me and I shake my head. We're not about to play soothsayer or create false idols. When I tell myself this, I can feel my face blanch. Lord, is this experiment corrupt? Steadying myself, I clear my throat. I mustn't let exhaustion and fear begin to dictate the preordained course. This clock, designed by a man who in turn served You, could well be the key to bringing these wretches to the gates of salvation.

"Listen to me carefully, my dear ones," I tell them. "The Captain of the Day that you see in front of you is only just one tiny part of the magic that is the Great Voice. He is the simplest little stick in the very big longhouse in which the Great Voice lives." They stare up at me as they huddle, shivering, on the floor. "The Captain of the Day tells you when he speaks that you must believe in what the Great Voice asks you to believe. He does not feel that he should enter a dialogue with you now. He tells me," I say, pausing and pointing to the clock, watching their thin faces turn to it, "that he speaks for the Great Voice. And so when you hear the Captain of the Day call out, he is telling you that the Great Voice waits to speak with you when your body stops and you go into His world."

Joseph takes his finger from his mouth. "So we must die in order to hear the Great Voice?" he asks.

I nod. "To fully hear Him, yes, you must."

"Well, I hope this voice is a really good one," someone mutters, and a few others laugh and cough. Even in their sickness, they still feel the need for levity.

"His is a very good voice indeed," I say.

Gabriel shouts, "Captain of the Day! Speak to us!"

The clock chimes five times.

"What did it tell you?" Joseph asks.

"The Captain of the Day told me," Gabriel says, placing his finger on his chin, "that now it's time for you all to stand up and go home for the night."

THE BEAST THAT TRACKS US

This winter of the new illness has pounded us into the ground, but the ground is too frozen to bury our dead who begin to pile up in lifeless longhouses. We are being consumed alive by an invisible animal, one that slips into our lungs and makes us splatter blood when we cough, one that turns our eyes the colour of burning coals and our throats so swollen we can no longer swallow. Each house shutters itself to the winter storms battering it. Each extended family uses this as an excuse for not opening our doors and letting our neighbours come inside. What we truly fear is the beast that tracks us. What we fear is that he hides in our friends' clothing or even in their breath. I watch as these families shake with chills and then feel as hot as if a fire burns just under their skin. The medicine people take turns coming through the longhouses with their turtle-shell rattles and powders, but even they are unable to stop this animal from its task. And now the animal has slithered into my home.

I've kept a close eye on Snow Falls for any signs of soreness or cough, but she appears to be fine. I urge her to drink tea made from the roots that Gosling gives me. I urge everyone to drink it, but there is only so much and Gosling can't possibly find any more in deep winter. It's my brother, Fox, who first begins coughing, suffering a fit late in the night when the sound of it jolts me awake as surely as the footsteps of a Haudenosaunee. I imagine everyone's eyes snapping open when he coughs again in his sleeping place near to mine. His wife whispers to him and he mumbles something back but ends up coughing even more. I try to sleep when he settles but I can't the rest of the night.

When the weak light of morning finally sifts in through the smoke holes, I wake Snow Falls. She likes her sleep, and I'll allow her as much of it as she needs to keep her strong, but today I have a task for her.

"Daughter," I say, "will you go see Gosling?"

She looks up at me from her sleeping robe, her hair tangled. "What do you want from her?"

"A favour," I say. "The illness has come into the longhouse, and I need her medicine."

"Shouldn't you ask her?" Snow Falls says.

"You're good with her," I say. "And I've asked too much of her already. Sometimes it's the woman's place to ask another woman for what she needs."

"Do I need her medicine?" Snow Falls asks.

"We all do." I hesitate for a moment. "Snow Falls," I say, "I want you to ask her if you can stay with her for a little while."

"Are you upset with me?"

I laugh, shaking my head. "No, not at all," I say. "I think only of your strength. Nobody has the power to protect everyone, but Gosling … I believe she isn't like most."

"I don't want to leave," she says. "I want to be here."

I think about how life has changed so fully in the few years we've been together, how she was once a young wild animal who's grown up, still wild, but with the patience now to at least let a stranger approach without her striking out. "You can learn much from Gosling if you were to stay with her," I say. "She has much to pass on."

"No," Snow Falls says. "Right now, I need to be here. I'll learn what I need by staying."

"It won't be easy to bear, what you'll soon witness and feel," I tell her. "We will lose some of those whom we love."

Her eyes darken. "I know," she finally says.

"Will you still ask Gosling if she has any more root medicine for Fox?"

Snow Falls nods and climbs from her mat.

I BEND OVER FOX with Gosling's tea. She's already told me it might be too late. I must try, regardless. He's delirious and doesn't recognize me, his face thin and glistening with sweat. He calls out to his wife, who stands behind me, clutching her hands. When I bring the cup to his lips, he pushes me away and some tea dribbles down his cheek.

"You'll have to hold him down," I tell her. She kneels and secures his head with both hands while I pin his arms with my knees. Again, I bring the tea to his mouth and begin to force it in. He's calmer now, and takes small swallows. When I'm nearly done, he coughs, spraying our faces with droplets of tea and spit. I let his chest settle, then feed the rest to him.

There's nothing else to do except keep his beaver robe on him and wait, hoping the sickness doesn't spread to the rest of us. But it does. The next day, I hear his wife and three children coughing and crying as well. Slipping one small root into my pouch in the event that Snow Falls becomes ill, I boil the rest and take the tea to Fox's family.

I keep watch over them all day and into the night, praying to Aataentsic and her benevolent son, Isouheka, to allow them more time to walk upon the earth. I pray to you, dear wife, to bring this message to Sky Woman and hope that she will listen.

By the time morning comes, two of Fox's children lie still, their faces seized by death. One by one I carry them out of the longhouse wrapped in their beaver robes, and I leave them in the cold of the porch so their bodies don't deteriorate before they can be buried.

Fox and his wife remain unconscious, waking every so often to call out or moan. When they soil themselves, I do my best to clean them up. I try to force a little ottet into their mouths, but Fox is the only one who will take any. That evening when it would normally be time for supper, I see their oldest child has gone still. He was Fox's pride and was becoming very skilled with a bow. I wrap him tight in his beaver robe and carry him to his siblings outside.

Snow Falls approaches me as I sing quietly over Fox and his wife, who themselves are growing still. "Is there anything I can do?" she asks.

I shake my head. "I only ask that you go to visit Gosling until the worst of this passes."

"Would that make any difference?" she asks.

She's probably right but I don't tell her as much. "Please don't argue with me at such a time," I say.

Snow Falls turns to go. It's for her own good.

I awake at dawn to the hushed hum of a mourning song. Opening my eyes, I realize I'd fallen asleep on Fox's family's sleeping mat. Fox lies beside me, his eyes wide open, singing as he cradles his wife in his arms. I can see from her stiffened arm sticking out of her robe that she passed to the next world in the night. I listen to him sing for his three children and his wife. I'm sweating, I see, even though the unattended fire has gone out. When I cough, my breath plumes out in front of me. With all the strength I have left, I pull myself up, a wave of coughs rattling my chest, and reach my hand out to touch my friend's head before dragging myself to my own sleeping mat. Shivering now, I crawl under my robe and hope that someone will get the fire going once more.

———

I'M BURNING UP and can't breathe. Someone has rekindled the fire and moved it under me so I roast. I can see the faces of my two enemies who I was sure were put to death. They kneel over me, smiling. They try to put something down my throat. Poison. My arms are as heavy as tree trunks, but I try to push them away. One pins my arms down and the other takes my head and pours hot liquid into my mouth. It burns and I spit it out. They pour more and hold my mouth closed so that I'm forced to swallow. They want to kill me. I begin to hum my death chant.

Now I wake because I'm shivering so violently that my teeth might break. I can see that a fire still burns, but there's no noise. It must be night. I'm sure I'm alone and everyone else has died. I'll soon die, too, and try to sing my death chant, but I shiver too hard for it to come out of my throat. I wonder where my two enemies are, if they're close and waiting. I hear the footfall of someone approaching. Lifting my head as high as I can, I see it is the young one, Carries an Axe, the son of Tall Trees. He wished last summer to come on our trade mission but I decided he was still too young. He puts more wood on my fire. He hopes that if I live I'll recognize his kindness and his courage for taking care of me in my illness. I need another beaver robe. Mine is so thin with age. I want to call out to him but the shivering won't allow it. Instead, I shut my eyes.

I can feel my body lift up from my mat and float around the room and then out of the house and over the village. No fires burn. We are all of us dead. I allow myself to float away from the village and follow the Sweet Water Sea, frozen and white below me, to another village, and it, too, is dead. It's deep at night as I float over the land, looking for some kind of light, some warmth, something to pull me down from the sky. Night sky only, and snow glittering in a half moon.

I fly above the world all night, searching for any suggestion of life. Sometimes I see the animals who hunt in the dark, the wolves circling a pregnant deer, the owls swooping low for mice that venture out of their nests, the yellow-eyed lynx on padded feet silent behind the hare. I float over the white of the inland sea, and when I look down my eyes penetrate the ice so that I see the big fish who circle slow in the frigid water, their hunger dulled by the need to keep moving, the big fish circling in their schools so that the smaller fish are forced to swim through them, a reminder of what they will once again eat come spring.

My teeth begin chattering with cold again so I rise toward the half moon, but it gives no heat. I fly across the frozen world, searching for something, some firelight, and I'm about to give up hope, my energy leaving me, the land below growing bigger as I speed above trees close enough that I understand if I get much closer I'll crash into them and their sharp limbs will tear me apart. I'm falling now, and my teeth chatter and I need warmth but only see the dark outline of tree and rock coming up fast. I shut my eyes despite now knowing that they've been shut all along. But then behind my eyelids I see the light of flames and when I blink and open them, I see strange stone houses beneath me. I aim for a tall smoke hole shooting red embers into the sky and slide down it right into the fire and I'm finally warm again and from the warmth of this fire I see familiar faces. The Crow and his two helpers. They sit at a table full of food and laugh with one another. Other Iron People with their hairy faces come in and out of this strange house. An odd round object ticks with the rhythm of a drum, and Snow Falls and Carries an Axe sit near the crows, watching it. When one of the crows calls out to this round object, it answers with the strangest voice. The smile on Snow Falls' face makes me smile, too. I'm warm here and the sight of food makes me feel full and none of these men or my girl are sick or even suffering a cough. I can close my eyes and rest in this warm hearth. In this place, despite my surprise, I feel safe.

———

I OPEN MY EYES. The longhouse is still. I don't know from the thin light if it's early morning or early evening. My fever's broken. I can smell the sickness on my body and when I try to sit, my skin still screams. Someone in the shadows coughs and then a child cries. This is worse than the other illnesses that descended on us, the one that turned people's skin into weeping blisters. I force myself to sit up. My throat burns and I need to drink water.

Climbing from my mat, I see that someone has kept the fire tended and then I remember Carries an Axe. Fox's family's spot is empty, but I can make out a few huddled forms farther down the longhouse. I dip a small birch bucket into the larger one that holds the water. Someone must have filled it with snow not very long ago. As I sip the water, the cold of it soothes my throat. I'm so thirsty I want to gulp it down but know this will only cause me to throw it up. My stomach's too tender for that. It feels like it'll tear if I cough one more time. Taking another bucket of water, I pour it over my head, and this brings some life back into me. I strip off my breechcloth and leggings and wash myself by the fire's light and warmth.

Outside, I see night's coming, not morning as I had hoped. Wandering about in the twilight, I feel as if I'm still in a bad dream. The snow has stopped falling, but it's deep on the path. Fires burn in fewer than half of the longhouses. The beast that is this illness has been very cruel, and it's not yet finished its feast.

Smoke drifts above Gosling's home, and when I enter, she and Snow Falls are sitting by the fire talking to Carries an Axe. Each of them seems well and all three smile when they see me standing at the door.

"Come sit by the fire and warm yourself," Gosling says.

"Your fever broke at last," Snow Falls says. "We left you not long ago when we recognized this."

"You fought hard when we tried to make you drink the root medicine," Carries an Axe says. "You called me your enemy. In your fever, I think you thought I was Haudenosaunee."

I sit by them. "How has your family managed?" I ask him.

"My father and mother still live." He stops and wipes an eye. "I lost my two sisters, though."

I fear he might cry, but he chooses to continue.

"My father's well enough to go out and hunt deer with Fox. Fox didn't want to leave your side and so my father asked me to sit with you while they were gone. We need the fresh meat."

"How long did my fever last?" I ask.

"Four days," Gosling says. "For a while it didn't look like you were going to make it. Here, you must eat." She reaches for her kettle and pours some broth into a birch cup.

We sit quietly for a while before I speak again. "This sickness isn't done with us yet. I dreamed of a safe place for you to go, Snow Falls."

"I don't want to go anywhere," she says.

"In my dream," I say, "Carries an Axe was travelling with you."

The two look at each other.

Gosling notices, too. "And where did you dream they should go?" she asks me, sounding amused.

"To the village of the crows," I say.

Even Gosling looks surprised. "Every dream doesn't have to be followed," she says.

"This one was powerful," I say. "Everyone looked strong in my dream."

"Some dreams," Gosling says, "demand that you listen to them. Others are simply images of what's to come, not of what needs to be done."

I think about this as I sip my broth. "I don't understand," I finally say.

Both Gosling and Snow Falls laugh. "You're right, Gosling," Snow Falls says. "What you say about men."

I look at Carries an Axe, who also seems confused.

"Gosling means," Snow Falls says, "that your dream might have simply been the fulfillment of what you desire, and not what should be done."

I look at Snow Falls, then at Gosling. "My daughter is now the teacher?" I ask, and Carries an Axe covers his smile with his hand.

"It's your dream," Gosling says. "And she's your daughter. The decision is between the two of you."

I think of Fox's dead family, of all the dark longhouses in our village, of how long it will take once the snow melts to bury our dead.

"I wish for my dream to be fulfilled," I say. "Carries an Axe, I ask you to accompany Snow Falls to the place of the crows."

The two glance at each other once again before Snow Falls turns to Gosling, who simply smiles.

"Maybe I will join you on that journey," Gosling says, looking at me.

"But I didn't see you there in my dream," I say.

"Maybe it's because I didn't want you to see me," she says.

It's decided, then.

———

NOW THAT THE GROUND has thawed, every family in our village takes care of their dead. I help Fox to bend his family's legs and arms into the position of children in the womb and we lovingly wrap them tight in their beaver robes so they'll stay warm. I help Fox to carry each member of his family to the ossuary that the community has dug. We will bury our loved ones together today so they'll have company, and we place our most prized possessions in the ossuary with them so they'll have what they need in the next world.

Fox climbs down and makes sure that each family member is beside the other, each of them touching, each of them surrounded by the objects in life they cherished. The sewing awls that his wife was so particular about and the bone scraping knife given to her by her mother, her corn pestle and the stone bowl in which she ground it, the kettle traded from the Iron People for a hundred beaver pelts in which she cooked for her family, and for me, over so many seasons. Fox's son has his bow and quiver placed across him along with Fox's most treasured knife. His daughters have shiny beads and cornhusk dolls and eagle feathers and their hide pouches that Fox had made for them. He places his most reliable fishing net with them, too, and then takes off his tobacco pouch and places it on his son's chest.

Families all around us go through the same ritual. We remain silent for now except for the small sobs that escape a few mouths. We have tightly wrapped our dead and given them what we hope they will need and all of us whisper to our loved ones that we'll see them in not too long and so please, we beg, keep an ear out for us when we cross over too.

Our once great village is now like a lost child wandering in search of its parents. We all circle the ossuary as one body, looking down at all of our dead. The women begin to call out first, crying and shaking and singing, and the rest of us soon join in, pounding our bodies in grief and singing out for our loved ones, for their okis to go now from their bodies and to the spirit world. We pray for the one soul that will stay near us and the village, and for the other soul that will travel far away, the men beating their chests and their stomachs and their thighs and singing as loud as we can, some banging drums and others shaking rattles. The women cry out and weep great rivers of tears and we empty ourselves of the pain that's filled us since the sickness descended and we beg for the orenda of our loved ones to rise up out of the ossuary, for their souls to travel together to the better place. We weep hoping we have given enough to them that they'll manage in the next place and some of us cry because we want to be on this journey with them. When I look over at Fox, I know this is his truth. And now he knows the pain I have suffered for so long, my love, and he knows from watching me for so long that this pain never really goes away, just wanes and rises like the moon, and now when we look each other in the eye we are true brothers in our loss and in our desire to once again be with the ones we love and have lost.

———

FAR FEWER WOMEN now to begin preparing the fields for planting. Far fewer men now to clear the fields. Far fewer mouths, at least, to feed, Fox jokes bitterly. He and I do what we have done every spring since we were children, this sitting up late by the fire, planning our summer. Of course it's different now. For long stretches we gaze into the flames, saying nothing. Last summer was the greatest of our adventures, but we shall not see that again in our lifetimes. Our men were just as hard hit by the illness as our women and children. Half of the young warriors who came with us last summer are dead. And even if we had the desire and the energy to make a trip to the place of the Iron People, there is no way anyone who has a family left would be willing to leave them right now.

"The thought of that paddle," I say, "the thought of those endless rapids and the hunger and the threat of those who wish to kill us around every bend of river, I don't have the energy to consider it."

"You know you love it," Fox says. "You know that even if two or three young ones dared approach and asked to go along, you would say yes immediately."

Of course he's right. Still, we must stay home and lick our wounds this summer.

"You know," Fox says, "we'll lose out on our trade agreements that we've worked so hard to breathe life into."

"The hairy ones will wait a few seasons for us," I say.

"The hairy ones will see we supply them with no furs this summer and will go to our enemy for trade on that excuse."

"We have always been patient with them," I say. "They'll be patient with us."

Fox just looks at me until I'm forced to consider my words. "If it were up to me," he says, "I'd like nothing better than to descend on those crows and kill each and every one of them. Is there any doubt they're the ones who brought the sickness to us?" Fox clutches his hands so hard he shakes. "Bird," he says, "let's kill them all so that we can go back to life before them. If we kill them all, we'll save ourselves."

"I fear it's too late for that," I say. "When we first agreed to mix with them, we didn't know they were worse than weeds. And now that they're wrapped around us, they'll never let go."

"It's time for me to travel to their new village and pull some weeds, then," Fox says. "I'm not afraid of the work my woman once did."

I wish it were so simple, but there's no point in trying to argue with Fox tonight. He's in the deep water of his despair and all I can do is watch my friend flail like a child as the waves pull him under.

"We'll soon need to go to their village and bring Snow Falls back," I say. "She's now your daughter just as much as mine."

"You don't want me going there," Fox says. "I won't be responsible for what I might do."

"It's only a day's journey," I tell him. I'll leave soon, when summer is closer. For now, she's safe there, and there's so much to do here at home. "I'll be fine travelling it alone. It's most sensible, anyway, for you to stay to protect the village. We'll all spend a quiet summer together." I want to say more, something that might soothe him, but there are no words for that right now. There will never be words enough for that.

———

ALL DAY, I KNOW I'm being followed as sure as I know rain comes later this afternoon. And now, not far from the place where the crows have built their new home, the footsteps approach. Whoever's been trying to find me is close enough the birds around us have gone silent. I've climbed up a ridge near a stream I've been following. I lie down in the grass and wait.

With my knife in one hand and my club in the other, I stop breathing as the form passes. It's not Haudenosaunee at all but the familiar figure of my dearest friend. When I whistle our call, Fox stops. Standing, I tell him he's lucky I wasn't the enemy. He doesn't laugh. He looks exhausted.

"I've been trying to catch you for hours," he says.

"I know," I say.

"There's no time for being foolish. The Haudenosaunee have attacked us."

"What?" Summer isn't even fully here yet.

"They've already descended on our Arendahronnon brothers and put fire to them."

I think of the large village where we played the Creator's Game. "Do they need our help?" I ask, realizing as I say it how little of it we have to offer.

"They're already defeated," Fox says. "Stragglers started crawling in yesterday. They suffered badly. The village is gone, and the Haudenosaunee will celebrate tonight with more of our people than they'll know what to do with."

This is unprecedented. A village of hundreds of fires not only attacked but destroyed. They've never come so early in the year. It means they must have left their homes very soon after the ice left the lakes and rivers.

"Help me retrieve Snow Falls and Carries an Axe," I say, "then we must hurry back." We're next. There's no doubt in my mind.

As we move through the forest, all the questions and fears arise. Their raiding party must be very large. They must have heard we've been so stricken by illness and knew now was the time to hit us. The bad blood has finally boiled over, and it won't stop until one of us has crushed the other.

———

A HAIRY-FACED GUARD lounges on the ramparts over the crows' village, weapon in hand. Fox and I fear he'll mistake us for the enemy and fire upon us if we approach without warning.

"Do you know any of their language?" Fox asks.

I shake my head. "I'll just call out and wave so that he'll see we're friends."

But when I do this, his face goes white and he raises his weapon. I call out to him again and he turns his head and shouts something in his language, then a few other men peer at me over the ramparts. They, too, call down to where I can't see and finally a bearded face I recognize appears, one of the crow helpers, the one called Isaac. He says something rapidly to them and they seem to relax. He waves with his mangled hand for me to come in. Fox follows me out of the forest, and this surprises them even more.

Inside, I tell Isaac of what's happened. I speak too quickly. He doesn't understand. I slow down, explain as clearly as I can that our people have come under attack. I say their name, Arendahronnon, explain again that they've been wiped out. He smiles when I say their name.

Now he speaks in his tongue, and I don't understand.

I ask where the Crow Christophe is.

This crow just smiles as he repeats stupidly, "Arendahronnon. Arendahronnon." He looks excited.

I see an older Wendat woman approaching. "Dawning of Day, my friend," I say, "come here quickly. I need to find Snow Falls."

"I know where she is," Dawning of Day says. "We don't need to ask the crow." She smiles.

Why is everyone smiling so foolishly? My stomach tells me something's terribly wrong. "Tell me where my daughter is," I say more angrily than I had meant to.

Dawning of Day looks fearful now. "She left with the crows and He Finds Villages for the village of the Arendahronnon a few days ago," she says, her eyes now concerned.

"What?" There must be some mistake.

"The father, Christophe, took your daughter with him to the Arendahronnon to explain his Great Voice to them. Don't worry," she says. "They promised they'd come back soon. And young Carries an Axe followed to make sure they remained safe."

THREE

We all fight our own wars, wars for which we'll be judged. Some of them we fight in the forests close to home, others in distant jungles or faraway burning deserts. We all fight our own wars, so maybe it's best not to judge, considering it's rare we even know why we fight so savagely.

Watch now, then, how Aataentsic, sitting by the fire beside us, reacts to what she sees. We'll keep watching, too. We can't turn our eyes away.

In times of war, and especially in the aftermath, the question she begs is the one each of us needs to ask. How do you keep going when all that you love has been lost?

Or perhaps the question is this: What role did I play in the troubles that surround me?

Or maybe it's this: Will I see my loved ones again?

For those with grander ambitions, perhaps it's this: If success is measured in one way, then how should we measure defeat?

Aataentsic with her sparkling eyes watches as all of us around the fire debate this, even as our own eyes are drawn to what unfolds among the humans below.

THIS IS NOT MY FATHER'S DREAM

I've arrived at the village of the crows.

My father Bird's dream, the one that said I leave him for this place, this is the dream that sent me away. The illness of our own village raged when he dreamed it, and the morning I left, the bodies that lay piled high outside the longhouses had begun to thaw. The mean boy, the good-looking boy, Carries an Axe, he accompanied me on the walk to the crow village. And just as Gosling had promised, as soon as we walked out the gates, she was there, waiting for us on the path. I felt torn. I was looking forward to being alone with this boy for the day. But the idea scared me, too.

Maybe she came to watch over us. After all, I'm convinced she can see through me as easily as if she peers through clear water. She knows what I feel for this boy, the heat mingled with ice. And when, halfway to the crows' village, a blizzard tore up from the Sweet Water Sea, so brutal the winds pushed us to our knees, I was glad she was with us. I think that if she hadn't come we would have perished in that brutal early-spring storm.

The snow blew sideways and the world disappeared in a white sting. I begged Gosling to let us stop and rest but she ignored me, took over the cutting of the snowshoe trail for the three of us when Carries an Axe could no longer do it. I knew it embarrassed him that a woman showed us the way, but all either of us could do was hold on to Gosling's robe like children as she pushed ahead. I knew later that if we'd stopped to rest, we would have frozen to death.

When we finally crawled, our faces painted in frost from the wind, into that village of the crows, I saw that my father's dream wasn't right. This wasn't a place of safety or of plenty. Dawning of Day's longhouse stank with the same sickness that ravaged our home, and the hairy ones from that faraway land glared at me and licked their lips but wouldn't offer food.

At least Christophe Crow remained the same as we stumbled through the gates, our lips blue. He allowed me to stay in Dawning of Day's longhouse but sent Gosling and Carries an Axe to another past the palisades.

And here we are now as the snow finally becomes water, trickling into the creeks that in turn pour into the rivers that in turn rush into the Sweet Water Sea. The crows are very particular as to how the day passes, with every part of it arranged for us in advance. They expect us to be in the place called the chapel every morning just as the sun rises and they talk to us and to their great voice until our stomachs groan with hunger. After that, they allow us a small morning meal of ottet. We're left to wander about for a while, and I try to avoid the ones who have come over to assist the crows because I don't like how they look at me. I've already had the bad experience with one of them in their village so long ago, and I won't trust these men again.

In the afternoon we're expected to sit like children in front of a strange thing that they call Captain of the Day. Every long while, Gabriel Crow commands it to speak and it calls out. At first it was entertaining but I can see most of us here have grown bored with the trick, all except the one who is supposed to be my brother, Hot Cinder. He still gawks with amazement. Once the Captain has called out, Gabriel Crow tells us that it's told him to send us home. We go back to our longhouses then and keep each other company till it's time for bed before the next day comes and it's repeated all over again. I look forward to heading home.

Gosling couldn't stand this place and left not long after she arrived. She promised that she'd return for Carries an Axe and me, though, as soon as it was safe to go back. There is illness here and it has taken some lives, but it's far worse where we live, and so I'm forced to wait it out in this strange place. The others who are here, a couple handfuls of them, come from different places for different reasons. A few Anishnaabe wait out the winter before they return to their villages, and the Wendat here have mostly lost their families to the illness and have no other way to support themselves. There's a sadness hard to ignore.

In my boredom, I try to get to know Carries an Axe better. He's not so cocky without his friends around. I want to ask him if they survived but I fear for the answer. Instead we walk through the strange village, impressed by how some of the buildings are partly made with stone, others with thick wood of trees that have been cut to all look the same. Rather than live in large groups like us, these ones prefer their own much smaller residences. The crows continue to stay alone, and the different odd-looking and odd-smelling men live in small groups of friends in their little homes. To me, they mostly look the same with their hairy faces and sunken eyes, their skin the colour of a withered squash blossom. When they talk, I can see many of them have few teeth, and compared to the body of Carries an Axe, they look weak and pathetic. Their clothes, too, make them look the same, with their thin, dirty shirts and strange hide they wear that covers all of their legs and asses, even now that the snow's melted. Carries an Axe likes to make fun of their appearance. He's even claimed that he's held some of their clothes in his own hands and that their clothes aren't made from the skins of animals at all but instead are created by old witches with bottoms like spiders who spin out their thread that other witches then weave. I laugh at his silliness, and when he smiles, I can feel it low in my stomach.

This morning, we skip the crows talking in the chapel and wander out into the woods. We won't be fed by them for not showing up, but

Carries an Axe says he's been setting rabbit snares along some runs he found.

"We shouldn't have to rely on them, Snow Falls," he says. "I'm a good hunter. I can look after us."

When he says the word *us*, I feel my face heat up, but then I remind myself he speaks of everyone in the longhouses. I wish he stayed in mine, but Christophe Crow says Carries an Axe needs to accept the great voice if he wishes that comfort. Carries an Axe just laughs, and I know this angers Christophe Crow. But the Crow should be careful. Carries an Axe stays here to protect me to make good with my father. He doesn't need these crows and their ways. I've seen Carries an Axe's temper. In the chapel when Christophe Crow begins to seethe like rapids, his eyes darkening and his cheeks turning bright when he speaks of all the ways the Wendat and our world is wrong, I look at Carries an Axe and see that he seethes even more.

The two of us walk the trail leading to the river, and I recognize a few of the tiny trails running from ours that the hares use just as we people do to make their way through the forest. Soon it'll be planting time and I wonder if there are still enough of us left living to work the fields back home, and in turn I wonder if the sickness will continue there until they're all dead and if I will be forced to live in the strange village of the crows forever. But then, like sun breaking through the cloud, I see the hare up ahead lying on its side, the snare tight about its neck, the animal's eyes closed.

Carries an Axe grins as he leans down and unties the thin cord from the saplings on each side of the trail. He weighs the hare in his hands and looks up. "This will be our feast tonight," he says.

"Some feast," I say. The hare is a large male and will feed more than just us. "You'll have to do better than that to impress me."

"Well, then," he says, handing me the hare to carry, "let's see how many others I've managed to take today."

I take the snare cord from his hand and tie it about the animal's feet so that I can drape it over my back. "Yes," I say, "let's see what you can snare today."

By afternoon, we've taken two more rabbits and have been busy creating a stone weir to try to lure any spawning fish travelling up this smaller creek to take that route, just narrow enough I can straddle the bank and the rocks we've placed. With two more saplings, these ones cut long and sharpened at one end, Carries an Axe and I stand, me behind him, our weapons poised for the flash of their darting past. I try and try but my timing is off today, and instead of catching one I end up only blunting my spear on the stones at the bottom of the creek.

Growing bored, I stop trying and instead watch Carries an Axe in front with his back still to me, bent at the waist with his spear poised, clearly focused on getting one. I reach forward with my spear and poke him in his rear end. He jolts, slipping from his rock perch and landing in the water. He splashes about, trying to climb back out. I realize he's struggling and I stop laughing. He raises an arm to me and cries out that he can't swim and I need to help him. Moving as quick as I can on the slippery rocks, I reach for his hand, and just as I grip it his face turns from panic to laughter and he pulls me on top of him, the shock of the cold making me cry out.

He stands. The water barely comes up to his waist. Standing as well, I reach out and slap him.

"Why'd you do that?" he asks, looking like a hurt little boy.

Instead of answering, I climb out of the water, my teeth chattering, and stomp onto the bank. I'm going to run back to the crow village but then realize I might get lost. I sit on the ground like a child, feeling foolish even as I do it.

Carries an Axe climbs out, too. "You started it," he says.

I look up at him. He's right. Instead of letting my anger go any further, I stand. "I'm cold," I say, shivering, my arms wrapped around myself.

Carries an Axe looks at me, his eyes confused. I watch them slowly light up. "Let me warm you, then," he says. He walks to me carefully, as if he's approaching an animal he's not seen before. When he's close, he opens his arms, and I do, too. The skin of his chest is warm against mine.

———

CHRISTOPHE CROW is angry with me. "You've not been coming in the mornings to listen to the Great Voice," he says. Gabriel stands behind him as if to try and catch me should I bolt. We're in the longhouse, and Aaron and I had been sitting by the fire laughing about when he saved my raccoon from the old woman who wanted to cook him. Aaron isn't laughing anymore, though. He looks like he's been caught doing something he knows he shouldn't be.

"You will come tomorrow," Gabriel says. I don't like this one. I refuse to answer him and just keep my eyes on the fire.

Christophe Crow says something angrily to Gabriel in their language and then kneels to me. "Snow Falls," he says. "You and I have known one another for a long time now. We've been through much together. In some ways, I may even owe you my life."

I continue to stare into the fire.

"Snow Falls," he says. "I beg of you to look at me."

Not wanting to, I turn to him, his face close to mine. In the glow it almost looks like he has tears in his eyes.

"You are like a relation to me," Christophe Crow continues. "We've made such progress and as soon as it appears that you are ready to live forever in the good place, you turn your back to me." He continues to look at me, his eyes pleading. "Come back tomorrow so that you may hear what the Great Voice has to say."

"And what if I don't?" I ask.

"Let's not be like this," Christophe says. I see that he looks at Aaron. "I know that Aaron would very much like for you to come back."

I want to tell the Crow that I am for Carries an Axe now, and he is with me. I, too, look at Aaron. His eyes are trying to tell me something.

It's all making me uncomfortable. "I don't want," I begin but then stop. "I want to go home," I say.

"You will go home soon if that's what you desire," Christophe says. "After all, Bird is a powerful headman, isn't he? I can't keep you against your will." Christophe looks at Aaron and then at me again. "But I'm not sure how much of a home will be left when you return."

The words dig into me. "My home is still there," I say.

"Many have died in that place, though," Christophe says. "It won't be the same. Keep in mind it was Bird who sent you here. He knows this place is safe, that it's watched over by the Great Voice."

"That wasn't his dream."

"His dream wasn't to send you here?" Christophe asks.

"It was, but ..." I search for the words. "He didn't send me here so that I could be protected by the great voice. Those weren't his words."

"Then why did he send you here?" Christophe asks. I can feel Gabriel's and Aaron's eyes on me.

"To get me away from the sickness of the village," I say.

"And the sickness of your village was a hundred times worse than here in ours, wasn't it?" Christophe asks.

I want to get up and walk away. The Crow is twisting my words, is twisting my father's dream.

"I'll tell you what," Christophe says, standing from his crouch. "After the planting, come with Gabriel and Aaron and me to the village of your cousins, to the Arendahronnon. Join us on the trip when the spring is almost summer."

"And what if I don't?" I ask.

"Come with us and watch what we do," Christophe says. "That's all I ask. Join us so that we may introduce the Great Voice to your cousins. And when we are done, you can go home if that is what you wish."

I stand up now, too. "I'll travel with you," I say. "But then I'll head home." To show him I mean what I say, I quickly walk away, brushing past the crow Gabriel as I go.

WE'VE BEEN WALKING most of the day, Aaron leading. He knows this land well. He now assures us we're close to the village of the Arendahronnon. I hope so. I'm tired. Gabriel and Christophe Crow are having a hard time keeping up, and so we walk slower than we like. Hot Cinder joined us on the journey despite my not wanting him to. But he's been good so far, talking little and just focusing on the travel. I'd wanted Carries an Axe to come, but Christophe grew angry when I asked. I was about to tell Christophe I wouldn't go, either, but Carries an Axe assured me he'd follow from a distance and not let anything happen to me. "Go," he said, kissing me. "We'll make it an adventure. I want to test what kind of powers these crows have out in the forest. I'll follow you, and none of them will even know."

And now we must be almost there because I smell the scent of burning wood. Behind us, Christophe and the hairy crow don't notice anything. They just keep talking even though they seem out of breath, neither of them paying attention in a place where there's so much to be worried about.

Aaron signals for us to stop. I can see light through the trees farther down the trail, and that must be the beginning of the great cornfields of the Arendahronnon.

Something isn't right, though. I look at Hot Cinder, and he has his fingers in his mouth. All of us crouch and drop back into the shadows. But the crows keep talking and breathing heavily, their feet slapping the ground in awkward strides as they come upon us. They'd walk right by, but I reach out my hand to them and signal for them to get down and be quiet. When they huddle with us, their eyes are round.

The smell of burning wood is strong. I'd assumed it was the scent of men clearing old stumps with fire, but this smell's bigger than that. It's far more pungent. And when I pick up the scent of cooking flesh on the wind, too, the hairs on the back of my neck prickle. Then the wind blows toward us, and I think I can hear the gleeful shouts of men doing something that gives them great pleasure.

Aaron crawls to me and whispers that he's going to find out what's happening.

I shake my head. "Don't," I whisper back. "Something's very wrong."

He ignores me and rises. "Wait here unless it becomes unsafe," he says, then quickly moves toward the fields.

We wait for what feels like a long time. When he doesn't come back, I signal for Hot Cinder and the crows to stay where they are.

The scent of fire grows stronger as I dart from tree to tree. The trail's too dangerous to follow, and the light ahead through the new leaves grows brighter. I'm sure now that what I'm hearing is a war song, a victory song.

I crawl on my knees to the tree line where the three sisters have just begun sprouting. There's no way to take cover there, so I can't go any farther. But the open fields give me a view of the village. The palisades around it have been torched, and most of the longhouses within are burning or have already crumbled into ash. I'm shocked by how many warriors dance around the fires or torture the living. A large group of what must be prisoners sits on the ground with a few guards around them. It's too far to make out the looks on their faces, but I know what they must be.

Hundreds and hundreds of war-bearers have come from all the nations of the Haudenosaunee. Then I realize with a shock that some of my relations must be in this great war party, too. Something almost like homesickness washes over me, but then I watch as a warrior raises his club to a man on his knees with his hands tied behind his back. The warrior smashes the man's head and he falls over, his legs kicking in spasms.

All of it comes back. You, my father, and you, my mother, and you, my big brother. I don't belong to you anymore. And I don't belong to Bird's people. The idea then comes to me that I'll simply stand up and walk across this field and let them decide who I am. If they still believe I'm one of theirs, they'll keep me. If not, they'll kill me.

Just as I stand to walk across the field, I hear the chatter of a squirrel. It's Aaron, back in the trees and motioning for me to get down. I shake my head.

He sneaks over to me and whispers, "What are you doing?"

"I think these are my people," I say.

"They're no longer your people," he says. "Come with me unless you desire a cruel death for Christophe and Gabriel."

I won't be responsible for any more deaths, my father. As a gang of Haudenosaunee warriors pulls people from the group huddled on the ground and drags them toward a bonfire, I make my decision. Despite Bird's wishes, I'm not a Wendat. But I'm no longer a Haudenosaunee, either.

Back where Hot Cinder and the crows huddle, Aaron instructs us to head back down the trail as quickly and silently as we can. As we stand to move, I see Hot Cinder hesitate. I realize he is still part of this tribe, and I'm certain then of what he will do.

Just as I'm about to warn Aaron, Hot Cinder says, "Father Christophe."

The Crow turns to him.

"You're the only one who's been kind to me," he continues. "But those others, do you know what they did to me?"

We all stare at him, and I'm frightened his loud voice will give us away. Aaron tells Hot Cinder to hush, but he pays no attention.

"Two of the donnés," he explains. "One holds me down while the other puts himself in me. They say if I don't tell anyone, they'll teach me the secret of the Captain of the Day."

Christophe's eyes widen and his mouth falls open. "That isn't true," he says. "It can't be."

"You don't believe me?" Hot Cinder says. "Do you want me to show you where I bleed?"

"No, Joseph," Christophe says. "Come back with us and we'll punish those men severely for this terrible sin. The Great Voice will punish them for eternity. I promise you."

"There is no great voice," Hot Cinder says. "You'd best get moving now."

He runs away toward the village and the warriors who occupy it.

———

WITH NIGHT UPON US, we move quickly but keep losing the trail. No one speaks, though I'm sure we're all thinking the same thing, that Hot Cinder will have told the Haudenosaunee of our whereabouts, and that there's no doubt we're being pursued through the darkness. This keeps even the crows moving as fast as they can.

Exhausted, we stop to catch our breath beside a creek, and like a small herd of deer, we drop our heads into the water to drink. It isn't safe, though, because we can't hear if anyone approaches over the burbling of the water.

I lean to Aaron and whisper that maybe we should cut off the trail and find a safer place deep in the forest where we can hide and rest. "Look at the crows," I say. "They can't go much farther." Both are slumped by the water, their chests rising and dropping.

We urge them to get moving again, Aaron leading us up a small rise. I hope he's considering my suggestion. Just as we make it to the top, something large darts out from behind a tree and strikes him across the head. I run through faint moonlight back down the hill, my heart beating in my throat, and straight into the arms of a large warrior.

JESU, DULCIS MEMORIA

I watch three Iroquois build a fire in a copse of trees off the trail. The other two tied the four of us up and left us sitting in the middle of the trail as they apparently search to see if there are others in our party. Gabriel and I whisper a litany of prayers in Latin, but when the two Iroquois return, one walks up and slaps each of us across the mouth. We sit and wait as the five congregate to talk in the trees off the path. I begin to whisper my prayers again, and Aaron finally comes to. He looks around, surveying the situation, and after a few moments, rather than pray with us, he begins singing his death chant, much of it about his love for Snow Falls. My strongest convert, and he still slips back into his dark ways so easily.

Our hands are tied painfully behind our backs, our feet bound as well. The Iroquois tongue is difficult for me to fully understand, but from what I can make out, they will dispatch Aaron here and take Snow Falls, Gabriel, and me back to the village at first light, where I can only imagine the tortures we'll face.

Dear Lord, I believe this will be the last time I see the sun rise upon this earth that You've created, and I pray You make me strong enough to accept with dignity and with grace the pain I'm about to endure, for my physical body is simply the vessel that holds my soul. When that vessel soon is shattered, my soul will rise up to You. For this I am grateful.

All five warriors are frightfully painted and glistening. They are similar to the Huron in build and disposition, and it would be difficult for any stranger to tell them apart. Three of them now emerge from the trees and onto the trail and roughly check Gabriel's and my bonds, then reach for Aaron, whose voice doesn't falter, and drag him back to the fire in the trees. With even greater shock, I watch as the other two reach down for Snow Falls, pull her up by the hair, and walk her a little way down the trail. With dawning horror, I realize their intentions when one yanks her skirt up and the other flips his breechclout to the side, freeing his erection.

"The Great Voice commands you to stop!" I scream. Both are apparently taken aback by my ability to speak the language. They drop Snow Falls and approach me.

"So this charcoal has learned the words, has he?" one of them says. Their facial features are so similar I assume they're brothers.

"What you wish to do to that girl," I say, "will send you to a place where the worst caressing you've ever witnessed will pale by comparison."

The other reaches down and slaps me so hard that the spine of my nose pops and warm blood trickles over my lips.

"You are in no place to threaten us, charcoal," his brother says. Above his voice I can hear Aaron's song, and I know that they're cutting or burning him now.

"Snow Falls," I shout, "tell them who you are and where you come from!"

Right after me, Gabriel calls, "Tell them you're one of them, that they're your people."

The two warriors turn to her. She has crawled to her feet. "You're not my people," she spits at them. "No Haudenosaunee would dare rape a woman."

One of them hits me so hard on the top of my head that my eyes go dim, but not before I see them walking back to her.

I will myself to stay conscious. "Gabriel," I say, "we must stop this." But he knows as well as I do that there's nothing to be done.

"Let us sing a hymn, Brother," Gabriel says. His dark eyes sparkle. "Our own death chant."

"Yes, Brother," I say, "let us sing, then."

He lifts his voice into the first lines of "Jesu, Dulcis Memoria." He sings it in French rather than Latin, and I listen to him sing a few lines. *"Jesus, the very thought of Thee, with sweetness fills the breast. Yet sweeter far Thy face to see, and in Thy presence rest."*

I join in on the chorus and our voices rise as the sky breaks purple over the horizon. *"No voice can sing, no heart can frame, nor can the memory find, a sweeter sound than Jesus' name, the Saviour of mankind."*

The two warriors turn away from Snow Falls and walk back up the trail toward us, apparently humoured by our singing.

"Listen to that death chant," one says, pointing to us.

"I've never heard such a sour sound in my life," the other tells him. "They're like cow moose in rut!"

They both laugh at this, and as they do, I see a shadow flash across the trail behind them toward Snow Falls on the ground. At first I fear it's another Iroquois warrior I had somehow missed, but this man bends over her and whispers in her ear. I raise my voice higher in song so the two standing by Gabriel and me don't turn away. As the light grows stronger, I realize this is the young man who's tormented me for so long back at the village.

He slips off the trail just as the two warriors turn their attention back to Snow Falls, one again lifting his breechclout and pushing her back so he can mount her while the other laughs and urges him on. Rather than fighting, though, she wraps her arms and legs around him as if in desperate want. Gabriel and I continue to sing, and as the one on top begins to try to enter the poor girl, the young Huron steps out onto the trail, brandishing his war club.

"Sing louder, Gabriel," I urge. "Sing as loud as you can." He looks at me, confused, but there's no time to explain. I pray our voices cover up the sound of imminent battle that might alert the three warriors who torture poor Aaron to the enemy among them.

"O hope of every contrite heart! O joy of all the meek," we sing as the warrior watching senses someone behind him, an alarmed look crossing his face. "To those who fall, how kind Thou art! How good to those who seek!" He picks up his own club as the young Huron swings his down hard with both hands onto the man's head, sending him face first into the dirt. As loud as we can now, we wail, "Jesus our only hope be Thou, as Thou our prize shalt be!" The warrior on top of Snow Falls now realizes something's wrong and struggles to pull away, but she's wrapped about him too tightly. Taking his knife from his sheath, the young Huron straddles the warrior on top of Snow Falls and pulls his head back so that his neck's exposed. "In Thee be all our glory now, and through eternity." The young Huron runs his knife across the neck of the Iroquois, the blood in the pink light of dawn spurting onto Snow Falls.

The young Huron helps her to her feet. We've stopped singing, and I wonder what's happening to Aaron. The sun's high enough that I can make out the look on Snow Falls' face as she bends to the dead man who'd been on top of her and whispers something to him. She then picks up a club, the young Huron picking his up, too. They run up to us and the young Huron cuts our ties, making the sign to be quiet. Then he and Snow Falls creep toward the fire, slipping into the shadows, the thorn clubs in their hands.

"What should we do?" Gabriel asks. "Should we sing again? Should we run?"

"We shall place our lives in the hands of the Lord," I say just as shouting erupts in the trees.

———

WE POUR WATER over Aaron's wounds with our palms. Gabriel strips pieces from his cassock to bandage them. Aaron is missing two fingers from his left hand, the blood pulsing from them with each heartbeat. His stomach has been prodded with fire sticks, and the wounds are black from the cauterization. He gazes impassively up into the sky as we tend to him as best we can. I ask if he still has faith in the Great Voice. He won't answer.

Beside us, Snow Falls dresses the young Huron's wounds that he must have received while attacking Aaron's tormentors. I hear her call him Carries an Axe, a name I now remember. He took cuts to his chest and a blow to the head but still managed to kill all three warriors, I assume. His hands are shaking.

Snow Falls helps him to his feet and whispers to us that we must get going now, for certainly other warriors will be on this trail. Gabriel and I help Aaron stand, and he clenches his teeth but still doesn't make a sound. We start up the same rise upon which we were ambushed in the night, and we stumble past the dead Iroquois, their fire now just a smoking ruin.

For the morning we travel slowly, stopping frequently to catch our breath and tend to our wounded companions. My head throbs with the pain of it being bashed, and I can't breathe through my broken nose. I imagine we look ragged and bloody as we haul one another along the narrow trail through the hardwood forest, light filtering down through it in soft patterns.

By mid-afternoon, Carries an Axe cautions us to walk as quietly as we can. He's sure someone follows. My Lord, I don't know how much more of this I'm able to take. If the Iroquois catch us again, there's no chance of defending ourselves against them. All we can do is help one another down the trail and toward the safety of the mission.

When Carries an Axe stops, I follow his gaze and finally make out what he sees. Two warriors are outlined ahead of us, their backs to the sun so they're bathed in a halo of light. We've just come into a clearing and they stand, stone still, across it. Instead of dropping down or retreating back into the forest, Carries an Axe lifts his arms in the air and warbles out like a bird. The two return it and run to us. I brace myself for the last battle, and it isn't until they're upon us that I recognize Bird and Fox. I've never been so relieved.

Bird reaches for Snow Falls and holds her at arm's distance, studying her for injury. She looks back at him, but something in her has changed. I fear the Iroquois warrior did rape her in the short time he had, though I pray to You, Lord, that he didn't.

Bird speaks to her in a hushed tone. She shakes her head. Angrily, he tells Fox that two of their attackers tried to rape her.

Fox looks surprised. "They must have been rotten ones. That isn't Haudenosaunee behaviour."

"Not to worry," Carries an Axe interrupts. "They're all dead now. Your daughter is a better warrior than I am. She killed her first Haudenosaunee this morning."

I'm shocked. It can't be true that this young woman, only a girl not so long ago, has taken another life. I cannot judge her, though, when I'm so close to all of this. Without her actions we would each of us be dead. Lord, help me come to terms with this. I want to believe they acted to save us, not out of sheer revenge.

"Carries an Axe killed four of them," Snow Falls says in a flat tone.

Bird and Fox look at him, impressed. "I hope you kept the scalps," Fox says.

"There was no time," Carries an Axe tells him.

"There's always time for that," Fox answers.

"What there's no time for is useless talk," Bird says. "Haudenosaunee are creeping everywhere today."

We pick each other up once more and limp across the field toward safety.

CONFESSION IS ABSOLUTELY APPROPRIATE

Gabriel wants to know if I believe the claims of the boy named Joseph. "I fear," he says, "that his charge might have truth to it."

I ask why he thinks so. We've already told Isaac of the horrific few days we've just endured, leaving out some of the worst torture. He's been patiently helping us nurse Aaron, who'd suffered horribly but will thankfully recover.

"I think Joseph's actions speak volumes," Gabriel continues. "He didn't need to cast doubt among us if he only wanted to return to his people." Gabriel looks at Isaac, then at me. "Joseph's no actor. He's quite possibly a little mad. But did you see his expression when he explained what happened to him? Although I don't have any evidence yet, I believe him." Gabriel pauses again, as if for effect. "A sickness has slipped into our mission."

Isaac shakes his head. "It can't be," he says. "These donnés have sworn to live lives of abstinence and purity. To abuse a boy? I can't see it."

"Don't be naïve," Gabriel tells him. "The devil lurks just beyond the light."

"Brothers," I speak up, "this is indeed a grave development, and we shall indeed pursue it, but there are more pressing matters, matters of life and death pertaining to our mission we must immediately attend to."

"You don't find Joseph's charge a pressing matter?" Gabriel asks.

"Dear Gabriel," I say, "I don't wish to in any way suggest this isn't a dire accusation. It has great gravity. But the Iroquois have taken to the warpath, and we're ill equipped to defend ourselves." I explain to him that we'll have to focus on our survival as well as bringing justice, if indeed such an abomination has occurred within our walls.

I can see he doesn't like my answer but must abide by its logic. I turn from my two brothers and feel overwhelmed by the crushing enormity of it all. I need to remain strong, especially now that the devil presses not just from the outside but also from within.

———

WITH BANDS OF IROQUOIS still roaming, caring for crops outside the palisades carries a strong tinge of terror. We can spare only one or two soldiers to accompany the field workers while the others remain vigilant on the ramparts, keeping an eye on the dark forest surrounding us.

Since the encroachment of the enemy into this territory, all kinds of refugees have appeared at our gates, Nipissing and Huron, Montagnais, even a few members of a mysterious group who call themselves the People of the Cat. There are so many sauvages within our walls that it's a struggle to feed them. We can't sustain this for long, even in high season. What, then, when the autumn returns, and after that, the winter? As always, Lord, we are in Your hands.

To add to my worries, Isaac has been acting more and more strangely. He's now convinced himself he can win the sauvages over to the Cross by performing silly magic tricks he apparently learned as a child. He's even gone so far as to sew secret pockets up the arms and along the insides of his cassock. Now that the Captain of the Day has become yesterday's fancy, he attracts children's attention by fumbling around with his fingerless hands, pulling out, and often dropping, all kinds of objects from his cassock to the children's delight, rocks, or letters that he proceeds to read in French while the children giggle, even a shiny French doubloon. Yesterday, Gabriel and I witnessed him pull a small chicken from his robe.

"Why, that was impressive," Gabriel commented.

"Especially considering his limited grasp," I added, which made us both laugh.

"But in all seriousness," he continued, "haven't we already discussed the dangers of trying to win them over through sleight of hand? Doesn't this foolery cross into that witch Gosling's territory?" Isaac was now pretending to swallow a feather and choking.

"Alas," I said, "they're still children. As it seems dear Isaac is as well. And to children belong childish things." We have enough to worry about, and really, this all seems so innocent. Some levity is actually needed in these troubled times.

———

WHEN BIRD LEFT with Fox, Carries an Axe, and Snow Falls shortly after our safe return to the mission in the late spring, he feared for his village. Despite my wanting him to stay for the small protection he offered, I understood his rush to get home, his people, by all accounts, lying shivering in their blankets, waiting for death from the illnesses they suffered or at the hands of the enemy. We've heard nothing as summer approaches its apex. We hope this means all's well, but no one's willing to make the day's journey to find out.

We throw ourselves into strengthening our defences, fifty healthy men and as many sauvages all building up the palisades and digging a canal into the mission from the river that will both power a mill and give us a water supply inside the gates. It's an ingenious design, complete with a locking gate that can be opened only from the inside. Our guests are mightily impressed. Now when those who are brave enough to leave do so, they do it by water, exiting the village via the canal and onto the river, then paddling hard to the relative safety of their Sweet Water Sea.

I turn my attention, this summer, to the needs within the walls rather than the fear of what lies outside them. I've requested a meeting with each donné and layman, and have made the strong suggestion that confession is absolutely appropriate. When they come to me, one by one, hat in hand in the cool darkness of the rough-hewn chapel, I ask how each in turn is faring in this brutal land. Secretly, I try to weigh whether there's truly any validity to Joseph's claim. These conversations stretch over the course of three days, and many of the men are clearly uncomfortable about speaking. All of them appear stronger now from the work than they did in the idle months of winter, the skin of their bearded faces tanned, the stink of labour permeating their clothing.

For the life of me, I can't detect Lucifer's tail on any of them, and, one by one, they clumsily approach and kneel and mumble a few mis-spoken words. These, Lord, are surely not the best of the race that will be the first to populate this new world. Surely, better men are to come. But for the time being, they're all we have. My attempt at finding the truth feels like an utter failure.

This afternoon before supper, now that I have met with all of them, I ask Aaron to join us. The poor young man still physically suffers from his torments, limping and holding his left hand in his right. Daily I watch him mourn. He and Isaac seem to have created a bond, the both of them having gone through similar abuse. Isaac tells me Aaron suffers just as much from lovesickness as he does from his wounds. I tell Isaac that like all infatuations, this one, too, shall pass. We must continue to focus on Aaron's soul, not his earthly desires. Isaac should know this.

As supper is being served, a handful of sauvages come by, and I wouldn't dream of turning them away. We sit crowded around two tables pushed together, twenty of us sharing a watery stew and some week-old bread that must be soaked in it to become edible. After prayers, we all sit with the squeal of chair legs on the wooden floor. The men eat hungrily, noisily, and it takes everything in my power not to chastise them. After all, I've invited them here to speak of important things. I take note that most of them seem in a good mood despite the gravity of our situation.

Once all have quieted from their eating, I raise my hand to speak. "Gentlemen," I say. "As we all know, the Iroquois have declared war upon the Huron, and us French, as we are allies of the Huron." I look about the room at each man's face to make sure he understands the gravity of what I say. "From all evidence, the Arendahronnon village was very well fortified and consisted of fifteen hundred to two thousand souls before the disease of last winter swept down upon them. And now that the Iroquois have struck, the Arendahronnon people are no more."

I go on to explain that our village of maybe two hundred, many of us women and children, must focus completely and tirelessly on our fortifications, and especially on our prayers that the promised soldiers and laymen will arrive to bolster us this summer, because otherwise we'll be in great peril. "The Iroquois respect very little," I tell them, "but one thing that commands it is the Frenchman's musket." I've tallied the numbers, and we have twenty at our disposal, with twice as many men who are expert at using them.

I then invite the men to debate the best fortifications and how to realistically create them in as short a time as possible.

"We need higher ramparts," one donné says. "And with them higher and thicker palisades."

"The Iroquois simply put palisades to fire," another donné argues. "We need to build up the stone wall bases at least to the height of a man." Several of his fellows agree.

"What about a moat?" one asks, but others argue this would take too much time. I'm impressed by their willingness to offer ideas.

The best one comes from a young donné with a wispy moustache who points out that to build a wall around the village would take a year of hard work, but stone bastions at proper intervals might be built in a couple of months. The men heartily agree.

They call for more water, and one goes to the kitchen for a large jug. The men pass it around, continuing to debate candidly.

Aaron drinks deeply from his cup, and I notice he makes a strange face as he wipes his mouth. He doesn't understand French, so I fear he feels left out. After taking another long gulp, he waves for the jug to be passed to him again. A donné beside him refills his cup.

"Aaron," I say. Turning to the Huron tongue, I ask him if there's anything he wishes to say that I might translate for the others. He shakes his head and drinks more.

I'd have expected everyone to leave as soon as they could after supper, but they continue to talk, some of them laughing now, others with heads bowed, deep in conversation, a couple even crying. A man goes again to the kitchen to refill the jug, and when he stumbles a little, it dawns on me what's happening.

Standing, I ask, "What is it you're pouring from your jug?" The men who hear me go silent and look down while others carry on, apparently deaf to my tone. "What do you drink in your cups?" I shout, and this time everyone takes notice.

"It's simply a cider, Father," one of the donnés says, "made from the crabapples that grow wild around here."

"Pass me your mug," I tell the one closest to me. He does, but dares to take a deep drink before doing it. I put my nose to it and inhale. The scent of strong, cheap brandy burns my nostrils. "That's not cider!" I shout, throwing the mug across the room. "Who's responsible for brewing this devil's piss?"

I glare at them, all with their heads now lowered. Finally, a donné limply raises his hand. "It was I, Father," he says meekly. "I just wanted to bring a little pleasure into our lives during such a desperate and dangerous summer."

"There will be no spirits in this mission," I say, my voice shaking. "Nothing poisons camaraderie and obedience faster than your cheap brandy. We're on the brink of being overrun by a great Iroquois war party that roams all around us, and you choose to throw a party?"

The men mutter. Some dare to pick up their mugs and drink again. Gabriel, upon seeing this, stands up as well. "There will be no mutiny within these walls," he tells them. "Need we remind you of the punishment you will face, not only in this world but certainly in the next?"

"And if that's not enough to help you make your decision," I add, "the soldiers of this mission are under my direct command. Mark my words, I am not afraid to call upon them." Finally, I see the change in the eyes of the donnés. They bend their heads in subservience. The one who'd gone to refill the jug returns from the kitchen, sloshing a little brandy as he looks around the room, startled.

"You fool," I snap at him. "Pour out that poison right where you stand."

He's about to object but the man closest to him reaches out and takes the jug, pours it onto the floor. A few of the men groan.

"I command all of you to empty your cups," I say. The men look at one another and then at me. I stare back, Gabriel by my side. They look away and empty their cups.

I notice Aaron watches all of this with some amusement. He hasn't understood the specific words, but certainly he grasps the tone. When he sees me looking at him, he lifts his cup to his mouth and drains it. He wipes his lips with his damaged hand and tells me he'd like to speak now. He slurs his words.

"That's not a good idea, Aaron," I say. "The time for talking is over tonight."

"It's only right to let me talk," he says. He stands and raises his arms to the men around him. "My name is He Finds Villages, and I am a Wendat man." The donnés around him smirk or look away. "The one you call Father, this crow here"—he points at me—"he spoke to the Great Voice and the Great Voice told him to name me Aaron." The donnés mumble uncomfortably. "Because I have accepted the Great Voice and turned away from Aataentsic, the Sky Woman, and her son, Iouskeha, Father has told me that I will not see my loved ones when I die, that I will go to a good place but it will be without my people."

He looks around at the men who no longer watch. Some begin to talk and laugh amongst themselves.

"I was willing to do this because I love a young woman named Snow Falls. It was my understanding that when I walked away from Aataentsic and Iouskeha, she had accepted the Great Voice. And so I understood she and I could be together in the good place after death."

His voice begins to quaver now as more and more men turn away, talking to one another as if he isn't there. A few get up and stumble out the door. "But I'm not so sure of this anymore. I don't think she's accepted the Great Voice after all, and now I have been left alone."

The men still there ignore him. Aaron raises his arms higher. "Cousins," he says, "I ask you for your knowledge. I ask you for advice." More and more men stand and leave, muttering or laughing.

I want to help Aaron sit. I make a move toward him, but he waves me away.

"The crows tell me," he says to the few men left, "that I shouldn't listen to my dreams, that I should only listen to the crows and to the Great Voice. But I can no longer ignore my dreams. I dreamed the loss of these fingers." He holds up his mangled hand. "And I dream constantly that this is only the beginning, that there are still many unfinished battles. My dreams tell me that it won't be long," he says, "before fires consume this country."

The last of the donnés walk out. Aaron looks at us three Jesuits. "My dreams tell me the end of this world I know is near."

He sits down heavily in his chair and holds his head in his damaged hands.

———

THE LAST COUPLE of weeks, the donnés, by all appearances, have been behaving themselves, now realizing the grave danger we face as a few stragglers from the Arendahronnon village or its small outlying hamlets straggle in, bringing with them more news of the massacre in Huron country. I'm shocked by the brutal efficiency of the Iroquois, who knew to strike when the people were weakest and when they least expected a raid, never mind a full-scale invasion. Hundreds killed, and hundreds taken prisoner. The once proud Arendahronnon, the People of the Rock, are now just a handful of wide-eyed and starving waifs huddling in an outer longhouse of our mission.

We've taken the idea of building stone bastions at each corner of the palisades. For long days men lug stones from the surrounding fields while our soldiers keep vigil with weapons readied. I watch the slow progress of workers stirring a paste of sand and mud and lime into mortar, while others puzzle out fitting the stones together, and each day a little more of first one small corner fortress, then another, is built.

Will they be enough, though? Gabriel and Isaac want to believe the Iroquois won't attack, that for this season, their blood lust has been sated, that to attack the Jesuits would start a much bigger war against France itself, a war the Iroquois can never hope to win. But I'm not so naïve. Something started here long before we arrived, something that's now coming to beastly life. I truly believe, my Lord, that this won't end until one destroys the other.

Many of the sauvages have lost interest in the Captain of the Day, and it's become difficult to keep them focused on Christ's message when they're under this constant threat. It takes all my powers of persuasion to get them into the fields to tend to the crops, and I must constantly point out that soldiers with muskets, what they call shining wood, are always close and keeping an eye. This calms some, but the ones who've recently escaped death at the hands of the Iroquois refuse to leave the palisades. Who can blame them?

Isaac and Gabriel and I have taken to daily novenas, praying hard for You, our Lord, to deliver the soldiers and laymen and supplies promised to us. I've taken stock of the stores, and as I already suspected, even in what should be the high season, we are using far more than we produce. We cannot survive the winter at this rate, and if the disease comes back to haunt us, we will truly be in Your hands. But as always, my Lord, I place myself gladly and completely in those hands.

I'M IN THE CHRISTIAN longhouse, trying to explain the act of confession and its importance, when I hear soldiers shouting and clattering in their light armour. Delilah and Aaron look up at me, their eyes asking if the moment has finally arrived. The dozen or so others sitting with them in the shadows and smoke begin to murmur. After telling them all to stay here, I rush outside.

Rain has promised all day, and now in late afternoon it begins to fall. Despite the grey skies, I wince at the brightness compared to the inside of the longhouse and run toward where a few soldiers shout down from the ramparts to somebody on the other side while two others on the ground prepare their muskets to fire.

"What do you see?" I shout up to the soldiers above.

"A party of warriors," one answers. "I count five. Shall I fire to scare them off?"

"Don't," I tell him, "until I can see them."

"They're making threatening gestures," the soldier responds. "And one of them carries a musket."

I lift my cassock with one hand and scale the ladder as fast as I can, skinning my knee on the top rung. Once on the ramparts, I hurry over to the soldiers and peer through the logs of the palisades.

"Don't fire," I say. "They're our allies." A hundred yards across the field, Bird, his weapon in hand, stands with Fox and three younger warriors. He calls out in Huron, asking permission to come inside the gates.

WE HAVE VERY FEW OF OUR OWN

Fox and I are most impressed by the taller structures, one completed, the other three not, that stick out from the palisades at each corner of the village, all built of stone and impermeable to fire and arrows and even the shining wood. From the protected roof, a man can get as good a view as he would from the ramparts, but his perch is far more secure and it looks too difficult to climb. No doorway is visible, though I suspect there's one inside the village walls.

Fox slaps the side of the wall. "Certainly it's strong," he says, "but you could always climb up."

"Try it," I taunt him. I know how skilled he is, and it will be interesting to see if he can do it.

He puts his bow on the ground and walks around the structure, studying his options to the top as the men above peer down at him. I see that the crows have come outside the palisades to see what's happening.

Having made his decision, Fox places his hands on a stone above and pulls himself up, his feet searching out a purchase. Finding it, he again reaches above, and gains a few more feet. When he's halfway up, I shout, "If this were a battle, they'd be shooting down onto you or dumping boiling water or throwing rocks. That might make it a bit more interesting, yes?"

Fox ignores me and keeps slowly climbing. He's now high enough that if he slips, he'll seriously injure himself. Me, I hate heights. I'm a man of the earth and of the water.

Reaching his hand over the top, he flips his leg onto it and is suddenly standing among the amazed soldiers. "See, it's not so hard," he shouts down. He thinks about it for a moment. "But if I were to attack this structure, I'd break into the bottom and start a big fire to cook the enemy out."

"What about building some of these back at the village?" I ask.

"The way I see it," he says, "the palisades are still vulnerable to fire. Eventually, a driven enemy would simply make his way in and then walk through the door, no?"

He's got a point. But these stone towers might serve to slow the enemy down and tire him out. At the very least, they'd make the Haudenosaunee much more cautious about attacking.

Once Fox comes down, the Crow invites us to sit with him. He knows we haven't travelled this far for a social visit. I send Snow Falls off to go find any Wendat who are here and to listen to what news they might have. Carries an Axe, who seems devoted to her, had wanted to come along, but I told him he was needed to protect our homes. I myself had asked Gosling to join me on the journey, as her opinions and advice are important. But this village is too dismal for her. "My head aches just to think of that place," she said just before I left.

The building the Crow invites us into is made partly of stone and partly of carefully chopped wood. This, too, is impressive in its apparent sturdiness. Inside in the cool darkness, it smells of must. These people don't keep many fires burning, and the dampness would soon cause any Wendat lung troubles. Rather than on the ground, he has us sit on benches, our arms resting on the table.

I light a pipe, puff on it, and then pass it around. The Crow refuses, as is his strange custom. I'm so used to his rudeness that it doesn't much bother me anymore. He doesn't waste any time in speaking, though.

"What brings you to the mission?" he asks.

"We came to find out any news," I say, "and to share some."

I tell him that a small group of Haudenosaunee arrived at our village to ask us if we'd surrender and hand over the crows. When we refused, a skirmish broke out. "We chased them off and even killed a couple, but they made it clear," I say, "that if we remain your allies, we remain their enemy. They promised to return."

He appears pleased with my words. "They've left this country, then?"

I nod. "There are a few small parties still wandering around to harass us, but the rest, according to our scouts, have gone back home."

He looks relieved but wants to know when they will come back. I tell him it's hard to say but most likely not until the next summer. After all, they have their own crops and families to attend to. "But now is the time," I say, "to tell your people that we are in grave danger. All of us," I say, opening my arms to our surroundings. "If your war-bearers were to use their weapons and put pressure on the Haudenosaunee by attacking them at home, this would give us time to regroup and build up our strength. And it would force them," I add, "to think twice about leaving their home next year in such great numbers."

The Crow shakes his head. "Military issues are far out of my influence," he says. "In the years that have passed since the great chief Champlain died, it's difficult to get those who are in charge to give us what we need. They promise, and we wait and hope. My duty, as you know, is a very different one from war."

"But your duty will cease to exist by this time next year," I tell him, "if your people don't act soon."

"I can send a message of request," the Crow says. "But I have little faith it will accomplish anything."

I ask that he send it anyway and offer a few of our strongest travellers to carry it.

"There was the promise," he says, "of more of my people coming this summer or autumn. More war-bearers, more shining wood, more supplies."

This is welcome news. "We also come to trade with you for more of your weapons and ammunition," I explain. The Haudenosaunee respect and fear the shining wood, and Fox and I are convinced that even ten or twenty can help defeat a much bigger force.

"We have very few of our own," the Crow says without hesitation. "We can't possibly trade any away." He thinks for a moment. "But I might be able to spare a little gunpowder and shot."

Fox looks at me. "I told you this would be his answer," he says. "Are you telling me," he says, looking at the Crow now, "that you can't trade any? Surely there must be a few extra that you don't need. We can trade food, furs, whatever your people want."

The Crow shakes his head again. "I'm sorry," he says. "We hardly have enough to protect ourselves."

"We've suffered hard from the sicknesses this last winter," I say. I don't wish to say out loud that more than half of us are dead. I do tell him, though, that we have very few warriors left with any experience and our only hope of making it through what surely comes is to gather together. I feel I'm on the verge of begging now, and this makes me angry. We kept the crows and taught them how to survive in our world, saved their lives more than once, and now we're being treated like this? Still, I bite my tongue. "If and when your others make it here, can you tell me that you'll trade with us for some of your weapons then?"

The Crow thinks for a long time, pulling at the pointed hair on his chin. "If they arrive safely, and with ample supplies, then yes, I think we could trade with you."

I will take him at his word, and tell him as much. Fox and I stand to leave. We'll visit with any of our cousins who are here tonight and then leave at first light. Nothing else is left to accomplish. My stomach doesn't feel right, though, leaving it to the Crow to not only insist that his people put military pressure on the Haudenosaunee but also to honour his promise that we might obtain even a few of their weapons. Maybe I'll send Fox to take his message to their head chief, because it must get there. But just the thought of Fox not making what now is an incredibly difficult journey allows me to realize he's too important to put in such danger. I'd go myself if it were at all possible, though I have to admit I no longer have the stamina that the younger ones do.

Maybe it is time for Carries an Axe to prove himself. Not that he isn't beginning to. He, I think, might even be worthy of my daughter.

As we turn from the table, the Crow clears his throat. "What if?" he says, standing too. "What of this idea you speak about, this coming together?" He looks at Fox and then at me. "Wouldn't it make sense for our two villages to become one, at least until the threat passes?"

"You'd so easily give up," I ask, "what you've started here?"

"Actually," he says, "I thought it would make sense for your people to come here."

I look at Fox, and he's scowling yet again. "I'd rather die naked and freezing than come here begging for protection," he says.

With that, we walk out and into the sunlight.

———

THEY'VE BUILT A waterway into the village from the river, and as the light glitters across it something deep inside me makes me stop and gaze upon it.

"Look at that," Fox says. "What are they up to?"

I'm not even able to answer. It's as if I've seen this. "I think I've dreamed it before," I tell him.

We walk the length of the stream to the palisades and back again. "It's a good idea for drinking water," Fox says.

I'm still wondering about its purpose when a couple of the hairy ones call down from the ramparts to others standing by the fence, who then lift a heavy piece of wood from the gate and swing it open, and I watch, amazed, as two canoes come paddling into the village. The men then swing the gate closed and wedge the wood back in place.

"Well," I say. "I've never seen anything like that before."

Again, Fox won't admit being impressed. "I bet the mosquitoes are especially bad," he says, "with all that stagnant water just sitting there."

I laugh, but even as we walk away I can't help but glance back at this little river.

We wander the village, taking in the strange sights. A number of houses keep the men who've come all this way, and the crows have built a large place for communing with their great voice, a shining cross inside on a platform, and many benches to sit upon. Another building stores corn in one room and small game in the other. If this is all of their supplies, the crows will be in grave trouble this winter. But most fascinating is that within the palisades and behind a fence are a few poorly built longhouses and Anishnaabe wigwams.

We wonder why these houses are separated from the rest of the village until we find Snow Falls sitting with the young one called He Finds Villages and Dawning of Day in front of a well-built longhouse. They explain that only Wendat who have accepted the great voice can live in the better houses.

"Why don't you come back with us, He Finds Villages?" I ask. He had such promise before he went to the Crow.

"I'm useless now," he says, holding up his left hand to show us where the fingers were severed. "Since I took the name Aaron, the world has been a more troubled place." He laughs at his own words, words that none of us find funny. He picks up a birch cup and even from here I can recognize the smell from that night long ago in the hairy ones' fortress.

"You like the taste of that?" I ask.

"It numbs the pain," he says, holding the cup up to us.

Both Fox and I shake our heads. "I still remember the headache it gave me the night I tried it," he says. "And that was a long time ago."

He Finds Villages holds the cup out to Snow Falls. She looks at it, then at him, and finally, as if rousing herself from a dream, she shakes her head as well.

"He's been drinking that stinking water and talking nonsense about himself for days now," Dawning of Day says. "The hairy ones make it from apples and stir all kinds of strange poisons into it." She looks at He Finds Villages. "They find it amusing to watch this one beg for it whenever he runs out."

"In part, I like it because the crows hate when anyone drinks it," he says, as if he hasn't heard any of our conversation.

I shake my head at this foolishness. "Snow Falls," I say, "it's too late in the day to head home, but we'll leave at dawn tomorrow."

She nods. "Do you wish to come home with us?" she asks Dawning of Day.

Dawning of Day looks at her. "Will my family accept me back?" she asks.

I knew it was going to come to this. "I need to tell you that your family travels with Aataentsic now," I say. "I'm sorry for your loss."

"All of them?" she asks. Her voice shakes. "That can't be right."

"If it's any peace," Fox says, "my family walks with yours now, too."

Dawning of Day looks at me, and then at Fox, and finally, at Snow Falls. We watch the understanding cloud her face, her brow taking the weight of the news. "Were they buried properly?" she asks.

I nod.

"I should stay here for now," she says.

———

THE SUN UP, Fox leads us silently down the path, strung behind him at wide intervals so we can disappear into the forest at the first sign of trouble. I had an even harder time than usual waking Snow Falls this morning. When I entered the great voice longhouse and shook her, she cried out and pushed me away. She's never been easy to wake, but getting her up today was exceptional. Aaron slept nearby, snoring. A flutter in my stomach told me something was wrong, but we had to get going.

Now, as we move up a ridge that will give us a view of the valley we'll soon cross, Snow Falls stops and throws up. Holding her, I urge her to do it as quietly as she can for fear of alerting any enemy who might be around. My first thought is that she's pregnant. I ask her as much.

"No, Father," she says, again trying to push me away.

I can smell that stinking water on her now that we're so close, and suddenly, I understand. She partook of it with He Finds Villages. The pain she feels serves her right, and maybe the long walk today in her condition will teach her something. I stand from her and move down the trail, slow enough that she'll catch up. I look back and see her crouching there. She wants to tell me something, but I know her well enough that if I return to her side, her mouth will tighten up like a mussel. Despite not wanting to, I push ahead.

BLOSSOMING

My brain beats against my skull with each step. I've been poisoned. When Father asks me if I'm pregnant, I try to push him away with disgust, glimpses of last night and waking up with Aaron on top of me and of pushing him off and of feeling a burning. I'm so scared that my stomach won't stay steady, and I can't stop the foul water and heat that rush up from my belly and out my mouth. I'm so embarrassed to be weak.

The rest of the day I do everything I can just to keep up, no longer even caring if the enemy is nearby, for they will kill the pain in my head. I swear to myself that I'll never touch that stinking water again. Just the thought of its smell makes me gag. Beneath the pain throbbing in my head, something even scarier scratches away. Worried about what Aaron did to me last night, when I know no one is looking I reach down and touch myself there. I'm sore and bruised. I remember sneaking out with him and tasting the poison, then tasting it again. I remember trying to be quiet sneaking back into the longhouse, and when I lay down the earth kept moving. I remember forcing myself to keep my eyes closed, even when I felt his damaged hand begin to explore my body. I try to remember more, but there is nothing. I'm so scared as I walk along the path that despite the heat and my sweating, I shiver. What did he do to me? What will happen now? What will I tell Carries an Axe?

I can tell how upset Father is, walking ahead of me so fast he often disappears in the bushes and trees. At the open spaces we all sit on the edges and watch for enemies and game. After the last rest when they push ahead again, I can't go on anymore, so I kneel down and pray to Aataentsic and even to the great voice, hoping one of them can hear me. I'm not sure how long I sit here, so tired my head begins to nod and I'm no longer fearful of being left behind. I cradle my head in my arms, and when I open my eyes again I'm staring into the large brown eyes of a deer that's standing so close I can reach out and touch it. We're so close I see its eyelashes, its nose quivering with my scent. Then it bounds away, its white tail twitching, when Father appears and motions for me to hurry up.

I put one foot in front of the other for the rest of the afternoon. Finally, when we reach the outer fields, I'm too tired to even care that so few of them have been sown this year with the three sisters. The village feels lifeless. Normally in the early evening, families would be visiting with one another and sharing meals, but not many longhouses have fires burning and the few people I see look like ghosts.

The loss doesn't truly strike me until I walk into our longhouse and see that Fox's place is empty of his wife and children. He and Father stand outside, smoking their pipes and talking. I've never been so happy to see my own sleeping mat. Carries an Axe hasn't come by yet, and I consider going to his family's home, but the call of my beaver robe is too strong and I crawl under it, soon falling into the darkness night brings.

———

CARRIES AN AXE and I wander down by the river. He has both his bow and his club, worried about Haudenosaunee raiders. We watch the water go by and talk about the summer. I feel like we've grown up so much since the last one.

"Did you miss me?" he asks.

I shake my head, then look at him. He looks hurt. "Of course," I say.

He leans over to kiss me, but rather than the heat he so easily builds in me, I feel scared. I tell him we shouldn't right now.

"Why not?" he asks.

I lie and tell him I'm too frightened of the enemy sneaking about.

Carries an Axe goes quiet then, like he's shut off all thoughts of me. I don't like it. I lean over and kiss him on the mouth. "It feels too open here," I say. "Let's find somewhere safer, somewhere we can hide."

He smiles and stands, reaching down for my hand. I'm nervous about what we're about to do again. But I know now we're going to do it. It's only been a few times, both of us fumbling and giggling and trying too hard. Maybe this time will be a little better. I decide I want to find out, even though thoughts of the stinking water and of Aaron wake me from sleep like lightning every night.

As he leads me up a hill to a cliff hidden by trees, a view of the big water and the waves crashing on the beach below, I want to tell him about my fears. But then he'd immediately head to the crow village and kill Aaron. As we lie down and begin to kiss again, I push away all these worries and let myself go.

———

THE SUMMER PASSES with the women in the fields, the men always watching for dangers we can sense but not see in the shadows of the forest. Rain falls and the crops grow, but so many of the fields haven't been planted. Gosling, I'm surprised to see, has stayed with us all summer, which isn't typically her way. She usually disappears for long stretches to visit with her people to the north. Most days, she works with us in the fields. She likes to make fun of us, of this work, of herself for doing it. "This isn't natural," she says, wiping her brow and looking up into the hot sky. "We Anishnaabe don't slave like this in the summer when the world is kind to us. What a backward people you Wendat are."

She's taken, too, to spending more time with me. It only dawned on me recently that Father must have asked her to. He watches Carries an Axe and me closely, and I know he'd be upset to learn of what we do with each other. She has no mother to teach her what she should be careful about, I can just hear Father saying to Gosling, so will you at least try and explain to her what a young woman needs to know?

But Gosling knows that when I spent last summer in the longhouse of the women, Carries an Axe's own mother was one of the ones to teach me. I know Father worries. All fathers should worry about their daughters. It's the way of the world.

Sleeps Long is happy for us, I can see. "You and my son will soon take up what so many who are no longer with us always wanted," she says to me tonight as we sit by her fire. She and Tall Trees are having another child, and she rests her hands on her belly that's beginning to show. "The sickness killed many dreams, but your dreams will be realized." She reaches out to stroke my hair. She's smiling, but when her hand touches my head, her brow furrows. "Your dreams will be realized, yes?" she asks, the uncertainty in her voice strong.

I nod and want to say something that will calm her. I don't have the words. "I've learned to live each day, is all," I say, speaking the truth without wanting to.

"In these times, I guess this is all any of us can do," she says. "You're a wise young woman, Snow Falls. You're more than worthy of my son."

———

WHEN THE RAIN COMES this afternoon, we head in from the fields. I enjoy the feel of the drops on my face, but the other women move quickly, trying to get inside before the storm starts in earnest. I can feel it on the wind. A good one is coming.

Once we're inside the safety of the palisades, the wind picks up. The rain's no longer pleasant as it begins to pelt. I start to run for home but see that Gosling kneels by the door of her place, sheltered by her roof. She sees me too and waves. I walk up, soaked, and she makes room for me to enter.

The fire's hot and warms my skin. I squeeze the rain out of my hair as Gosling comes to sit beside me.

She has something in her hand. She reaches out and opens it. A porcupine-quill box, the top of it a beautiful flower, blossoms from her palm.

"For you," she says.

I look at the box and then back into her eyes.

She lifts her palm closer to me. "For you," she says again.

I take the present into my own hands. I turn it around and then remove the lid. It's empty.

"This is a gift for you and Carries an Axe," she says. "Your lives will soon change."

I look to her, my eyes questioning what she means.

"There's rarely the need for your man to know everything," Gosling says. "Happiness comes when you share only what you both know you need to share."

I want to tell her I don't understand, but she already senses this.

"There are times when you are not to blame for the actions of others," Gosling continues. "When your trust is broken, or someone who is your friend takes advantage out of desire."

Now I begin to follow her thinking.

"This quill box," she says, "is made to hold what's important to you. You will know what it is when the time comes."

I thank her for it, and tell her how beautiful, how perfect it is.

"You must begin preparing for what comes," Gosling says. "It's time for you and your betrothed to build your nest."

I want to ask her what she's talking about, sliding my hand down to my stomach. I look into Gosling's face. She smiles.

IT WAS NICE OF YOU

Isaac's been sitting with Aaron, keeping him calm and away from the brandy. The two seem to understand each other best. We've been forced to bind his hands and feet, as he'd turned into a wild animal last night, at one point taking a knife and slashing at his arms. I assume it's drink that demonizes him so, and the men who make it have been rounded up and placed in chains. I warned them once, and despite the grumbling of the other donnés, I will not allow this poisonous disobedience.

Isaac and Gabriel have bandaged Aaron's wounds, and we wait for him to explain what possessed him. All last night he moaned and howled and clearly it has something to do with his hurting Snow Falls. I told him she was fine and in the company of Carries an Axe and her father, but this only made him grow more agitated.

I walk outside along the periphery of the mission. We've been hard at work building residences for the expected arrival of the newcomers. Possibly a hundred men will soon arrive, many of them well-armed soldiers. This should give any Iroquois war party second thoughts. The Huron women have been tending to the fields, and the crops, while not plentiful, are in good shape. Sauvages from the north have been coming in to trade with us, so our storehouse holds plenty of game and a number of furs that these strange people are willing to barter for cheap knives and glass beads. This was Gabriel's shrewd thinking, to put word out to the various tribes that we have plenty of goods to trade. All in all, we are in fine shape now that the mornings arrive a little cooler each day, hinting of autumn. I will send hand-picked men out with the Huron to hunt for deer and other wild animals when that season comes. I tell myself we'll be fine. We've gotten through on much less before. It's the threat of the Iroquois I can't put out of my mind.

I'd sent two donnés along with three sauvages to deliver my letter to the governor of New France, suggesting what Bird had so cleverly conceived. Even a small force of soldiers with their superior weapons can be sent to harass the Iroquois this autumn, perhaps setting fire to their crops and thus making them question the wisdom of a full-scale war come next summer. I say extra prayers each morning and evening for the safe return of my messengers. They'll have to paddle and portage quickly and silently. The travel alone is brutal enough, never mind the constant fear of capture and torture.

When I return from my walk, I see that Isaac has untied Aaron.

"Is that wise?" I ask in French.

Isaac nods. "He'll be fine."

I turn to Aaron, who now sits up in the bed, looking confused and mildly angry. He absently rubs his bandaged arms. "How do you feel?" I ask him.

His answer is a grunt.

"Do you wish to speak about what happened last night?"

Again he grunts.

"Is there anything that would make you feel better?" I ask.

He smiles, but it isn't a kind one. "Give me more of that stinking water," he says.

"The men who gave you that have had their limbs bound and will soon face a torture," I say. "The poison has been poured into the earth and if you don't believe me, I can show you where it turned the grass brown. There'll be no more of it."

"I need it," Aaron says. He stands, agitated. He's a strong young man, twice as wide as poor Isaac. His once shorn hair has grown out so that it's all the same length now. It makes him look younger than he is.

Isaac extends a mauled hand to him, and suddenly I understand their bond. "I know what you feel," Isaac says. "Many of us have felt this when we get too close to it. The pain it causes will go away, and then the desire for it will grow. But that, too, will leave your body."

"Just give me a little bit and I'll be fine," Aaron says.

I shake my head. "There is no more."

He steps toward me with what I think is hostility, but his eyes are pleading.

Isaac holds his hand out farther, and Aaron stops. "Let's go for a walk," Isaac says. "You promised to show me that tree whose bark helps a body's pain. This might be a good time to find it."

Aaron glares at me for another few seconds, then drops his eyes and follows Isaac out the door, his stride uncertain.

———

GABRIEL AND I stroll the fields with our heads bent in discussion and our hands clasped behind our backs. The harvest draws closer. I wish the debacle of the secret distillery was behind us, but this rough period of unhappiness refuses to pass. As we take measure of the corn's height and health, Gabriel questions the donnés' character.

"It seems many of them came to this place," I explain, "as a way to escape prison for different crimes." There are those, though, both Gabriel and I understand, who are truly good men who have come to help spread God's word. "Just as we must weed these fields so the crops grow well," I say, "so must we continue to weed out the troublemakers, those ones who wish to distill spirits."

Gabriel nods. "With only ten soldiers and four times as many donnés and laymen, it might prove difficult to keep them in line if they decide to rebel."

"This is the way of the world, though, isn't it?" I say. "We must find something more positive to keep them focused. Besides, more soldiers have been promised any day now." But as I speak this, I fear that we've been forsaken yet again.

"We've not yet punished the distillers," Gabriel says. "They've been in chains for weeks. Something must be done."

I've not been able to force myself to have them whipped. It's clearly becoming obvious to the rest that my distaste for punishment is a weakness. Then it strikes me. "I've been meaning to lead a small delegation to Bird's village," I say. "They need to know we still exist, that we still speak for the Great Voice. Why don't I take the prisoners with me?"

"Are you joking?" Gabriel asks. "You really wish to travel in this climate of hostility? You know that Iroquois raiders wait all around us for exactly that type of foolishness."

"I'll deal with several problems at once," I say. Aaron's as good in the forest as any Huron I know. I'll ask him to guide us, and force the prisoners to accompany us as punishment. "It's high time the donnés understand the dangers that fester in this land," I say. "Fear of the evil around us will lead them back to the fold, don't you think?"

Gabriel shakes his head. "Brother," he says, "I hope you don't mind if I'm left here to keep watch over the flock while you travel."

"Of course," I say. "I'll be fine."

———

MAYBE I STRIKE OUT for Bird's village as the first frost threatens because the realization sinks in that no help is coming from New France. If this is the case, I'll need to convince Bird we'd all be better off if we joined together.

Aaron leads us on the day's walk, and I've kept the travelling party small, just the four ringleaders of the distillery, Aaron, and myself. If we're to reach the village before dark, we need to move quickly. For the first hours, their eyes are wide in terror of Iroquois waiting behind every tree to jump out and brain them.

When we stop for a rest, I whisper stories to them of the tortures I've witnessed and all the horrible ways one can die at the hands of the sauvages. They need to understand we are in grave danger and that their drunken disobedience can't continue. What I've not told them is that I plan on offering their services to Bird for the winter. I think it's best he keep them so they may learn something of this world they now live in. I also want to separate them from their friends and allies at the mission.

Two are very young, maybe eighteen or nineteen. The boy with red hair has been trying to grow a beard to make himself look older. The other, blond and sickly thin, is the one who plays the fiddle music. The distiller and his helper are as old as I am, both of them with missing teeth and their hair falling out from the lack of nutrition.

In the afternoon I see Aaron stop ahead of us. He looks down and then all around, turning his head slowly. When I join him, he's standing over the remnants of a small fire.

"Iroquois?" I ask.

He nods. "We must be very careful now," he says.

The four donnés join us. "What's this," the distiller whispers.

"An Iroquois fire. A recent one," I say, letting the words sink in. He looks as if he's about to faint. "We must be vigilant," I say, "and stay as quiet as mice. They hear everything."

We move slowly through the afternoon when all we want to do is run as fast as we can. Not until we reach the edge of Bird's cornfields does my heart begin to calm.

———

BIRD PROVIDES US an abandoned longhouse near the palisades. I'm shocked by how the village has suffered. So few of the houses are occupied. This evening, I gather all of us together and bless our temporary home, followed by my blessing each man. We bend our heads in prayer. Once we've finished, with a fire roaring in the hearth to warm the cold air and to burn away the sadness of the many families who died here, I tell the donnés they should make the longhouse as comfortable as they can, for this is where they will shelter this winter. I expected a strong reaction, but when the young blond one begins to cry and the others complain bitterly, I'm caught off guard.

"This isn't a death sentence," I tell them. "There were many punishments I'd considered, but this one will actually teach valuable lessons."

"You can't leave us here with these sauvages," the red-haired boy says as he tries to comfort his blond friend, who's now collapsed on the ground.

"I beg of you, Father," the distiller says. "Allow us to come back to the mission. We will take the lashes, as many as you think fair, if only you allow us to come home."

"Please, Father," the other says, opening his arms to the room. "You can't expect us to live like this. In this place? Surely these sauvages will kill and eat us."

I shake my head. "They'll teach you important lessons about how precious life is," I say. "And you'll be strong and teach them the resilience of the Christian man."

———

BIRD CALLS FOR ME in the morning. He lights and puffs on his pipe, and when he offers it to me, I refuse. Fox sits nearby but won't join us at the fire.

"How has the harvest progressed?" Bird asks.

"Good, I think," I say. "But the fear there won't be enough to get us through winter will always be near."

He nods, contemplative. "Our harvest will only be enough for our mouths. There will be little trading this year, which is a shame. We need much after the sickness."

I look around me at the nearly empty longhouse. "It hasn't been easy for anyone, but especially for you," I say. "And this is why I come to visit. I've brought with me four of my people in the hopes you will keep them as servants for the winter. They're hard workers. Let them collect your firewood and your water. They are in need of helping you."

Bird looks at me inscrutably. "You bring me the gift of four of your people?" he asks. He laughs to himself. "You think that passing on four of your problems is a gift?"

"What do you mean, problems?" I ask. "They are not problems." How does Bird intuit this? "They're strong, for the most part, and they can be used by you in any way you like."

"We need no help," Bird says. "But I feel you do."

"Bird," I say, "listen once more to me. We are two small villages that together can become a large one. You yourself said the Iroquois will return in force next summer."

"What of my request to ask your war chief to surprise them in this season?"

"I sent the messengers as you requested, but they haven't returned yet, which makes me fear for them."

"And what of the new arrivals? Did they come?"

I shake my head. "I fear the worst for them as well."

"And so you come instead with your gifts for us," Fox says, his voice surprising me. He stands, and despite his small stature, I fear no man more. "You bring us four dogs instead of something useful?"

"They can be useful," I tell him. "They're meant only as a sign of my good faith."

"That's kind of you," Bird says, "but we respectfully ask you take them home when you leave."

"We need no more sickness from you," Fox tells me.

"I simply come to request our two villages join forces," I say. "If we're to survive the Iroquois, we must work as one."

Bird tamps out his pipe, then stands and stretches. "It was nice of you to come all this way to visit," he says. "And I thank you for your offer, but we can't afford four more mouths to feed."

"Or the sickness they carry with them," Fox adds.

"I ask you to consider what I suggest," I say. "We built extra lodging in my village in the hope of our new arrivals. There's room for more. We can come together there as one."

Bird shakes his head. "When the Haudenosaunee attack you next summer, if there are any survivors, let them know they might be welcome here."

I wait for more, but he turns away so that I'm left standing alone, my right hand grasping my left uselessly.

———

AARON HAS GONE missing now that it's time for him to lead us back to the mission. I gather the four donnés, who crowd around me, grovelling.

"I've made my decision," I tell them. "And this decision directly affects your futures."

The men look at me with pleading eyes. "Tell us, Father," the young blond says. "Please tell us we can go home."

"I've decided to take you back with me," I say, "if you promise to abstain from your evil practices."

The men nod and hold out their clasped hands.

"If I'm to let you return to the mission, you must kneel now and repent."

They race one another to find the ground with their knees. "We do, Father. We do," they all cry out. I look down at them, as if still weighing their fate. Their eyes bulge with the desire to come back. Raising my right hand, I make the sign of the cross above them as we speak the Lord's Prayer.

We wait the entire day for Aaron to reappear. Children begin wandering by the longhouse to get a glimpse of us. Apparently they've been told not to come too close, for whenever I call out to them, they run away. A few men sit on their haunches at a safe distance, watching.

They want to watch me, as well as the ones I've brought along. When I can't stand to wait any longer, the night threatening, I walk out into the village to ask after Aaron. We must leave first thing in the morning. But everyone I encounter turns away without saying a word.

When I've given up and go back to the longhouse, something's coming from it that I've not heard in many years. I stop and listen. It's an old song, one from my childhood. The melody is simple and beautiful. It's about a shepherd guarding his flock from the beasts in the darkness, and the light of morning soon approaches. One of the men sings it in a lovely voice. It is a song my mother once sang to me.

And then, as I conjure her face for what must be the first time in years, her dark hair framing it, a woman's voice joins in the song, hushed at first but then becoming louder and more sure of itself. I'm stunned by it. Whoever's singing has the voice of my own mother. It's so eerily similar that hearing it almost brings me to my knees. Shocked, I start for the longhouse. It must be one of the young donnés who is able to sing so angelically.

Tears in my eyes, I enter as quietly as I can, wanting to witness this small miracle. I look at the fire and the men standing around it, the distiller singing as the other three sway and listen. That's when I see her. Gosling stands beside the distiller, watching his mouth intently as she sings along with him. When the song comes to an end, all the men hoot and applaud.

"What an amazing mimic," the redhead says.

"To think that she can't even speak French, and yet I sing it to her just once," the distiller says, "and she masters not just the words but the melody."

Gosling looks to where I'm standing in the darkness. "Did it bring back memories for you?" she asks in Huron.

I can't find the words to answer.

Gosling smiles and begins to sing it once more.

———

WE'RE FORCED TO SIT and wait another day before Aaron eventually returns, bursting into the longhouse panicked, telling us we must leave this very instant.

"You can't behave this way and expect me not to be upset," I tell him.

The donnés grumble. Gosling left soon after she spoke to me the night before, and the men blame me. She's cast a spell on them. They've been unceasing in begging me to go out and ask her to come back. Of course I refuse.

"We must go now," Aaron says again.

"What's the rush suddenly?" I ask. "You've kept us waiting for two days, and now you decide it's time?"

Aaron simply picks up his bow and his club, waving us to follow. Outside, he sprints through the gates and into the fields, the five of us trying not to lose him. He keeps a desperate pace until I call out to him to slow down. He waits on the path, breathing heavily.

"What's come over you?" I ask.

Aaron looks behind me, as if worried we're being pursued. "Snow Falls is pregnant," he whispers.

"What?" I say, taken aback. "What business is that of yours?" As soon as these words leave my mouth, it all begins to make sense. "Are you the father?"

"I don't know," he says. "But Bird will kill me if I am." With that, he races down the trail.

———

NOW THAT AUTUMN'S coming, moving to keep warm is actually pleasant. The donnés don't know how lucky they are. Staying with Bird and his people would certainly have taught them much more about obedience and fear.

We reach the mission gates well after dark, Aaron steady in his direction, which impresses all of us, and the donnés praise his skills. They slap him on the back, but he doesn't seem to notice.

Inside our residence, finally, I sit with Gabriel and Isaac, all of us bursting to share what's transpired.

"I tried to give our four to Bird," I say, "but he would have none of it."

"Never mind that," Isaac says. "We have important news, good news, I think."

He's smiling, but Gabriel is his usual frowning self.

"Well then," I say to the both of them. "Please do share."

"The soldiers and more donnés arrived two days ago," Isaac blurts.

I look at both of them. "This is extraordinary news," I say, clapping my hands. "We must go immediately so I can greet them and pray over them."

"In due time," Gabriel says.

"What's the matter, Brother?" I ask.

"We were promised over a hundred souls, but only seventeen arrived."

"Will the rest come soon?" I ask. "Were they held up by weather? Are they lost?"

"No," Gabriel says. "There are no more."

"What?"

"The governor decided he could spare only this many," he explains. "And to make matters worse, our messengers were ambushed and killed. The Iroquois have made it clear they're determined to get rid of us and our allies."

GO NOW

I find out with the first frost that Snow Falls is expecting a child. It isn't Snow Falls who tells me but Gosling. It appears my daughter is too afraid to let me know this herself.

"Am I to assume that Carries an Axe is the father?" I ask.

Gosling looks at me in a way that makes me suddenly even more upset. "That is for Snow Falls and you to speak of," she says.

"What's that supposed to mean?"

"You should never question your daughter's goodness," she says.

I ask where my daughter is, but Gosling claims not to know.

"Maybe she's with Carries an Axe," she says. "He's a good one for her. Indeed, he was a foolish child not too long ago, but he's become a man, and he's grown well."

"They're barely adults," I say.

"They were forced to grow up quickly," she answers. "And they do what's natural, especially in a time like this."

I snort and walk out of my longhouse. I walk the whole village looking for Carries an Axe, and I can tell by the way people avoid me that trouble's hovering in the crisp air. I see He Finds Villages and rush up to him. The strange young man with the missing fingers looks at me in horror and bolts away. I'm not sure what these charcoal are doing to make the ones who listen to them act so strangely, but it doesn't befit a Wendat. My search for Carries an Axe continues. He's lucky I can't find him.

MOST OF THE FIELDS have been harvested now, and we can see clear to the forest beyond where the leaves shine gold and red. Snow Falls won't say anything, and so we just simply walk, looking for any ears of corn the women might have missed. Conveniently, Carries an Axe is off on a deer hunt with his father, Tall Trees, and I've still not confronted him. Snow Falls has been staying with his mother, Sleeps Long, who is herself pregnant, or with Gosling. Snow Falls says she needs to be around women and there are none left in our longhouse. I can feel myself losing my daughter in bits and pieces each day.

And now soon, when the women decide it, Snow Falls will move into Sleeps Long's longhouse, as is our way. And soon it will be Fox and me, alone and bitter, two grumbling old men acting like a married couple in our bickering. I think I might ask Gosling to come and live with me as a wife. I'm tempted to speak of this with Fox, but then I realize I will only hurt him. There are few women alive now who aren't already married or in a position to take him as a husband, despite his abilities and his reputation. In the spring, I'll force him to travel with me to another Wendat community and make himself available.

"Did you want this?" I ask Snow Falls when the silence gets too much.

She won't answer me.

"Am I to take your silence as no?"

Still nothing.

"Was it forced upon you?" I ask, stopping her now and taking her arm, turning her to face me.

Snow Falls erupts in tears. "I love Carries an Axe," she says.

"Did he force himself on you?" I ask again, my hand, I realize, squeezing her arm too hard. I let her go. "Please, Snow Falls," I say. "I'm not upset with you. You're not in trouble."

Her mouth quivers. She opens it to speak but cries even harder. "Not Carries an Axe," she says in heaves. "Never. He'd never make me do what I don't want."

"Someone else did? Is this what you're trying to say?"

She looks at me, pleading, and then looks away.

"Tell me who it was," I say. "Was it a crow? One of their stinking people?"

"No," she cries. "It … it was no one." She sits down in the field, wiping her eyes with the back of her hand. "This is very difficult for me," she says. The tears have finally stopped. Her voice is already calmer. "I love Carries an Axe, and I will have our child."

"Well, there's no other choice, is there?" I say.

"Gosling told me there are certain roots that will take care of the problem, if that's what it is." Her voice is flat now. The crying child in her has disappeared like morning frost in the sun. "But I've decided to have this child, and Carries an Axe has agreed as well."

I nod. "This is your decision, after all," I say. "For you will be the one to raise it."

"I hope you'll show the child love," she says.

I laugh. I think I might learn to be excited about becoming a grandfather. "I will," I say. "I promise you."

———

AUTUMN PASSES UNEVENTFULLY, the leaves turning, then more and more of them dropping with each windstorm off the Sweet Water Sea. The harvest wasn't a big one, but as Fox bitterly pointed out last spring, there are far fewer mouths to feed. Still, I worry, my love. My life has become one long worry.

I'd wanted to trade corn for furs with the Anishnaabe and Montagnais and any others who might have wanted to in the hope of building up a stockpile and sending a smaller, quicker force next summer to the French while the more experienced warriors stay and protect the village. If the Haudenosaunee give us even a year's reprieve from attack, I know we can gather our wits and our strength. It'll be a gamble to send any men out to the French come summer, but it has to be done, and I may have to go as the envoy. After all, they'll listen to me. I'm sure of it. I'll bring the Crow to translate and explain the importance of the Crow's Iron People harassing the Haudenosaunee to keep them off balance. My daughter will be protected by Tall Trees and Carries an Axe. I'll let Fox decide if he wants to come with me or not. If I know him at all, he'll be more than eager.

———

NOW THAT THE SNOW has come, Fox and I sit by the fire and plot new ways to trade with the fur peoples.

"We can promise them an overabundance of corn the next time if they agree to give us furs now," Fox says. "I remember my father telling me he was forced to do it during a very bad season, and the traders were willing."

"You know, though, they've come to rely on our food as a staple in winter," I tell him. "Not too many will be happy to wait a full year on the promise of twice as much."

"We could always invite them along on the summer's voyage," Fox says.

This is interesting. While he and I both know it's dangerous to show our trade routes to our allies, never mind planting the idea in their heads that we might simply be middlemen and unnecessary in the next years, Fox and I have to do something to protect our people's position.

"Now that's an idea worth discussion," I say. "Why not take it one step further?"

Fox waits for me to go on as he plies the fire with a stick.

"Do you think it a good idea," I say, "to ask any who are willing to fight alongside us if it comes to that next summer?"

Fox smiles. He knows the Anishnaabe are great fighters, as are the Montagnais. Stories from our past when we once fought instead of traded with them are still often told around winter fires. "We need friends for what comes," Fox says. "But what's in it for them?"

"They want our crops to keep growing so their winters aren't so difficult," I say. "They want to feel secure against our common enemy. And they are never ones to back down from a good fight. What else could they desire?"

We laugh for the first time in days. This is all worth consideration. It might just be what saves us if the Haudenosaunee come in force again.

———

THE SNOWS FALL steady for a whole moon's cycle now, and the winter will be a heavy one. When we should all be sleeping deeply and dreaming of the spring, the nights, I know, will be restless as we wait to see if our enemy will live up to last summer's word. Some nights, Fox and I are sure they will. Other nights, as we debate with one another the ability and sheer planning of one more venture that size, we calculate there's no possible way for them to do this a second year in a row.

"Just think of what would be owed if so many warriors were to leave their homes so soon again," Fox says. "So many villages having to agree on the same course, the fear of leaving their families unguarded, the loss of work time. This last must have been the one year it was possible. Two years in a row?" he argues, surprisingly. "That rage burns bright for only so long." I'm impressed by this and want to say as much, but I fear that it will only rip open a barely stanched wound. "They'd have to be driven by something bigger than that to attempt such an undertaking twice," Fox says.

He does have a good point. But he's used to me counter-arguing. "Maybe it isn't rage so much as hunger for wealth and control that drives them," I say. "Can you imagine the prizes they paddled home with last summer? The prisoners, the three sisters, the furs and wampum?"

The two of us sleep little at night as we banter by the fire, swaying one way and then the other, never believing much of anything for long. I watch the creases of Fox's face deepen as each passing day grows shorter. I know how much my friend suffers, how the pain of his loss still feels so heavy he can't breathe. I want to tell him it does grow lighter, if only a little bit, but I know he knows this pain will never go away. This pain, I'm beginning to realize, is what all of us must share.

———

TALL TREES AND Sleeps Long have promised to come to my longhouse soon, now that the shortest days of the year are here. It's about time. Snow Falls, my thin little daughter, has been showing what she and Carries an Axe have managed to create for the last while now.

"Tall Trees and his woman will come to you when they come," Fox says, showing a little of his old drive. "You should be focused on teaching your girl what she needs to know."

I'm shocked by the words. This would be your job, love, not mine. Tell me what to tell her, yes?

Tonight, at last, Tall Trees sits by the fire on one side of me, Sleeps Long on the other. He holds a beautiful beaver robe, the soft dark hair of it shining in the fire's light. Sleeps Long holds a wampum belt that glitters like tiny wet shells on a summer beach.

"We apologize that it's taken so long to come to you on our son's behalf," Tall Trees says. "I had to go to great lengths to procure a robe worthy of your daughter. And Sleeps Long, she sewed this belt by hand."

Both are magnificent. I light a pipe and we talk about little things. "I believe that your son will be good for my daughter," I finally say, tamping out my pipe and taking the beaver robe in my hands, admiring its thickness. Then I reach for the wampum belt and am surprised by its weight. "Your skills are the finest I've seen," I tell Sleeps Long.

She looks away, pleased. "I learned from my mother's sisters," she says.

"And so I suppose a feast is in order," I say. It's as simple as that. They are two adults now and will soon bring new life to us all. We haven't had a feast in this village in a very long time.

Tall Trees allows himself to smile. I hand-picked this one years ago for a reason, and if the son is to become anything like the father, my daughter will do well.

———

I WELCOME ALL who can fit into my longhouse and have asked many women to cook for us. The kettles are full with everything I have. Tomorrow I will have nothing, and this makes me feel light and happy. Carries an Axe and Snow Falls sit beside one another with gifts scattered about them, clay pots, furs, shell beads and deerskin pouches, amulets and utensils, tobacco and pipes, knives, arrows, a new bow for each of them. There's a glow in this longhouse, my love, that hasn't really been here since you last walked in it. My two in front of me smile and laugh. We all needed this as much as they do.

I try to keep my speech short because I want people to eat as the cold wind blows outside, shaking the walls. I tell the story of how I brought Snow Falls here to our village so long ago, when she was a wild animal and was afraid of nothing, how she scared the other children and many of the adults. People laugh and others nod. And then I become serious, speaking of how, one night, on a river far from here, she took a stone and a clamshell and cut my finger off. I hold my hand up so that my guests may see. And then I tell them how she mistakenly cut her own off, too, and this was the deal that was struck that can never be broken. I speak of how her bravery to do such a thing to a man who'd killed her family astounded me. I tell the crowd who listens so carefully that it took me a while but finally, when I understood her rage, I tried to help her control it.

I can see Gosling, half in shadow, looking at me as I talk. I tell my guests how I did not raise the child alone, but how different women took her to them and taught her and how this helped to truly settle her. I look down at Snow Falls and see something I've never seen before. She's crying with happiness.

And then it's time for me to speak of Carries an Axe, how I knew he was something special not just because his father is such a splendid war-bearer but because he once asked to come with me on the long voyage to the Iron People when he didn't yet even have the wavy hair. Women cover their mouths and giggle, and men laugh out loud, shouting Ah-ho! And then I tell the story of how Carries an Axe single-handedly killed his four Haudenosaunee captors, and with the help of Snow Falls killed a fifth but was in too much of a rush to take their scalps. Again people laugh, and I finish by saying that despite this, I knew then he was good for my daughter. I then ask for people to eat until they can't eat any longer, and then eat some more.

As is the custom, I refuse the food but instead make sure everyone has everything they desire. It's a good night for me to watch the people eat and sing and dance and make more speeches for the couple. As I watch Carries an Axe stand and dance for his new bride, I pray to Aataentsic and Iouskeha that they watch over my two and allow them a long life together.

Like all good evenings, this one passes too quickly and is over before I know it. The guests leave in twos and threes until finally only our two families are left. Snow Falls is exhausted and Carries an Axe tries to act attentive, but he is tired, too.

"Go now," I tell them. "Go to your new mother's house, Snow Falls." They stand and we hug. As she gets to the door, I remember something and ask her to wait. Climbing to her sleeping platform, I reach up and cut down the great raven she's kept there.

"You can't forget this," I say as I hand it to her. "Is this not the first gift Carries an Axe ever gave you? Tie it above your new bed to keep watch over the three of you. It seems like good protection."

She smiles and takes the bird in her arms. Then she and her husband turn away, leaving me standing in my longhouse, my arms at my sides.

———

ON SNOWSHOES, Fox and I track a large buck all day. The snow's deep and the animal knows we're following. He's not dropped his antlers yet. We can see from his scratchings on the trees that he's big. His heavy rack will slow him. The snow already has. We're catching up.

We come to a creek bed and see that his tracks have dropped down into it. Fox knows this creek. It arcs toward the big water and comes back close to here like a snake before curving away again. He tells me he'll cut through the bush if I keep following the tracks, and if Fox gets to where he needs to, I'll flush the animal right to where he'll be waiting. I slow my pace so as not to send the buck running.

The travel's difficult in the deep white of the creek bed, but I stay mostly on top of it, my snowshoes only sinking in to my knee. I try to control my breath. I walk with my bow ready and an arrow notched. The day's bright and cold. At night, the trees have already begun to pop. In not too long we'll tap some of the maple for their sap that we'll boil down to a sweet syrup. A grey jay cries out at me, chattering away as if he scolds. I see the prints of hare criss-crossing the creek. This is a good place. Fox and I should set some snares and stay here the night. Now that my supplies are gone, I'll need all that the forest is willing to give.

Up ahead, the creek curves just as Fox had said it would. I can see from how the snow's sprinkled so finely around the buck's deep tracks, all the way up to his chest, that he can't be much farther ahead. As I round the curve, I see him now, stopped, looking back, just out of range of my arrow. I freeze. I hope Fox is within range, though, and if not, that I don't scare the deer up into the forest where he'll certainly gain an advantage and make us chase him through the night.

The buck snorts, a long white cloud of steam pouring from his nostrils. He paws at the deep drifts that surround him. Something is agitating the animal. He must sense Fox is close by. I like this. I try to will him to charge me. If he does, I'll simply draw my bow, aim for his broad chest, and let the arrow fly.

Instead of charging, the buck pushes up the creek bank, snow flying, and disappears into the bush, flashing the white underside of his tail. The feeling of losing him makes my belly sink. I have little energy to keep pursuing but now I'll have to.

As I push toward where he disappeared, I hear a commotion, branches snapping and then a warrior's shriek, the deer now bounding back out onto the creek bed, trying to clear the deeper drifts. Behind him, I'm astonished to see Fox, bounding too in his snowshoes, in pursuit. The deer, fighting the deep drifts, sends huge clouds of steam from his mouth and nostrils, but Fox, light and quick, seems to float over the snow as he gains ground, the deer now in the middle of the creek, Fox nearly to him.

I can see the flash of a knife in his hand in the sunlight as Fox makes a tremendous leap and latches onto the animal's back. The buck's massive, his antlers pointed and sharp as he shakes his head and jumps, trying to dislodge Fox, who's got one arm barely around the animal's neck. Fox lifts his other arm and drives it down, plunging the knife into the buck's side as many times as he can, trying to hit the lungs, the animal grunting now. I can see from here the blood dots in the snow as I hurry to help. As I gain on them I watch the flash of knife again, this time aimed at the animal's neck. Blood spurts up into the sunlight, and the deer's eyes, brown and wide in anger and fear, look right at me.

Finally, making it to the struggle, I'm breathing hard, but I must pounce, too, grabbing the animal's antlers with both hands, trying to twist its head down to the ground so that Fox can make the important cut to the neck. The buck's still full of strength, though, and I only manage to allow Fox to slip off him. He falls on his back into the snow, and now it's just the crazed deer and me, and I'm holding on to his antlers, knowing that if I let go, he'll use them to gore me or will crack my head open with his sharp hooves.

Twisting as hard as I can, my eyes looking into the buck's, my arms shaking with the strain of it, our nostrils flared and snorting white puffs of air, I begin to feel the animal losing his balance until finally he twists onto his side and then his back, me holding on hard as I can. I can sense more than see that Fox is up now, my face full of snow as the buck kicks his legs violently, trying to right himself. The animal lets out a bellow right into my face, his spittle covering me, his eyes wide and tongue sticking out. I can feel the kicks get lighter, then lighter still, until finally the animal is twitching more than kicking. But I know not to let him go just yet.

When I have nothing left, I loosen my grip on his antlers and just lie on my back, trying to catch my breath, the great deer's head resting upon me. I stare up into the sky, a few chickadees flitting by, flashes against the blue. A raven caws out, and the world feels still again. I can smell the strong tang of fresh blood, the stink, as well, of guts from the animal's opened cavity.

When I'm able, I crawl out from under him to see Fox already bent to the gutting, blood on his face.

"Wouldn't it have been easier to just shoot it with a few arrows?" I ask.

He laughs. "Probably. But I pulled so hard on my bow that it snapped."

"Impressive," I say.

The animal's innards steam in the cold air, and I, too, bend to the careful cutting and scraping out. As I begin to quarter it, Fox builds a fire. Soon, we're cooking a piece of loin over it. The walk back home with such a large animal won't be easy, but it'll feed many mouths. We'll construct toboggans to pull it, and the story of how we got it will be a good one to tell.

———

RATHER THAN BEING greeted with happiness when Fox and I have finally made it back into the safety of the palisades, all we encounter are stricken faces. We deposit our kill at the longhouse and I go out in search of the problem. We've only been gone a few days. What could possibly have happened? The potential troubles flood in. The death of an important person. Someone else with the telltale cough. The sighting of an enemy. A healer's bad dream.

I find Gosling in her small home, sewing by the fire. I sit by her.

"Something's wrong with the three sisters," she says before I even have a chance to ask.

"Tell me."

"The women have discovered a rot. Some are saying that it spread from house to house."

Gosling reaches beside her and passes me an ear of corn. Even though it was carefully picked and hung before being placed in a basket with the other ears, when I pull back its husk, I see it's covered with a grey fuzz, and underneath it the kernels have turned an oozing black.

"How much has been affected?" I ask.

"Most of the village," she says.

If this is true, it means certain starvation before spring. "What of the other two sisters?" I ask.

"It wasn't a good year for them before this," she says. "The squash seems to be infected, too, but the beans, from what I've heard, are still all right."

I want to ask her what to do, but the question will sound foolish coming out of my mouth. Instead, I say, "We must put out the word that the bad corn be burned."

Sitting beside the fire with Gosling, the two of us silent, all I'm left to do is contemplate the calamity of it all.

ARE YOU ALL RIGHT?

The bliss of what's so new to us doesn't last long. Not a month after I take Carries an Axe and he takes me, the village is visited by another sickness, this one killing the corn. It's almost as bad as if another illness had descended on the people themselves during this moon of the popping trees. The days have grown as short as they can and now just begin to grow longer again, but one would never know it by the way the sun teases, only coming out for a little while some days. The people, though, are panicked, and we've burned all the sick corn to try and stop the illness from spreading, the few kernels on the cobs that were still good popping from the fire, the children rushing to grab and eat them. It's a fun game to them as their parents feed the fires and pray.

Medicine people try to dream where the sickness has risen from, and what caused it to come to us at an already desperate time. They sing and shake rattles and burn offerings, trying to divine what can be done. But still the disease spreads. The women rush to build new birch baskets to hold the dried corn or hang it high above us in the longhouses on rafters, hoping the smoke that rises will coat it, bless it, protect it. We all begin to eat just enough to get through the day, our stomachs moaning. Some of the children begin to cry at night. The village comes together to take note of how much we have, but it turns out to be little, and it will last no longer than one moon's full sink and rise.

"This will leave us in the coldest month without the three sisters to feed us," the oldest healer says, and so the men, my husband included, double their hunting efforts, staying away for days at a time. And still they come back with little.

As if in defiance of my body being fed less, my stomach seems to grow bigger every day, and Carries an Axe is off on the hunt the morning I first feel the baby kick. In his place I have Sleeps Long put her hand on my belly, and she smiles and tells me right away that it will be a girl. She herself is due any day now. Her stomach pushes her deerskin dress taut. I go out to find Gosling to tell her the news, the wind howling and snow blowing, the sun shining behind it, making the flakes glisten and dance.

She's not home, and so I head to my father's longhouse to see if he's returned from his hunting. He and Fox brought back a large buck, and he's kept a haunch just for me. He wants his grandchild to grow strong. He doesn't know, though, that the extra meat he gives me I in turn give away to the children in Sleeps Long's house, my new home. I see smoke from his fire caught by the wind and racing away from the longhouse, and so I rush in to tell him the news. I see he sits with Gosling. They're holding hands. She laughs, and his face doesn't look like I've seen it before.

"It's true," she's saying to him. "You wanted this, and so I found a way to make it happen."

"Is it truly possible? I thought, I thought …" He looks at her, his face like a boy's, looking younger than I've ever remembered seeing it, his eyes wide and his mouth slightly open, clearly not believing what he's just heard. He's about to say something more but looks up and sees me. He beckons for me to sit with them.

"The baby moved today," I blurt, truly struck now by what's happening in my body.

Gosling and my father smile. "Let me know when it moves again," he says. "I want to feel my grandchild for the first time."

I want to ask them what news Gosling has given my father to make him act stunned like this, staring at me smiling, one hand rubbing the other, his eyes distracted, looking from me to Gosling, then back to me again.

"Here," she says, standing to scrape some stew from the kettle by the fire. "We've been saving this for you."

I don't want to accept the bowl, but my stomach groans and Gosling smiles and my hands take it. I sit by my father and eat much faster than I mean or want to. He still sits there, quiet, but not himself, either. Gosling sits back down to join us.

"What's news with you?" I ask casually.

He opens his mouth to speak, but shuts it again.

Gosling laughs. "He seems to have lost his tongue," she says.

"Shall I tell her?" my father asks.

She shakes her head. "Not yet," she says. "This is Snow Falls' time."

"Tell me what?" I ask and push his arm. "This isn't fair. Tell me what?"

Gosling laughs again, and just as she does, I feel the flutter in my belly and then the push, as if by my eating something, I've awakened it.

"Here!" I say. "Give me your hand. Here." I take my father's hand and place it on my stomach, right above my belly button.

His eyes go wide and for a second time today he looks like I've not seen him before. He smiles. I think he's speechless.

"Would you like to feel, Gosling?" I ask.

She hesitates. Both of them are acting so strangely. They're like children, unsure of what to do. Finally she leans toward me, reaching her hand out, a small smile on her face. The baby's stopped moving, though.

She takes her hand back and rubs both of them together quickly, as if heating them up. "I do want to feel your child move," she says, leaning forward again and placing her hand on my belly. My stomach feels like I once felt when a bolt of lightning struck too close. The hair on the back of my neck stands up, and a tickle runs into my belly that isn't quite uncomfortable, just strange.

"What makes it feel like that?" I ask.

"It's just an old trick my mother taught me," Gosling says. "You can focus your orenda, you know. Maybe you're feeling mine?" She laughs. "There it is," she says as my baby stirs once more. Smiling, she moves her hand slowly over my belly, and the child inside, as if waking from a nap, moves its arms and its legs. I'm sure of it.

I look at Gosling in amazement, and she looks back at me, her face relaxed. Closing her eyes, she hums something, and the baby continues to squirm and push. I'm between that place of liking and not.

Gosling's eyes dart open.

"What is it?" I ask as she continues to rub my belly as though she's searching for something, her eyes glazed. "Please," I say. "Tell me what it is."

Gosling focuses again. Looking down at her hand as if it doesn't belong to her, she lifts it from me, and I suddenly feel heavy.

"Shh," she says when I ask her again what the matter is.

I look to my father, his forehead wrinkled with concern. He wants to say something, I can see. But he waits.

"It's nothing," Gosling says.

I don't believe her. "What did you feel?" I ask.

She says nothing. I push her further. "Do you really want to know?" she asks.

Suddenly, I'm not so sure. I nod anyway.

"You are going to have a girl," she says. "That's all."

"Sleeps Long told me the same," I say, feeling relief.

Gosling nods at me, and now I can see it as clearly as if she's saying it out loud. This isn't the only news.

"You will have a girl," my father says, clapping his hands, breaking my stare.

When I look back to Gosling, she's already standing. "It's time for me to go," she says.

———

CARRIES AN AXE finally comes home with just a few hares and partridge to show for his days away. He's a good hunter, but the world seems like it's turned against us. I can feel the worry, even a slow burning fear, when I leave our longhouse on my walks. Everyone knows what comes, and yet none of us, as hard as we try, can prevent it. The talk has turned to whether or not we go to the village of the crows before we run out of food. Some say that they would rather die than beg from the charcoal. Others argue that in their time of need, we looked after them. The least they can do is repay the favour. This debate divides the village. It's the last thing we need right now, but too many people worry about their children and their families.

Tonight, Sleeps Long and I listen to our husbands talk about it all.

"We might have to go there," Tall Trees says. "There's little other choice."

"I won't beg from them," Carries an Axe says.

His father explains that we won't go to the crows with empty hands, that we still have furs and labour to offer in exchange. He says rumour has it that none of the regular winter traders, the Montagnais or Neutral or Anishnaabe, have come to us because they still fear last winter's sickness, and now word has gotten out that our corn has become tainted.

"What I've heard," Carries an Axe says, "is that the crows and their people offer their kettles and knives and beads in exchange for furs and meat. They now have what our trade partners want." I can hear the anger in Carries an Axe's voice. "Don't you see," he says. "The crows have slid themselves like snakes between us and our allies."

Sleeps Long and I look over at them. Tall Trees smiles. "What better reason to go to their village, then?" he asks. "If you think they've taken from us, then you must go to them and speak your truth."

Tall Trees is wise. I see what he's done. His son has to now temper his anger and agree with his father about the importance of going to the crows' village. I'm impressed until I realize we'll all be making the journey back to the place that has caused me such pain.

NEARLY HALF THE VILLAGE decides to go. This is no longer the place of many longhouses. I'm sad to see how few of us are left. Now that deep winter sits upon us, and we travel with the old and the very young, the walk will take two days instead of one. When the skies relax and the weather relents a little, we set out, a long line, clad in deerskins and beaver robes, snowshoes upon our feet, the men ahead cutting trail and dragging toboggans of supplies so that those who walk behind will find it easier. Ahead of the men who cut the trail, our scouts sneak through the forest, seeking signs of enemy raiders and looking for good places for so many to camp overnight.

For half a day, the rest of us who've decided to leave trickle out of the palisades, but not before we say our goodbyes. And then we wander out in groups of five or ten or fifteen. It's as if our home exhales half its breath this day but can't find a way to breathe in again.

When it's my time to go, I walk to my father's longhouse and find Fox inside, sitting by the fire. He looks almost like a boy squatting there, but his size never stopped him from being one of our greatest war-bearers.

He stands when he sees me. I approach him.

"I'll see you in spring when we return to plant," I say.

He nods. "Tell your father I don't think less of him for going with you. I would too, to protect you, if you were my daughter."

I want to tell him it isn't too late, that he can come, too. But I can't imagine him living within the walls of the place of crows. It would kill him. That or he would strike out in rage.

"It won't be long," I repeat. "Only until the winter breaks."

He nods again. And then he does something he's never done to me before. He takes my shoulders in his hands, as if he cups a bird's egg in each one. He looks at me, his eyes glistening, before pressing his forehead to mine.

CARRIES AN AXE walks with a group of us women. His job is to protect us, and I love how his chest puffs out with the mission. Not knowing what else to do with my raven, I'd tied a length of sinew to his feet and slung him over my shoulder, his length nearly as long as me. The women laugh and caw out to me as we walk through the snowy fields toward the forest.

"Why don't you make it fly," one teases, "so it can carry you to the crow village?"

If only she knew. I don't mind being teased. They mean nothing cruel by it.

As we reach the edge of the field, we all go quiet. It's time to be careful and to pay attention now. I glance back at the village once more and the thought arises that I'll never see it again. I push it away and focus on the journey.

My father's up ahead with the trail cutters. He'll leave a sign in the forest for me. "Keep an eye," he said. "I'll snap branches from a spruce and arrange them by a birch not long before it's time for all of us to gather and make camp. I'll strip the branches and place them in a curved line beside the trail. You'll be the only one who knows this means you're within a short walk to the night's shelter. And you will amaze everyone when you announce this and it indeed comes true."

All day we walk, our progress measured. We can only go as fast as the slowest in our group. Despite wanting to speak with Carries an Axe, I know not to waste the energy or take the chance of alerting an enemy scout. I feel twice my normal size, and it's hard work to keep up, but Carries an Axe is always nearby. At the sun's peak, we stop to build a small fire and warm ourselves.

"Do you want me to pull you by toboggan?" he asks. He can tell I'm struggling.

I shake my head. "Don't be silly," I say. "I'll be fine."

He reaches into his pouch and pulls out a piece of dried deer meat. "Chew on this slowly as you walk. It'll keep you going."

We push on through the afternoon, and to keep myself occupied, I chew on bits of the meat, trying to make it last as long as I can as I look for the sign my father says he'd leave me. I'm not paying attention on the slow walk, and as afternoon begins to darken, the toe of my snowshoe catches a root and I tumble forward, slipping down a short embankment beside the path, my torso banging along rocks or old stumps buried just under the snow.

When I try to push myself up, I feel a sharp pull in my belly. Right away I lie still and whisper to my baby.

Careful, I say. *Are you all right?*

The other women call out to Carries an Axe, and he is down before I can fully catch my breath. He kneels by me without saying a word, placing one hand on my shoulder and another on my belly. I look into his eyes, trying to keep mine from giving away fear. He stares back. We both know when I'm ready for him to help me up. The sinew holding the raven snapped as I rolled down the small hill, and when I pick him up, I see that one of his wings hangs at an odd angle.

"Don't worry," Carries an Axe says as he reties the sinew and places the bird back over my shoulder. "We'll fix it." I want to believe him, but I don't know how we will.

We walk even slower now along the path, the women gathered around me like a flock of geese protecting their young. The pain in my belly recedes, but still something doesn't feel right. When they ask, I tell them I'm fine.

As dark begins to threaten, I see a large birch up ahead, and when we near it, I see the stripped spruce branches my father told me to look for.

"We're near the camp now. I'm certain of it," I say.

The women look at me.

Sure enough, within a short walk, we smell the smoke and then see its light in a dense thicket beside the trail. The women are impressed.

"How did you know?" one asks.

"My raven took flight when you weren't looking," I say. "Then he came back to report to me."

———

TONIGHT, I'M SLEEPLESS with the worry. My stomach no longer hurts much, but something in my body warns me. A fire burns hot in the middle of the clearing, and different families lie huddled together for more warmth under our birch roofs, the front of our lean-tos facing the fire. There are camps of us like this all over the area, our guards walking about and keeping an eye so that we might sleep peacefully.

"I can't sleep either," I hear a voice whisper close to me. Carries an Axe lies behind, his arms wrapped about me. My father sleeps in front of me. It's Gosling, burrowed like a mouse inside his robe. I didn't know she was there. Her face is close to mine.

"I fell today and worry I hurt my baby," I whisper back. "It didn't seem like much of a fall, but I felt something pull."

Gosling doesn't say anything, but this doesn't surprise me. She rarely wastes her words.

When I think she must have gone to sleep, she finally whispers again. "You know that I didn't tell you everything the other day," she says.

Rather than answer, it's my turn to not speak.

"This is because I myself am not sure what I saw in my head when I touched your belly." She pauses. "I saw a young woman, about your age. Her face was pocked from a sickness, just like yours. But she lived in a crow village. A large one. She wore the charcoal clothes of the crow, wore one of their sparkling necklaces around her neck and a long cloth the colour of night that covered her hair." Again, Gosling stops.

"Tell me more," I say. "Was she happy?"

"I can't say, but she didn't look to be. She knelt like the crows do and whispered their words. She knelt in front of a very large carving of the one they love so much who was tortured and nailed to wood."

"What else? Tell me more."

"There is no more. Only that I could tell the crows held her in great regard. They told others to pray to her when they were sick and then they'd be cured. None of it makes sense to me."

I want Gosling to tell me more, but again she says there's nothing else, just the imagination of a crazy woman.

As the fire burns low and the cold begins to creep up from the ground and into our sleeping robe, I shiver. I can tell Gosling is still awake.

"If there is anything else you remember, will you tell me?" I whisper.

"I can tell you something now I've told no one but your father," she says.

"What?"

"I too am pregnant. In the late summer I will give birth to your father's child."

I want to ask how this is possible. Despite her beauty, I believed she was beyond the age to become pregnant.

As if to answer my thought, she says, "There's a reason you Wendat say we Anishnaabe have magical abilities. If one wishes for something hard and long enough, there's no reason it can't come true."

THE MISSION THRIVES

They begin to trickle and then flood into the mission. The first arrive shortly after morning prayers, the guards on the ramparts shouting down in warning. Gabriel and Isaac and I rush out and up the ladder to look over the wall. I recognize Huron from the village where I once lived, standing just in front of the tree line, a dozen or more of them. In their language, I call to them that it's safe to come forward, and then, scrambling back down the ladder, I order the gates opened.

They come in with apprehension, looking about them at the buildings so different from their own. I recognize one of the older ones, a woman who used to tease me mercilessly.

"Welcome," I say. "What makes you travel all this way in such conditions?"

"The three sisters became sick and perished. We came here so as not to starve."

I look at Gabriel. He gives me the knowing look back. "Our stores are in good order," he says. "There should be enough for all."

He's right. The northern tribes have been coming to us all winter in order to trade and to get a glimpse of this new community. "Are many more of you coming?" I ask.

The old woman scratches her head. "Perhaps half the village."

I almost fall over. This must mean at least a couple hundred souls after the last year's decimation from diseases. I turn to Gabriel and Isaac. "We have trouble on our hands," I say.

More and more pour through the gates just as a February storm arrives, the wind blowing hard from the northeast and rattling the walls. There isn't enough room for all the refugees. I open up the empty buildings to them, and people cram inside the longhouses and wigwams, others constructing temporary shelter as quickly as they can before the brunt of the storm arrives.

By afternoon, a fierce gale blows off the Sweet Water Sea, and we worry that some will still be stuck in the storm. They have the same ability as the forest animals to burrow down into the landscape, I remind myself to ease the worry.

At nightfall, I order the gates shut and locked. But I worry nonetheless, excited and nervous as I fight my way through the howling winds from place to place, checking in on all the arrivals, the sauvages crammed in but happy in every structure of the mission, talking and smoking pipes and laughing as if the storm outside doesn't even blow. They all must be starved. Their faces are thin, and the old people's cheeks are hollowed, yet they're happy to be out of the cold and ice and wind, and so maybe this is enough for now. I will have to sit down with Gabriel and Isaac tonight and sketch out some better long-range plans. It strikes me then that this might not be a temporary visit. Lord, is this Your plan that begins to come to light? Is this my chance to finally bring souls to You?

I return, half frozen, to our own small residence and find Isaac and Gabriel at the table, already discussing the complexities of this newest challenge.

"I don't see how we can possibly feed all these new mouths," Gabriel says as I stand as close to the fire as I can, my cassock steaming. A wind rattles the roof and sends a gust down the chimney, flattening the fire for a moment.

"We have faced greater difficulties," Isaac says. "I'm happy so many have chosen to come to us in a time of need."

"We'll have enough," I say. "You know this by now, don't you, Brothers? He will provide."

THIS MORNING, shouts coming from the Huron alert us to bad news. Gabriel reports to me that a family of four was found huddled outside the gates, frozen to death. Rushing through the palisades, I turn around the corner to see a horrific sight. Four bodies, ice formed on their faces, lean against the wall. The man, clearly the father, has his arms wrapped around his wife, two small children between them. Huron who must be relatives stand near them, singing and praying. Not sure what else to do, I order my men to bring them inside where they can thaw and be prepared for burial, but the men struggle trying to pull them apart. The bodies are frozen together.

Eventually, with great effort and the sound of tearing, the father comes free, and I watch as three men struggle to carry his awkward, crouched form into the mission. The mother and children won't separate, and so a small group of others simply pick them up as one and carry them inside as well.

An old Huron woman asks me what I plan to do with her son and daughter-in-law and grandchildren.

"I will allow them to thaw so you can perform a burial for them," I say.

She thinks about these words. "We will not be able to bury them till spring, and so I don't know why you want to thaw them." Her face is a mask. Their faces always are when they confront the death of a loved one. She won't allow her tears to come until the funeral.

"Please tell me what I should do with them," I ask.

She tells me to have them brought to the longhouse where she stays, and so I give the directive.

I remember my thoughts last night, my attempts to ease my worries by telling myself that the sauvages who didn't make it in would be fine. Did I order the gates closed? At what time? My Lord, it dawns on me that this is my fault.

The chapel is emptied of its temporary residents now that the storm has passed. I walk up to the altar, my face hot, and I kneel. What have

I done, Lord? What have I done? Give me Your guidance now. This is my fault. I did order the gates closed, fearing an unseen enemy. But the unseen enemy is Satan, and he was victorious last night. Why didn't I leave the gates open for stragglers? What if there are more out there, frozen in the snow? What did I do in my haste and my fear?

Sick with guilt, I can barely keep myself up. I'm responsible for that family. Forgive me. Please, Lord, forgive me.

———

FOR THE NEXT DAYS, I'm debilitated with the weight of what I allowed to transpire. I'm unable to sleep for the frozen faces that haunt me. I even go into the chapel late tonight with a spruce switch and pull down my cassock, exposing my back. Praying to You, I flail myself mercilessly, but the welts I can feel rise up are no justice. I strike myself until I can feel the warm blood begin to speckle my back. This is nothing, either. I consider walking out into the night so I may feel what that poor family did, the pain of the cold as it slowly cuts its way through the skin to the bone.

In the morning, a deep malaise has set in, and when I don't arise from my thin cot, Isaac comes to ask after me.

"Père Christophe," he says. "Are you all right?"

I don't have the voice to answer.

"Is there anything I can get you?"

"I'm feeling unwell. Please leave me alone to rest."

For two more days and two more nights, I lie on my cot, getting up only to relieve myself the first day, the second day not even able or needing to do that. When I sleep, it's fitful, and I see Satan's face peering in my window, looking down at me and grinning. He's taken the upper hand. I know this now. But I feel useless to stop him.

Just as the light begins to wane on the third day, my bones aching and my back a scream I ignore, I hear a light knock on my door.

"Enter," I call out in a hoarse whisper.

Gabriel's silhouette appears at the door and behind him, the taller, muscular silhouette of Bird. I try to sit up, but my body refuses me.

"Bird needs your counsel," Gabriel says. "As do we."

He stands aside and Bird walks in, hulking over my cot. "You're ill?" he asks.

I nod.

"You need to find your strength," he says. "The people need guidance. Your bearded ones won't listen to us as they say you're the only voice they'll obey. My people need to build shelters. We can do it outside the palisade walls, but we prefer to be within them. Twice now I've had to prevent some of my men from fighting with yours."

Slowly, my body crying out, I raise myself to sit. I try to find my voice, but nothing comes. I signal Gabriel for water. He brings me a jug and a cup. I drink deeply.

My voice is a scratchy whisper. "I'm not sure what I can do."

Bird stares at me. "You can climb out of your bed now," he says. "We put our faith in your offer to come here, and it's time now for you to get up. There are already some dead, but far more will follow if you don't stand. And I can tell you that many of them will be your hairy ones."

With that, he turns and leaves. He's right. I've shamed myself enough. I stand, dizzy, and walk unsteadily to my door.

———

EVERY MAN AVAILABLE helps with the cutting of trees, the peeling of bark, the collecting of firewood, the building of residences, the expansion and digging of the palisades as best we can into the frozen earth. The weather holds bright and sunny and the temperature drops so that more and more donnés report frostbite. I scold those who simply pretend in order to get out of work duty, giving them the odious jobs of heading into the forest to cut trees. To a man they are scared stiff of the wilderness that surrounds us, imagining lurking Iroquois in every shadow.

I know it's simply to assuage my guilt, but I throw myself into it as well, working alongside the men from first light until well after dark, watching as the Huron show us how to erect longhouses. Each night I crawl into bed exhausted, the vision of that frozen family forcing me awake even before the sauvages, ready to head outside once more to the back-breaking work.

I've ordered the storehouses open, and I put Gabriel in charge of handing out food to all who need it. If I were to leave Isaac this task, I fear the rooms would be empty within days. I've never witnessed Europeans work with the sauvages before, and I'm mightily impressed by what I see. Within days of my shaking off Satan's spell, we've built enough longhouses to house the influx of Huron through winter. It is true, Lord, that hard work leaves little room for the ill will born of idleness.

In these first weeks with this warming of relations between the two groups, though, I begin to notice that the donnés are less inclined to attend Mass each morning or even to show up for the shorter evening prayers. Some mornings, there are more empty benches than full. I try to decipher whether this has something to do with the sauvages who've descended like a flock of birds en masse, with their skewed sense of time and of propriety and of work ethic, so often drumming and singing late into the evening, or stopping their work suddenly and without notice to wander away and smoke their pipes or go hunting. This lack of structure seems to be wearing off on my men.

Gabriel, Isaac, and I discuss what can be done about it.

Isaac is of the mind that nothing needs to be altered. "Just look at how much has been accomplished in such a short time," he says. "The Huron have built their longhouses, many have gone off to hunt, and they seem content. Is this not enough?"

"But what is our mission?" Gabriel asks. "Just to offer them comfort? Haven't you noticed that our hard-fought converts no longer come to Mass anymore? They've slipped back so quickly into their old ways."

Gabriel's right. The blessing of this arrival may very well prove to be a curse. "And so, Brothers, what to do?" I ask.

"To me, it's simple," Gabriel says. "If they live within these walls, they must abide by our rules."

Isaac's face grows red. "Do you believe it's really that simple?" he asks.

"I do," Gabriel says.

"And so what do you propose?" I ask of Gabriel.

"That we be stern. If the sauvages are to partake of our kindness, our generosity, then they must abide by our rules." Gabriel glares at Isaac. "They must agree to come to listen to the Lord's word. They must make an effort to understand us. They must conform to our ways."

"But they never asked this of us when we were the ones at their mercy," Isaac says, shaking.

"And that is their weakness, isn't it," Gabriel spits.

I fear the two will soon be at each other's throats if I don't intervene. "Brothers," I say, standing up and between them. "You must understand you're both correct. But this still leaves us with our dilemma. Our mission is to bring them to Christ. I'm sure you each agree with that."

Gabriel nods, but Isaac is too upset to react.

"We still need to provide safety and comfort," I say. "And especially spiritual guidance. Remember, both of you, we all came to this dark land long ago so that we might shed light upon it. The Lord's light. So let us come together as brothers again and agree that the saving of their eternal souls is our utmost priority."

I look at Gabriel, whose eyes are turned away but whose countenance tells me he agrees. Isaac looks at me, his mouth an angry line.

"This is our mission," I say, slamming my fist into my open palm, my voice rising with emotion. "We all swore we were willing to sacrifice our lives for this, did we not?" I ask. "What could be more blessed than to offer our lives for those less fortunate? If this is the case, my brothers, it is indeed our time. The sauvages have come to us asking for help. The help we can give them is far greater than they can ever know."

Gabriel stands when I've finished. He reaches his hand out to Isaac.

Isaac, sweet Isaac, hesitates but then takes it as best he can with his mangled grip. We stand together, our hands interlocked.

"We will focus harder, and work together as one to take them into the fold, yes?" I ask.

Gabriel nods. "Yes, beloved Father," he says.

Isaac looks at both of us, his face lightening from the burden. His eyes go wide. "Yes," he says. "I am willing to die for them."

———

THE MISSION THRIVES as March comes in cold and blustery. It's almost what I imagined all these years I've dreamed of our two races coming together. The donnés and the sauvages certainly avoid one another more than I like, but I watch interactions take place between the two as they carefully approach one another to try to communicate or trade. I've put word out that the donnés are obliged to attend daily Mass, and they've returned, for the most part, to the fold. Gabriel and Isaac and I now spend our days amongst the longhouses of the Huron and the wigwams of the fur peoples, speaking of the Great Voice and urging them to come to the Great Voice's house so they may understand better.

While it isn't a perfect society yet by any means, I see it truly becoming something. Bird, though, has spoken of how this is only a temporary visit, and that when spring comes soon, they'll go back to their own village. This is indeed a cloud on the horizon of my plans. But I haven't given up hope yet that many might wish to stay in the comfort of the mission.

Aaron is one of the few sauvages who's stayed close to the fold since the arrival of Bird and the rest. He attends daily Mass and avoids much interaction with his own people. This morning, after Mass, Gabriel and I stand on the steps of the chapel and discuss this when we see Snow Falls, clearly heavy with child, wander by.

"I understand why Aaron stays away from them," I whisper to Gabriel and then tell him Aaron might possibly be the father.

Gabriel is shocked. "Have they truly no shame?" he asks.

"Just watch," I say as I see Carries an Axe walk up and take her arm. Her pregnancy is so obvious now. "I'm not sure who the father is, and I'm not sure she does, either."

Gabriel shakes his head. "Can we allow this kind of behaviour within the walls of the mission? Shouldn't someone speak to her? Or better yet, speak to her father?"

Young Snow Falls, you are a disappointment. You've been my bane since we both first arrived here so many years ago. As soon as I think I begin to understand you, have even won you over to Christ, you surprise and shame me by biting my hand. And now, as you proudly flaunt your immorality, you've shown me you are not at all what I'd hoped you'd become. But I haven't given up all hope for you.

"Maybe the question we should ask ourselves," I say, "is this. Is she Mary Magdalene, the young whore who'll come to see the light? Or is she just a young whore who doesn't even know who's fathered her child? Personally, Gabriel, I don't want to believe the latter."

As I watch you walking away from me with Carries an Axe on your arm, I've made up my mind, Snow Falls. I'll allow Gabriel to speak to your father about how you flaunt this latest power you must think you wield over young men. Gabriel will make it clear to your father, and to Carries an Axe, that your behaviour is not to be condoned.

"Yes, dear Gabriel," I say. "Maybe it's best you speak to Bird about all of this. We can't allow their immoral behaviour to go unchallenged. But be careful with your words. He can have quite a horrible temper."

IT'S TIME

A sense of contentment has actually settled here in this strange village of crows, my love. We've built enough longhouses for all, and while they might not be as good as ours back home, each of us has a roof over our head and a hearth to keep warm by. We had not brought much in the way of food, yet the crows were generous, and this has impressed us. They know we won't stand owing them, and all will eventually be made even. Who better than you to know a Wendat never forgets a kindness? The hunting here has been good, and we've added much to the meat and hide supplies. We'll make it through this difficult winter.

I miss my friend Fox dearly and wonder how he and the rest of the village manage. We left them with most of the food on the assumption the crows would have enough. Fox and I will see each other soon, when the planting moon comes. That isn't so far away, suddenly. The moon of the last snows has arrived. In another moon's cycle, we will travel back and prepare for summer and hope that the Haudenosaunee stay home as well.

That is also the month that Snow Falls is to have her baby. She's been having some pain lately, and only finally admitted she slipped and hurt herself weeks ago when we walked here. She's been asked to rest, and her new mother, Sleeps Long, who gave birth just after we arrived here, watches over her.

I have something to tell you now. It isn't as if you don't already know. But this is to be the year of new babies. I'll be a father again. Gosling is the mother, and I hope you look down and see our happiness. I've not told anyone yet. Not even Fox. That time will come soon, as Gosling begins to show.

———

LIFE IS SO EASY here I grow restless. I consider the idea of making the day's journey to see how Fox and the others back home manage. The snow's wet as it begins to melt and makes travel difficult and miserable. Still, I feel the pull of needing to move my body that aches from its memories of adventure. I'm not willing to leave Gosling or my daughter for long, though.

Gosling has picked up on this. She isn't happy at all in this crow village, but she understands that the group's needs outweigh her own. Unaccustomed to living in such large families, she maintains her old style of living alone in a wigwam. More nights than not, I'm with her.

"You'll soon burst if you don't find something to keep you occupied," she says tonight after I've returned a third time from collecting more firewood. "Why don't you gather some young ones and take them out hunting and snaring? You know the crows guard their food cache as carefully as squirrels. They'll remember every nut they've offered us and then use it against us when the next time comes that's in their favour."

"I wouldn't feel right," I say, "leaving you alone in your condition." The words come out before I can stop them.

"And what is this condition I suffer from?" Gosling asks. She's been short-tempered with me lately. I can't blame her.

"It's not what I meant to speak." I stop now in order to choose my words more carefully. "I worry for you and my daughter both." Again I think. "I don't want to leave for any length of time. I'll be honest. Something keeps waking me in the middle of the night."

"I'm sure it's just my groaning belly," Gosling says. We laugh. She looks at me now, her eyes sparkling in the firelight. "I'll be honest, too, and tell you I don't want you to stray far, either, despite knowing you want to."

I wait for her to tell me more.

"I lie awake as well, and not just because of this." She touches her belly. "Perhaps it's only because we're forced to live so close to them, in this awful place. But most nights, I feel something's very wrong."

"Then we have to pay even more attention, don't we?" I lean to her for a kiss.

———

THE CROW GABRIEL asks me if my daughter is married.

"How does that concern you?" I ask.

"It's obvious to all she will give birth very soon," the crow says, "and the Great Voice demands she wed the father."

"Sometimes our differences aren't so many," I say. "Our children are well cared for. You know that."

The two of us sit alone in the place where they speak to their voice. It's drafty, with the fire barely burning in the hearth. I can hear snow water dripping from the roof into puddles on the ground. He'd asked me here to speak of important matters, and so I'm left confused. I'd expected a meeting to discuss the terms of my people's stay with the crows now that it's almost time to leave. I'd expected a conversation regarding what is owed.

"I don't want to be the one to stir the kettle, but maybe I must in order for us to see what lies below the surface," this crow says. "I've been told that Snow Falls, how shall I say it," he says, placing his fingers on his chin, "that your daughter isn't sure who the father of her baby is."

I stand from my bench then, kicking it back so it clatters onto the ground. "What did you say?"

The crow also stands, now alarmed. "I mean no harm, Bird," he says, holding out his arms.

My fists are clenched. "What did you say about my daughter?"

"Simply that there's a rumour Aaron might be the father. Or maybe it's Carries an Axe."

I walk toward him.

He stumbles backward. "I mean no harm, but don't you think it's important to rectify the situation?"

I lunge for him, and he trips over a bench. I pick him up by his stinking robe and lift him to my face. "Where did you hear this lie?" I ask, so close I can smell his foul breath.

"I imagine everyone knows," he stutters. "I thought you did, too. I mean no harm." He's shaking in my hands. Or maybe it's because I'm trembling with anger. I tense, then pitch him away so that he flies back and crashes into more benches. He scrambles to his feet and flees from the room, and I consider going after him. Instead, I turn around and stalk outside.

I make it clear to everyone I see on my slow walk around the crow village that I look for He Finds Villages. This explains his odd behaviour that day so long ago when I walked up to him and he ran away. Does Carries an Axe know? Why didn't my daughter tell me there were two boys? I will find out the truth.

I go to Gosling. I find her standing in front of her wigwam and wave her inside. As soon as we sit, I ask if she knows anything about this. She looks at me as if she wants to apologize for something.

"It's true, then?"

"Bird," she says, "listen to me. Snow Falls came to me in a time of great need. It was after your return from this place last autumn. Your daughter was concerned that He Finds Villages had pushed himself on her while she slept."

"She's a deep sleeper, but not that deep," I say, my face burning.

"Remember how ill she was the morning you walked back from here?"

I do remember. I remember it all in a rush, my concern, my even asking if she was pregnant.

"He Finds Villages and Snow Falls drank that foul water. She was unconscious."

"I will kill him then," I say, standing.

"Carries an Axe doesn't know any of this," Gosling says. "Think about him. Think about your daughter. Think about your grandchild and what's right for all of them before you act."

Her words hit me as I walk out the door.

Despite my looking everywhere and asking everyone I see, I can't find the boy. The snow's mostly melted now, and the village paths are a ruin of mud. I can't stand this place any longer and walk out the gates, the hairy ones watching me.

———

FOR TWO DAYS, I hunt for He Finds Villages. I've even gone so far as to wait by that place where the crows caw each morning while the others sit or kneel or stand according to some strange plan. He's disappeared. No one I speak to has seen him. The second evening, when I think he's run off into the forest for good, word spreads that he's been found. Gosling tells me.

"He's by the river."

A small group of hairy ones has gathered at a small stone-and-wood house along the palisades, the water of the river rushing by on the other side. They part way for me when I come up.

I walk through them and enter the small building. In the dim light of dusk, I see He Finds Villages. He appears to be floating, his legs off the floor. A chair lies on its side. His neck is bent at an angle, and his face is bloated. His head is cocked as if he's just asked a question.

The Crow pushes by me and walks up to the body. The other crow, the damaged one with the missing fingers, follows right after, crying like a child. Together, they try to lift the boy up, but he's long dead. I watch them fumble with his body, useless in their attempts to free him from the rope that holds him.

GOSSIP TRAVELS AS FAST in this village as in any other. It appears that no one is quite sure why the boy killed himself, but everyone is certainly sure I hold the answer. After all, I was searching for him not so long ago, and it wasn't with kindness. But I won't speak. I've been avoiding Snow Falls and Carries an Axe out of necessity. I put on a stoic face, but inside I'm shaken by all of this. I won't speak of any of it to my daughter or her man. Gosling's right. Some troubles are better left alone.

They bury He Finds Villages outside their cemetery fence. Dawning of Day stands with Gosling and me, explaining it all. A large group of us stand here, watching from a safe distance. At first, I think he isn't being buried with the others who've died because he's Wendat.

"No," Dawning of Day says. "There are many Wendat buried within that fence. He took his own life, though. According to their great voice, he won't be able to go to the good place anymore."

"Where does he go, then?" Gosling asks.

Dawning of Day shrugs. "Some place that is between this world and the other. It isn't where everyone burns in fire, and it isn't where everyone has everything they want."

Near me, Snow Falls weeps, her head on her husband's chest. I watch him wrap his arm around her. I can tell he doesn't know. The crows talk in their strange language and make their signs and then throw dirt into the hole. When it is over, all of us walk away, sad and confused.

GOSLING'S ANXIOUS TONIGHT. Half a moon's passed since the boy's funeral, and the first buds will soon show on the poplars. It's time to go home. It's not just Gosling who's restless. We all are. She sleeps fitfully beside me, calling out and then hushing herself. When I try to sleep, I imagine wolves circling a deer, tensing to pounce.

Well before dawn, I'm so agitated I'm about to crawl from our robe when I hear someone running up. I reach for my club.

"Bird," a man whispers. It's Carries an Axe. "Gosling," he says.

She wakes and sits. "It's time," she says.

We run with Carries an Axe to the longhouse. He's too panicked to answer when I ask what's happening. Rushing inside, we see Sleeps Long near the fire, kneeling with my daughter. Snow Falls cries out.

"She's early," Gosling says, crouching beside the two.

"Tell me," I say.

Gosling looks up. "It'll be fine," she says. "Leave us to this. Go outside and light a pipe with Carries an Axe. Explain to him what it's like to be a father."

IT'S A WISE CHOICE YOU MADE

Maybe it's the suicide of He Finds Villages that makes the baby want to come out too soon. What am I to think of all this? I've tried convincing myself that Carries an Axe is the father, and want to believe it, and I bolt awake less and less in the middle of the night from dreaming that Carries an Axe has found out and has left me to be alone. But with word that He Finds Villages has hanged himself, my body immediately feels sick and the pains in my belly, not long after, begin to come.

I try to will away the pain that sears through me because I know it's too early. But when I can't anymore, I tell Sleeps Long I think the time might be coming. I've already been told by those who know of such things that I need to stop walking about and I must command my body to lie still all day long. I'd begun going mad from the boredom of it. But as soon as the pains came shooting through me in earnest, I could only beg the boredom to please return.

Gosling makes me tea that helps some of the worst pain. She and Sleeps Long whisper to each other out of my earshot and turn their concerned faces to me. A wave of anguish comes and washes over me, then slowly recedes until I feel like I might be able to stand up again if only I were allowed to. For two days this pattern repeats itself till I almost get used to it.

Tonight, I have to get up to pee, and Sleeps Long accompanies me out of the longhouse to our place in a clump of cedar. "Slow down," she says. "This isn't a race, you know."

I squat, barely able to crouch now that I'm so large, worried I'll wet myself if I'm not careful. How did this happen? When did I become the woman that I used to make fun of and despise? It's so difficult. I remind myself how happy I'll be when this thing that grows inside me finally comes out of my body and I can have me to myself again.

As if I summoned something I shouldn't have, when I stand from my squat, the shooting pain is far worse than any so far. It makes me fall to the ground. It's as if the child in me took my thought for a challenge and has lit a fire inside my body. I scream out when the next pain shoots through me, and Sleeps Long rushes over and tries to pick me up.

When I'm standing again, bent over in pain, I feel the warm trickle of what I fear is blood running down my legs. I reach my hand and smear it, raise it to my face. Thank you, Aataentsic. It's a clear liquid.

Sleeps Long sees what's happening to me and carries me from the cover of the cedars. She calls for help, and my husband comes running. Together, they carry me back to the longhouse.

It's as if the earlier pains were just warm winds blowing over my body. I lie on my mat and must bite a piece of thick hide that Gosling places in my mouth. I see my husband's face hovering over me, but Sleeps Long sends him outside. Now the raven we've tied over our bed floats above me, its one wing lame, hanging down, its other out in a graceful curve as if in flight. My lower body feels like it's being torn in half and put to fire. I can't stand it.

But I must. I slip in and out of consciousness, jolting awake to screams that I realize are my own. The raven continues to hover above, and so I imagine myself climbing up and onto his back, wrapping my arms around his neck and whispering for him to fly me away. Just as Gosling once showed me long ago, I can feel the pulse of the raven's muscles under his feathers as he begins to slowly beat his wings, the broken one not quite as strong as the other. The pain shoots through me again, and I beg the raven to beat his wings faster, to take me away. He looks back to me, twisting his neck slowly to my face, looking at me with one shining eye, his eyes the gift from Sleeps Long. I can see my face in the eye, the fire in the hearth behind me burning, and I look frightened, my hair long and matted, my face drawn despite the weight of the pregnancy. The raven begins to beat his wings faster so that he floats now, freed from his tether, and either he grows bigger or I grow smaller, but soon I can barely wrap my arms halfway around his neck, and I must hold on to the feathers or else fall off. The raven, still turned to me as he beats his wings, one sparkling eye staring, opens his beak.

Are you sure you want me to fly you away? The others can't come with you right now. They might soon. They will later. Are you sure?

The pain rips through me. I nod.

The child you carry inside won't come with us.

I think of the baby. I see the face of He Finds Villages. I see my husband's face hovering over me with concern. I will stay.

Take one of my eyes. It will help you see.

In my pain, I reach up and pull the shining shell from the eye socket of my bird.

It's a wise choice you made.

When I open my eyes and look down my body, I can see Gosling's head near my spread legs. "It's a wise choice you made," she says, smiling. She tells me that despite the pain I will feel, I must push. The baby wants to come out now. I do as she tells me, and each time it feels as if I'm forcing myself inside out and ripping myself apart.

When I think I can no longer take it, Gosling tells me to push once more, and I do, grasping my fists on my robe, my eyes squeezed shut. I try to will my body to open. I scream when I feel the rush of it bursting out of me. I look, and Gosling is smiling, her hands busy. The sound of crying, and I think of my little raccoon. My body feels empty, but my hand hurts. I lift it to my face and open it. In my palm lies a bloody shell. The sun breaks through a seam in the birchbark wall. I close my eyes.

CARRIES AN AXE lies beside me, cradling my head in his arms. Gosling sits beside us, holding the baby wrapped in rabbit furs. She hands it to me. "Here's your little girl," she says.

I pull back the fur to look into the face of my child and am surprised by the thick charcoal hair covering her head. The baby's eyes are closed, the eyelids almost translucent, and she moves her mouth as if she's feeding. I look at Carries an Axe. His eyes are wet as he touches his child's face. She opens her eyes then and starts to cry.

"She's hungry," Gosling says. "That's all."

When I place my girl's mouth to my nipple, I feel a small shock. We two are one again. She nurses, and I let the pain of the last days slide away like spring snow from the longhouse roof. I still hold the shining shell in my hand. I turn it over and over. I look up to the raven that hangs above me and see that he's missing an eye. In my delirium, I must have reached up and pulled it out. Not wanting to lose it, I look around and see the quill box from Gosling resting near me. She told me I'd find a use for it. I ask Carries an Axe to open the box, and I drop the shining shell inside. He closes it. I lean into him, dozing off along with our child.

GHOSTS FROM THE TREES

For two days, my daughter sweats and screams and bleeds. For two days, I prepare myself to lose her more times than I can count. Her baby is too soon and too stubborn. It wants to come out, then it won't. Exhausted this night, I finally fall into sleep, lying on the porch of the longhouse, Carries an Axe pacing beside me. It feels like only moments that my eyes are closed, but when I open them, my body shivering from the cold, the sun breaks, shooting rays of light through the stakes of the palisades.

I'm alone, but I can hear voices inside. They seem happy. A woman sings a sweet song, and a baby starts mewling, upset and hungry. My body aching, I push myself up to greet my grandchild.

Shivering by the fire, I watch as the women fawn over the baby girl, bundled in rabbit furs. My body complains from the last days' tensions and my falling asleep in the cold. I tell myself we can now leave this village for our own as soon as Snow Falls has her strength. It's time to go home.

Gosling and Sleeps Long, her own baby on her hip, gather what food they can and heat the kettle. My stomach groans, and I realize I'm starved. We all are. It's time to celebrate now, Snow Falls sleeping lightly by the fire, her new girl on her breast. When she awakes, we'll eat to her growing strong again, to this new life's growing strong, to the strength of the people. I crave my home, but this place will suffice for now.

The smoke rises up to the ceiling of this longhouse, the light filtering through so that I feel like I'm still in the dream world. The women laugh and the kettle bubbles and I'm finally starting to feel warm again. I reach for my pouch and search out my pipe.

Twisting a stick into the fire to light it, I look up as Gosling's eyes meet mine. She smiles. Her stomach, I see, is starting to show. A late-summer child. I light my pipe and puff, beckon her to me. She sits and takes the pipe, puffs on it.

"It will all be all right?" I ask.

She nods slightly.

Sleeps Long sits with Tall Trees and their son, my son. They eat from their birch bowls. I get up to serve Gosling and me, but before I do, I kneel to my daughter and stroke her head. She opens her eyes. Her child sleeps, making soft sucking noises. Snow Falls smiles. When I smile, she closes her eyes again. I stand and ladle food from the kettle.

We all curl up and sleep in the longhouse, the fire keeping us warm through the spring day, waking only when the baby cries out and then nodding back into sleep again.

My eyes open even before I hear it. I can tell by the sun that late afternoon has arrived. The rest of us, exhausted from the last days' trials, still dream. And then it comes. The voices of the hairy ones, shouting down from the ramparts. I lurch up, Tall Trees and Carries an Axe right behind me. We're at the gate and climbing the ladder, pushing past the guards, who stare down and point.

In the empty fields, my dear friend Fox stands and searches the men above him for a familiar face. His own is smeared in blood and his body's blackened by soot. A handful of others huddle near him, in just as poor shape. Still more appear like ghosts from the trees beyond.

Fox finally finds me. We look at each other. His eyes, they tell me everything.

FLITTING IN DREAM

The day passes as if in a dream, all of us sleeping, then me waking to feed before we fall back to sleep again. We're exhausted from the stress of these last days.

At some point in the afternoon, my child and I awake to the shouting of men, but we continue to doze, not wanting to hear or know of anything that might be wrong. Just a little more rest. That's all I ask.

I awake to darkness, and for a moment I don't know where I am until I feel my baby squirm beside me, waking as well. I place her on my breast and listen to the fire pop and to the voices of men, hushed and serious. I think I'm still dreaming when I hear Fox's voice. Isn't he back at home? What's he doing here? I begin to question whether I've somehow ended up back home after all. I want to get up, but my body is too sore. Instead, I listen carefully for what they talk about.

Our village overrun. A vicious surprise attack. Hundreds of Haudenosaunee. Too early in the year. Nobody expected it. I don't quite believe what I'm hearing. I force myself to a sitting position, careful to balance my girl, my body crying out. My legs are weak. I look down at my child's face in the firelight. She's beautiful. The hair on her head is so thick and dark. She suckles and raises both hands, making fists. A tiny bit of milk runs down her chin that I wipe away. I walk to the fire, where I stand behind them so they don't take notice of me. I want to hear what's going on without their leaving anything out for my sake.

"They came so fast we didn't even get the gates shut," Fox says. "Who'd expect an attack in early spring? Many of them carried the shining wood, and they knew how to use it."

Tall Trees shakes his head, and my husband crouches silently beside him. "I wouldn't have believed it if it weren't coming from your mouth, Fox," Tall Trees says.

Bird asks the hard questions, apparently not for the first time. I can see he's having difficulty with what he's heard. The village taken after a short skirmish, maybe a dozen managed to escape, possibly more, but this is all Fox saw with his own eyes. The Haudenosaunee must have left in late winter by foot to make it here at this time of year, an unprecedented and near-impossible feat with such a large group.

"That," Fox says, "or they wintered on our land without us knowing it. It doesn't matter now. What does matter is that their allies supplied them with the same weapons we've always asked of the French. This new imbalance worries me greatly."

"We must go in force and try to save whoever's left alive," Bird says. "We must leave right now."

Fox shakes his head. "The destruction and violence was unlike anything I've ever seen." He pauses, having a hard time speaking. "Very few will be left."

"And so what does that leave us with?" Carries an Axe asks.

"We can surrender to them," Bird says, "or we can fight. I don't see us surrendering." He looks around him. The men clearly agree. "We must finish this war, then. There's nothing left now to do but that."

I look down at my tiny child, her eyes closed, lids flitting in dream.

IT'S TOO LATE NOW, ISN'T IT?

I send out scouts, led by Fox, to report on any enemy sighting or movement. If I know the Haudenosaunee, they'll revel in their victory for at least a few days, taking their time with the prisoners they choose to caress, sending other prisoners back to their land to be adopted by those at home. I don't imagine they're done with us yet. They're so close to ridding themselves of the Wendat. Now that most all our brother nations have surrendered or been defeated, all that really stands between them and their goal is this group of us, the people left in this strange crow village. If I were my enemy, I'd certainly strike while I had the chance.

Carries an Axe has been asking to go out and scout as well, but I tell him he's needed here to protect his family and the others. There will be plenty of action for you soon, my new son.

Stragglers from our village continue to trickle in. I keep hoping for more to show up but now, a few days after the news of our great defeat and slaughter, I've lost much hope. All told, I've counted maybe thirty survivors, including Fox and the ones who appeared that day. I'm numb. I feel like I suddenly live under water. I think we all do.

But we must fight through it. We throw ourselves into the strengthening of the defences, the collecting of wood for fuel, the rationing of food, and the planning of where to keep the women and children and old people when the battle rages.

This little river that the Iron People have dug into the community will serve us well. I stand by it and study it in the sunlight glinting off its stillness. We'll have more than enough fresh water to drink and to put out the fires the Haudenosaunee will start. But something about this strange creek continues to intrigue me. I feel something deep in my spine when I catch a glimpse of it, and I don't know why. Clearly, I've dreamed of it. I will ask Gosling what she thinks its significance is. There's no time for reflection, though. I do everything I can to keep my mind from what might happen, very soon, to so many of us.

———

FOX COMES BACK with Tall Trees to tell us what they've seen. The Haudenosaunee have sent out small bands of their own scouts to scour the territory. Fox found the markings of where a few of them slept less than half a day away.

"I can see what they're doing," he says. "They're finding the most efficient route here."

I ask how long he thinks before they come to us. He says as soon as two or three days.

The night's discussion around the fire is dominated by the question of how to get the women, children, and infirm to somewhere of safety. Where that might be poses only the first great problem. How they can be guaranteed this safety outside of the palisades is another. What they are to do without shelter or much in the way of food is still another. We can't afford to send more than a few men, as we will need every one.

"I question if it's sensible to do this at all," Tall Trees says. "I for one am not willing to let Sleeps Long and our baby far out of my sight. Where would they go?"

"The islands in the Sweet Water Sea aren't so far from here," Fox says. "Wouldn't this be a good hiding place?"

I know these islands, three of them, one large and two smaller. While fishing in spring, I've stayed on them. "It's an interesting idea," I say. "And if we had the time to make a camp for the women and children, at least some protection from the wind and rain, I might say yes. But we don't."

Carries an Axe clears his throat. "I say we use the islands as a last resort," he says. "I won't let my wife and child stray outside of these palisades without me, either. If the worst happens and we need to flee, let's put out the word to meet on the largest of the islands."

"Well, the young man doesn't speak from his ass," I say, making the others laugh. It feels good. "I agree with you, my son."

The others do as well.

———

I SIT BY THE FIRE with Christophe Crow and try to explain to him that the Haudenosaunee will attack soon. He's stunned, unable to focus. He doesn't want to believe it.

"Do you think they'd make such an enemy of the Iron People?"

All I can do is nod. They would, but he doesn't want to hear it. "At least let us be prepared," I say.

"At first," he says, "I didn't want these war-bearers that my people sent me coming here. I thought they'd bring the worst of my people and their ways with them. But now," he says, "if we're to be attacked, they'll probably be the ones to save us."

I ask him again if there is more of the shining wood for his war-bearers to share with ours. "We have to act quickly to train my men," I explain.

He shakes his head. "Very few of the men who were promised came last autumn. They brought very little with them. I'm sorry."

I tell him to come with me to the head of his war-bearers and let him know that Wendat and Iron People alike now have to plan our defences together. The Crow, as if he's just waking up, nods and climbs to his feet.

———

FOX AND I WATCH from the ramparts as the hairy ones teach some of ours how to load the shining wood and how to aim it. I won the argument that it's good for all to know how to use what we have at our disposal. They fire a few times to get my men used to the thunderous bark and the smoke. I have a group of younger ones, little more than boys, searching out the good hardwood for arrow shafts and scouring the riverbank for flint for the tips. They've already filled every kettle, bucket, and container they could find with water from the little river and placed these near all the buildings. The Haudenosaunee will no doubt launch a fire attack first to cause panic and confusion.

My own shining wood rests in my arms, a gift so long ago from their great chief. I've used it rarely. If I hunt with it, the sound scares game far away, and in a time of war, the first firing is impressive, but in the madness of struggle it's very difficult to reload, taking too much time to make bark again.

"I'll do what I can to help you prepare it if you need me," Fox says, nodding to the shining wood. "Me, I'm going to rely on my bow and my club and my knife."

We turn from the view below to the forest in the distance. The sun's been our friend the last days, any traces of snow long gone. The rich dark earth of the fields heats in the sun's warmth, and the wind blows its scent to us.

"I don't think I'll see another spring again," Fox says.

"Don't be so morose," I tell him. "We have many more springs of fishing together. The Haudenosaunee will come here and think twice when we wipe out their first wave. They'll have had enough quickly once they try us the first time."

I look around me as if I see it from my enemy's eyes. The palisades appear well built even if there's only one row of them. Despite this, the stone corners of the village are something daunting that they've probably not seen before. We have only three sides to defend as a river runs along the back. I want to believe the enemy will be turned away and decide to leave.

"I'm not sad if I don't see another summer," Fox says, pulling me back to the two of us standing here. "I'm not being morose. I just tell you when it comes, that day, it will be a good one to die. I look forward to being with my family again."

"Well, you're just going to have to wait a little while longer to see them, my friend," I say. The time presents itself to tell him, and so I will. "Gosling," I say, "she's pregnant."

He looks at me flatly, but then his face breaks out in a grin. "I knew the two of you were much too close to simply be friends." His grin turns to momentary confusion. "Isn't she," he says, careful with his words, "isn't she past that time? I mean, understand it when I say that she's beautiful. I've long dreamed of having her." He realizes what he's just said. We both laugh.

"My old friend," I say, "there's a reason the Anishnaabe are known for their magic."

Evening is close when we climb down the ladder and walk to where Christophe Crow and his two others stand talking by their holy house. All three are visibly nervous, especially the one called Isaac, who mashes his club hands into his face. When I get closer, I'm surprised to see he's sweating.

"It's true?" he asks. "They come this way?"

I nod.

He moans, and the dark one, Gabriel, reaches out for him. "Be strong," he says. "It's time to pray and to reflect and to prepare."

Isaac doesn't seem to take comfort in the words. I can't blame him. He knows what will happen if the Haudenosaunee are able to overwhelm us.

"When the assault begins," Christophe Crow says, "we think it sensible the old ones and the women and children stay with us in the place of the Great Voice."

I look at the building behind him. It might be large enough. "Why there and not somewhere else?" I ask.

"It's a solid structure, and close to the waterway and food supplies. We have most everything we need there."

Fox shrugs. "It's as good as anywhere, I guess," he says.

I nod. "It might be any time now," I say. We'll tell them all to gather there."

I'm uncomfortable, even after all these years, allowing the Crow such proximity to everything I hold dear, but it's too late now, isn't it? Fox and I turn away then, the one called Isaac shaking and crying, and head out to spread the word and to check once again that all is as ready as it can be.

A COMET'S LIGHT

Something must be done about Isaac. Gabriel and I stand on the porch of the chapel, speaking quietly, Isaac inside with a cool towel upon his head. He's been chewing the bark from a willow, claiming it eases his pain. He's been learning all kinds of sauvage potions and cures and remedies, is becoming quite good, it seems, at pointing out the plants and roots and fungus that can help or harm.

"I understand his fear," Gabriel says. "But this is too much to bear. We have enough trouble to contend with."

"He faces his mortal terror," I say. "And he's losing." We must figure a way to help him pull himself out of it, to help him strengthen his backbone.

"He responded strongly when we all agreed we were willing to die for the Huron," Gabriel offers. "I think we should raise this conviction again, that we should grasp hands in a circle and pray with him right now. He just needs to see that he isn't alone in his fear."

Gabriel's right. This is indeed what we'll do. "The hardest part for him," I say, "is the waiting. It's the hardest part for all of us. I think they know this, too, and they use it as a weapon against us." I ask that before we pray with Isaac, Gabriel take a brief walk with me to survey the defences one last time.

We walk as always with our hands clasped behind our backs, but instead of bowing our heads in conversation or in reflection, we study everything around us. The sun's just set, and the sky flames orange and red at the western horizon, incrementally turning from pink to purple as I look east. Soon it will be black. There'll be no moon in the sky the next nights, and the timing couldn't be worse. We want to be able to see the enemy sneaking across the fields. Will tonight be the night? It's the same question I've been asking myself the last few evenings.

Numerous soldiers and a handful of sauvages walk the ramparts, looking intently in the direction from which the enemy might come. We have two dozen soldiers and three dozen donnés and laymen to fire thirty or so muskets, and maybe eighty or a hundred sauvages ready for combat according to the last report I received. At most, a hundred and fifty men against a force three times as large, by all accounts. I pray to You, Lord, that the palisades remain standing.

As we pause by the waterway, I look up to the darkening firmament, just as a comet streaks across it before fizzling out. I'm considering my childhood habit of making a wish when I see another, and then another zipping overhead. I grab Gabriel's arm. Within seconds, dozens of flames lick the sky above us, many dropping into the mission. Voices erupt up on the ramparts, and the thundering boom of a musket makes me jump when I look over to see what I just now realize is a flaming arrow land on the roof of the granary, the thatch of it already beginning to crackle and catch. Men shout and fling pails of water, extinguishing the flames.

Arrows fly in, thick enough to begin lighting our way as Gabriel and I rush to the chapel, women and children and old people running from the longhouses to join us. I stop and shout, "Gabriel! Shepherd them into the chapel. Keep an eye for arrows landing on the roof and prepare to put fires out."

"What are you going to do?" he shouts back.

"I want to make sure all the women and children know to come to us."

I run off toward the sauvage quarters, the arrows continuing to fall with sparkling thuds. One whistles so close to my ear that I can feel its heat. The men on the ramparts fire their muskets toward the tree line, more out of panic than aim, I fear. Those on the ground shout to one another for more water and begin forming lines as first one roof then another burst into flames. It appears, as I run by, that they're putting the fires out as fast as they start.

Rushing into the first longhouse, I shout in Huron for the people huddling there to hurry to the place of the Great Voice. Looking terrified, they begin collecting their few belongings and slinging children onto their backs. They hurry by me in twos and threes as I tell them to be careful crossing the village.

I run to two more longhouses and do the same thing. We'll be crowded there for all the souls, but I believe it best to keep all of us close for the safety in numbers. I'll make sure that all available hands will stay vigilant for arrows lighting the thatch or the wooden walls. This is the best plan, is it not, Lord?

Once the Christian longhouses have been cleared, I run through the gate to the heathen side just as the nearest roof explodes in flame, a number of arrows hitting it simultaneously. The dry bark of the roof acts as tinder, and before I can even get to the door it's a roaring fire. Hearing screams, I pull open the door to a thick wall of smoke that knocks me onto my back. Crawling on my hands and knees, I shout in the haze and choking smoke, the roof above ready to collapse any second. A child cries out somewhere close by and I feel for it with my hands, hot cinders falling down and burning through my cassock. I feel a leg and grab it, the child screaming. It must be the mother's face that appears in the smoke, grimacing, and I grab her, too, dragging them back to the cool air. Just as we claw our way outside, the longhouse caves in, the screams of those engulfed by the pyre the most horrific noise I've ever heard. I bless myself and whisper to You, Lord, that their suffering passes quickly.

By the time we get back to the chapel, the arrow attack has slowed, the odd one flaming in and hitting dirt before it sputters out. As I'd guessed, the building is full of frightened Huron and a smattering of other tribes, babies crying and women talking in low, excited tones to one another. Some peer outside, and it dawns on them it's safe to head out into the better air from the stuffiness of the building.

Fires burn here and there, a few longhouses already smoking ruins. Some of the donnés' small residences are wrecks as well. The ramparts are so still I'm frightened our soldiers have somehow mysteriously disappeared, but then I see movement in the shadows and realize they lie still for good reason as they watch and wait for an attack.

I take these few quiet moments to join Isaac and Gabriel in the chapel.

"Brothers," I say. "Let us pray." I recite the Hail Mary and then whisper words of encouragement to Isaac. "We will be strong for them, for the innocents. We must be brave for the small children who we love. We will act selflessly for these people in the understanding that our life's work is finally coming to fruition. We must remind ourselves now, here where our peers can hear us, that we will die for them if this is what the Lord deems necessary. I commit my physical body," I say, my voice steady, "to these ones for whom we travelled so far. I will die for these ones in the hopes that their souls may find the light of Heaven."

Gabriel takes his turn now, and I'm surprised to hear his voice shaking. But he finds his strength as he, too, commits his life.

When it's Isaac's turn, he looks up at me and then at Gabriel, his eyes wet with tears. "I no longer cry tears of sadness, only joy," he says. "For I know I will die for these ones, and not only for myself. We will die for something greater. Thank you, my brothers, for now I understand my role. Now I realize what I must do."

A calm has settled over him that I've never seen before. His back's straighter and he no longer looks about him frightfully like a whipped dog. Together, the three of us recite the Lord's Prayer, and just as we finish a great cry goes up from the ramparts, followed by the thundering of muskets.

I HEARD HIM

I'm with Carries an Axe and our child, resting by the fire, discussing possible names for her. We consider the names of those close to us who've recently passed, wondering if our child might hold any of their spirits.

She has the eyes of my grandmother, Carries an Axe says.

I wish I'd known her. I wish I'd known my own grandmother. I push the thought away. "We could name the child after her, maybe," I say. "What was her name?"

"She Is from the South," he says. We think about this, gazing at our baby who's awake now but still unseeing. Without speaking it, we both know this isn't the right name. We laugh.

As the baby begins to cry and I lift her to my breast again, a loud thunk strikes the roof. As soon as I look up, I see a tear of fire that spreads so fast I'm left breathless.

Carries an Axe jumps up and begins pulling me to the door. As the crackling above grows louder, I yank on him and tell him to hold the baby, then run back and pull my broken raven from its tether above our bed.

"Are you crazy?" Carries an Axe shouts over the flames.

Thinking quickly, I grab some moss for the child and her rabbit furs. Underneath them, Gosling's beautiful birchbark box shines in the light from the blaze above. I grab it, too, then bound for the door.

Our baby wails, I can see from her open mouth as we hurry away from the heat of the flames that now begin to consume the longhouse. I watch as everything we have, our few sad possessions, burn up in the night.

All around us, men yell and arrows slice through the air, burning the colour of the summer sky until they hit the ground or a long-house before they explode like a small sun. Carries an Axe shields our baby with his body as we make our way through the panic of people. Leading me to the place of the great voice, he shouts over the din, "Their roof is strong, but stay near the entrance in case it catches on fire." He passes me our child. "Do you hear me? Don't get caught inside in the middle of that place or you might not get out if there's a rush for the door."

I nod, my baby screaming in my arms now, and Carries an Axe runs for the ramparts.

The murmur of women hushing crying babies and the smell of sweat and fire and something more pungent below it push at me as I walk in the door. The chapel is a large outer room, another one attached to it where the crows claim the body of the great voice resides in a big, shiny box. The crows have their small fires burning so we have enough light not to trip over one another. Outside, the shouting and the occasional boom of shining wood puncture the air. We all wait with held breath for the arrows that will hit our structure. I stay near the door as Carries an Axe requested, and as I see fewer and fewer arrows light the night sky, I decide it's safe to venture out a little way with a few of the others, breathing in the cool air.

Eventually, most everyone inside comes out now that it's grown quiet again. We talk and some laugh, but the tension that hovers above us, crushing down, keeps us quiet and ready to flee back into the crows' house. I hear some of the older women discussing how the Haudenosaunee are merely testing us, harassing us with these arrows, trying to cause us to panic while they hope to destroy as much as possible.

"When they sneak up to the palisades in the middle of the night and put them to fire," one old woman says, "then we should be worried."

I see that a few of the buildings have burned down. The Haudenosaunee have announced themselves. There's some sense of relief just below the fear now.

I see Christophe Crow walk by, and so my baby and I follow him. He walks into the holy house and meets with Gabriel and Isaac. They each take turns whispering to one another as they hold hands. It's a strange custom of theirs I've grown used to. I watch as Isaac speaks. Something seems to come over him. It's as if he grows taller in front of my eyes. He feels so intense it's like he's burning. The other two notice this as well. I fear for poor Isaac. All the tension and fear have made him loose in the head, I think. He knows well the cruelties the Haudenosaunee are happy to inflict. I'd be scared, too, if I were to have to face it a second time.

Just as they release each other's hands, a sudden thundering makes me duck my head and cover my daughter's body. It takes me a moment to realize that many shining wood are firing at once. Over the screaming men and the splintering wood, I panic, thinking I can hear Carries an Axe calling to me. Women run back into the building as I try to get out, shielding my baby from the pushing and jostling. Outside, thick smoke obscures the ramparts, but I see men lying on the ground below them, some writhing in agony, others motionless. What's happened? Is Carries an Axe among them? I'm sure I heard him cry out for me.

Once it goes quiet again, with my child in my arms I run out to those on the ground, slowing as I get to them. Three of the hairy ones have great oozing holes ripped in their chests. One man's face is missing. Gagging, I cover my daughter's eyes from the sight, even though she can't see yet. Warriors shriek outside the gates. More shining wood booms. I see a young Wendat lying broken on the ground near the palisades. No. Weaving through the dead or wailing men, I reach him, his face in the dirt. This isn't Carries an Axe. He's taller and leaner.

I'm about to move on when I hear my name shouted. Looking above me to the ramparts, I see it's my father.

"What are you doing?" he demands.

"I heard Carries an Axe," I shout back. "I think he's been hurt."

"I just saw him. He's fine. Leave now!" Bird yells just as men around him make their shining wood roar.

I run back to the safety of the holy house.

PLUGGING THE BREACH

The enemy sends in the odd volley of flaming arrows throughout the night to keep us from sleeping. Small bands of them who dare to sneak close to the palisades scream out as loud as they can in order to keep us ungrounded. We answer by leaning over the walls and firing arrows or shining wood down at them. A short time before dawn is to break, my head nodding, I hear the strange sound I've become accustomed to over these last years, the three crows rising from their light slumber and chanting their prayers in their strange rhythm. I don't want to admit it, but I've grown to like it.

Fox's voice startles me. "They just don't know when to be quiet, do they?" he says, and we laugh. He then goes silent and cocks his ear.

I wait for him to tell me what he hears. And then I hear it, too. The soft scrape of a blade cutting something.

He motions to me and I follow him down the ladder, carrying my shining wood. On the side of the village near the river, the sound grows louder. We hunch in the dark and listen. My eyes begin to adjust. That's when I see it for a heartbeat, the flash of a blade. I touch Fox's shoulder and point. With the moments passing, it becomes apparent what we peer at. Someone on the other side of the palisade, just a few lengths of a man away from us, has found a weakness, a group of logs that weren't dug into the earth deep enough, tied by leather thongs that he now cuts through with his knife.

We lower ourselves onto our bellies and crawl silently toward the logs, the darkness still protecting us. I have a plan and let Fox lead. When we're close, we see that a few logs are leaning at an angle, creating a gap almost big enough for a man to slip through.

Again I touch Fox's shoulder, giving him the sign on his skin that I'll strike first and he should follow immediately. I aim my shining wood at the break in the palisade and then pull the hammer back with my thumb. Staring down the length of it, I steady on the break in the logs. My finger pulls the trigger and the shining wood speaks, sparks shooting out from it followed by a kicking roar and flash of light. I can hear the men on the other side scream as Fox and I stand with our clubs and run to the break. Fox beats me to it and launches himself halfway through.

"You dropped three of them," he shouts, struggling with something I can't see. "Pull me back through." I grab his legs and waist, yanking as hard as I can so that he slides safely out onto our side, dragging a severely wounded Haudenosaunee behind him.

"Take that rope quick," he says, pointing to a strip hanging from the gap.

While he holds the moaning man up, I wrap the leather tight around his wrist.

"Now tie him to those logs. Quick, before any more come."

I do what Fox asks, the warrior now hanging in the palisades, his body plugging the breach.

"That might give them pause if they try to come in this way again," he says, braining the enemy with his club. "You'll not keep me up all morning with your crying."

I BESEECH THEE

I gently wake Isaac and Gabriel. The fighting has grown quiet and they, along with most of the women and children, have fallen into a light sleep. We must maintain our routine, though. The three of us will give thanks for the new day, and then we'll hold Mass, just as we do every morning.

We stand in a circle and sing the Lord's Prayer in Latin before preparing for Mass, opening the tabernacle and removing the Hosts and the chalice that holds the spring water that will become Christ's blood.

As I'm about to ring the hand bell to awaken the sleeping ones, the boom of a musket not so far away shatters the still air. Babies start crying, and I hear people shuffling to their feet throughout the chapel. The night sky lightens to a grey hue. There won't be any sun today.

Gabriel returns from investigating the musket that was fired so close to us. "The sauvages killed one of the Iroquois and have strung him up on the palisades," he reports grimly. "They fall into their barbaric ways so easily."

I gather all who can fit into the chapel as the light grows strong enough for us to see one another, and it beams through small arrow holes in the roof, the dull rays kissing the heads of many of the women in front of me.

I bless myself, and the faithful follow suit, and then I see that a group of donnés and soldiers, their faces blackened, have joined us in the chapel, too, removing their hats and helmets, the unconverted turning to look at them.

I pray for all our souls, beseeching You, Lord, to take care of us in this time of great crisis. Smoke from still-burning houses drifts in, and a few people cough in fits.

My sermon will be kept short. As a couple of babies begin to cry, I speak in French and then in Huron of how we must stay resolute in the face of the aggressor, that we must face our greatest fear with the deep understanding in our hearts that if the enemy is to take our physical lives, You, Lord, will welcome our souls into the eternal place with open arms.

"I beg Thee, Lord, to hear our prayers. Amen."

The congregation who understands responds with "Amen," and then it's time for Isaac, Gabriel, and me to prepare Communion by blessing the Host and chalice. As congregants line up, shouting erupts outside, and I watch how the neat lines of the faithful fall into immediate disarray as women push away from the door, men fighting to make their way to it, the shouting outside growing louder, followed by the booming of muskets again.

READY BESIDE ME

We'd expected this when dawn came, but even I'm shocked by how many Haudenosaunee warriors pour from the trees, their faces painted like ours in the colours of blood and squash blossom and charcoal.

Every available man in the village waits with shining wood or bow atop the ramparts or down on the ground, aiming through cracks in the palisades as the enemy advances across the field. I watch their progress as they come roaring over it, thick lines of them struggling through the mud but still keeping a good pace.

"Look at how many of them have the shining wood," Fox says.

"Just wait until they are close," I say, "and keep your head down when they fire." That's when we'll have them in trouble. "As they try to reload, we'll stand and shoot down upon them." The only problem with my plan is that there are so many enemy that they come in waves.

A few of our war-bearers fire their shining wood too early, passing them down to be reloaded and now standing helplessly on the ramparts wondering what to do. The Haudenosaunee are halfway across the fields now, close enough I can begin to make out their grimacing faces, their mouths open in a howl. They are brave to attempt such an assault. And they will pay.

Without warning, the whole group of them comes to a halt and the world goes quiet but for their panting breath. What are they doing? Hundreds of war-bearers just standing in the middle of the field, their chests heaving, stare up at us. And then a group of them parts for a tall, muscular one, his entire face painted the colour of blood. He raises his arms.

"I am Tekakwitha," he says, "and I have been given the solemn duty of asking you this only once. Will you surrender to us?"

To put down our arms and allow them in means that most all of us men will face the caressing while our women and children are taken away to become Haudenosaunee. Everyone in this village knows that.

As if Fox reads my mind, he speaks. "I'd rather die a war-bearer than a prisoner. If they kill us today, they'll take our women and children anyway. Me, I'd rather go to Aataentsic smiling and on my feet."

I let out my fiercest shout, my throat tight.

Tekakwitha drops his arms and is swallowed up by his war-bearers, who, answering my scream, advance once more.

"Wait!" I call out to the men around me. "Wait until they fire first and keep low, then return it." My shining wood is cocked, my bow ready beside me after I take that first shot.

Their warriors are now close enough to shoot at us, and they drop onto one knee, aiming up. Others arrive and stand behind them, still others pulling back on their bows, ready to release.

"Drop your heads!" I shout just as the first blasts rip into the grey morning air, the noise so loud it draws my breath from me. I cover my face with my forearms as the sound of iron tearing into the wooden stakes sings out, and some men above and below scream as the wood splinters and pierces them, the smoke of the shining wood bitter enough to burn my nostrils. I see some men stand to return fire too early, and a second wave of blasts erupts, sending them flying back off the ramparts as they hit hard ground with a thud.

"Now," I tell Fox, and we both stand, surprised at how close the Haudenosaunee are below us, their faces, some painted like charcoal with snow dots, others in strips like blood, all of them with long feathers tied in their hair, look up at us or frown down at their weapons, struggling to reload them. I choose the biggest warrior I can see, aim, and fire at his chest. The lead ball rips through the wooden breastplate he wears as he flies onto his back. In the time it's taken me to shoot once, Fox is already notching a third arrow and takes down an enemy who decided to run away from us.

I grab Fox and pull him hard just as arrows slice through the air, sticking dully into the palisades or flying overhead. Only then do I realize my ears are filled with a dull pounding as if I were standing close to a waterfall.

I can feel more than hear the thumping as Haudenosaunee chop at our defences with their axes as quick as they can. Those who are able pour boiling pitch down onto the heads of the ones below. The screaming and thundering are a throb in my ears.

Rather than reload, I pick up my bow and, peering through the palisades for the right moment, I stand, the arrow ready, and fire into another Haudenosaunee. At least now the waves have stopped approaching. The ones who have decided to brave this frontal assault are all crowded below, shouting and firing back at us or working their axes on the logs of the palisades.

Pushing Fox's shoulder, I point out to him where a group is trying to get the stakes to burn, laying torches at the base. We both stand and aim, taking out two of the men, which causes the others to retreat.

As our men all along the ramparts continue aiming down from our better vantage, the Haudenosaunee begin to pile up, and more and more start retreating to the tree line, falling back and then stopping to fire at us, covering their others who in turn run to them. In this way, the siege ends for now, the sudden silence falling like a blanket over us. I watch Fox's mouth move but I can't hear him. It's as if someone's stuck cattails in my ears.

WILL HIM TO WAKE

When it's quiet enough to do so, we women head into the fresh air again and watch as our men swing open the gates so that a group of warriors can make their way out. I wonder what they're doing and why they'd want to leave the safety of the palisades until they begin returning with bows and arrows and knives and shining wood in their arms. There must be many dead out there. A few men stand up on the ramparts, shouting out, celebrating the retreat of the enemy. My baby wakes with a start and begins to cry.

"Hush, my girl," I say as I rock her. "Why don't you and I go find your father and wish him a good morning?" As if she understands, she stops crying.

Many are dead on our side, too, I see as I walk along the palisades, looking for Carries an Axe. Men have begun to collect the bodies, dragging them to one of the buildings where I guess they'll keep until it's the right time to bury them. I picture all of the dead men inside the building, stacked like ears of corn on top of one another. Again, my fear that Carries an Axe is gone washes over me. I can picture him in there, his body squeezed between French and Wendat warriors. I need to stop being stupid. The Haudenosaunee might come back any time now, and I want my husband to see his daughter, if only briefly.

A group of Wendat are talking and smoking pipes up ahead. I ask them if they've seen Carries an Axe. One with a large cut above his eye, the eye itself swollen shut, points to a ladder. I look up and recognize my man's fine legs as he stands watch, peering over the fence.

When I whistle, he looks down, and a smile spreads across his face. He says something to the man beside him and scrambles down the ladder.

"Let's go for a walk," I say as he gently takes our daughter. His cheeks are blackened from the smoke, and the paint on his face needs tending. We go toward the river where it'll be safest and find a patch of grass to sit upon.

"Our child needs a name," Carries an Axe says.

I nod, taking her from him and telling him to lie back and rest his head on my lap. He looks exhausted. "She'll find her name," I say. "There's no need to worry about that right now."

Within a few breaths, my husband's fallen asleep, his chest rising and falling deeply, his eyes darting beneath his lids. The baby begins to stir, and I put her mouth to my breast. In the distance, somewhere outside the village in the forest, I hear the sound of wood being chopped. It makes me wonder. My head tingles when I gaze at my husband, and it feels as if I can't breathe deep enough to get the needed air in. I want this feeling to go away. I whisper to Carries an Axe, "Please be careful." I want to wake him up, but he needs the sleep. Still, even though it's selfish, I will him to awake.

A VERY DANGEROUS PLACE TO BE

After the morning's vicious attack, our day is spent tending to the wounded. More and more come to us, and we've opened the large dining room of the refectory since it's the biggest available and as removed from the palisades as possible. French and Huron alike moan out or lie unconscious on blankets or furs or simply on the cold wooden floor. A few of our countrymen who've been trained in such things do their best to treat the burns and the bullet wounds, the bodies pierced by arrows. Ultimately, though, the most we can do is offer a little comfort and water to drink.

Several of our sauvage women have come in to try and help, the sorcerer Gosling included.

"What does she hope to do," Gabriel whispers, "shake more sand from their bodies?"

When she sees us looking at her, she smiles, one that appears genuine. She's bending over a warrior who took wood shrapnel to his face and eyes. She's asked another woman to hold him steady as she plucks long slivers from his cheeks and around his eyes as he shakes but remains silent. When she stands to stretch, leaning back, I can't help but notice that her stomach seems to be rounded. She couldn't be. Surely she's too old. But it's hard to tell with these people.

So far I've counted thirty of our own dead since the battle began last night. Another twenty or so lie too wounded to be of service. By my estimation, we've already lost a third of our men.

"How much longer do you think we can sustain such assaults?" Gabriel asks, as if he's read my mind.

I look around the room and see Isaac knelt to a wounded Huron, speaking to him while he holds his hand. "Let's get some air and talk," I say.

The sky remains low and seems to threaten rain. "Wouldn't a good storm be a blessing," Gabriel says. "Especially if they plan to launch more flaming arrows against us."

I only partially listen. "I don't think we're going to survive this," I say.

Gabriel stops walking.

I turn to him. "I don't mean to be fatalistic, but I've heard how many of the Iroquois roam out there. They've already done great damage to the palisades. It's just a matter of time before the defences collapse or burn up."

"So what do you suggest?" Gabriel asks, frowning.

"That we prepare to leave our earthly bodies and be welcomed into Heaven. If we are captured alive, it'll be very difficult for a couple of days." I can see the fear flash in his dark eyes. "It will be especially difficult for Isaac. But I ask you to be the one who prepares him. He seems to have gained resolve. We must keep it that way."

Gabriel nods. "I'll speak to him again this evening." Clearly, he wants to say something more.

"If ever there was a time to talk," I say, "it's now."

"Would it be a sin," Gabriel asks, "if indeed the worst comes in the next while, that we ask Isaac to man the ramparts in order to bring our men comfort?"

"But that's a very dangerous place to be," I say. "It's far too easy to be killed in the thick of it."

He nods. "I know," he says. "But if Isaac were to die in the helping of our soldiers, wouldn't he ascend to Heaven that much quicker?"

Now I understand Gabriel's line of thinking. "And it would save him the hellish tortures that he's already survived once," I say. "But is it immoral?"

The two of us walk again, contemplating this as axes ring out in the wilderness, reaching us on the wind.

THE DEAD BELOW

All day we've listened to the Haudenosaunee out in the forest, chopping down trees. "Are they building their own village?" Fox asks.

"Maybe they've decided to live in peace with their new neighbours," I say. Despite our laughing, neither of us can figure it out.

I look down at all their dead below, most of them stripped of anything valuable now, their bodies starting to bloat in the afternoon warmth. There'd been talk of hauling them away as they'll begin to stink by tomorrow morning, but it makes more sense to leave them there where the living will have to trip over them as they try to get close to our walls.

"How many are there?" Fox asks. "I've counted over fifty, but I got lost after that."

I tell Fox I haven't counted, but obviously we've killed more of them by far than they have of us. They've come with such great numbers that they knew they could risk this loss in order to test our resolve.

All in the village have been tense today, as all are expecting another attack. Nothing so far, and as it gets closer to dusk, I know the enemy's decided to wait until the darkness of night. We're left to sit here, straining our eyes as we stare into the forest, the Haudenosaunee felling trees.

———

OUR EVENING MEAL consists of the same ottet we'd normally eat on our summer voyages. Fox reflects out loud on some of his favourite trips. Still, he says, his most enjoyable by far was the one when Snow Falls chopped off my finger. I smile, but I'm preoccupied.

"I'm willing to bet that as soon as it's dark enough," I say, "the Haudenosaunee will launch another flaming arrow attack."

"I'll take you up on that," Fox says. "They'd never be so predictable. My bet is they'll try another big assault."

We agree to wager our best pipe, and sure enough, just as dusk settles to darkness, the flickering of arrows overhead and landing in the village begins once more. The attack seems twice as large as yesterday's, arrows coming in heavy and hitting longhouses too quick for us to put the fires out. Already it appears most of the village is on fire or in a smoking ruin. With the women and children and old ones in the crow house, I've ordered our water-bearers to stay close by it. It's all we can do now.

"Looks like you won this one," Fox says.

"Unfortunately, I think we both did," I say as Haudenosaunee rush out of the darkness, their shining wood booming and arrows striking against the palisades.

This assault's so heavy we no longer have the luxury of waiting with our heads down between rounds of fire. All of us now stand and pour everything we have onto them. I'm running low on arrows and decide to reload my shining wood. As I squat down and finish ramming the stick into its mouth, Fox grunts and crouches beside me, holding his side, the long shaft of an arrow sticking out of him.

Laying down my weapon, I examine him as he grimaces. The arrow has pierced the sturgeon tattoo on his stomach and its tip pokes out of his back.

Fox tells me that the arrow must have shot through the crack in the palisades. "All I felt was a punch and the burning."

It'll be easier to continue to pull the arrow through him than pull it out. "Hold on to a log," I say. He does, facing away from me. Taking my knife, I trim away the feathered fletching.

Hoping that it hasn't pierced his liver or his stomach, I begin to pull, and Fox moans out. It doesn't want to move. Firming both my feet, men all around me shouting and fighting, I pull hard as I can, and the arrow begins to move before it slips right out of him. He collapses onto his stomach, and I stand to fire my shining wood at a Haudenosaunee below me, chopping with his axe at the wall. I can see I've shattered his shoulder as he spins down to the ground, crying out.

Bending back to Fox, I reach into my pouch and take fingers full of tobacco out, stuffing it into the wound that pours blood out of his back. I then cut a strip of hide from the pouch and stuff it into the hole to slow the bleeding.

"Turn around," I say. I do the same to the front of him. I believe that the arrow didn't strike anything vital, or Fox would have already gone still. Instead, he pushes himself up to standing and asks for his bow.

For a second time, we repel their attack, sending them scurrying back to the woods, our war-bearers roaring. Looking around, though, I see we've lost many more.

Fox tugs at me, pointing to the crow house, smoke still rising from the partially burnt roof. "That was close," he says as we watch people fill buckets in the little river and pitch water onto the roof and walls.

The world goes quiet for the rest of the night but nobody sleeps. The only noise we can hear as the sun begins to show is a few wounded Haudenosaunee singing their death songs, the crows soon joining in the chorus with their morning chant.

IN THIS TIME OF GREAT TROUBLE

I stand in the house of the crows, the roof partly burned away so the sun's rays now sparkle across the water pooled upon the wooden floor. Christophe Crow stands in his place on a small platform, facing us. Above his head, he holds dried ottet in his hands, formed so carefully that it's round as a moon.

My girl, you are so pretty. You are so fragile, and yet I see in your outstretched arms the strength you'll one day possess. I've never seen a head of hair so thick and shiny in a child only just a week in this world. Will you help me pray to Aataentsic that your father survived the night?

People who follow the great voice begin to crowd around us, lining up to take a part of him into their bodies. Christophe Crow told us earlier that we need to prepare to die soon if this is what the great voice decides.

Sleeps Long, standing beside me holding her own baby in her arms, scoffed at that. "Has he so little faith in our men who stand outside and protect us? Maybe he should stop hiding in here." Now, as the people come to eat from Christophe Crow's hand, she pushes away. "I need air," she says. "Meet me outside and we'll bring some food to our husbands."

I watch as the people, those from their faraway land mingled with ours, wait anxious in the line to take the bit of food into their mouths, as if worried there will be no more when they reach the front. The faces of those who take the ottet and turn from the crows seem sated, even calm. It's then I make the decision. I will take some of this food into my mouth as well, this food that Christophe Crow has tried to get me to eat for so much of my life. I will take this food if it helps to protect my husband. The crows always say if I speak what I need to the great voice, if I take his body into mine, then he will answer my prayers. And so I line up, and I pray to you, Great Voice, that you protect Carries an Axe in battle, and you push our enemies out of our land, and you allow my husband and me to grow old together as we watch our child bloom along with the three sisters.

As I get closer to Christophe Crow, I repeat my desire over and over, and when it is my turn and I stand in front of him, his hand holding a piece of the ottet torn off the moon, he looks down at me, confused.

"You are willing to accept the Great Voice?" he asks.

I nod.

"In this time of great trouble," he says, "there's little room to act like a child."

I look up at him.

"I normally wouldn't believe you, and instead think you were playing another game with me."

"I worry my husband will be killed today," I say.

Christophe Crow's eyes change then. He nods, and as he holds out the ottet, I open my mouth.

———

I FIND MY HUSBAND alive and talking with his mother and father near where we sat yesterday. Sitting down with them, I begin to cry. This makes me feel weak, but Carries an Axe holds me while his parents look away, holding each other. Both my husband and his father look exhausted, their faces strained beyond their years. An arrow glanced off Tall Trees' arm and he wrapped it in a bloody bit of cloth one of the hairy ones gave him. Carries an Axe is proud that nothing has touched him yet. "Don't worry," he says, "their arrows can't find me."

We lost many war-bearers last night. I listen as the two men talk, but I'm so tired I fear I'll fall over and crush my child.

"Here," Sleeps Long says, reaching out for my girl, "let her visit with her relation." Cradling her own daughter in one arm, she takes my daughter in the other. Carries an Axe takes me, and the two of us lie back in the grass, drifting off as the spring sun shines down on our faces, dreaming we're not in this strange village of war but home after a good day of planting.

THEY WILL SOON SHOW US

All of us who still stand in defence of the village, maybe half the original number now, had fully expected the Haudenosaunee to do one more great push as the sun broke. I had feared this more than anything because I was sure it would have broken us. But by noon, the world remains quiet, the odd arrow slicing its way in, hitting dirt or the side of one of the buildings left standing.

No one's slept for more than a few moments at a time for the last two days. The sentries are so tired that some have begun seeing the enemy in the shadows or hearing them climb the walls.

Now that we have a chance to walk about and calculate the damage, I see how well the stone structures at each corner of the palisades have served us. The French placed many of their shining wood in each one, and the constant firing down upon the enemy from their protected position is what has saved us this far from being overrun. The bodies piled below them prove their worth. These are something I won't forget.

But the palisades themselves have suffered miserably. Stretches of them have been hacked or burned so that a group of focused men could push their way through. Those with any strength left work to repair them, tying the weakened logs together and digging new posts in behind the damaged ones.

"Why do you think they've gone so silent?" Fox asks as we take our turn as sentry once more on the ramparts. He's pale from loss of blood.

I look at the dead below, their number doubled since yesterday. Indeed, their bodies have begun to stink. The Haudenosaunee, I realize, won't leave until this is done.

"I imagine, old friend," I say, "they'll soon show us this new trick they've been working on." I look behind me at the smoking ruin of the village.

With the sun already passing its height, we sit and wait, our heads nodding in the spring day, a beautiful one with a slight breeze. I've collected as many arrows from the dead as I could find, and my shining wood is loaded. Fox sleeps beside me. I know my friend, though. He will awake suddenly, as if he has no idea what dreams are.

Down the ramparts I hear a familiar voice cry out. Opening my eyes, I see that it's my new son, Carries an Axe. He points to the field and shouts. We're in for it again.

Fox and I stand. He's slower than me with his side clearly paining him. His leg's bright from the blood seeping onto it. I look across the field and see something I've never even imagined, a wooden palisade as wide as four men with their arms outstretched, slowly making its way across the empty field.

"What are we witnessing?" Fox asks.

It's then I can make sense of it. The Haudenosaunee have strapped together a great shield of logs to protect their advance, the men behind lifting it and walking it, putting it down to rest before lifting it and walking it forward again. My stomach sinks further when I see a second one emerge from the forest.

"Well, my brother," I say, looking over to Fox. "We're in for a fight now."

We watch the advance, all of us behind the palisade quiet. As the two walls creep closer and closer to us, one on either side of the field, I find the tension of the last days slides off me. I listen to what I think are waves rhythmically hitting a sandy beach before I realize it's the blood pumping through my body.

Once again, I shout for the ones around me to prepare but not fire.

The wall in front of us is within range of our arrows but I see how useless it will be to fire. There must be a way to breach it. I ask for Fox to please figure it out.

He laughs. "If they come too close to our wall, we'll just push theirs down on top of them."

Despite his joking, I wonder if it might possibly work.

The Haudenosaunee walking behind the ones who carry the wall start firing shining wood and arrows at us, but now that we're in their line of sight, so are they in ours. We exchange iron and arrows without much consequence when I hear a strange, familiar voice shouting out, asking us to fight hard. I glance behind me and see the crow named Isaac walking back and forth, looking up to us in his long robe, his arms out, his fingerless hands raised.

Shaking my head, I turn to Fox and shout as more shining wood explodes, "Tell me again why I thought bringing them among us was a good idea?"

Now that their wall is close to ours, their men dart out from its protection with torches and axes to attack our palisades and gate. We fire down and pour boiling water or pitch onto them, their screams by now something I've grown used to. I look over at the closest stone bastion and see that the hairy ones have a good angle and shoot as fast as they can at the ones behind the moving wall. But still, it creeps closer to our own.

Despite our great effort, the enemy below now hacks at the palisades, and it can't be long before they break through. "Fox," I shout, "go down and pass poles up to the ramparts."

He knows not to question, and despite his wound, he's slid down the ladder before I can turn back to the fight.

He and another are soon handing up lengths of spruce and poplar hoarded to strengthen the palisades. I grab one and, reaching out, jam its tip against the enemy's wall and start pushing with all my might. Quickly, the others see what I'm attempting, and putting down their weapons, they take up poles of their own, a gang of us now pushing against the top of the enemy wall so that we begin to feel it give way.

A man shouts out beside me, and I see Isaac struggling to hold his own length of wood in his fingerless hands, but it slips from his grasp and falls to the ground. He looks at it for a moment, then places his nubs onto my hands, and together we push, watching as the wall that the Haudenosaunee built topples back and onto the ones crouching behind it.

With a roar, we pick up our weapons and fire down upon the surprised enemy, sending most of them scurrying back to the tree line.

This is a great victory, I think. This turning them back might be enough to send them home.

I look for Fox to share this with him just as I hear men screaming and wood splintering down the line. The enemy's second wall leans against our own and, as if in a bad dream, our palisades give way, collapsing into the village.

NOW WE'RE EVEN

Dusk settles as we prepare to fight up close. I hold my club in one hand and my knife in the other. Fox stays close beside me, and we move up to where the palisades were destroyed. It looks like the Haudenosaunee surprised even themselves, as only a handful jump through the breach and are quickly overrun by us. But we have no time to repair the damage they've done and instinctively gather by our ruined wall, their war-bearers on the other side shouting and whistling, readying themselves to charge in. The French have been left up in their stone buildings to keep firing upon any enemies who try to hack or climb in at other places. We're in trouble. It won't be long now.

I tell Fox we'll help defend as long as we can but then have to get back to the crows' house and try to get the women and children out of the village and to a safe location. I think hard about how it is we're going to do this. Aataentsic, please help me with that answer. Fox and I know what'll happen now as we brace and the Haudenosaunee begin roaring on the other side, sending themselves into a frenzy. We'll get all the people we can out of the village, even if we have to chop a hole through the palisades, and then we'll fight until our last breath in the hope they can disappear into the forest and eventually make it out to the islands.

Carries an Axe and Tall Trees stand side by side near Fox and me. We all look at one another and then at the palisades. The Haudenosaunee begin to climb through. Despite his injury, Fox is the first to pounce and meet them. He swings his knife and hatchet so that he pushes back a half-circle of the enemy. They try to surround him, try to get around him, but he stabs the first one who gets too close. This gives the other three of us the chance to jump in as well, swinging and cutting, trying to avoid their knives and hatchets and clubs as best we can. I feel a knife slice my arm but ignore it just as another Haudenosaunee swings his club toward my head. Rolling out of the way, I see Tall Trees kick the attacker so that the man falls back, and then Tall Trees is on top of him, crushing his skull with a hatchet.

Two men have attacked Carries an Axe. I lunge at one with my knife, aiming for his lower back, the warrior screaming out and falling to his knees. The other one glances at me, and Carries an Axe swings his own hatchet, splitting the man's skull. We hear shouting over the din and see several Haudenosaunee raining down blows on Tall Trees. By the time we get there, he's on his knees, his face covered in blood. Carries an Axe screams and rushes the men, stabbing and slicing, his hatchet a blur as two and then three fall to the ground. But the other men keep swinging down on Tall Trees till I can see, as I myself bring my club down on one of their heads, that he lies flat on the ground, bleeding into the dirt.

When we have killed all the attackers, Carries an Axe kneels down by his father. I turn at the approach of an enemy running at me with his hatchet raised and, ducking his swing, slice through his belly with my knife. When I turn back, I can tell Tall Trees is dead.

Carries an Axe stands up and says, "My wife will be proud that I tried with my all today, yes?"

I nod, and just as I begin to run to him so that together we can find Fox and get the women and children out of the village, an arrow slices straight through Carries an Axe's neck. He falls to the ground, and as I reach him, he's choking on his blood. His eyes are wide as he drowns in it, and I see there's nothing to do for him as I hold him and he pushes against my chest, begging me to help. Let it be quick. Please, let it be quick. He pushes harder with both hands against me as if it's me who's killing him, and all I can do is hold his shoulders as the life pumps out of him in spurts until finally he goes still.

As I make my way to stand, a scream of pain shoots through my leg, and as I look down, I see an arrow sticking out of my thigh. I try to stand but fall over as a Haudenosaunee runs up, both hands raising his club above me. I lift my arm with my knife to try and stab him but swing pathetically. He smiles, then tenses, and just as he begins to swing down a body flies into him, knocking him over. Fox rolls on the ground with the much bigger man and, slipping around to the man's back, takes his knife and slits across his throat.

He stands and runs to me. I think he's going to help me up but instead snatches the arrow and pulls it out of my leg. I roar with the pain.

"There," he says. "Now we're even."

THIS IS MY BODY, WHICH IS FOR YOU

It is with a happy heart, dear Lord, that I tell You that each day I have tried to live by Your word, and each day I have always sung Your praises. I am blessed to find myself in a foreign land surrounded by a people in need of Your guidance, and I am closer to becoming the man I've long wanted to be. Please accept me into Your kingdom with open arms, for, after treading so close many times in the past, I now understand that Your kingdom is near.

Dear Superior,

I write to you with a heavy heart that shall soon be enlightened. I write to you with the understanding that most probably you will never receive this epistle which I fear will be my last. Our mission is under siege by the Iroquois, and they are bent on our destruction.

While I have in no way fulfilled what I had once as a young man hoped to fulfill in this wilderness, I can't imagine an earthly paradise grander than this one. Despite the darkness that constantly threatens this place in which I find myself, I have had the immense privilege of living amongst a people at once craven and prone to the basest of appetites, and more generous and even gentle than any I've ever had the pleasure to know.

I've tried to shepherd these people toward the good pasture, and it has been a blessing to be aided in this effort by two young Jesuits, each gifted in his own right. Please pray for us all, and in those prayers ask that we soon will rest in His arms.

A horrible battle rages outside the mission palisades, and I've tried to comfort not just the dying but also those who fear what comes. We huddle now, hoping the enemy won't get in. The damaged roof of the chapel offers scant comfort from the screams of the wounded. The afternoon wanes, and I myself fear the coming darkness worst of all.

I look around at the small group who still holds faith in this place. One of my oldest converts, Delilah, hardened into a shell in recent weeks, sits glumly alongside a handful of Huron and a couple of Algonquin fur people. And then there is sweet but damaged young Snow Falls, her newborn wrapped in rabbit skins and sleeping now in a covered basket beneath the table upon which the tabernacle sits. It was my suggestion to put the baby there when Snow Falls wandered in just as the fighting grew hot again. It seems the safest place in the event more arrows fall upon us.

I try to maintain a hopeful countenance, but any words I speak are punctuated by men shouting or dying or killing. Instead, I bow my head and pray, hoping the others might follow me and find a little solace. As the afternoon wears on, people come and leave, always rushing. To where, I have no idea.

Gabriel has been out tending to the wounded and finally returns with Isaac at his arm. Gabriel looks at me.

"There were many close calls," he says, "but our brother managed to escape unscathed." Gabriel shakes his head and sits.

"I helped the Huron prevent one breach of the palisades," Isaac says breathlessly. "And it worked. But the wall at the far end of the village has fallen to a second attack." He stares at me, his eyes bloodshot. "The time has come, Père Christophe. The enemy is inside the gates."

I'm at once drawn to and repelled by his crazed eyes, this fever that's overcome him. I hear the distant shouting of men fighting within the walls of the mission. "What is it time for, dear Brother?" I ask.

He looks at me as if I'm stupid. He wants to say something but bites his lip as he scratches his head with the stump of his hand. "We still have time for Communion," he says.

He's right. "Please, Isaac," I say, "prepare the Eucharist."

I take my place and ask that we all join hands in prayer. We gather in a circle, all except for Snow Falls, who seems hesitant. "You partook of the body of the Great Voice this morning," I say. "You are ready to partake of it again."

Everyone flinches as a musket fires nearby. I offer my hand to her. She stands and comes to me.

Isaac returns, clasping a dish between his arm and body. "Thank you, Brother," I say, reaching for it.

He pulls away. "Père Christophe," he says, "will you please allow me to serve the Eucharist?"

Another musket fires close by. I nod.

Isaac bows his head, and the rest of us follow. He whispers what I recognize as one of his favourite Gospel passages, rooting around in the dish until he's able to grab a Host in the fold where his thumb once met his palm. "For I received from the Lord, that which I also delivered to you," he whispers, "that the Lord Jesus, in the night in which he was delivered up, took bread, and having given thanks, broke it, and said, This is my body, which is for you: this do in remembrance of me."

Isaac places the thickness of it into his mouth and chews, struggling to swallow. He moves then to Delilah, who gazes blankly back at him as he again fumbles to grasp a Host. She opens her mouth obediently when he finally manages.

And then he turns to Snow Falls, managing to grasp a large Host more quickly now. The bleat of her baby echoes from under the tabernacle and she turns to it, but Isaac whispers and she turns back to him to accept the Host in her mouth.

When it's my turn, I see that Isaac shakes and sweats, and I fear for the commotion he's about to cause. Almost dropping the dish he pinches between his chest and arm, he manages once more to grasp a Host and raises it to my mouth. I accept the offering, but a bitterness explodes, making my mouth salivate and my throat close.

I gag and spit it up into my hand. "What's wrong with this sagamité?" I ask.

Isaac looks at me. "We are dying for them, Père Christophe." He shudders and then spits up onto himself. "The village falls soon, and it's best to die for them now." He looks at me with a sudden clarity I've not seen in him before. "To allow us to be tortured before death is a brutality I can't allow."

I look in horror at Snow Falls and Delilah. Both sit on their haunches, holding their bellies.

"What did you put into the Eucharist?" I ask Isaac.

"Ingredients that will act quickly," he says. "Death-cap mushroom and water hemlock. I tried it on a dog, and he passed within minutes."

I slap him. "Are you insane?" I shout.

Delilah begins to cry and moan, and the others in the circle have stepped back, all but Gabriel, who throws himself between us. "What's happened?" he asks, confused.

As the sound of nearby fighting erupts outside, a group of frightened women and children rushes into the chapel, Sleeps Long and Gosling among them.

"Isaac has killed them," I say, pushing him out of the way and grasping for Snow Falls, who's collapsed onto her back and begins to convulse.

DID I DO THIS TO YOU?

I know something's wrong as soon as I enter, even before I see the crow Isaac and Dawning of Day lying dead on the floor. What has happened? Have the Haudenosaunee already attacked?

Christophe Crow rushes to me. "Quick," he says. "Your daughter." He's crying. No.

I shove through the throng of women and children who've come here as the fighting begins to spread throughout the village. Sleeps Long crouches beside my daughter, holding both of their babies as Gosling furiously tries to push charcoal into Snow Falls' mouth.

"What is this?" I roar.

"Isaac went mad," the Crow tells me. "He ate poison and fed it to Delilah and your daughter." I kneel down and Gosling looks at me. Her eyes, they've always told me the truth.

But this can't be true. My hands begin shaking and I see sharp colours. "Save her," I whisper.

My daughter's body quakes. Her eyes are open but don't look like they can see anything. Blood drips from the side of her mouth, and her lips are black from the charcoal. She looks like she shivers to death.

"I'm sorry, my love," Gosling says.

I stare down into my daughter's face, wondering how it rains in here but not outside until I realize that I am washing her in my tears. My daughter. Oh, my daughter. Did I do this to you?

Sleeps Long takes my shoulder. "Here, hold her," she says. She hands me my tiny granddaughter. Her eyes are open, too, and see nothing either, not yet. I cradle her as my daughter begins to convulse more strongly. I lie down beside her, the baby between us. She reaches a hand out and touches her mother's lips, cuddles her face into Snow Falls' cheek. My daughter. Did I do this to you? Did I cause such pain to all of us? What if we'd never come across your family on that winter day? What if I'd never killed your parents and taken you for my own? Would all this bad blood between your people and mine have turned so poisonous?

I take my daughter's hand in my own. "I'm sorry," I whisper in her ear. Her hand squeezes mine, as if she can hear me.

DRUMMING INTO THE OTHER WORLD

As Christophe Crow gathers those in the room into a circle, I watch as Isaac Crow walks toward the shining box, my baby sleeping in her birch basket underneath the table. But instead of going into the shining box for the round ottet, he reaches into a secret pocket in his black robe that he sewed for when he did tricks for the children. He pulls out a dish and some other ottet and sets them on the table. He then rips the bread into chunks and places the pieces in the dish.

He comes back to the circle and whispers words in his tongue before eating a piece from his dish. He then offers it to Delilah, who chews, her eyes blank, and then he offers it to me.

My baby wakes and begins to cry just as Isaac is about to feed me. He tells me it'll only take a moment. The large piece that he stuffs into my mouth with his damaged hand tastes horrible. I want to spit it out and look at Delilah. But she chews without complaint. I don't want to be rude to the crows so I chew as fast as I can and try to swallow the bitter-tasting food quickly. Immediately I feel pain in my stomach and wish I'd let myself cough it out.

Christophe Crow's face shows that he doesn't like the taste, either. He spits out his ottet, and that's when I kneel beside Delilah, who's already on the ground, and try to make myself throw it up. Nothing but spit comes out. The inside of my stomach feels like it's been sliced in half and begins to burn. Christophe Crow slaps Isaac and rushes to me. Isaac collapses to the ground.

Christophe Crow sticks his fingers in my mouth, and I gag so hard that I spit out red. "You must throw it up," I hear him say as I fall over onto my side when the pain gets too great.

I stick my own fingers down my throat, but the ottet seems to have lodged itself deep inside me. I can hear my baby screaming under the table now, and I struggle to crawl up and to her. The fire that shoots through me drops me flat.

My baby. My child. Help her. I don't know if the words are in my head or coming out of my mouth. Help her. She's screaming. I see Delilah on her back, her body doing little jumps. Her legs kick the floor. Christophe Crow leans over me, and the sparkling necklace I've known for so long hovers in front of my eyes. I want to grasp it. I want to touch my father. Delilah's legs drum out on the floor. I remember my mother now, my brother, drumming their legs into the other world. My legs begin to drum now, too.

My father dangles above me, one arm pointed to where the sun rises and one arm pointed to where the sun sets, his legs crossed comfortably over one another, the halo of blood around his head. My baby still cries but not as hard now. The sound of her gets closer. Gabriel Crow stands over me with my baby in his arms. A burning knife cuts through my guts. I can taste blood in my mouth. My body vibrates. Gabriel Crow hesitates, then leans down to me. I reach up when my body stills and take her in my arms.

I'm not sure what I'm seeing anymore when my eyes open, the pain now a great rush of boiling water through my body. I can't feel my arms or know if my daughter's in them. I want my husband here beside me. Faces hover, all of them crying. But none is my husband's. My body kicks then stills again. When my eyes are closed, I see Carries an Axe walking with me through a field of new corn, hand in hand. Our baby isn't with us but I know she's somewhere safe. When I open my eyes again, Christophe leans over me, touching my forehead, my chest, both of my shoulders. I see Gabriel, and Sleeps Long stands above me weeping, her baby in one arm, mine now in her other. I see

Gosling, who forces my mouth open and stuffs charcoal into it. I can tell from her eyes that she knows it's too late. I see Fox, who leans to me and touches my forehead. I see my father, Bird, his face blackened and the paint of war on his cheeks nearly smudged off. I've never seen him cry. His tears splash on my face. Please don't cry, Father. It means I'm dying. He has my daughter in his arms now, and he lies down beside me. My daughter's tiny hand tickles my lips and, as I close my eyes, I feel my child's warm breath upon my cheek.

THAT PLACE DANCING WITH FIRE

I pull myself up from my lifeless daughter. Fox speaks to Sleeps Long. I know what he tells her. Her body acts as if it wants to collapse, but her face remains a mask. She comes to me.

"They died bravely," I tell her.

She nods, and when my granddaughter begins to cry, Sleeps Long passes her own child to Gosling and takes the baby from my arms. "She's hungry," Sleeps Long says as she removes her breast from her loose top. Snow Falls' daughter sucks hungrily.

The fighting outside gets closer. By now a few dozen women and children have made their way to us. Fox approaches. "We have to get them out," he says.

Gosling gently rocks Sleeps Long's baby, cooing to her. "I recently dreamed," she says, looking at me, "that one day, years after our child is born, you will take him to the same rocks where you had your own dreaming."

I'm about to say we can speak of this later, that we must get out of this place.

"You know those rocks," Gosling says. "The ones with the ancient paintings of men in canoes being escorted by Mishipishu."

I can suddenly see them as vividly as if I stand in front of them. I'd always thought the men in canoes were being pursued by the water lynx, not guarded by him.

A few men shout outside. "Fox," I say. "Come with me. I have a plan."

I limp out of the crows' house as fast as I can, dragging my leg and keeping a careful watch for prowling Haudenosaunee. I lead Fox away from the fighting and to the little river that comes into the village. In the darkness, we see the canoes lining the banks. We were fools for not noticing what was right there before us. But isn't this always the way? As Fox and I run to the gate, I explain that we'll have everyone lie flat in the canoes while the men swim behind them, guiding them out. "Even if the enemy sees the canoes from a distance," I tell him, "they'll think they float empty." We'll sneak out right under the noses of the Haudenosaunee and then paddle to the Sweet Water Sea and the islands.

The two of us lift the heavy log from the gate and swing it open. The river is a black line in front of us on this moonless night. I let Fox go first as I limp back, my leg dragging badly, to begin the departure.

———

IT'S ALL WORKED OUT WELL. About half of the people have made their way safely to the little river and, if all goes as planned, they'll reach the islands tonight. I stand in the crows' house with Fox, listening to sounds we don't want to hear. Haudenosaunee warriors have drawn closer, and I'm amazed they haven't overrun this building already.

We've been sending out a group at a time to lessen the chances of being spotted but can no longer risk the delay. With the fighting out front, Fox has broken a hole through the back wall facing the little river. I usher the women and children through it and Fox leads them to the canoes. Our last handful of warriors wait there, and as each canoe fills and the occupants lie flat, the men slide into the water and guide each one out to the main river and freedom.

I remind the women to keep their children hushed. I've tried to get Gosling and Sleeps Long to leave already, but they refuse to go without me. I want to shout at them to stop being stubborn.

Finally, there are few enough left that we should fit into two canoes. Fox is waiting by the hole in the wall, and in the darkness the shouting and now triumphant singing of the Haudenosaunee grow louder. I ask him to help me carry my daughter's body and her small bundle of possessions with us. We race as fast as we can to the water, pain shooting through me with each stride.

I urge Gosling and Gabriel Crow, a few old women who have difficulty climbing in, and three children who look around with big eyes to be as still and quiet as they can. The two canoes are loaded, my daughter beside my woman. Christophe Crow stands on the bank.

"Fox," I whisper. "Is that everyone?"

He nods. "I think so. Sleeps Long and the two infants were in the last canoe to go out, yes?"

I've lost track and tell him as much. Then I point behind us at the warriors carrying torches toward the crows' house.

"We'd better hope she was in that canoe," he says.

I motion for Christophe Crow to get in. We need to go now.

He stares down at us, then shakes his head. "I will stay," he says.

His helper, Gabriel, rises to his knees. "You must come with us. They'll torture and kill you."

"So be it," Christophe says. "There are many still here who will need to be comforted."

Light flares in the sky and we turn to see that the Haudenosaunee have put their torches to a small building on one edge of the crow house.

"Please, Father," the helper begs. "Come with us. You'll be needed on the islands."

Again he shakes his head. He reaches into the arm of his robe and pulls out the papers on which he makes his markings, then hands them to Gabriel. "May it one day return home," he says. He lifts his hand to us and makes his sign before walking up the bank and back toward his house, his large frame lit by the blaze ahead.

Just as I slip into the freezing water to begin to push one of the last canoes out of the village, the Haudenosaunee erupt in screeches. I try to climb back up the bank, but my bad leg's gone dead. Fox sees me struggling and pulls me the rest of the way. We lie on the ground and watch their war-bearers drag a woman out of the crows' house. My heart drops. It's Sleeps Long. She must have thought we were coming back for her when she saw us gone.

"No," Fox spits. Two of them take the babies from her arms and lift the tiny bundles in the air. She lunges for them but is knocked to the ground.

I try to stand, but my leg won't allow it. We can see the tall form of Christophe Crow walk up to the men and reach for the babies. This must surprise them, this charcoal appearing out of nowhere. One clubs him on the head and he crumples to the ground.

In the bright light of the burning house, another Haudenosaunee, the tall one painted red who I recognize as their chief, Tekakwitha, walks up, and the men stop their whooping and listen to what he must say. They hand the babies back to Sleeps Long and then Tekakwitha escorts her away.

"We have to get her and the children," I say.

"What do you propose you will do," Fox asks, "drag yourself over and beat them with your useless leg?" He looks at me for a few moments, then reaches into his tobacco pouch. "Here," he says. "Take this." He hands me his favourite pipe. "I'll expect it back when I get to the islands." He rises to a crouch, his knife in one hand, his hatchet in the other. "You can't walk," he says, "but I imagine you still remember how to swim. Now take those two canoes and go."

With that, my old friend sneaks away and is swallowed up by the shadows.

Shivering, I push the canoes out of the village of the crows in the middle of the night, and when it's safe, I climb into one, the last crow left paddling the other. Together we wind down the black river, turning to look back only once at that place dancing with fire before we push forward again and enter the Sweet Water Sea.

THE STOLEN FRUIT

My mother used to tease me that I grew into a Brittany giant because as a child I'd sneak into our neighbour's apple orchards every day to steal the ripe fruit hanging just above my head. I tell this story now to my Iroquois captor, Tekakwitha, because I can see it infuriates him. It's not the story itself, Lord, that makes him so angry, but that I tell it in French. I think he considers this an insult.

Tekakwitha, clearly the captain of these raiders, is as tall as Bird and me, with a scar that runs across his cheek and to his mouth that gives him a permanent snarl. He wears his hair in the standard thin roach down the middle of his plucked head, the hair reaching to his lower back and decorated with a beautiful assortment of feathers. His face is painted a solid blood red. He has me tied to a stake in my ruined chapel, the walls still somehow standing, though the roof's no longer there. He sits perched on the altar and watches the proceedings. He's already ransacked the tabernacle and claimed the tin chalice from which he drinks.

Now I want to tell him the story of how my father drank his cheap and strong apple brandy and how he used to tie me to a post like this one and beat me mercilessly for stealing neighbours' fruit until the blood ran down my back. But Tekakwitha clearly doesn't want me to speak my tongue anymore. He orders his warriors to squeeze my face until my jaws pop and my mouth unhinges. While one digs in with his dirty fingers, pulling my tongue out as far as he can, the other takes a red hot blade and saws it off at the root. Feeling the blood run down the back of my throat, I wonder if this might drown me. But my persecutors take an iron poker from the blazing hearth and stuff it in my mouth, cauterizing the wound. The burning flesh smells like a cow's liver left too long on the fire. I am at the beginning of my second day of torture.

Yesterday morning, after Tekakwitha had me stripped naked, he held a mock feast in my honour and explained that he didn't expect it would take very long to make me scream and beg like a woman. He ordered that a dog killed in the fighting the day before have its scrotum cut off. Then one of his warriors stuck it in the fire for a few seconds before forcing it in my mouth. This cruel act reminded me how much, so long ago, I loved dogs. It was then I took his challenge to heart, Lord. It was then I promised You I wouldn't cry out no matter what they did to me. And I know You are here, watching me, Lord, for I witnessed a glowing armour descend from Heaven and wrap itself around me, covering my nakedness. I'm able to observe, as if from a distance, what these sauvages do to me and not shout out at the pain.

Yesterday, when I still had a tongue, I preached to the warriors who danced and sang all around me, telling them that, unless they accepted You, they'd end up in fires far worse than the ones they now stoked. They laughed at me as they complimented my grasp of their language and delicate accent as they prodded me with burning sticks and sliced at me with sharpened clamshells. By mid-morning, when I still hadn't screamed, their caressing became more vigorous. They forced me to walk the length of my chapel with my hands tied behind my back while they smashed my toes with rocks and pushed me into the fires they'd built and shoved burning sticks into my orifices. I knew my time on this earth was short and fought my fainting, but slipped into unconsciousness despite my efforts.

I remember awaking to cold water being poured into my nose, and I sputtered awake to the sight of them standing around me, patting me on the back and clasping my hands and smiling at me as if we were all the best of friends. A couple fed me pieces of meat tenderly with their own fingers while still others tipped a birch cup to my mouth. Then they untied me and let me hobble around before tying me to the post again, this time with my hands in front of me where I could see them.

Tekakwitha chose his ten favourite warriors to stand, and each time he nodded his head, one walked up to me and twisted a finger till it snapped, then took his knife and cut it off, staring into my eyes. I smiled at each man who came and whispered a prayer for his soul. I finally felt I'd begun to understand my dear misguided Isaac's travails. I just wish he'd not acted so insanely and caused such great harm.

Forgive me, my Lord, but yesterday after each finger was removed from my hands, and as each bleeding stump was cauterized by red-hot iron, my strength failed me again, and I sank to my knees unconscious.

When I awoke in a crumpled pile, my cheek against the rough wood of the post to which I was tied, I heard babies crying. Looking up, I saw Sleeps Long, the beautiful young wife of the warrior I'd named David so long ago, cradling her baby in front of Tekakwitha. He himself gazed down at the infant cupped in his own large hands. I could tell by her throaty cry that this was the daughter of my troubled saint, Snow Falls, wailing out her rage.

"Come here," Tekakwitha commanded of one of his warriors who stood nearby. "Look into her eyes and tell me you don't see a child worthy of being Haudenosaunee!" The warrior, not sure what to do, nodded dumbly and skulked away. Then Tekakwitha announced in a loud voice to all in my chapel, "From this day forward, this child is mine. And you and yours," he said, pointing at Sleeps Long, "will become mine as well. You will continue to nurse both this child and your own." I smiled at Sleeps Long to try and give her some comfort as warriors led her and her babies away, but I fear she didn't see me.

And now today, Lord, it is the third day of my captivity and of my torments. I smile at the coincidence, for did You not suffer for three days, too? Didn't you wait another three days before rising up to Heaven? The trinity is a fitting thought for me, as I can tell that my physical body will not survive until tomorrow. And still I have not cried out. Tekakwitha is perturbed. I can see it. If only I had my tongue so I might tell him more stories.

They've built up the fires in my chapel so hot the air undulates as if I crawl through the desert. They've given me no water, and I swear my tongue is swollen, even though yesterday I watched an Iroquois roast and eat it before my eyes. I still have my eyes. The warriors applaud and hoot when I push myself up the pole and onto my feet. I look down at my body, now reddened and blackened, blood pulsing from my untended cuts with each heartbeat. My hands are especially ugly, the fingers gone, the stumps swollen twice their normal size, now just oozing charcoal knobs.

I can no longer speak, but I can praise You with song, my Lord. At first, the sauvages who rest in the chapel must mistake my humming for moaning, for they rush out and bring Tekakwitha back with them.

But I smile at him as I hum the lovely hymn "Ave Verum Corpus" as loudly as I can, and although I can't speak the words, I hear them in my head, Lord, I hear them in my heart. *Hail, true body, born of the Virgin Mary, who having truly suffered, was sacrificed on the cross for mankind, whose pierced side flowed with water and blood.* Tekakwitha himself approaches me with his knife drawn, and jabs quick so that I barely feel the blade penetrate my own side. It's as if he knows the words I sing as the heat turns to fire and I double over silently in pain.

Three warriors, two of them wearing French breastplates, the other a brass helmet, lace hatchet heads together with chain they must have taken from my dead soldiers. They smile at me and speak gently as they place their creation in a fire. Others have come in with a large kettle of water and set it over another fire. Tekakwitha smiles at me, and I smile back. The afternoon sky above us is beautiful, a blue so clear it's as if I peer into the shallows of the Sweet Water Sea. I can feel its coolness. I know, now, what soon comes, Lord. Please continue to shield me.

Tekakwitha calls out and warriors stream into the chapel, singing in a high tone, dancing in their swooping gait. Many of them carry objects from my mission. One swings a rosary, the next wields a wooden chair, and another holds a squawking chicken up above his head while others point and shout and laugh. Still others have put on cassocks and pantaloons and leather shoes they wear on the wrong feet, and a few brandish muskets taken from my men. I watch all of this in wonderment.

But then I see him, dancing in the circle around me with the others, glancing at me, holding what he was so long enamoured of in his two hands. Young Joseph the betrayer, Hot Cinder, dances by, and the mission clock, the Captain of the Day, is his special prize. If anything makes me want to scream out, my Lord, it's the sight of this naked boy passing by me with accusation in his eyes.

Tekakwitha stands as the warriors call out and drum and dance. Realizing that my physical strength is leaving me more quickly than he'd hoped, he orders his men to cut me from my stake. They lay me gently upon a beaver robe, careful as they pour cold water down my throat while others rub the few parts of me that aren't cut or burnt. One chews a piece of venison to pulp and then places his mouth on mine, feeding me as a bird feeds its chicks. The chapel's quiet as the afternoon lazes into dusk. The men around me are excited but respectful. When I am ready, I begin to hum "Ave Verum Corpus" once more, and I sit up on the robe, surrounded by these people.

Joseph stands, the Captain of the Day still firmly in his hands. "This charcoal," he says, pointing to me, "has magic. They all do. They can command this thing to speak." He raises the clock above his head so everyone might see it. "They'd ask it to talk and it talked. It would tell us when to come to eat and when to go home to bed."

"But don't the sun and moon tell us the same thing?" someone shouts, and people laugh.

"It spoke like this," Joseph says, and he O's his mouth and makes a *gong gong gong* sound. The men are amused, but he sees they don't believe him, so he walks up to me on my bloodied beaver robe and demands I make the clock speak. It has wound down to silence. I reach out to take it, to wind it up, but then I remember I have no fingers. I drop my mangled hands in my lap. Joseph stares down at me as if I'd just cut him to the bone. He drops the clock, and it hits the robe with a muted chime.

When dark arrives, they help me stand and tie me to the post once more. Tekakwitha has asked Joseph to tell the seething crowd a story. And so he does.

"The charcoal," he says, "tell a story that when you are born, you must have water poured upon your head to protect you."

Men behind him pick up the kettle from the fire with a pole and carry it forward. Joseph steps aside while they lift it above me and slowly pour the boiling water over my head and body. I can feel the thin skin of my pate bubble then tear away. I shut my eyes tight so I might at least be able to see into death. The water courses down my body and spares nothing from its rage. I pray to You for help, Lord, as my skin begins to melt. It's as if I can feel the nerves of my body deaden, and I begin to hum my hymn once more.

"And they tell another story," Joseph says, "that to speak to their great voice, you must wear a bright rope about your neck." He points at my crucifix, the one given to me by my dear mother, that Tekakwitha now wears.

Other warriors dig the chain of white-hot hatchet heads from the coals. Two of them carry the necklace on pokers and lift it over my head, draping it around my neck, the metal searing into my shoulders and chest. I hear the sizzle of my flesh and smell the stink of burnt meat, and the weight of this fire sends me slipping down the pole to my knees. I open my eyes and try to stand again but can't. The Iroquois all around me cheer and shout encouragement, but I no longer have the physical strength. I remain kneeling.

"Are there other stories worth telling?" Tekakwitha asks.

"There are many," Joseph replies, "but the ones I've told seem to me the best."

I droop now, my Lord, at the base of this pole. Thinking I can see You, a shining light beginning to brighten the eastern horizon, I call to you by humming my hymn.

As if in a dream, I watch as my donnés and soldiers who have survived are dragged, tied together, before their new master. They cry and beg or stare as if they're already dead. Tekakwitha declares in his language that they'll be kept alive and traded to the Iron People for Iroquois prisoners. My men are shuffled away, many of them sobbing, as they look down on me. I try my best to smile at them so they know I don't suffer too badly.

Now, Lord, I am sure I see Your light glowing above me where the roof of the chapel once hung.

Tekakwitha speaks to the warriors gathered around us, praising my strength and my fortitude, for no one would have believed I'd make it this far without begging for mercy. "But I myself," he says, "will give it one more try." The warriors lift me to standing and tie me to the pole so my arms are above my head.

He takes a burning poker from the fire and slips it into my ear. The crackling I hear is a forest fire rushing up. He then pushes the poker into my eye so the flames leap and turn that one eye's vision red then black. I hum my hymn once more. *Hail, true body, born of the Virgin Mary, who having truly suffered, was sacrificed on the cross for mankind, whose pierced side flowed with water and blood.*

With my good eye, I see Joseph come to me, holding a knife. He looks me in the eye, and then cuts deep into my sternum. I can feel his hand enter my chest.

May it be for us a foretaste of the heavenly banquet in the trial of death.

I can feel my life slowly pulsing in his hand.

O sweet Jesus, O pious Jesus, O Jesus, son of Mary, have mercy on me. Amen.

I watch from above now as Joseph smiles, lifting the red weight of it to me so that, as my sight fades, I may glimpse what he holds in his hand. He bites into it, and I can see myself again, a small boy reaching for a branch, grasping then biting into the stolen fruit.

A RAVEN'S EYE

Word spreads to the last of the Wendat, to all our nations, all the survivors chased from their longhouses and living in the forest like frightened hares, that we come together in the Sweet Water Sea. But as word spreads to our own people, the Haudenosaunee picks up our scent, and our most worthy enemy follows us to that island. I'm forced to bury my daughter in a rush in those early weeks of panic.

Maybe it's because summer's arrived, and their own families call them home. Or maybe it's because, after the great letting, they finally take pity upon those of us on the island. The Wendat who suffer the most are those who don't surrender to them and who travel to the mainland to try and hunt or find missing kin. Roving bands of the enemy wait like wolves for those who wander and tear them to pieces. And so we stay on this island, welcoming any Wendat family who manages to make it across the water in leaking canoes.

Gosling tells me, now that her stomach's large, that the island we try to scratch out an existence from is haunted. "This is why the Haudenosaunee won't come onto it," she tells me.

The women plant the seeds of the three sisters they'd so carefully wrapped in deerskin and carried with them. But the soil of this island is too sandy, and the summer sun beats down upon us, scaring off the rain. We're left to dig for roots or try to catch fish in what nets we can make, or hunt the few deer and smaller animals that make this place their home. For the first summer in living memory, we begin to go hungry.

Gabriel Crow seems lost now without his Father, Christophe, just as I feel lost without my daughter and Fox and all the others who were close to me. Rumour has it the Crow was caressed for three days and never uttered a sound except for his strange singing. I find this hard to believe, but that man surprised me in a hundred different ways. I never thought I'd say this, but I miss Christophe Crow as well.

I give Gabriel his due, though, for throwing his back into the labour of building shelter and some semblance of palisades without complaint. It's as if he, too, works for his absent friend. On this island that takes two days to walk around, we've built fifteen longhouses, and the families cram in. We've strained the resources of this place that protects us, and we're forced to scavenge on the other islands. I took Gabriel with me to the two smaller ones nearby in search of mussels and crayfish, and he announced he'd call our new home Charity, and these Faith and Hope. I don't have the heart to tell him our island already has a name. Gahoendoe.

As summer wanes, we prepare for what we know will be a nervous autumn and a brutal winter. The waters separating us from the mainland, now a liquid palisades to keep the Haudenosaunee away, will freeze into a pathway of ice for them. And just as bad, there are no crops to feed us through the long dark nights of snow and howling winds. But we'll make it. We always somehow find a way.

———

IN THE EVENINGS now that autumn approaches, the scent of hardwood fires hangs longer than usual in the air. When I wake I can feel the ghost of frost beginning to wake, too. Though Snow Falls' baby decided to come early, as if she couldn't wait to get out in the world, now it's as if Gosling's and my baby has decided to take some extra time to luxuriate in his mother's womb. I've grown anxious, taking walks along the beach, staring out at the bright skies and looking for signs of enemy smoke on the mainland, then lighting my pipe before walking back again.

Gosling forces herself to rest, and to wrestle the boredom she cures and cuts birchbark, sewing together small boxes she decorates with porcupine quills from her bundle. Instead of keeping them, she gives them away to the children who come to spy on her. Today, as I walk up from the beach, a young girl walks out of our longhouse with one in her hand. "The woman in there gave me this," she says, holding it up for me to examine.

I smile.

"She gave it to me, but she's making strange noises like she hurts," the girl says.

I hurry in to where Gosling squats on her mat, water puddling at her feet. She looks up at me. "Leave me now and get the women."

I run to fetch them.

For a long time I pace outside, stopping myself from peeking in whenever she cries out. I begin to worry when it goes quiet for a long time, but then I hear the cry, the cry so similar to that day not so long ago when my daughter gave birth. I rush inside.

The women around Gosling are busy with their hands, wiping the baby gently and wrapping it in a fur. One lifts it to me. "Meet your new daughter," she says.

"Daughter?" I ask. "Are you sure?"

She looks at me strangely, but then Gosling begins moaning out again. "Leave now," the woman says.

I stand outside, gazing at this red-faced bundle in my hands, fearing Gosling won't be all right. But then I hear more crying inside, and when I go back in the same woman says, "Now meet your new son."

———

TODAY, A SHOUT from the sentry goes up. Both Gosling and I have been having restless dreams. My experiences these last seasons have taught me to always expect the worst. I pass my daughter to Gosling and touch my son's cheek. I look at my woman, but her eyes give me nothing. I hurry out to see what has triggered the sentry's alarm.

Down on the beach, the sand cold under my bare feet, the sentry points to a lone canoe moving quickly over the rolling water, the waves silver in this dull light.

"Who would dare such a crossing in winds like this?" he asks. "I fear the Haudenosaunee are playing a trick."

We watch as the warrior slices through the waves, his paddling strong. He has the cut of a scout. "He certainly knows what he's doing," I say to the sentry. I recognize his stroke. How many summers has he paddled beside me?

I walk into the water as Fox pulls up to the shore. His canoe's loaded with hide-wrapped packages. "I come with gifts," he says.

That evening by the fire, all the others from their longhouses join us. Fox tells of his adventures, how he single-handedly harassed the Haudenosaunee these last months, how the rumour spread he was a vengeful ghost, how he took many unsuspecting enemy by slitting their throats or firing an arrow from his perch into their chest. The people sit by the fire and listen, enthralled. And then Fox pulls out gift after gift. Beaver robes for the mothers. Sturdy bows and knives for the men. He hands out painted gambling stones, even a hairy one's shiny breastplate. He gives away sewing awls and wampum beads and pretty shell necklaces. He gives until there's nothing left to give.

When he's done, he glances at me with a strange look upon his face.

"What is it?" I ask, balancing my daughter on one knee, my boy on the other.

"I just never pictured you doing this again," he says, smiling.

"I find it suits him well," Gosling says, laughing. "These are now your relations, too."

Fox grins. "There's one more thing I have for you," he says, then digs into his pouch before cupping something that must be very delicate. When he opens his fingers, a flower blooms.

Gosling gently takes it from him. "I made this for Snow Falls," she says. "Where did you find it?"

"The night you all paddled away from the crow village, I sneaked back into their holy house," Fox says. "Beside where your daughter died, Bird, I found this quill box. There's something inside, but I'm not sure what it is."

I watch as Gosling opens the box and stares. I lay my children down on their furs.

"Show me," I say. She passes it to me. An object glints in the bottom of the box. Something deep in me recognizes it as I shake it out into my palm, a shell the size of my nail, delicately shaped and polished, days of work to the one who would have such patience.

"Tell me," Fox says. "What is that?"

I hold the shell out to him. "It's the missing eye of Snow Falls' raven."

For tonight, we have food and we have warmth and we have the company of one another. We have our family who still lives, and we have the longhouse to recline in. I look about me as people talk and laugh. For the moment, I can see, we aren't worried about tomorrow. What more could I want right now, my two children sleeping in their furs and my old friend Fox beside me? Gosling watches all of this, too. She knows what will come, and I believe we're now ready.

I pull two pipes from my pouch and hand Fox back his favourite. I twist a stick in the fire and hold it steady for him as he inhales. I light my own. Once I've puffed, I hand it to Gosling, our smoke curling up and into the shadows of our longhouse.

———

TODAY, I TAKE GOSLING and the babies to a secret place, a small lake on the island. It's the rare day of late autumn that breathes one last summer's breath and it's warm enough this afternoon to fool the bull-frogs, who've come out to sing. We spear what we need and cook them over a fire as the stars begin to appear above. We eat to our content and lie with one another as Gosling feeds each child in turn.

Once they sleep wrapped tight in their bundles, she points out the star that always leads her people north to their home. I show her where Aataentsic slipped through a hole and fell to earth so long ago.

"I can see how our world will go," Gosling says.

I wait for her to tell me. I've been waiting for this all my life.

"The Wendat have suffered enough these last years," she says, "but still it will be a difficult winter. The Haudenosaunee, though, will refuse to come onto this haunted ground."

"Will we live?" I ask. "Will you and I and our children live till next spring?"

She nods. "We were destined to," she says. Gosling tells me how the others who make it through winter will scatter to the winds. Some will go back with the crow Gabriel to the place he calls Kebec. Others will be adopted into the Anishnaabe of the Nipissing, and the Algonquin, and yes, the Haudenosaunee, too.

"You and me," she says, "our family." She touches our children's heads. I smile. "We will know by next summer that it's most sensible to head north and be taken in by my people on their side of the Sweet Water Sea." She tells me I'll never farm again and neither will my offspring or their offspring. Never again will we eke a living from the earth but instead do what her people, the Anishnaabe, have always done. We'll go back to the forest, and we'll live by what it gives us. She laughs when she tells me the nearest I'll ever come again to farming is teaching my son and daughter to collect wild rice into our canoe. Gosling tells me all this as we lie back beside this lake on an island on a greater lake that itself rests upon Turtle Island. She tells me all this as she traces the patterns of stars with her finger so that in front of my very eyes warriors and deer and mythic beasts come to life and then dissipate again into the black sky.

"I'll tell you one more thing," Gosling says, "and that will be all for tonight."

I nod like a little boy.

"Your family, my family, the family of Bird, we will keep wandering north in pursuit of the animals and to avoid the crows and their followers who'll continue coming to this land. Eventually we'll stop near a frozen salt sea because we can't go any farther."

I listen as she tells me the story of the Birds who will come after I am gone, how they'll be great warriors and great hunters and great seers. On this night she makes me see that life goes on despite so much of it around us having so brutally expired. We hold each other beside this lake, the frogs' singing gone quiet now, the fire warm, the stars turning above us in their slow and dizzying walk.

Just as I begin to drift off, I tell Gosling I've been dreaming about Snow Falls and I fear my quick burial of her was not to her satisfaction.

"Is anyone ever truly satisfied on the day they're buried?" she asks.

"It's just that I interred her so quickly," I say, "and without what she might need."

"Then you should do it again," Gosling tells me. With those words, and for the first time since the troubles began, I fall into a dreamless sleep.

———

IN THE MORNING, I head to a copse of maple whose leaves make the trees seem to shimmer in fire, and I bend to the work of taking my girl back out of the earth.

When it's time to unwrap her from her mat and thin beaver blanket, the only one I owned, the sun breaks through the trees to shine on Snow Falls' face. I'm stunned. She's as perfect as she was on the day she left us. I touch her face glowing in the sunlight and see that it's hardened to a shell. My daughter, I took you from your people when you were still just a child, and you really were a special one. I never doubted it, even on those days when you tested my patience beyond the boundaries anyone should be tested. I touch your face once more with my hand that misses a finger.

I dig your grave deeper and line it with the robe Gosling sewed together from all the scraps of fur I've collected these last days, then bundle you up like you're a child ready for sleep before putting you back in your resting place. Around you I arrange the things you might need, birch baskets and a pair of pretty moccasins, quill barrettes for your hair, sewing needles, a bow for hunting small game, and best of all, the great raven that Carries an Axe once gave you so long ago and Sleeps Long helped you stuff, its one eye sparkling in the autumn sun. I lay this across you, and it's nearly your length, this strange object Gosling made sure to spirit away with her from that crow village. Finally, I take the small quill box holding the raven's missing eye and tuck it between you and the animal's wing. This eye, it'll allow you to see in the other world, my girl. And this raven, my daughter, it'll protect you. It will allow you to soar.

WE HAD THE MAGIC, the orenda, before the crows came. We'd never questioned this before their claws first grasped our branches and their beaks first pecked our earth.

Most of us will admit we were taken aback by how quickly the crows adapted. When you fall asleep laughing in the evening, it's difficult to awake crying in the sun. But this isn't just about sadness, or pity, or blame. We're all party to our own wants as well as to our own shortcomings.

Aataentsic, the Sky Woman and mother of the Wendat, she still sits by the fire watching with her eyes of polished shells. Aataentsic doesn't like to give much away, but if you watch her expression close enough, sometimes she does.

And so when the crows arrived to caw that our orenda was unclean, at first we laughed. Aataentsic did, too. But she didn't laugh for the same reasons. She'd already foreseen the nests the crows had begun to build as they plucked the odd feather from our hair or begged a strip of hide from our bundle even as we looked into their eyes. Aataentsic laughed because she is just as imperfect as we are. She laughed because we couldn't see our own demise coming.

But hindsight is sometimes too easy, isn't it? And so maybe this is what Aataentsic wants to tell. What's happened in the past can't stay in the past for the same reason the future is always just a breath away. Now is what's most important, Aataentsic says. Orenda can't be lost, just misplaced. The past and the future are present.

ACKNOWLEDGMENTS

This novel has been deeply enriched by the work of many scholars, historians, and elders. The list of books I've consulted over the years is too long to share here but I do need to name some: John Steckley's incredible *Words of the Huron*, and Allan Greer's concise edition of *The Jesuit Relations: Natives and Missionaries in Seventeenth-Century North America*, specifically his chapter dealing with Jean de Brébeuf's description of the Feast of the Dead offered me insight and sometimes the words I needed. Bruce Trigger's masterpiece, *The Children of Aataentsic* and Elisabeth Tooker's *An Ethnography of the Huron Indians, 1615–1649* were very helpful to my early research. In addition to this, Emma Anderson's *The Death and Afterlife of the North American Martyrs*, Conrad Heidenreich's *Huronia*, and Georges Sioui's *Huron Wendat: The Heritage of the Circle* are must-reads for anyone wishing to fully understand the era and the people.

On a personal note, I wish to deeply thank John Steckley, Allan Greer, Emma Anderson, Conrad Heidenreich, and Georges Sioui for reading different drafts of this novel and so generously offering their insight. *Chi miigwetch.*

Writing can be pretty lonely most of the time, but I feel very fortunate to have had the company, support, and kindness of David Gifford, Gord Downie, Jim Balsillie, Mark Mattson, Jim Steel, John Wadland, Chrys Darkwater, Nick Mainieri, Julian Zabalbeascoa, David Parker, Mike Pitre, Buddha Blaze and A Tribe Called Red, Robbie and Leslie

Baker, Brian Charles, Gerald Kennedy, Kim Samuel Johnson, and William and Pamela Tozer. Also, many thanks to the Banff Centre and its Indigenous Arts program. I will thank you all personally by showering you with exotic gifts. And to those I've undoubtedly forgotten to mention, thank you, too.

I continue to be blessed by working with the most passionate and astute people in the publishing industry today. For all of you at Penguin, especially Stephen Myers, David Ross, and Lisa Jager, I love working with you.

Nicole Winstanley, thank you for recognizing something in me a long, long time ago. We've worked together from the beginning, and there's still so much more to come.

Gary Fisketjon and Sonny Mehta at Knopf, thanks for believing in me. Gary, I had more than a few nightmares where green ink played a central role, but this novel is so much stronger because of your insanely keen eye.

Francis Geffard at Albin Michel, you've also believed in me from the very beginning. *Merci beaucoup, mon ami.*

Eric Simonoff, wonder agent and agent provocateur, I'm thrilled to be working with a man who loves the written word so much.

And always, to my great big loud and beautiful family: without you, I'm not much.

Mom, you never cease to amaze all of us.

My son, Jacob, as well as all of my nieces and nephews, you keep me relatively young.

Amanda, you've always brought out the best in me. This is a splendid journey we've chosen together, yes?

ABOUT THE AUTHOR

Joseph Boyden's first novel, *Three Day Road*, was selected for the *Today Show* Book Club, and it won the Rogers Writers' Trust Fiction Prize, the Amazon.ca/Books in Canada First Novel Award, as well as numerous others. His second novel, *Through Black Spruce*, was awarded the Scotiabank Giller Prize and named the Canadian Booksellers Association Book of the Year; it also earned him the CBA's Author of the Year Award. Boyden, of Ojibwe, Irish and Scottish roots, is a member of the Creative Writing faculty at the University of British Columbia in Vancouver, Canada, and the Institute of American Indian Arts in Santa Fe, New Mexico. He divides his time between Northern Ontario and Louisiana.